THE
Gardener's Daughter

Sara Hammond

THE GARDENER'S DAUGHTER

Sara Hammond

Copyright 2015 by Sara Hammond

1

"Damn Lord William," Anne muttered. In all her seventeen years, she had never cursed. She was surprised at how gratifying it felt to do so. "Damn him," she said again through clenched teeth. She wished she could scream it. After all, it was surely his fault that she was sitting in the cold mist of a May morning waiting for a coach that would take her away from the family of the Duke. Too late she realized her mistake of thinking of them as her family. They were the family- not her family.

The afternoon before, Anne had bid her farewells to the members of the noble household. When they spoke, there was a new indifference and haughtiness; they seemed relieved by her departure. Though she had shunned Lord William, he had still had his revenge. She might have felt maudlin if not for the fact that she traveled to join her father.

A lock of hair escaped her bonnet and blew into her eyes, irritating them close to tears. "Do not let them make you cry."

When the swaying lights of the London bound stagecoach appeared over the rock wall at the end of the field, her anger gave way to fear. She watched the livery boy hoist her trunk up to the driver, and with no further ceremony, she departed.

The journey became tedious by the afternoon. Anne's bones ached, and she was tired of the stiff position she assumed, ever conscious of strangers with whom she shared the coach. Travel was slow as the carriage was interrupted by stops to change out horses, leave off or pick up passengers, and stops for a meal. In addition, there were the more difficult sections of the road. The foot man would jump from his footboard on the back to aid the top-heavy mass of the coach up hills, between ruts and small creeks still swollen with spring rains.

Anne listened to the rhythmic beat of the horses' hooves. Each revolution of the coach's wheels was progress. She tried not to think of the hours that had passed and those still left to go. In the past, when she journeyed to London, she had been a nursemaid traveling with several children in a private coach. Those trips were broken up with stays at various manors. This journey was so different; long, uncomfortable, and lonely.

For the beginning of her trip, Anne sat inside. As the coach filled with other riders, she was bumped to a seat outside because her fare had been less. She did not miss conversation, as she was not accustomed to speaking to strangers. She did not wish to explain her journey in the way she had been forced to when an elderly matron sat directly across from her inside the coach.

"So dear, to which stop are you bound?" The wrinkles on her face bunched around her mouth as she spoke. Her wine colored hat perched on her head like a bird nest. Two bedraggled feathers, long ago removed from their avian source, protruded from the rear of the nest. With the polite answer, "just outside of London," the woman let loose another question, and another, and still one more.

"Where are your parents, dear? Is there not anyone accompanying you? Is it quite safe for you to travel alone?" she asked.

From where Anne sat, the light fanned out across the edge of the old woman's face, illuminating thick powder sticking to the hairs of a generous jowl. The angle of the light also revealed a white mustache of powdered hairs above the old woman's reddened lips.

Anne looked down, hoping to avoid the barrage. She saw that the woman wore shoes one size smaller than her feet might have preferred. The bulge of her foot where it met the shoe was a cruel lump.

Anne replied curtly, "My father will meet me." She wished she could have been as rude as the old woman, but she knew to hold her tongue.

"Humpf" was all the woman replied.

Riding atop the carriage, the weary young traveler felt a safe comfort leaning against a large leather case strapped beside her. The jostling of the long trip had settled into her joints with a dull, ever-present ache. No sooner had she snuggled into the case, than she drifted off for a much-needed nap.

"Low branch!"

The footman's shout permeated the heavy layers of fatigue. Anne stumbled between fast asleep and soon to be awake; the place where dreams were created. It was a fortunate event that she did not respond, thus missing the removal of her bonnet by the tree limb that combed its way across the top of the stagecoach, leaving her covered with a shower of leaves.

Pushing herself upright from the suitcase, she was met with the foggy realization that she was awake, quite sore, and heartsick, still in transit by stagecoach. The vague remnant of a dream played in her mind. It was the scene of an elderly woman surrounded by flowers handing her a paintbrush. That was all that she could recall.

As she was about to take the brush from the wrinkled hand, the shout of the coachman tore her away. She deserted the recollection of the dream, stretched and wondered how much further they had come.

Passengers exited as the stagecoach neared London. The driver saw that the young girl was now awake and sitting up. He instructed her to move to the inside of the carriage. After traveling more than one hundred sixty miles, Anne felt empty as if her life dwelled somewhere on a far horizon. It was a lonely thought she hoped would end with her arrival.

"We're very close now, miss." She heard the driver call down to her as she forced her eyes to stay open. She appreciated his care during their stopovers.

While she had waited in line with the other riders at the first inn, she noticed some of them exchanged money before they were taken to rooms down a hall or up the stairs. When it was Anne's turn, she learned no room had been set aside and when she emptied the few coins she had in her purse, the innkeeper shook his head.

"We are not operating a charity here. A farthing will get you a meal tonight. Rest there on the front bench until your coach leaves." With that, he had taken her coin and waved her off.

Feeling a mixture of embarrassment and disillusionment, Anne settled on the wooden bench. The coachman brought a blanket and assured her he would wake her for their departure early the next morning. With hours more of discomfort, it frightened Anne to realize how vulnerable she was without the family's protection. She had slept little with the unusual noises, arrivals in the night and departures before daylight, as well as the cold draft and odor of manure that wafted over her every time the door opened and closed. The next night was much the same though she waited in a warmer corner by the kitchen where the thick smell of rendered fat made it difficult to breathe. Once again the noise of voices and the movement of maids continued into the night and started up before dawn.

Now that the driver had informed her of the proximity of her stop, nothing could keep the bubble of anticipation from rising in her throat. She became alert once more, sitting up and looking out for the first view of her destination.

Spring of 1806 came late, but more verdant than ever. The square outside her small window was bordered by roads on two sides, and the shimmer of water in canals on the other two. In stark contrast to all the green of the surrounding grasslands, Anne's eyes rested on the light grey parish church with a modest steeple, which stood alone on the green. The church looked much larger than it truly was.

The coach pulled onto a smaller road. From this lane at the back of the manor, the carriage could circle back to the main road. The driver was certain the young woman was not a relative of the master or mistress, so he felt this stop would be appropriate. He was reassured when a man in an apron came forward to offer a hand with her things.

As Anne took in her surroundings, she became aware that she had arrived to chaos. Men scurried back and forth. Shouts and clinking metal tools played a percussive symphony. Her stomach tightened with knots of expectation as she started up the path from the driveway, shyly aware of the men around her.

Meeting this moment with a mixture of hope and trepidation, Anne did not condemn the decisions that had been made. All she knew was that she had done nothing to initiate the change. She followed directions, innocent to the idea there could be any other way. These were her first steps in her life without a guide.

As she started out from the carriage with Lucas, the cook's husband and steward for Lord Greville, he smiled a warming smile that gave Anne the boost she needed to proceed down the path. She dawdled, taking in everything that was under construction around her. As she stepped onto bare soil, her feet sank and she almost stumbled. She let Lucas pass, carrying the trunk containing most of what she owned in the world. He dodged the stakes that were hammered into the ground indicating the new garden bed.

"The wife is so excited about your return," he called over to Anne, "she spoke of nothing else all morning."

Piles layered with bark, manure, and leaves lay ready for planting. Anne knew these plots would be used to raise crops that loved the warmth given off by these decaying mountains, providing heat when the English sun could not. The smell of freshly turned beds surrounded her, bringing to mind fond memories of her family, the one of which she had been a true part.

The pale grey cape and bonnet of a lady looked very much out of place amidst the blacks and browns of soil and unfinished pathways. The young woman walked up the damp earth corridor to the cottage in the back corner of the garden, once again impeding Lucas' progress as he hurried around her and back to the driveway. Her manner of dress protected her from nods or cap tipping by any of the workers. It would be improper indeed for any of them to look her way or be caught paying her attention. They might easily lose their jobs for such an infraction.

The area of the garden was small enough that it could be taken into view all at once. Anne found the size agreed with her. This garden of the noted horticulturalist, Lord Charles Francis Greville, son of the Earl of Warwick, created a coziness that the larger gardens of His Grace, the Duke, did not. Off to the left, Anne could see the top of the nobleman's large glasshouse where Lord Greville collected plants from all over the world. The most exotic specimens were housed in this hothouse for protection.

"There we have it," said Lucas, returning from the cottage after delivering her things. "Your father will be glad to see you safely arrived."

"Thank you, Lucas. I am very happy to see you all, as well." Anne fumbled with the strings of her purse for a coin to reward him, but Lucas pushed her hand away, not willing to accept her offering. It was a subtle reminder of how changed her life would be. She held no position here.

The new arrival made her way to the little cottage. She removed her gloves and shed her cape. When she peeled off her bonnet, a mass of dark curls cascaded off her shoulders. The damp, dark inside of the roughcast house was uninviting. Anne took another step in, allowing her eyes to adjust. The sparse furnishings appeared especially bare and drab in the dim light that came from the one small window. The dank surroundings did not repulse her, but reminded her how humble the dwelling was surviving so many years.

She noticed her father's sweater hanging on the chair. The dull brown color matched the soil in which he toiled. Anne longed to see her father. Tossing her bonnet on top of her other things, she rushed out into the bright sun.

Though not yet mature in years, the girl's face held a classic beauty that masked her youth. The dark waves of hair that framed her face was notable, but it was her eyes, her late mistress had told her, that would always be "her best feature." Though Anne took after her mother with her dark auburn hair, she did not inherit her mother's blue eyes. Instead, her eyes were the darkest brown, and they glistened like the reflection of sky that waited on the surface of water deep in a well. The look in her eyes was kind and innocently gentle. There was no malice in her expression, and her smile prejudiced anyone in her favor.

Anne saw her father coming towards her out of the crowd. Her heart warmed to his squinty eyes and wide smile. She was pleased to see an expression of obvious delight, so rare from him. He moved with a slow bent gait that reminded her of how close she had come to losing him last winter.

As Anne stepped forward to meet him, she could smell the manure in the wagon just beyond them. The men sought the head gardener's directions almost immediately. She patted his weathered and misshapen hands with her delicate white ones.

"We will talk later," she insisted. "We have plenty of time."

"I am glad your journey was safe," he replied, standing clear so as not to soil her dress. Anne did not know that her gestures and calm voice brought forth images of her mother, catching her father off guard.

The stay with her father would solidify a relationship that was based on short visits and vague recollections of a family that once included her mother and brother. Anne's memories of her mother had been reduced to just a handful of images, mostly following her in the herb garden. The last image she had of her mother was at the nursery door, waving a kiss her way. By evening, Anne was informed that her mother had taken ill with the same epidemic that had taken her brother's life and infected many of the noble family and most of the village. All of the Duke's family were spared, due in part to her mother's careful nursing.

For fifteen years, George Blake had worked as undergardener below the head gardener, William Speechley, an authority on growing everything from pineapples in the hothouse to grapes in the field. As George Blake felt he could no longer stay on at the manor where memories of his wife and son haunted him, the steward found him the position at Charles Greville's manor almost immediately. It was said that Lord Greville was assembling a fine collection of plants, due in part to his friendship with Joseph Banks, the famous sponsor of voyages of discovery.

George had meant to take Anne with him, but the daughters of the Duke objected to removing the little girl. They found she was a welcome addition to the servant staff, and they could not ignore her plight. Her mother was the midwife who had attended most of the births in the household, and the woman who had nursed their children back to health. Anne was to remain until such time her father could provide a better situation for her. That time had never come.

Sitting in the cottage, Anne pulled her thoughts back to what remained of the day. She found one of her day dresses in the trunk, changing from her travel suit and the tight boots she had worn for the last three days. She dragged her trunk into the smaller room and began to unpack the rest of her few belongings.

That evening, there was quiet conversation and soft laughter in the little cottage at the back of the manor.

"There was only Jane to see me to the stable where Henry, the old groom's son, waited to take me to meet the stagecoach. He is quite grown now and very tall. It was still dark, and most of the household were asleep."

"Hmm, no one from the house?" George Blake looked at his daughter across the table. Last winter, there had been no discussion of her leaving service with the noble family.

The story of her departure remained to be told. "My trouble came from Lord William. I avoided him as much as I could. They have sent us both off, though I did nothing wrong. The ladies knew that, but still I was removed, and here I am."

Anne's father did not question her further. He knew these sorts of things happened to those in service, but he felt his ire would get the best of him if he knew any more. Sure of his daughter's innocence, he never spoke of the Duke's family again.

Her father told of the newest plant arrivals and his intentions for the new vegetable beds. When he spoke of the flowers, he mentioned the rose bushes' need of weeding and his failure to thin the fast approaching blooms. They passed an hour enjoying these subjects without investigating any of them at length.

There was no discussion of Anne's future. A letter of character was forthcoming from the Duke's household. Without such a document, her present would be separated from her past, a frightening prospect. Bedtime came early as Anne saw her father yawn more than once at the table and then make his way to his platform in the corner.

"When does the master return?" Anne asked.

"Soon, too soon," was all her father remarked as he turned away from her.

Anne was feeling the effects of her trip. Her body was stiff as she stood. She crossed the room to where her father stretched out and leaned over to give him a kiss on his bristly cheek. He gave no sign that he had received the kiss, but Anne was still comforted to be in the same dwelling with him.

Settling into her narrow bed, the tired girl thought of her father's employer. She had only vague recollections of Lord Greville. He sent a note during the gardener's illness wishing him a speedy recovery. That one effort caused her to believe he was a good man. She was curious to meet him though it was doubtful she would have the chance. She had no connection to his household and thus no reason to approach the lord.

Anne rolled onto her side, crunching the thin mattress of dried ticking. She looked out the window at a blurry image of a star. She heard Jane's words the night she realized her life was about to change.

"They will send you away." Jane had predicted.

"No, they have sent him off. I have done nothing wrong," she had protested.

"Still, he will return one day, and his mother and aunt will not want any temptation to remain. I am so sorry, Anne."

With those words, Anne realized everything she knew was impermanent. Now, lying here in the small, dusky room, it had all come to pass. Tomorrow, as she waited for a letter of character and a new appointment, she would take the disruption with as glad a heart as she could, pleased to spend time with her father. Nonetheless, an element of anxiety remained. Finally, sleep came to relieve her.

2

*A*nne slept through the night without waking. She was not summoned. No children stirred to bring her from her sleep. When she woke up, guilt jolted her upright. She examined the close, bare walls, remembering where she was. When she stood to gather a shawl about her shoulders, she let out a shiver as her feet touched the cold, stone floor. Hurrying to seek out her father in the next room, her legs gave way, and she grabbed the edge of the bed to steady herself. Her muscles had turned to jelly during the night.

She had intended to join her father for tea, but seeing morning light coming through the window, she knew he would be gone from the cottage hours before. She could hear the sound of shovels and the murmur of conversations from the garden where laborers toiled. She was ashamed to have been so lazy. She could not remember a time she had slept so long into the day. It was a luxury she had never been allowed.

Anne looked around to see that the small dwelling was in need of a thorough cleaning. Every corner held a web of some sort. A thin layer of dust covered every surface. She would eat a dry biscuit and drink a quick cup of tea before she set herself to the task of cleaning. All morning she made her way around the room, moving furniture to sweep and drag a wet rag across the wood floor removing months of dirt and gravel. She took the time to carefully remove several spiders, as she knew on the whole they were good workers in the garden. She washed down all the dusty surfaces and cleaned her room from top to bottom.

Toward afternoon, Anne went to the kitchen where she met the head housekeeper, Mrs. Lambert, in the hall. The housekeeper always looked exactly the same to Anne. She wore the black dress of a widow even if she never claimed to be one, no grey or lighter colors in her wardrobe. The bit of hair that stuck out from her starched cap was perhaps her only attempt at style. Anne decided Mrs. Lambert applied sugar water to the carefully arranged the curls, only five of them, that encircled her forehead. Those curls never moved. The housekeeper smothered Anne with a hug to her thick chest.

"Oh, look at you, what a pretty picture you make. How happy your father is to have you here," she said.

Anne wondered if Mrs. Lambert knew the reason for her unexpected return. If so, she would probably make no mention of it. If not, Anne wished she could speak of her innocence. She had never been asked by anyone. This, however was not the time.

"Mrs. Lambert, I am expecting a missive from his Grace's daughter, a Letter of Character."

"Oh dear, they did not prepare one for you upon your departure?" The housekeeper asked.

"No, I suppose they were busy with other duties and my departure was somewhat sudden." Anne wished she could feel comfortable enough to add her story, but she had just arrived and her insecurity outweighed her need to explain.

Mrs. Lambert was distressed to hear Anne's claim. It was very doubtful in her mind that the family of the Duke would send such a letter now with the girl removed from their home, their sight, and their minds. Poor thing.

A peck on the cheek came from Cook as she came from the kitchen. Cook smelled like sugar and spice. She was rosy from the frizzy red hair that escaped her white cap and her shiny, round, pink cheeks to her pudgy pink fingers. Anne loved that she was almost always smiling, and found it contagious.

Anne was also met with curious gazes from the maids. One new girl gave her a look so positively evil Anne had to look away. Anne smiled as genuinely as she could, but did not look the girl's way again. She had no wish to draw a negative opinion from anyone so soon upon her return.

By the end of the week, the garden projects were completed and the large crowd of workers disappeared, giving Anne more freedom to wander, finding new parts to the garden. It was the rose garden that became her favorite. Anne loved roses best of all flowers. The smell of roses reminded Anne of her mother. Anne began to look at this part of the yard as her garden. After all, she said to the budding bushes, "I do pay you the most attention."

What impressed Anne most about this rose garden was the large vase set on a pedestal in the middle of the thorny bushes. Anne was not sure if it was stone or made from clay or if it was truly as old as it looked. The shoulder of the vase was decorated with chains of small balls carved into the outside as if strings of pearls were hung from its neck. Below the necklace decoration was a carving of a god figure, repeated in various positions. Anne folded her arms as she finished her study of the vase.

"If I owned such a piece," she announced quietly, "I would be inclined to keep it indoors where it could not suffer from the elements!"

Anne made a ritual of sitting in the rose garden every day. When a chain of rainy days descended upon the property, she found the rose garden looked even more enchanting. The wet bushes were glorious as they shined back the silver of the overcast sky. The dripping rain came off the shoulders of the vase creating what looked like a fountain.

Anne found the east corner of the hothouse where plants were stacked into a thicket of foliage to be another favorite. New specimens arrived each week from a man named Banks. Anne watched her father unpack each one from a box filled with moss or peat. He would pot it up if necessary, and then place the new treasure in a special spot in the greenhouse.

"This gloxinia does not wish for sun. I have tucked it under the fig for now," her father explained.

Anne liked to imagine the wild places from which the plants had originated; hot, humid jungles, islands with soft sandy beaches, or rocky, snow-covered mountains. Anne's father told her just enough to send her imagination reeling, but he never had enough time for the questions that piled up in her mind.

Anne and her father formed new habits around each other. She tended the cottage as her father had never done. She kept busy sewing curtains and making a tablecloth from an old sheet she found in a cupboard. Though a mouse had borrowed one corner of the material for nesting, she was still able to salvage a large piece. She stuffed pillows with rags for the bench where her father slept, and dried and stuffed new ticking in their mattresses.

As mistress of the small abode she shared with her father, Anne proudly cleaned the dishes Cook had given to her, the cracked and chipped pieces no longer in service for the master. Cook offered her preserves and fruit, complaining that Anne did not eat enough. These complaints may have stemmed from the fact that Anne and her father did not approach the round form of Cook or the even larger frame of Mrs. Lambert.

Anne was very drawn to the plump chef and her husband, Lucas. They paid her the most attention of anyone at the manor. Having raised children of their own, they had a parental soft spot for Anne. Without a mother, Cook knew even a well-behaved, young adult such as Anne needed occasional direction. She knew George Blake to be a kind man, but he was elderly and not at all familiar with the job of parenting.

When Anne paid her visits to the kitchen, she heard bits and pieces about Lord Greville and his return from Wales. She wondered if he had any connection to her previous employer. Anne's main concern, after the well-being of her father, was her assignment to a new position where she might care for a new family of children.

"Does the master entertain?" Anne asked, thinking of her previous residence and the constant flow of visitors and family coming and going and the grand events held in the village yearly.

"Rarely," Cook replied. "He has visitors to his library or the gardens, but they do not stay or dine here."

The weeks passed, the stakes marking the beds were removed. Young plants appeared, popping out with vigorous enthusiasm. Vegetables flourished in the new soil, spreading their leaves and forming blossoms. The lawns were once again green, and the paths clean with a fresh layer of flagstone or marl. The tropical plants were settled in the glasshouses, and what arrived alive had survived, a fact of which her father was most proud. The construction on the manor house was completed, and all the scaffolding removed. The driveway was tidy with a new gravel coating. Everywhere in the garden there was progress, but for Anne, no letter arrived and so time dragged on.

Three weeks after Anne's arrival, the master came home late one afternoon. The gardens and the grounds were quiet. The servants lined up on the drive to receive him as he descended from his carriage. He must surely have been tired, Anne knew, as she herself had been weary after her long trip. Still, he took the time to acknowledge each and every one of his staff assembled there.

Anne stayed back by the hedge that lined the path where she could watch the arrival and this formal greeting. She was anxious to catch a view of the master, the son of an earl, once a Member of Parliament, and the owner of the most amazing collection of plants that Anne had ever seen. She was not part of the household. She had no cause to be acquainted with the nobleman.

Charles Frances Greville appeared of average height. He looked thin to Anne but not lanky. He shared bows with Robert, the footman, and the livery boy. When it came time for him to greet her father waiting at the end of the line, he took her father's hand and bent even closer to speak with him. Anne noted that he spent more time with him than anyone else assembled.

George Blake's place in the hierarchy of help would have usually been considered lower than most of the other members of the household staff, but not to the horticultural-minded nobleman. In Lord Greville's small household, the levels of house servants were not so well defined. Cook held a station high on the ladder as she was queen of the kitchen. In a house with no wife or matriarch, Mrs. Lambert's position as head housekeeper indicated even more distinction than in most. She truly kept the house and the activities of the household in order. She reported directly to his lordship. The one person who did not form the receiving line was the master's valet who had arrived the day before without ceremony or acknowledgement. Anne barely knew of the man's existence.

James Coleman had duties relating to the task of taking care of his lordship's toilet, clothes, and personal affairs. Coleman kept his master's belongings in tiptop shape, as he felt doing so would be reflected in the good opinion of others. The elderly manservant was a staunch advocate of keeping things exactly as he thought they should be, and he considered the master quite liberal when it came to his dealings with the world. James Coleman was a stickler for etiquette and not fond of change.

The servant loved his master, and Lord Greville felt a bond beyond master and servant. When Charles was young, Coleman had served his father, the Earl, and though the manservant must have been much younger, the valet had seemed elderly even then. Coleman had served the lord's brother from the time he inherited the title of Earl of Warwick until he came to serve Charles several years ago.

Coleman was given a bedroom and sitting room at the end of the hall at the top of the kitchen staircase. The privilege of his above stairs apartment included his desire to receive his meals in his room and not with the other household staff. Coleman rarely made appearances below.

The only time Coleman was seen below was when his lordship called upon him to act as butler. As the senior male in the household, he was more than happy to do so. Previously, Lord Greville had employed a hall man, Arthur, who answered the door, handled cards and messages, and polished boots and silver among other duties. He had died three years before, and although the master had intended to hire a new man, he had never done so.

Those few times that Lord Greville did receive guests, Coleman would guide them into the drawing room to await their call to the Lord Greville's library. More often, the guests were led straight back to join the master. Coleman was pleased with butler duty as he felt a part of his dear master's life. Moreover, Coleman feared that if he did not answer the door, the master would appear on the drive alone to meet his guests or, even worse, answer the door himself.

Mrs. Lambert had accepted the valet's arrival seven years ago with some reservation. They established their separate territories; she would tend to all matters of running the house, and he with running of the man. They had come to terms with one another. Most of the household had little or no dealings with the valet. The exception was Sybil. She began her employment with Lord Greville a few years after Coleman. Her recommendations made her the head housemaid immediately. She took care of the master's bedroom and sitting room, his bath, and the library.

Sybil knew her place and was careful not to overstep her position in regards to the handling of the master's personal effects.

She cleaned the top of Lord Greville's dresser without moving a thing. She never rearranged piles, nor removed any scrap of paper or book from his bedside table.

Even if Sybil carried finished laundry to the master's room during the day when he was apt to be out or in his library, she left the pile on a table at the door. Coleman would retrieve the pile and place each item of clothing in its appropriate spot. It was not Sybil's place to handle anything so personal, and Coleman made sure she was aware of the fact.

So while Lord Greville dismissed the bulk of his household staff, James Coleman watched from the second story. From his vantage point he could see a young woman tucked just behind the edge of the bushes along the drive. He wondered what she was about, but went back to his unpacking of the master's clothes.

As the line-up broke apart, Anne saw Lord Greville give her father one last pat on the back, smiling and nodding his head. Anne wished to be introduced to the nobleman though she knew the odds were slim that she would be. There was no reason for such a meeting.

3

*O*ne month had passed since Anne had been dismissed from the family of the Duke. The ladies had taken to Anne in an exceptional way, allowing her freedom to enter their household and their lives. She was a quick learner and a very pretty girl. As the women who were involved with providing for orphans at the Foundling Hospital had explained to the Duke, "we cannot take care of the wild children of London, and neglect this girl who lives right under our noses."

The Duke's household included many other children aside from his own grandchildren. Several great nieces and nephews shared the grand manor. Anne had been allowed to accompany the younger children during their schooling. She had taken the opportunity seriously, as Jane had advised, earning the esteem of the schoolmaster. Over time, the teacher came to look on Anne as his best pupil, helping her to pursue reading and mathematical tasks far beyond those of the other children.

In addition, Anne received cast off clothes and shoes. She was allowed to take books from the extensive library, a privilege that allowed her to pursue her education and interests. Usually her meals were taken with the children. She slept in the play room within earshot of any child who might cry out. She kept her few possessions in a bureau in the hallway. It had been left to Anne to tend to the youngest children. Mostly she played and accompanied them except when they attended music, art, or riding lessons.

Anne learned by watching. She practiced walking before mirrors when she was alone, imagining being a part of their lives. When she was in the presence of the noblewomen, however, she barely dared to look up when they spoke to her about the opportunity to earn a better situation in life than that to which she was born.

Although Anne believed she would stay on with the family in the same capacity, it was not how providence played out. The interest shown by the Duke's nephew, Lord William, disturbed her future. Anne was thrown into a situation with which she had no experience.

That rainy day, the nephew had ordered his lunch brought to him in the library rather than his coming to the dining hall. He insisted he desired to continue reading. The maid brought a platter of food, curtsied, and left it on the desk. At the same time, Anne came into the room to replace a book.

The library contained several aisles of book shelves, stacked higher than she could reach; walls of books Anne loved to linger between when given the chance. Past these bookshelves, the room opened up to an area by a fireplace with a large desk where the Duke's nephew was seated. Anne saw the young man before he saw her. She ducked between the tall bookshelves to hide and then make her retreat, but it was too late. Her stomach knotted as she heard him call out to her. He had a nasty habit of tormenting her.

"Stay," he barked, as if training a dog. "I want you to stay here while I eat." He made a show of sitting in the oversized chair puffing up as if he were someone of greater importance.

"Come, sit by me," he commanded, pulling over a stool with his foot and indicating for her to sit. "Better yet, let's play pretend."

Anne knew better than to defy his order. He had hurt her in the past. He spoke with a familiar sinister tone that made Anne shiver as she slowly approached the desk.

"I will be the Duke," he smirked, scratching his newly whiskered chin, "and you will be…"

"The Duchess?" Anne asked.

"No silly," William replied with a sneer, "You are a nobody. No, you shall be my mistress. Sit here," he instructed, pointing to his lap.

Though his words stung, Anne moved to his side of the desk and sat, though more and more reluctant about the game. If she did not obey, he could pinch her on the underside of her arm, pull out a lock of hair, or worst of all, demand she sit idle in the corner until one of the maids came and found her, usually not in a mood to hear any explanation for her failure to return to her duties.

So she sat on the nephew's lap. It was just in this position, with his hand slowly wandering up to cup her breast that his aunt, Lady Henrietta, found them as she came into the library unexpectedly.

"It was inevitable," the mistress muttered. She sent Anne to her study where she waited, anxious to tell her side of the story. When the lady returned, she did not seem angry and did not ask Anne to explain.

"Your pretty face has attracted a young man beyond your station. This will not do." Lady Henrietta let her voice trail off, thinking to herself.

The lady had spoken in a perturbed fashion that Anne would soon understand. That had been all that was said at the time. The young man was whisked off for a stay with relatives, and Anne was soon to learn her fate as well. From the moment that she and the nephew were found in the library, attitudes changed.

Now, a month later, and a day after Lord Greville's arrival, everyone was employed except for Anne. She set off to the kitchen to witness how the master's arrival had affected the activities there. She had barely poked her head through the door before Cook was scolding her.

"No, no, no! I've no time for you today. Busy, so busy," she muttered, making a sweeping gesture with her hands as if to whisk the girl back out the door. Anne turned on her heel to head back out the door before tears could form. Cook looked up just in time to see the sadness on her young friend's face.

"Wait! I have something to show you." She was quick to create a reason to bring the girl back into the kitchen.

"Look there, in the box." Cook pointed at a split wood carton sitting on the counter.

"They look like giant strawberries, so much larger than the little wild ones," Anne spoke softly.

"Try one." Cook pushed the box of berries toward her.

Anne reached in and chose a smaller one shyly as they were certainly the master's treat and not her own.

"Delicious, hey? Now, take another one and be off with you, I have plenty to do this morning."

Anne left the kitchen feeling relieved. She retrieved her drawing supplies and headed off to sketch in the hot house. From the Blake's cottage, she could walk outside the entire length of the walled garden. During the colder times of year, George Blake kept fires breathing up the flues inside the wall. The location of the small cottage was ideal for her father's nightly duties, close enough to stoke the fires without bothering the household.

The greenhouse stood along the south end of the property facing east and west. The walled garden ended where the glasshouse began. She hopped over several ditches carved into the ground where water slowly made its way from the canal.

With her sketch folder in hand, she was not thinking of anything in particular. She assumed there would be no one in the enclosure. Her father had mentioned the master's intention to be away. She was disappointed when she heard rustling and saw movement of someone in the center aisle. She thought to turn and make a quick departure, but she was alarmed by what she heard.

As she listened more attentively, she identified the repetitive grunts to be choking sobs. There was a man crying by the bench. It was the first time she ever remembered hearing a grown man cry. Young boys screeched and yelled their cries. Babies complained in squeals. These throaty groans were heart wrenching. The discordant noise seeped into her heart. She felt his anguish as if it were her own.

Anne was privy to a very intimate view of the man. She felt embarrassed for him and tried to look away, but empathy pulled at her. She could not control her fascination and looked closer. The image was interrupted by a puzzle of leaves.

It was Lord Greville. She hardly recognized him. He wore no wig. She could not see his face straight on, but his profile was composed of finely etched features. He held his brow in his hand, his arm stiff with his elbow braced on the bench as if his head might fall off if he did not clench it so.

None of what she saw of his face came as any surprise; he was much as she had seen the day before. She was only surprised to find he looked so much younger and unimposing than she had always imagined him. His nobility did not protect him from such sadness. The scene would affect her judgment from that moment on.

Anne knew there was much talk and gossip about Charles Greville. Cook's assistant gathered her "most reliable" information from the wife of the butcher. It seemed there was no one for whom the greasy-handed woman did not have some tidbit of unbecoming information. The tales that the butcher's wife passed on about Lord Greville revolved around his previous mistress, his once meager allowance, the inheritance from his uncle, and his unsuccessful search for a wife.

Anne wondered which of these might be causing the hollow moans and short gasps for breath she heard coming from a few feet away. He appeared crippled by pain, making it impossible for him to hold his frame fully erect. She believed he sensed her presence or maybe he heard her breathing because he looked up to stare straight at her. She thought he most assuredly had seen her. She remained paralyzed. She stared back through the lacy pattern of leaves and waited to be discovered.

Instead, the lord threw down the papers he was holding and rushed from the glasshouse, slamming the door behind him. Anne stood aghast for the first few minutes after his exit. It took several more minutes before she was able to move. Her arm was numb from holding onto her sketch paper and pencil box so tightly. She moved to the table where he had been leaning. She looked at the papers he had tossed, fully expecting to find a notice from a bank or perhaps a letter with sad news. What she found surprised her. She put her hand up to her mouth to suppress an exclamation. On the top sheet of paper was the drawing of a flower. It appeared to be an orchid on a long vine with opposite leaves. At the end of the bench was such a plant, but there was no flower that she could see.

Anne stared at the sketch, especially the stem of the plant where it appeared to be made of letters, an "E" and an "a" at the end of the vine. Other swirls suggested letters in between, perhaps a name. It was a poor attempt at drawing an orchid. It looked like a face with a big nose. Anne looked to see any other notes or cause of his discouragement. The drawing was the only paper that was not blank.

She should have felt ashamed at her investigation. Instead she considered she had a special connection to the man. Having witnessed such an intimate scene, she wished for an explanation. She gathered her things against her and slipped out the door as quietly as she entered, drawing the door closed with a shaking hand.

4

Anne spent the afternoon mulling over the morning's events, much disturbed by what she had experienced. She sat in the cottage on one of the three chairs surrounding the table. There must have been a fourth Anne surmised, but three remained. They would seldom need more than two.

The ceiling was low and the room quite dark. The glass in the one window was no longer translucent, but milky and opaque. Anne had scrubbed the surface in and out, eventually accepting that the surface would never be clear again.

The walls on each side of the small window held a few small crocks and utensils that pertained to food preparation. Above her father's bench was a shelf where he kept a few tools. Anne had carefully dusted a knife, an old pipe, and a small collection of books he had been given over the years. At the end of the shelf was a silhouette of his wife, her mother. The paper cutout was tattered and barely recognizable to anyone other than those who had loved her most. Anne had held the picture close wishing for her mother's protection and advice more than ever.

The cottage was the oldest structure in this corner of Paddington Green. The flint and roughcast walls and thick thatched roof were a remnant of a time gone by. The charm survived. Most of the out buildings on the property were built of thick planks of wood with slate roofs. The larger, newer structures were constructed of stone or brick.

This front room was the original building. The thickness of the walls indicated layers of plaster applied many times over the years. The floors had originally been packed dirt. Now thick planks had been added to lift the small hovel out of the soil. Without a human occupant, Anne was sure the cottage would be reclaimed by its surroundings. Brambles would overtake the roof, reducing the dwelling to a pile of stone.

The opening to the other section of the cottage had most likely been the back door. This room was timber framed, much newer by several decades with a flagstone floor. Anne occupied this second room, while her father continued to sleep on the bench along the front wall. Anne's room held a bed, a small three-drawer dresser, and a chair that had belonged to her mother. Tight as this room was with these few furnishings, she relished the fact that, for now, it was hers.

The Blakes had this cottage to themselves. Unlike many of the staff who lived together in small rooms along the hall behind the kitchen, they had privacy here. For the time being, Anne set up housekeeping for her father who required so little. Soon she might be living elsewhere.

As Anne sat at the table, attempting to calm her thoughts by darning another one of her father's holey socks, she could not help but ponder the troubled state of the manor's lord. She was ashamed of spying on him earlier, but eased her guilt by admitting it had occurred quite by accident. Anne wished she could blurt out what she had seen to her father, but she would respect the gentleman's confidence. When her father finally did arrive, she approached the subject timidly.

"I saw the master quite distressed in the glasshouse today.

"You did not disturb the master, surely Anne?" her father asked. He looked up to glare at her while removing his boots.

"Oh no, Father, I was leaving when I saw him upset," she said, skirting the truth.

"It was the orchid," mumbled her father, rubbing his shins and the backs of his legs while seated by the stove.

Anne was peeling carrots and turnips, thinking her father would ignore her and how she might try a different tact. She was surprised when he answered.

"What did you say, Father?"

"The orchid upsets the master," the old man said. "It has bloomed and no one observed it."

"Which orchid is that?" Her interest was piqued. Her father's explanation agreed with the drawing she had seen on the greenhouse bench.

"The vine, the vanilla. The bud was not expected so early."

George Blake was a man of few sentences and very short conversations. He was a man of action. Her father's reply indicated to Anne the importance of the event, a flower blooming.

"How was it missed?" She had looked at that vine and had seen no sign of a flower. The orchid's vine was an impressive sight, barely tamed. It wound around a wooden post vertically for several feet and then horizontally for several more.

"The flower opens in the morning and if the bloom fails to be pollinated during the day, the blossom will not open again. It wilts and dies by nightfall." As Anne listened, she had an uncontrollable reaction.

"No, that cannot be! One day, that is all? The poor thing is discarded so easily? Oh! Nature can be so cruel." Anne jumped up. Carrots and turnips tumbled onto the floor from the fold of her apron. Anne startled back to the chore at hand. Her father was spared an essay on the errors of nature. She wanted to continue, but it was difficult from her position on all fours fetching vegetables under the chairs.

"Settle down, Anne." The elderly man was unsure of how to control this sort of outburst.

"Will the orchid have another flower?"

"The first bud was early. There are others, very small, more than a month away. We will watch more closely." He gave her a motion with his hands telling her without a word to stop talking. No sound, just a movement with both hands and a stern face. She knew his meaning and went dutifully back to work on their meal.

She could not believe that the orchid's flower could be the cause of the agony she witnessed in the greenhouse. There had to be something more to the emotions that erupted from so deep inside the master. She had only to think of the letters on the stem to think otherwise. It had certainly been a name.

Anne wished to talk more about the day's event, but her father ate in silence and she let him have his peace. She would look elsewhere for answers. Shortly after dinner, her father took to his bed in the dark corner of the cottage. Anne cleared the table and brought out her paper and pencil. She began to sketch a picture of the master. It was the only way to settle her thoughts. She had no problem drawing the hunched figure. The picture was etched into her mind.

"Come quickly Anne," her father said, as he shook her awake sometime in the pitch-dark night. Anne came out of bed with certain urgency, knowing her father had awakened her for some pressing purpose. She grabbed her shawl and slippers on her way. A hailstorm was raging outside. Somehow she had slept through the loud tapping. Her father jogged out the door toward the greenhouse. Anne ducked her head and followed through the screen of ice pellets, unable to look up. She kept her eyes focused on the path covered with slippery little balls. She was chilled as her thin nightdress and shawl blew back as she ran.

Inside the greenhouse, the noise of the hail was deafening. Her father grabbed a lantern and hurried toward the middle of the glass building. Rain and hail slid down in a cascade where the roof had broken. The cascade of ice and water from the edge of the hole landed on plants below sending mud out onto the floor. Anne's father scrambled to move the plants from under the waterfall, and Anne joined in without further instruction. When they were finished, she thought she would retreat to their cottage. As she turned to leave, more glass crashed behind her. The surprise startled a small cry from her throat. When Anne turned to look, she viewed a horrible sight; Lord Greville's body was sprawled on the floor.

Anne and her father tiptoed through the jagged sheets of glass to where the master lay prone. Luckily he had been knocked to the side. Somehow the framework that held the glass panes had given way, striking the nobleman down. Part of the hothouse skeleton was still swinging precariously above the lord. When she knelt down beside him, she saw blood gushed from a wound somewhere on his forehead. She did not tarry long, but ran off to the cottage and back in an instant. Her father had not moved an inch from his position at his master's side.

Anne checked the man's pulse, which remained strong. Relieved that he was not dead, she began to treat his wound. The blood was flowing freely as Anne knew an injury on the face was prone to do.

"Your coat, Father," Anne demanded. The old gardener ripped his jacket off and covered the lord as Anne began to doctor the cut, curious to know the extent. Swelling was creating a bulge above the bleeding, so she acted quickly. She opened a tin that held a poultice of herbs as she dabbed at the blood. The source was a long cut just above his right eyebrow. Anne cleaned the edges of the wound and applied the sticky poultice pressing lightly with a patch of clean rag from her collection. She did not worry if the lord would be offended or have an opinion at all about her treatment. She worked to stop the flow of blood without consideration.

As she laid clean bandages across the cut, she leaned closely to the unconscious man. She studied his face. Was this truly the same man she had seen crying so piteously? He looked so peaceful and yes, handsome. The hard-etched features of his noble face were relaxed into a softer expression that drew strange emotions from Anne. She stroked the hair back from the area of the wound. Her heart went out to his unknown anguish in the hothouse more than the cut on his brow.

His eyes began to flutter. They came open and he looked directly into Anne's face with a quivering smile. Anne smiled back, pleased to see the master come awake.

"My angel," he said, and Anne saw his eyes close again and his head relax. He slipped back into unconsciousness. Anne finished her bandaging, tying a strip of linen around the master's head to hold the poultice in place. She warmed at the lord's expression. Ah, to be so adored, but this man did not know what he was saying, she reminded herself. Though she thought she should pat his hand and speak to him, she did not, worried he would startle awake and then what?

Her father had darted off to find Lucas and now returned with the burly manservant. Lucas picked the lord up gently and off they all went to the manor. Anne looked about, but there was nothing to be done until daylight. The violence of the storm was spent. Only a mist of falling rain sprinkled on her as she left the greenhouse and headed home, no longer feeling the cold.

As Lord Greville sat in bed with the most wicked head ache he had ever endured, he tried to remember what in Heaven's name made him go to the greenhouse in the middle of a storm. Yes, he heard glass breaking, but all the more reason not to go. Now, he watched as Coleman fussed about offering more Laudanum and worried sick about the small wound above his eye. He would take no more tincture as punishment for his stupidity.

He raised his hand to his forehead to touch the bandage there. The lump surrounding the cut had reduced down to a small hill across the top of his eyebrow. It was hot and sore. There was a pounding beat as if a drum sat between his ears instead of his head.

He had no memory of ever entering the greenhouse or even the walk to it, but he did remember the apothecary, John Parker, who came so quickly, remarking how well the wound had been cared for. If the dear doctor did not tend it, who did?

"Coleman?" He called out.

"Yes, my lord?"

"Who brought me to the house last night?

"Lucas carried you and George helped with the doors." Coleman replied.

"Was there anyone else?"

"No sir, not to my knowledge."

Neither of those men would have cleaned and bandaged the deep cut on his brow, and yet someone had. As he sat back on the pile of pillows Coleman had fluffed and stacked behind him, he had an overwhelming feeling of adoration without a source or a recipient. There was more to the incident, but it hurt his head to think too closely on the subject now.

"Coleman, pull the drapes, the light is killing me," he yelled in frustration.

Closing his eyes to the brightness, Lord Greville saw a face. Startled at first, he opened his eyes again to the darkness Coleman had provided and the face disappeared. He closed his eyes again and the image returned. It was a young woman unknown to him. There was an angelic look on her face and she leaned close to him, close enough he might have kissed her. Surprised by the vision, he opened his eyes again.

Unexpectedly, peace came with her look and he wished to see her again, but when he closed his eyes, she was no longer present. "Where are you, my angel?" He asked the back of his eyelids. There was no reply. He opened his eyes to Coleman leaning over him, not nearly as pretty as the vision, his stern look in no way angelic.

"You called for me, my lord?"

"No, thank you, Coleman." He was embarrassed that he might have called to the young woman. He heard the crunch on the gravel of the approaching grocery cart. The morning was progressing without him. He knew more plants were to arrive in the next day or so, and now he had the damage from the storm with which to contend. His headache was waning as he sat in the dark.

"I think I will rise," he announced to his valet.

"Do you think you should? It may be wise to rest today. In fact, the physician will be here later and you could stay abed until he arrives." Coleman wrung his hands as if the lord's decision tormented him.

"No, my good man, I think I am ready to face the day. I need Robert to hire the carpenters and glaziers to start the repairs in the greenhouse as soon as possible. By now, George has cleaned up the mess, and the damage has been assessed. I wish to make myself available to any questions concerning the repairs, costs, and the time required. Please let Lambert know I will be coming down for breakfast."

As Coleman leaned out into the hall to tell the maid of the master's plans, the lord closed his eyes one more time, but sadly, the girl was gone. He smiled to himself to think such a lovely person lurked about the edges of his mind. The brain was an amazing organ!

32

5

*I*n the morning, Anne hurried to the manor's kitchen to learn of the master's fate. She still had questions, so many questions, whirling in her head. She felt her connection with Lord Greville had only strengthened. Her resolve to discover his heartache had grown keener. As she entered the kitchen, she was pleased to hear a circle of maids talking about their master.

"The physician said he was lucky that the blow to his head had not fractured his skull. Evidently, the cut was sufficiently closed that he did not need to treat it further. When Lucas came to bed, he assured me the master would recover as he had left him sipping brandy and complaining of a headache," Cook commented to the group. Everyone agreed they were glad the master was not more seriously injured. Anne smiled to herself, knowing her aid in closing the wound had been successful.

"He is the strangest man I've ever worked for," said Becky, the young, well-endowed downstairs maid, the one who looked on Anne with such negativity.

Sylvie agreed by nodding. Anne liked Sylvie very much. She was older and had a steady view of the world and her position in it. In Anne's short time at the lord's manor, she had developed a friendship with the maid despite the difference in their ages. They had conversations about all manner of subjects, whereas Anne never shared a comment with Becky.

"He told me not to worry about his dresser as it would always be a little untidy." Sylvie went on. "He said a quick dusting and a sweep of the floor should be fine as long as the windows were kept washed. He was most cheerful as he took the time to attend me. Of all things, he wants the windows clean so he can see his garden. It is Mr. Coleman I have to worry about," Sylvie said.

Cook looked up from her chopping, saying, "When I first started working here, his lordship instructed that he didn't need fancy dinners while dining alone. He sent compliments to the kitchen for the simplest dishes. He informed me that vegetable soup was always his favorite," Cook added. "It doesn't come much easier than making a good soup. He even complimented me on my pie the first evening I ever was the cook here. I can't remember ever receiving a compliment on a pie. I came to work here five years ago, and I will stay until they carry me away in a box," Cook pronounced.

Anne turned from the sink to face them, in case they had forgotten her. She worried the conversation might end there, but she was relieved when Becky took it up again.

"He is not so high and mighty," she said. She pushed up her nose with her finger, making a nasty grimace. She ignored Anne completely.

Sylvie merely smiled and said, "I am happy the master will recover, though I fear Mr. Coleman may not!" The group laughed in unison as Sylvie left with a stack of freshly cleaned and folded linens.

"He loves the garden more than the furnishings in the house, I believe," said Cook. "He never fusses over tableware, but insists on a vase of certain flowers on the table. He is a different kind that one, and I am glad for it. Not so stuffy here." She turned to go to the pantry, leaving Becky and Anne sitting there alone.

Becky turned her attention to Anne, moving closer with a sneering smile. Anne leaned back slightly.

"You know about his past, hey?" asked Becky in a lowered voice with know-it-all nonchalance. "Some say he is not truly a man." She raised her eyes and then looked down below Anne's waistline. She nodded her head and then burst out laughing at Anne's expression of shock.

"What are you saying, Becky?" Anne asked. Anger was welling up inside her.

"Some say that he likes men more than women, but others say it is just a problem down there," she said pointing between her legs. "Maybe Lady Hamilton gave him the foul when she had him!"

Anne did not know to what Becky referred, but she knew it must be abhorrent by her cackling laugh.

"You should not talk that way," Anne scolded.

She knew it was not kind or Christian, but she could fairly say she did not like Becky. She thought Becky's manners rude and coarse. Anne studied Becky. She wore her low-collared dress loosely as if it were too big. Her apron hung crookedly around her neck. She pulled her hair tied back, but it did not look as if she used a comb or brush to do so. Her skin showed scars of past blemishes especially around her mouth and chin. She had bright eyes; but something in their set was not attractive, but menacing.

Anne had seen the part-time laborers wink at each other as they made jokes when Becky paraded by. The maid, in turn, laughed and spoke louder than necessary. She enjoyed any bit of attention the men might pay her despite the vulgarity of their remarks.

Becky continued making lewd comments about the master, but Anne no longer listened. She was squeamish around any such talk, and she knew Becky enjoyed watching her squirm.

"Becky, stop! You should not speak in that manner." Anne walked away, feeling her vexation might cause her to do something rash.

Becky only smiled and left the kitchen with wax and a rag, casually wiping woodwork as she went. Cook returned to her stove, stirring and sampling as she added spices that sent the aroma of rosemary and thyme up into the air.

Anne turned her attention to Cook. She felt comfortable talking with the ruddy-cheeked woman about any subject, and thought she might dare to stretch the conversation toward her needed answers.

"Cook, do you suppose the master misses his past lovers?"

"Anne, have you nothing to do but ask me simpleton questions about the master? You have spent too much time talking with Becky. Mix the pie dough, and mind you, use the fresh water as it is the coldest."

"Yes, but I wish to understand. I saw his lordship so sad yesterday in the greenhouse. I wondered what might make him so unhappy."

"I have no thoughts on the matter. His past is just that, past. The woman was married to his uncle, and is now widowed by him. With the death of Lord Nelson, she lives a life quite separate from that of Lord Greville. I do not think he despairs for his decision to send her off or his present unmarried state, he keeps busy enough."

Anne mulled over Cook's comments, absorbing the information. Cook had spoken of Emma Hamilton, Lord Greville's famous mistress. Becky had done so, as well. If Lady Hamilton remained in their thoughts, perhaps she was in Lord Greville's, also. Anne thought of the name spelled out on the stem of the flower, "E" "m" "m" "a". Though it was an important discovery, Anne was not satisfied and pressed Cook for more. "What do you think would make him cry?"

"You saw him crying, dear?" Cook looked up from the pot she stirred. Anne stopped cutting the lard into the flour to meet Cook's expression of concern with her own.

"Yes. Father says it is because an orchid bloomed that he didn't see, but I think there must be more." Anne looked out the window thinking. She hoped she had not said more than she should, but Cook was one of the only people Anne could trust to answer such a question.

"Well, he loves his rocks. He might cry if one were missing, I can imagine. Don't you worry about Lord Greville. He has come from harder times. He has money in his favor. Perhaps what you saw was joy."

"No, what I heard was not joy." Anne knew she should stop. She would be stepping over the threshold of the man's privacy. She didn't want Cook to dwell on what she had revealed. Anne would need to wait for some later explanation.

As she turned to leave, she saw a young man waiting at the back door. She looked over at Cook.

"Get the door, Anne. He has come with our delivery."

Anne opened the door to a stack of sacks with a head at the top. The face greeting her was handsome with dark skin, black hair, and stunning light blue eyes. There was a dark shadow of moustache on his upper lip. Anne knew she was blushing, her racing heart heating her face from within. He gave Anne a smile that was inviting and friendly enough to be returned by one of her own.

"Excuse me, miss." He was forced to pass in front of Anne and close enough to brush her body.

"What have you there, Tom?" Cook inquired.

"I have two sacks of flour, one of sugar, a bag of soda, and your salt is on top." The young man tilted himself to look at the pile in his arms as he answered Cook's inquiry. Anne wondered at his strength, carrying so much at one time.

"Leave the salt and soda here on the counter, take the rest to the store room," said Cook, dismissing him and returning to her work.

As no one moved, she turned back to Anne, "Help him with the salt and soda and get the door for him. Just leave the sacks on the table for now. The door is not locked."

Anne was flustered. She found it difficult to change her place and move around Tom. It was necessary for her to lean forward into him to remove the smallest parcels from the top of his armload. He ducked a little to help her. As she withdrew the bags, his face and hers were no more than inches apart. When she looked up, she was met with an alluring gaze that once more flushed her cheeks red.

Anne started out ahead of the delivery boy. She felt the boy's eyes upon her. Her body stiffened knowing he was watching. He brushed by her again, and then it was her turn. She walked behind him to the cool room. His adolescent body did not show any sign of strain as he carried the unwieldy stack of bags. His black hair stuck out of his cap above his ears and across his back along his collar. It was as wavy as hers, but unlike her, he was able to crop his short.

Anne looked down the length of his lean body. He was tall, but not thin. He possessed tight muscles she could see on his arms and imagine on the rest of him. She tripped and realized her thoughts were not on where she was going. Just then, Tom turned to let her go first. He caught her looking low on his body. He lifted his eyebrows and gave her a wily smile. She hurried past him to get the door.

She fumbled with the door latch, not pressing down hard enough to lift it completely the first time. She budged the door and it did not move, pushing back at her with equal force, she amost lost her balance. Embarrassment choked her as she tried again. She hoped his arms could endure her ineptitude. Finally, the heavy door swung open, and she entered the dark room ahead of him. She moved half-empty sacks to the side of the table where Cook directed the goods be placed.

Anne stood in the narrow corridor between the walls of shelves built of roughly hewn planks. Some held boxes where potatoes, squash, onions, apples and other fruit would be stored after harvest. Sometimes meat, cheeses, and butter were kept in the room during the colder months. The room was a remnant of some previous dwelling. The interior was cool and dry. No moisture entered through the thick layer of stone, straw, and plaster. The walls inside the room were smooth, and kept white and clean. There was no musty smell, no mold, and no mice.

"Here." She pointed to the empty tabletop. Tom controlled the load as he allowed it to roll slowly off his arms. Even so, the weight shook the entire stack of shelves. The delivery boy separated the sacks into two piles. He made a great show of straightening them from horizontal to vertical.

Tom finished with a flourish of straightening and wiping his hands. He rubbed his arms where the bags imprinted their weave into his skin. Anne stood behind him in the dark long enough to feel an awkward heat starting up her body. She could not move forward as he blocked the exit. She waited for him to turn, but he did not make any effort to leave. He kept his eyes on her as if he waited for her to speak.

Before she could, he asked her, "Are you a kitchen maid here? I have never seen you before, I would have remembered!" A devilish smirk lifted the corners of his mouth.

Anne looked down quickly, embarrassed by his attention and her own. He had asked a difficult question as Anne did not work for Lord Greville.

"Yes" seemed like the easiest answer for now.

"You are lucky. I hear the lord has money enough. There are those who pay poorly or deny wages. Some even punish their servants with lashings."

It seemed to Anne as if the delivery boy spoke from experience. She thought that perhaps such a slow return to the kitchen might warrant a beating. She should be getting back rather than dawdling in a dark room alone with him. Surely, Tom had other deliveries to make, though he seemed in no hurry.

"You are very pretty," he said, taking a step toward her.

Anne looked to the side. Though she felt an excited flutter in her stomach, she had little experience with this sort of thing and she feared his advance, thinking of the Lord William. Tom sensed her discomfort and gave her one last quick smile.

He turned around bumping against Becky, who arrived from the driveway.

"Oh, there you are." She came up to Tom, stopping inches in front of him. Becky could not see Anne's smaller frame hidden in the darkness, but she did note the strange look on Tom's face.

"What, not glad to see me, my love?" Becky pushed him back into the dim threshold. She stretched to him on her tiptoes waiting for a kiss. Instead, he managed to side step enough to prevent her advance, miss her lips, and give her a view of Anne who struggled to keep her balance as she was pushed back by the other two.

"Oh, I see we are not alone. Are you previously engaged?" she asked accusingly. Tom ignored the question and veered around her out of the storeroom. He swaggered back to his wagon where there was still one box of fresh goods to haul into the kitchen. Becky glared at Anne with a sneer of loathing. She gave Anne an ugly grunt of a laugh, which conveyed a pitying condescension. It hurt Anne as much as if Becky had slapped her. The maid skipped off to Tom without shame for her obvious interest.

Anne felt her stomach twist with a cramp of embarrassment. She watched the pair for a moment until Becky looked back. She regretted Becky's interruption of the encounter. Though she had been uncomfortable, it had been thrilling at the same time.

She quickly closed the storeroom door, leaving it unlocked as she had found it. She escaped into the kitchen long enough to tell Cook the goods were put away, but short enough to keep from revealing any of the emotions swirling in her head. She hurried out the other end of the kitchen before Tom could return.

The incidents with Lord Greville and her curiosity about his connection to his past lover, and now Tom's attention in the storeroom gave Anne plenty to mull over. Somewhere, though, she heard Jane's admonishment, telling her not to forget her place. To find a new position in service was her calling, and soon she would be leaving to employment elsewhere leaving all this behind.

*A*nne avoided her compulsion to go to the glasshouse. She wanted to remedy the mishap of the day before, possibly entering with more noise so that she might alert the master, excuse herself, and then perhaps have a chance at an introduction. Perhaps she could ask after his injury. She gained no further information to explain the master's behavior. The suspense perpetuated her empathy as well as her curiosity.

In addition to staying away from the greenhouse for the next few days, Anne limited her trips to the kitchen, as she feared a confrontation with Becky. She knew Tom would not return for over a week, so she did not worry about a reunion there. Becky, however, seemed to always arrive when Anne visited Cook. Anne worried Becky might read her inner feelings; her attraction to the delivery boy with his gypsy-dark hair might be obvious to the maid.

Boredom continued to set in. Anne had not received a letter from Lady Henrietta, and no message came from a new employer. Daily she thought over her position with her previous employer. Surely, she had been well liked when she worked in the Duke's household. Was there any reason she should give up hope? She would decide they were just much engaged and would soon attend to her plight. As the days added up, she was beginning to doubt her optimism.

Limited to the garden, Anne visited the roses. The rose garden was tucked in the back corner of the yard near a path to the drive that was seldom used. Beyond the path, a hedge hid the bins of soil, manure, leaves, and straw her father stored along the edge of the tool shed. Anne felt the roses needed care and she was thinking of doing the work herself. Surely, a bit of weeding and cultivation would take only one hour. She would wear her father's old clothes, so as to appear to be one of the undergardeners. At any rate, there was no one about to see her at this late hour.

The weeding progressed well enough, as Anne bent over working the mossy topsoil into an aerated looseness using a small hoe her father had built for the purpose. She worked around the base of the bushes, but not deep enough to disturb the roots. She was careful to duck under the branches, away from their cruel thorns. Worms wiggled here and there to find new tunnels in the freshly turned earth.

Anne was daydreaming while she worked. She had thought about Tom and then imagined conversations with Lord Greville yet to take place. She was so absorbed, she failed to hear approaching footsteps. Before she was aware, Lord Greville, in the flesh, was standing directly behind her. He came up the path so quickly, she had no time to escape. She could not make the gentleman's acquaintance in this situation. She was trapped.

"Hey there," Lord Greville called. He held a hand to his brow and looked with a squint into the rose garden.

"Hey there," he called again, squinting harder to focus in on the small gardener on his knees working in between the bushes.

Anne froze and then held her arm up in response to his call, showing that she had heard. She dared not look up or turn around. Her loose clothes, her father's breeches and sweater, did not fit well.

The outfit hung on her as a blanket might, heavy and awkward. She could not move easily in the bulky clothes, and certainly she could not stand up without hiking up her pants and tucking in her shirt. She could imagine the conversation as she held the dirty hoe in her hands, "Hello there, I am the one who bandaged your cut." She decided she would remain on all fours despite the master's desire to speak with her.

The lord waited for several seconds until he realized that the waved arm was the only response he would receive. He cleared his throat, invoking an overseer's tone, but still said nothing for a moment. He thought to bend into the rose garden to get a closer view of the man, but it was unseemly that he should do so.

"Excuse me." Charles found himself addressing the gardener again, somewhat apologetically for what now had become an obvious interruption.

"Have you seen George of late?" He was still waiting for the gardener to turn and address him, or better yet, rise from his work and bow in recognition of the superior status of the inquirer. Nothing happened. Perhaps the gardener was deaf. No, he had waved his arm and certainly his back was turned, so he must have heard.

Luckily, Anne had seen her father raking along the drive. She was very glad to know of her father's whereabouts. She wanted to direct the master away as quickly as possible.

Charles' puzzlement was interrupted by a pointed finger at the end of a slender hand. The signal made the lord turn his gaze in that direction and catch a glimpse of someone up ahead. That was the information he had asked for, even if it was delivered in an unusual fashion, and he hurried off, glad to be finished with the non-verbal worker.

The Right Honorable Charles Frances Greville, as master of this property and employer of all who worked here, muttered to himself as he walked away. He was miffed that the laborer failed to jump to his feet and tend to his bidding. A master walked a thin line between an amiable relationship and wielding the upper hand. If he lost control, laziness and disrespect might follow. Once lost, it was difficult to gain a good measure of work out of any servant.

He had to think, was not the gardener doing as he had no doubt been instructed? Charles decided he would speak with the man on his way back to the house. He continued down to the drive. There he found the hunched over figure of George swinging a rake, collecting leafy debris into piles.

"Ah, there you are," he called out.

"Yes sir." called George in reply, finishing the last circle that drew the leaves together into a central pile. He looked up and leaned on the rake.

"I am expecting another shipment of plants from Banks tomorrow. Several of the specimens are from the New South Wales collection. Not sure just what will be in the crate or in what condition they will be."

"Yes sir," George repeated, staring at the ground as if he were not paying attention.

"We will find them a spot in the hothouse, yes, George?" Charles added a bit of merriment to his voice hoping to assure George of his total confidence.

"Yes sir," George said again. This time he added a note of assurance to his answer. With George, his "yes sirs" were the best Lord Greville could expect and fine enough if one listened closely for the intonation in the old gardener's voice.

"Say, I spoke briefly with the young man working in the roses."

George's cheeks flushed knowing there was no such man working in the roses. He pictured Anne in his clothes. He almost panicked, but held onto his humble apology until he knew how angry his lordship might be. George wondered how the interview

46

could have possibly proceeded and yet yielded such a civil manner in his master.

"Actually, we did not speak," Lord Greville said. An uncontrollable smile came across his face covering for his embarrassment. "He was quite busy with the weeding I suppose. Huh! Who is the young man? What name do you address him by?" demanded the lord.

George collected himself after hearing that they had not spoken. He was relieved Lord Greville was still unaware that it was, in fact, his daughter. He would plead confusion and ignorance, characteristics an old servant could use to his advantage at this point.

"Do not know for sure, sir." The gardener looked as if he were thinking, and then shook his head as if he were not able to answer the master's question. "We have had many young men helping these past weeks." The elderly man took up the rake again, holding it tightly.

"Well, he seems to be the only other gardener here, but no matter." Lord Greville was reluctant to pursue the point any further. He watched the elderly man begin to rake as if he were not standing there at all. Had he lost control of these servants already?

"I intend to speak to him on my way back to the house. My sisters will be visiting soon; we will want the garden to ourselves on those days," Charles blurted out in frustration. He could only imagine his sisters and their reaction to a waving gardener.

George waited until Lord Greville moved off to draw in a breath. He wanted to moan, but he slowed his raking and wiped a tear from his cheek. He had feigned ignorance. He had lied to the master.

The lord intended to reprimand the rude young man upon his return. The young man's insubordination was becoming more irritating with each step back down the path. The rose garden was empty. There was no sign of another gardener anywhere. The lord felt dissatisfied with himself for not dealing with the situation in a firmer manner.

In addition, he was uncomfortable with George's reaction. Was the elderly man so unaware he did not know who worked with him in the garden? The experience left Charles disquieted.

The smell of the roses met Lord Greville's nose as he took long steps to the library door. He had not noticed the smell when he passed the rose garden itself, but now the odor was unmistakable. He turned back to glance at the roses. Odd, there was not one flower as of yet. The scent on the air was distinctly that of roses. Disgruntled, he left behind the garden, the rude gardener, George's confusion, and the scent of roses as he entered the house in search of Mrs. Lambert for a discussion of next week's events.

Anne crept back to the cottage. She redressed and busily prepared a dinner. Only half an hour later, her father came in from his duties and went straight to the bench to remove his boots. Anne was thankful to be busy separating meat from the bones of a rabbit, leftover from Lord Greville's supper of the previous day.

She was not certain how much had been said by Lord Greville about his interaction with her in the rose garden, but her father's lack of greeting spoke to the state of his mood. She knew her father would be displeased with her behavior. She was prepared for a deserved reproof. As her father still said nothing, she bravely took up the subject.

"I'm so sorry, Father. Lord Greville did not know who it was. I suppose I should not have been there working at that time of day. I did not expect him." Anne tried to explain.

"You did not expect him in his own garden? It is not for you to expect him or not. Keep clear, Anne!" Her father answered sharply. Anne could tell he was greatly annoyed with her, as he never raised his voice.

"The master's return makes it necessary for you to stop your wandering, especially dressed as an undergardener! Lord Greville could dismiss me for such actions. I lied to him." George's voice quieted as if worn down. "I do not care to lie to any man, but certainly not the man for whom I hold the utmost esteem and my living."

Anne stood quietly facing her father. She kept her head bent and thought hard about what her father said. She was truly sorry, but the tears collecting at the corners of her eyes were due to her father's tone, not remorse.

"I can only imagine how you were able to keep your identity from him. This will not do, Anne," he said firmly.

Anne's father instructed her while he struggled with his boots. It was evident he was tired and his body strained. He did not implore her further. He shook his head and closed his eyes as he looked away from her.

"Yes, I know, I did not think of the circumstances. Lord Greville came down the path so quickly. He did not discover who I was, and I was able to guide him to you without speaking." Anne thought how ridiculous her pointed finger must have appeared.

Her hand! Oh no. Her heart skipped. She had not thought of her hand without a glove. Horrified, she swallowed to calm her stomach.

"I don't want you to walk anywhere in his garden. You must stay out as his sisters will be visiting one day soon. It will not do for you to be caught walking about."

Anne could tell there would be no discussion. His words were final, and she would do as she was told. She could feel that her world had just grown smaller with denying her visits to the roses. Time would pass, and her father might rescind this punishment. It would be best to leave the conversation for now. It had been a close call and she did not want to make trouble for her father.

"You should not go about the glasshouse either," her father continued.

This was too much for Anne. Without thinking she added, "Perhaps I should just take up needlepoint and stay here in the cottage all day." She was not accustomed to being rude to her father, but the idea of never entering the glasshouse was unbearable. Sitting deep in the foliage of the hothouse was one of her last escapes from the nothingness in the rest of her life.

What was to become of her? What was left for her to do? What would occupy her days? She had her drawings of course, but what did she chose to draw? Her subjects were almost always in the garden. This was too much to ask. She could not obey and feared he would insist she stay away.

"You must be careful not to offend the master with your roaming. When he was away, that was allowable, but upon his return... I see that I have been too lax, allowing you such freedom. There are appropriate activities for you, and acting as gardener is not one of them."

"What are those activities, Father? What can I do to help? I cannot wait for a governess position any longer. I want to assume some usefulness, some reason for my being. I have nothing that is needed of me."

George Blake sighed and sat by the fire to rest his legs and aching feet. Anne hated to upset her father, especially at the end of another busy day. She came to his side and sat by him on the floor taking his foot into her hands and rubbing his heel softly.

"I am sorry. We have each other, and that is enough for me for now. It is enough for any daughter to have such a good father. I should not complain, but I would like to contribute. We will speak of it no more."

Anne meant what she said. She had no desire for other company, and though new friends had been slow in coming, she could take comfort in knowing her life was simple and without the fear of utmost poverty so many without employment were experiencing, but she wished for a new start. Her stay had become extended. She did not want to tax her father anymore tonight. She would pray for a change soon.

As the week came to an end, Anne kept away from the garden altogether. She finished her sketch of the lord in the greenhouse and began to add color. She sketched another drawing of the roses on the vines. She had only her daydreams of an introduction to Lord Greville and another conversation with Tom to occupy her thoughts. She no longer dwelled on thoughts of her life just months before.

When Sunday came around, Anne was thankful for the diversion of attending church. She walked to church each week with Sybil, as her father had yet to attend church. The plants were his excuse. After church, they would take a turn or two around Paddington Green. Many people did so if the weather was fine. The girls stayed on the grass side of the road and steered clear of the canals, unsavory territory for two young women alone.

The two were engaged in conversation as they met a crowd of several persons walking in ones and twos. Towering above them all was a young man with a tuft of light gold hair peeking below the brim of his hat. He was looking over the crowd at Anne as the two women waded through the wave of people walking in the opposite direction.

The blond boy did not attend their church. Anne knew she had not seen him in the congregation. He stuck out from the rest; he was so tall, well dressed, and self-assured. As the girls passed, Anne let her eyes settle on him for just an instant and in that time, a moment he seemed to be waiting for, he tipped his hat to acknowledge her look. Anne was mortified that the boy caught her paying attention. When they came around the opposite corner of the square and met him once again, Anne could not control the silly smile that crossed her lips. This time they looked at each other and gave a nod.

"Say a greeting to him, Anne. He looks right at you every time we pass. You could speak of the weather or the crowd of people, but certainly you could begin with 'how do you do?' I think he is the dairyman's son. He has an air about him that suggests more, but I believe he is the one who delivers milk to Cook each week."

It surprised Anne to hear this. Although she did not think he was a nobleman, she did suppose he was the son of a merchant, quite well to do. A dairyman's son with such mannerisms seemed out of place, but she knew little of the trade, really.

The women made their way around the Green one last time and saw the tall blond head coming toward them as they turned toward the lane that led back to Lord Greville's house. Anne noticed the boy hurried to meet them before they could leave the square. It seemed he would say something as his approach took a straight line to them. He almost came to a stop as he was only a few steps away, but then he started his walk again and passed them by.

Sybil and Anne trotted up Lord Greville's drive, giggling together. Anne stopped on the lane and took a peek back toward the Green, trying to control the hiccoughs of laughter. There in her view was the tall boy with the gold hair looking after them. Anne turned back to Sybil with a new series of giggles, a bit thrilled to be the object of the boy's attention.

7

*E*ach night, after her father was asleep, Anne made a trip out to the opening in the hedge where she had a clear view of the manor and Lord Greville's library. Peering into the darkness, a light through the windows was obvious. She would know Lord Greville was still awake. With that, Anne could predict a later hour of rising for the nobleman. If she vacated early, she could visit the greenhouse in the early morning hours.

The near discovery in the rose garden had been an awakening. It was a foolish risk, she realized now. The mishap could have dealt serious consequences for her father's employment and her own future prospects. She folded her father's old sweater and pants, and put them on the shelf at the end of his bed. She would not wear them again.

She would not visit the greenhouse this morning though she had seen a light the night before. Not only had she been disturbed by the yet to be solved mystery of Lord Greville's sorrow, but as much as she hated to admit it, her mind had strayed to thoughts of a certain dark-haired delivery boy. Another order was due today, and she had not fully recovered from the previous episode with Tom in the storeroom. She would make her way to the kitchen a little later in the morning.

Reliving those few moments with Tom remained exciting. She pictured him taking the step toward her over and over. She swooned at the look in his eyes, but remembering Becky's face at the end was not so pleasing. Becky was the conclusion of many a good daydream, Anne lamented.

She also thought about the dairyman's son. She saw his head sticking up above the crowd, tipping his hat to her. She was flattered by his attention, but it did not spark the same emotions as the incident in the dark storeroom. The blond boy's eagerness to be acquainted put her off.

As Anne imagined how she should approach a reunion with Tom, she practiced acting coy. As she acted with a rehearsal, she knew she could never perform such expressions as genuine. She thought of being brazen, but then she thought of Becky once again. She could never act in such a way. She found there was a limit to these contemplations.

Anne kept herself busy putting a new hem on a dress. Soon it held her complete attention. The sound of the horse crunching up the gravel driveway did not alert her. At the end of the full skirt's circumference, Anne realized a great deal of time had passed. She hurried down the path and past the hall door to check for the cart on the drive. Seeing it there, she rushed into the kitchen, shocking Cook with her sudden entrance. Anne was disappointed to see packages already on the kitchen table.

"Well, there you are!" the older woman declared.

"Tom is finished." Cook gave a side-glance in Anne's direction. Anne sat down flustered, looking toward the door as if the gypsy boy might still come through it. She wondered if she dared go out.

Cook noticed the direction of her gaze.

"Ah, Becky has helped him with the storeroom door, do not go out there."

Anne looked at Cook, astonished at her mind-reading. Another minute passed before Becky came in, stomped through the kitchen, and slammed the hall door as she left. Whatever had happened in the storeroom between the two had not been to Becky's liking. Anne was further surprised when Tom re-entered the kitchen moments later.

He looked at Anne with an odd expression. She pulled her sad expression into a welcoming smile. She noticed a bulge under his vest that Cook could not see from her vantage point.

Cook looked up from her work, glancing at the boy, "Yes Tom? Is there something else?"

Tom looked dismayed. He saw Anne watched him from the table.

"No, just wishing you both a good day." His smile did not cover the guilt Anne saw on his face.

"Thank you, Tom," Cook answered. Anne turned slightly toward him and offered another smile, hoping to encourage conversation. There would be no further interaction. Tom departed as suddenly as he had returned.

Anne chided herself for the silliness of her actions. She had wasted so much time thinking of her conversation with Tom. All her plans for an interlude were reduced to a dull smile and nothing more. Tom would not be back for another seven days.

All the long week, Anne kept in seclusion as her father had instructed. She fussed about the cottage cleaning walls already spotless, sweeping a hearth already clear, and washing linens not nearly soiled. She let her mind wander to castles and princesses, but only conjured up an angry master and a worried father. She learned nothing more of the master's health. She visited Cook only two times in the week, and she missed a walk on Sunday due to rain.

As the day and then hour of Tom's delivery finally approached, Anne made herself more useful about the kitchen, hoping to have a chance to overlap with the delivery boy again.

"Anne, you have been here all morning. I am quite finished with my work, bless you."

"I have little to do, and my father says I am to keep clear of the garden."

"And it is a grocery day," the chef added slyly. Her puffy cheeks ballooned out with a big smile.

"I-," Anne began, but at that moment Sybil arrived with a summons for Anne from Mrs. Lambert.

Mrs. Lambert wished to match the style of new upstairs draperies with any of Anne's memories about drapes at the Duke's estate. Anne tried to have patience as she spoke with the housekeeper. She was still hoping to return to the kitchen in time to see Tom. She gave short answers. In the end, Anne gave a description of one fabric used for curtains and some chairs in the main dining room. It was a design she had favored over the rest in the house and seemed to supply the kind of information that suited Mrs. Lambert.

"They were an off white, not cream exactly, but more like milk than snow. The stripes of small flowers were royal blue, but thin and spaced every inch or so. The stripes came together where the folds of the curtains curved in and out, so the blue stood out."

With that, the housekeeper dismissed her, but minutes too late to see Tom. It would be more than a week before the young man returned and by then, any interaction would seem farfetched.

With another week, came the only other highlight, another Sunday. Yet there was no blond boy following Anne and Sybil on the square. It allowed the women to have intimate conversations. They talked about Sybil's sisters who worked for a great family in the north. In addition, Sybil inquired after the reason Anne had left her previous employer.

"They let you go? With so little cause after all those years?" Anne hated to admit that yes, it seemed they did her an injustice. In addition, she still had not received the letter of reference or news of a position as governess. The future held no reassurance for Anne. Her talk with Sybil only made it more evident.

"My sister had such a situation." Sybil hurried on to say. "She was given some boots by a fellow servant and tricked into thinking they were discards from the daughter of her employer. As she wore them for the first time, the young lady recognized her boots; my sister was labeled a thief. In the end, the truth came to light and the other girl was let go. The daughter gave my sister the boots. The mother said it was as a reward for their misjudgment, but the daughter made it clear that she could not think of wearing a shoe in which my sister had put her foot."

Anne wanted to speak to Sybil about Becky, but she feared Sybil might think her petty. She wished to continue her relationship with the older maid without impediments. Sybil treated Anne as a younger sister. She understood Anne's plight, her idleness, and how helpless Anne was to do anything about her situation. Anne did not bring up the subject of Tom. An element of shame prevented her from speaking openly, and in addition, she feared any news of her interest might get back to Becky. On their last turn around the Green, Sybil teased Anne about the dairyman's son.

"He hasn't been out walking since we ran away. His reluctance to speak to you has increased your interest."

"Indeed it has, though I do not wish to mislead him by showing more than I feel."

"You should be pleased to have such a suitor, Anne," Sybil advised.

That night, as Anne lay awake in bed, she could not control the slow tears that wet her pillow. Nothing was going as she hoped.

Spring gave way to summer; the sky opened up and the temperatures increased. All around the garden, her father's efforts were evident as foliage and flowers crowded together. For Anne, life stayed very much the same. Longer days meant only more time with nothing to do.

In the afternoons or evenings, Anne sewed napkins and handkerchiefs. Sometimes she could help Cook, but when neither occupation called, she worked on her drawing of the master. That one disturbing image still haunted her, but she preferred to remember how he appeared lying on the hothouse floor, handsome and at peace.

One consolation to time's progression was that her father had reconciled with her visits to the garden when the master was not about. Anne imagined meeting Lord Greville. She thought to make amends for her behavior in the rose garden, but she also knew the subject must never be approached. No such meeting would occur today as Cook had informed Anne that the master would be away for several days. There was no need to pick berries or extra produce, as no meals would be prepared.

Though Anne thought she would enjoy a morning of drawing in the garden, she produced nothing but scribbles. She took the path back to the house planning a visit with Cook before heading back to her small domain. She started toward the back hall door, but a glint of glass caught her attention. The two massive doors, arches of leaded glass, that led from the garden into the master's library stood wide open.

Extending her walk past her intended destination, Anne stood directly outside the room with the very open doors. The sun was not yet around the corner of the house, so the interior was not bright, but for one small slice of light. Anne could see the lord's desktop which held piles of papers. The view made her wonder if there were any sketches of an orchid sitting there or any other clue to the man's discontent.

She knew Lord Greville was not at home, as Cook had mentioned. Anne would not bother a thing, just take a quick look. She let her feet take her one after another until she stood behind the very desk she had been looking at only seconds before. She scanned across the desk for any drawings. The top sheet of paper in the pile on one side of the desk contained notes covered with numbers and odd symbols. Piled on the other side were letters with elegant penmanship. She did not look closer as guilt seeped in, preventing her from meddling further in Lord Greville's private affairs.

The wall to the left of the desk held books from floor to ceiling. It reminded her of the Duke's library though so much smaller in size. The shelves and a glass front cabinet beyond held what looked to be rocks, which was surely possible, as the master was known to be quite a collector of mineral specimens.

Anne panicked when she heard the rhythmic noise of feet coming down the hallway. She stood frozen with fear. Sybil passed by on her way upstairs with a basket of laundry. Unnoticed, Anne let go of her breath. Surely, if she had any sense she would vacate the place immediately. Instead, she looked around the room from behind the desk.

Anne's attention traveled up from the doorway to a large portrait of a woman. Anne was puzzled by the woman's costume. The white robe she wore was gathered under the breast with a tight golden belt accenting the curves of her body. Anne studied the muscles of her arms as the woman clenched a knife in one hand and hung onto a wreath of leaves on her head with the other. The background beyond the figure was a foreboding grey and dark red. The artist had painted the woman's shawl blown back off her shoulders as if she stood in a tempest. The woman's beauty was arresting. Anne could not take her eyes from her features; they were so perfect. The angle of the light in the painting shone a non-human aura to her face, suggesting a heavenly view of a goddess. She glowed from the dark canvas with the light the artist had given her. The draping of fabric for her dress was so true to life. Anne pulled a paper from her folder as she balanced it awkwardly on her hip. She was thinking she might sketch the woman's face. Anne fumbled for a pencil, but then remembered she was standing in the lord's library and thought better of the idea. She would not easily forget what she had seen.

This must be Emma Hamilton. Anne tried not to dislike her for her beauty. She would not disdain her because of the rumors. Such a woman must have been difficult for the master to surrender for the promise of fortune, as people said. Surely if Lord Greville looked into this face each day as he sat at his desk, he must still feel a deeper attachment than Cook had suggested.

Had Lord Greville suffered a broken heart? Had relief from his debts been enough to send his mistress away without regret? Why had Lord Greville never married? Anne longed for answers. She recalled the sobs in the greenhouse. She pictured the letters on the stem of his drawing - had he written Emma's name? With one last view of the room and smiling at her discovery, Anne pirouetted back toward the open doors.

Just at that moment, Lord Greville dashed into the library. He had forgotten notes for a meeting. The lord was alerted to another's presence by the dark silhouette in the bright doorway. The figure appeared to have no features whatsoever as he failed to realize she was turned away from him. He could see the form took the shape of a woman in a simple dress. The master of the house cleared his throat, ready to ask the identity of the unknown person in his library. Instead, "Excuse me." was all he uttered.

The clearing of a deep male throat frightened Anne. She took three quick steps, escaping the room to the wide-open doorway. The question came from the master, yet she was too unnerved to turn her body and look at him directly. She took two more steps, grabbing the doorframe and pulling herself through the threshold. Anne turned only a quarter of the way back toward her father's employer, looking down with a bit of a bow. "Sorry," she murmured, hurrying out to the refuge of the garden.

60

Anne ran down the pathway past the kitchen doorway and the rose garden to the back of the drive. She looked for somewhere to hide and found a break in the hedge where she waited for the sound of footsteps or calling out, but no one pursued her.

Charles Greville was not the type of man to talk down to his servants. He had never let one go. As the second son of an earl, he wandered the world with more tolerance than some. He had friends in all levels of society. Yet, he could not believe his inaction as he watched the figure disappear from view out his library doors, giving her time to escape, pitying her rather than demanding answers.

"Oh, I am slipping. To let a view of a woman give me such leave of my good senses." Charles rubbed his forehead and shook his head smiling at his own indolence. He should be enraged, but he had no tendency to be.

The girl was not part of the household staff as far as he knew, but he was not completely sure. In addition, she did not carry the tools of a housekeeper, but she did have something under her arm, a flat folder of some sort. He scanned the top of his desk, but there was no disarray. The papers he sought were still in their pile on the side of the desktop. What was the young woman doing in his house? He was puzzled.

He would mention the affair to Mrs. Lambert upon his return. No need to put the household in an uproar now, he had no time for it. The person did not seem dangerous. Of course, the incident could not go by unaccounted. There must certainly be an explanation.

The lord might have pondered longer about the apparition had he not been in a hurry to take up his notes and get to the coach. As he leaned across his desk, he noticed a paper on the floor. He moved around the end of the desk to retrieve it. The paper held the lines of a fine drawing of what he recognized immediately as the inside of his glasshouse. The corner bench and a few of the plants at that end of the building were familiar. In the drawing was a man who looked very much like himself. The man was bent concentrating on something on the bench where he stood. Charles looked up and out the open doors. Odd, had this ghost of a female made the drawing?

He took up his notes, smiling to himself. The irony of what he had found compared to the notes he had come back to acquire from the top of the desk did not escape him. The notes contained plant drawings from several artists within the covers of a book. Lord Greville planned to meet with his good friend, Sir Joseph Banks. They would discuss the work of a mutual friend whose premature death resulted in unlabeled drawings of flora found on the islands of Greece.

So strange, he thought. He looked up at the open door threshold once more before he exited. He pictured the long fingers of a slender hand on the doorframe. There was something familiar about the hand, but he could not place it at this moment. He recalled now that the silhouette showed uncontrolled curls coming loose from the ribbon tied at the nape of the mysterious female's neck; significant clues for later identification. For now, the enigma would be safe from exposure. The nobleman planned to be away for days. He slipped the drawing into the leather case with the other notes. It was the only evidence he had that the woman had been there at all, that and the definite scent of roses.

Anne remained hidden in the hedge at the back of the garden for an hour. After half that time, the trembling stopped. After another quarter hour, she began to experience shame and disbelief in her actions. For the last fifteen minutes, she began to fear the inevitable rebuke still to come.

8

harles Greville would make the visit to Warwick Castle that he so dreaded. The situation had more effect on him than he cared to admit. The financial issues were settled. On his return trip, he would stop to see his friend, Sir Joseph Banks. He looked to that leg of the journey to be the more uplifting part of his time away from Paddington.

John Stewart, the 7th Earl of Galloway, took possession of the Warwick holdings. He did so to avoid embarrassment caused by the foolish spending of Charles' brother, George, the current Earl of Warwick. John Stewart had been married to Charles' sister, Mary. She died when Charles was in his teens, and his brother-in-law had remained close to the family even after Mary's death and the sad death of each of their two children.

John Stewart, Charles Greville, as well as Charles' younger brother, Robert Greville, held positions on the Privy Council, trusted allies to the king. Charles had looked to John Stewart much in the same way one would look to an older brother, a relationship Charles did not have with his own brother, George. The two men saw each other on occasion at court, but had not engaged in a discussion of the distress in the family's holdings until they met privately just over a year before.

John Fitzpatrick, the 2nd Earl of Upper Ossory, also stepped forward to save the family's interests. Fitzpatrick's half-sister, Henrietta Vernon, was George's current wife. Their reckless spending had brought the family's name to the brink of disaster. Fitzpatrick had been aware of George and Henrietta's situation over the years. The two earls, Stewart and Fitzpatrick, would join in the project of managing the lands out of debt for George. The noblemen assured Charles that little had changed as they took charge of the affairs of the estate. As they were each family members, the estate was safe. Not knowing how long this arrangement might last, Charles felt everything had changed and would never again be the same.

"You will always be welcome, Charles." Stewart told him as they finished looking over the last of the tenant records.

"We want your family to visit the castle whenever they wish." For Charles, the term "visit" said it all. In that these gentlemen had taken over the financial mess left by his brother, Charles felt they deserved complete control of their new estate. Neither of the earls expected to reside in the ancient fortress, but still Charles did not wish to inconvenience these relatives with his coming and goings. He emptied his rooms of everything but the furnishings.

"Thank you, John, your understanding of our situation has been most fortunate. It has been a difficult time for George and Henrietta with the death of their child and the retrenchment. You have proven to be a loyal friend."

Lord Greville had no plans to return to Warwick anytime soon. There was no homesick longing for the place as the earls might expect. If he closed his eyes, he could easily picture the grey towers stretching up into the sky above the vast landscaped park. The structure intimidated several enemies over the centuries, and reminded the local populace of the power of the landowner as well.

The castle was as massive with quarried stone as it was thick with history. A millennium of events had taken place within the walls. Many were reminded by his sisters that their bloodlines "dated back to William the Conqueror," and in fact, the ancient leader was buried on the castle grounds. Even Charles felt humbled as he entered the courtyard.

Once inside, the family's quarters were much cozier with a fine view of the river Avon. Some memories were as clear as the water over the waterfall. Other memories Charles allowed to fade. He had stayed away from his family as much as possible over most of his adult life, returning only for an occasional holiday, wedding, or funeral.

With the inheritance from his uncle and his position in society repaired, Charles had returned several times to examine books and consult gardeners with his plans to build a greenhouse. He would avoid such impromptu visits in the future, at least until George might be able to resume possession. Charles had heard that it might take at least five years for the estate to bounce back from debt, but even he felt that might be an optimistic guess.

"I leave you now, as I hope to include a visit to Sir Joseph at Spring Grove on my return to Paddington."

"Please give Sir Joseph my humble regards. I have not seen him of late." Stewart said.

"His gout troubles him. It limits his activities out of the house, but never his interest. Still quite busy despite his health." Charles gave the nobleman a clench on his arm and the two men embraced briefly.

Charles was anxious to see the Banks family. The visits there were always comfortable in the way true friends make one feel. He no more shut the door before he was accosted by two boys, some of the Stewart clan. Obviously, they had been waiting for him.

Robert Stewart had sired sixteen children with his second wife. Charles lost track of the children's children, the Earl's grandchildren, years ago. It seemed to Charles that many of the grandchildren were of the same ages and names as the children and thus the confusion. Several children roamed the halls and the grounds during his stay at Warwick, and he merely smiled at them all, unable to guess to whom they might belong.

"We wish to hear something about the ghosts," the older of the two boys stated. It occurred to Charles that this boy might well be the future Duke of Marlborough, and the son of Stewart's daughter, Susan.

"Yes, yes, please Uncle Charles. Our fathers will not speak of it and everyone we ask says we must be too idle to be concerned with such things," said the younger and much smaller boy.

Charles noted the younger boy was almost shaking with enthusiasm for the topic. Charles sized them up and felt they were certainly old enough for some ghostly fun as Charles and his brothers had been at their age. The term "uncle" was not uncommon between them all, and Charles knew as an uncle he was expected to tease them relentlessly, but for now a good ghost story would do. He backed down the dark paneled hall away out of the candlelight. He stooped down to speak to the boys as if in confidence.

"Well, if you see anything unusual in this room here," Charles noted the room from which he had just exited, whispering for extra effect, "that would be Ralph."

"Ralph?" The two boys repeated simultaneously. One could tell the boys were disappointed in the common name given to the ghost. They so wished for something foreign with many syllables.

"Yes, his name would be Ralph Haywood. Do not fear him as he means no harm. He is very sorry and wishes only to make amends to all who will pay him any attention." Charles stopped there to let the boys absorb that much of the story. He checked their expressions for any signs of fear, but neither showed anything but keen interest.

"What? Is he guilty of a crime, perhaps a murder?" the younger one asked, making it evident he already knew something of the story.

"Yes, you have guessed it! It was your great, great, oh many greats uncle who was murdered. It is suggested Ralph comes here to look for his master to apologize."

"Oh, I think I saw the pen move from one location to another on the desk once, as if he were trying to write something," the younger boy said. He looked to Charles for affirmation and was happy to get an immediate response from his almost uncle.

"Now that might have been old Fulke himself, the Great Uncle. They say he tries to write a better portion into his will for Ralph who was angered by his small inheritance. For that reason, Ralph stabbed his master in the back, a cowardly act indeed."

"Was there not a female ghost also?" Again, it was the younger boy, Randolph was his name, Charles remembered. He was the eldest grandson and waited in line to be an Earl someday. He exuded the confidence of his position. The older one would certainly be George Spencer's son, another George, as was tradition.

"A female specter? I always thought it was Lady Jane Grey, who walks about. She will not bother or even notice you. She seeks her husband and his father. Lady Grey's arranged marriage and declaration as Queen of England cost the lady her life. Her reign lasted only nine days whereupon they were all three beheaded for treason. I have never seen the lady, but I am apt to walk about absent minded, not looking for ghosts."

Charles looked at the boys who displayed satisfaction with the answers he had given. He saw his chance to escape.

"I wish you best of luck with your sightings, gentlemen." He eased away, leaving the two boys giggling and elbowing each other with an "I told you so." Next time, Charles would remind them about the oubliette in the dungeon basement and the cries for help that so many thought they heard.

9

ord Greville knew he arrived at his friend's manor when rows of apple trees and beds of strawberries mulched with yellow straw ran along the lane. He felt the horses slowing as they came in front of the house. Charles could not keep the grin from his face, so pleased to see his oldest and dearest friend.

Sir Joseph Banks had been expecting Charles all morning, and yet he startled when his butler announced the arrival. Banks had been so absorbed in examining drawings that his clock watching had stopped, and he had forgotten about the visit altogether. Now that his friend was announced, he reined his mind in and away from the desktop.

"Come in, come in!" Banks shouted across the room from behind his massive oak table. The piles of papers arranged in rows had been under Sir Joseph's scrutiny all morning. Each pile contained hand colored drawings of plants with similar characteristics organized by their Linnaean names, keeping those of the same genus or family together. One feature, the way in which the flowers pollinated, determined the plant's uniqueness with a Latin name of its very own.

Carl Linnaeus had developed the method for organizing all living things. For plants, Linnaeus chose the male sexual parts of the flowers, the stamens, as the key indicator for the distinction of the twenty-three classes into which all plants were divided. The female parts, the pistils, further divided these classes into orders. Banks was passionate about adhering to these rules and assigning names accordingly.

The method of identification had arrived just in time to classify the new species coming into England from explorations across the globe. Working through the new collections could be accomplished in less time with less confusion or so Banks liked to think until moments such as these. He was a stickler for detail.

Sir Joseph Banks was a stout man. He reminded Charles of an owl with a slightly jutting brow crested with bushy eyebrows and an invisible neck where his head hooked to his shoulders. He sat hunched in his chair at the head of meetings as the great and wise overseer of the forest of information concerning the natural world.

Banks had the most engaging manner of anyone Charles knew. Lord Greville considered him the best of his friends; one to be trusted, but one who would give his opinion freely when asked or perhaps even when not asked. Banks put anyone with whom he wished to speak at ease, but he could also exude an austere presence, difficult to tolerate, when he was disappointed or dissatisfied with a fellow.

Suffering from acute gout, Sir Joseph stayed seated in his wheel chair and cringed a bit, as he straightened himself when Charles made his way across the room. The invalid flagged his servant over to remove the tub in which his feet were soaking. The manservant wrapped the bright red feet in hot, dry towels while Sir Joseph sipped on herbal tea.

Charles walked through the brightly lit room. He was surrounded by bureaus, some with glass fronts and some with

70

stacks of small drawers that pulled out as trays. Charles knew the drawers were full of collections of all the items in the natural world. There were shelves laden with rocks, shells, dried mushrooms, stuffed birds, bird nests. Vases of dried herbs adorned the top of most of the cabinets. The view was very like a storeroom in a museum or university; and this was only a part of the man's collections.

"Come, Charles. I have need of your help." Banks beckoned to his friend.

Charles felt shame for his laziness compared to Sir Joseph. He had accomplished little for the world, and less for others. If there were a ceremony to celebrate Sir Joseph's honors, it would take days to name them all he supposed. His friend was not only a member of several scientific societies but usually an officer. In addition to his titles, he was President of the Royal Society, a trustee to the British Museum, and curator of the royal gardens at Kew. He held numerous honorary degrees bestowed upon him by the best universities in the country. He had written numerous treatises about plants diseases, insects, and propagation.

Now Banks was often confined to this wheelchair, unable to walk, suffering from unimaginable torture in his feet and toes, and yet he took other projects to task. It was difficult for Charles to watch his old friend deal with the debilitating pain. At times, Charles' stomach bothered him to a point of distraction and he had repetitive headaches, but none of the symptoms was chronic.

There was a time when the arrival of a young and charismatic Joseph Banks and a handsome Charles Greville, sent a murmur throughout a crowd at a ball. Each had taken mistresses, and Banks had fathered a child at one point although it was never discussed. Unlike Charles, the death of Sir Joseph's father had provided Banks with considerable fortune and lands. For Charles, the death of his father, the Earl of Warwick, only lessened his small stipend.

Sir Joseph's marriage had come at the right point in Bank's life, Charles believed. Charles deemed Dorothea a superior woman. She matched Banks' mental abilities in a way that must have been quite satisfactory for his brilliant friend. To have a wife attend to you when you were in such a condition had to be a great comfort, also.

The Banks family was very close. Sir Joseph's wife and sister shared the responsibility as fellow mistresses in the households of Sir Joseph. They shared in their care for brother and husband without squabble or competition. The two women were inseparable. It was always a pleasure for Charles to spend time with them.

"Smith sent over the last few of Old Sibthorp's journals to work through. The letters are not easy to decipher, and there are numbers on many of Bauer's drawings to indicate the colors. Sowerby is anxious to start on the engravings." Banks heaved a sigh, weary with the project laid out across his desk.

"I am baffled by this euphorbia. It is well drawn, and it appears to be the dendroides. Still, I worry I am missing something in the drawing Bauer made and Sibthorp failed to finish labeling. They grow to an amazing six feet, Charles! There is no sense of how big the thing is from the drawing." Charles heard his friend's frustration.

Dr. Robert Sibthorp had been the Professor of Botany at Oxford. He died from complications of the tuberculosis that plagued him the last year of his life. As a fellow enthusiast of plant collecting and identification, he recorded hundreds of plants on his visit to Greece and the Aegean islands. Many were also recorded in Ferdinand Bauer's sketches. Their enthusiasm surpassed their ability to record every detail of the plants as so many new species were being discovered each day. Bauer had no time to paint them all and thus labeled them with a color code to tint at a later date. When Sibthorp returned to the area to collect more specimens, he had become quite ill and never recovered.

72

Charles leaned over the drawings. He was glad to be of assistance, but equally pleased that the project had not landed on his desk.

"I am sorry it falls to you, with so many tasks already, but you know you would not have had it any other way," Charles said. "I brought you some handwritten notes I had from Sibthorp. They might be of use to you and Smith in deciphering his writing." Charles handed Sir Joseph the papers. They were the very notes he had retrieved from his library desktop. He thought of the intruder briefly, but there would be time to speak of the incident later.

The executor of Sibthorp's will was his brother-in-law, Robert Hawkins. Hawkins had in turn hired James E. Smith at one hundred fifty pounds per year to sort through the notes and correlate them to plates, putting it all together into a book, which Sibthorp had planned to call <u>Flora Graeca</u>.

"As Hawkins pointed out to Smith, Sibthorp had no intention of dying or he would have marked his drawings rather than committing the information to memory. There are notes on this drawing for instance, but they are all about fishing! That is of no help to me, my good Doctor," Banks said, looking in the general direction of Heaven, as if Sibthorp might hear.

Sibthorp's artist, Ferdinand Bauer, had recently returned from another plant-collecting mission in which Sir Joseph took even more interest. The exploration of Botany Bay, so named by Banks and Captain Cook because of the huge amount of unknown flora, had rendered an amazing array of new specimens. Sir Joseph felt indebted to Sibthorp to finish this project before corroborating the new samples. With the aid of Smith and Hawkins, he would do so.

Franz Bauer, Ferdinand's brother, worked to record the plants at Kew Gardens for Sir Joseph. While Ferdinand traveled the world to find the subjects of his botanical art, Franz stayed in England working on a narrower selection of plants, creating an artistic record down to the miniscule parts, the organs of the flowers and even the seeds.

"The return of his brother and the death of their old teacher have kept Franz away from Kew of late, but we hope to get a chance to record as many of your plants as we can in the near future. I am especially interested in the orchids, and Franz seems keen to draw as many as he can for a future publication. First things first, though. I must finish this Sibthorp business." Banks stated firmly.

Charles Greville tried to act concerned with the identification of the euphorbia. The strange flower in the picture, which perplexed Sir Joseph, was indeed well drawn. There should be no confusion. Charles was certain Banks was overly wrought.

"Of course, Banks, dendroides would be correct," Charles stated, looking squarely at the drawing on the left.

"Not that one, Charles." Banks shook his head, "The one on the right." Sir Joseph pushed the drawings away and began a new conversation.

"Have you been to the castle or are you headed north from here?"

"I am heading back to town. Fitzpatrick and Stewart assure me they will do their best with preserving the grounds and the plants that remain alive in the glasshouse. The orangery is bare except for the orange trees, much too large to move."

"How does George fare with these arrangements?" Banks asked.

"Well enough. He seems to be able to keep to himself and ignore all that may be going on around him. It gives him more time to make his soap." Charles commented in a mocking tone, but Banks showed sudden interest.

"He is making soap? How interesting."

"I think it came from experiments in his laboratory. As I said, he keeps to himself. He may be drinking, I have no knowledge," Charles said, shrugging. "George will remain the Earl of Warwick, but he will have none of the privileges that come with the title until the debts have been settled. Certainly all rents from tenants and any farming profit will go to the debtors who have appeared with full accounts." Charles was perturbed by the subject.

"It is a new Greville everyone is whispering about. My critics in the past are now much interested in the harbor at Milford and wish to help me if they can. Foremost they are interested in turning a shilling into a guinea, of that much I am sure," Charles said. His tone and his expression continued to carry a sneer.

Banks gave his friend a look of scorn. Charles no longer owed him money and that relieved any previous tension in their relationship. Though some investors had stepped forward on the Milford project, Banks knew that, on the whole, London based shipping had failed to expand as Charles might have liked.

"I do not need investors," Charles said. "What I need are new merchants who wish to ship goods from my port. I need tradesmen, those who can make a tight barrel or twist a sturdy rope. That is what is lacking. I cannot expect seamen to come to Milford if they cannot purchase what they need locally. Shortly, I will visit the new London docks."

Charles changed the subject entirely.

"Frances and Louisa plan to visit Paddington to see the changes I have made to the grounds and the house." Charles was speaking of his widowed eldest sister, Frances, and his brother, Robert's wife, Louisa.

"They have not seen the front porch or the new layout of the walled garden. Frances likes the statuary, you recall?" Charles reminded his seated friend.

"Yes. I think they will be quite pleased. My ladies and I will return to town soon, also." Banks said. He spoke of his wife and his sister. "I have a visit to the surgeon; perhaps they could just cut the feet off! At any rate, there are diversions for the ladies over the summer. For me, I have my work here that can travel to the study there just as well. I must be satisfied with getting this work accomplished indoors, as I cannot visit my garden as I once did." Banks took a sip of his herbal tea before going on. He squinted at its bitterness as he swallowed.

"Our townhouse dictates no such responsibilities, so all the better to concentrate, but there are interruptions there that can be a nuisance."

Lord Greville wandered off across the room as a servant removed the nobleman's slippers and wiggled socks over the reddened skin and knobby toes. Charles examined a case of stuffed seabirds. Each had a unique patch of feathers on its tail or wing to differentiate it from the rest. He paused to look at them more closely, thinking of the birds at Milford and giving his friend time enough to be aided by his man.

10

$\mathcal{S}$ ir Joseph began to speak as soon as the manservant left the room. "The Society is taking up so much of my time, I feel as though I should probably say no to the next opportunity that comes my way if I am to do honor by the position of President."

Charles knew that his friend took his position as the head of the Royal Society very seriously. Indeed, with the leadership of the likes of Isaac Newton, the Society had always been on the forefront of scientific experimentation. Of late, however, the group had been inundated with antiquaries and learned men rather than those who actually conducted the science. Banks had met with some resistance as he urged the inclusion of a more scientific group of "Fellows," as the members were called.

Banks invited anyone whose pursuit of science needed recognition or discussion to appear before the best minds in England. The Fellows gave out several awards to leaders in scientific experimentation. The most prestigious, the Copley Medal, had been given to Benjamin Franklin for his paper on electricity and

Captain Cook for his observations in the South Seas. Much study went into the selection of the winners of these awards. It took up a great deal of the nobleman's time both at meetings and in his own library. Banks did not want to dwell on his problems with the Society, as he knew Charles was not interested in the politics of the group.

"I, too, desire to see your orchids when they come to bloom, so many of mine have not bloomed." Banks jumped back into the conversation he and Charles were having about the visit of Charles' sister. "I have moved several of the tree orchids into the baskets as your gardener, George, suggested. The roots grow out through the weave and there is new growth, a novel idea really.

"How are the newest plants I sent over? New Holland was a paradise Brown said. He thought New South Wales was more beautiful than his native Scotland. I have to agree, and it saddens me to think I will never see it again. I could not tolerate such a journey now." Banks again spoke with dismay.

"Brown brought back over one hundred orchids. He was the right man for the job. I am so proud to have recommended him."

Charles had heard enough. He admired Brown, but his friend's elation seemed to put Charles in his place even if that was not his intention.

Banks sat back in his chair, trying to relax. He once more shuffled papers on his desk, obviously looking for a certain document. He pulled a paper from the pile and leaned forward to rest his elbows on the desktop.

"Oh, before I forget, I am returning your Treasurer's Report to you for the Horticulture Society meeting. I will not be able to attend. The girls and I are off to Hokum and the shearing after my appointment in town. I hope the Duke of Bedford will grant me a tour of his garden. His Grace has a new hothouse."

Charles knew of Sir Joseph's plans to attend the event. Many thought Banks attended because he was Chairman of the Board of

Agriculture, but actually, Banks came to listen to the exchange of thoughts and ideas that flowed between the new and old farmers. The new farmers, wealthy landowners who had come to take an interest in farming, practiced new methods coming out of books. They had money to buy tools and hire labor. What they did not have was an inherent feeling for the land.

Charles placed the report in his valise. The drawing he found on the library floor remained alone as the only other business in the case. He took the painting out, as he wanted to show it to Banks for his opinion and curiosity's sake.

"I thank you for the orchids in advance; though I, too, have neglected them this spring. George and I wait patiently for the vanilla to bloom again. We missed the bloom that came last week. I was so busy; I took no notice of plants in the greenhouses my first day home."

Charles did not tell Banks how his concern over Prime Minister Pitt's death, the handling of Warwick Castle, his efforts to woo London merchants to his Milford port, and solicitation to him for funds from Emma of all people had overwhelmed him. He was recovering by pleading apathy for politics, ignoring merchants who failed to answer his request for an audience, and refusing to give Emma another penny, though on this last score he had put in a word for her.

"You must try to pollinate the vanilla, Charles! I will send you an article explaining the method."

Sir Joseph almost came up from his chair with his excitement. Banks was interested in the orchid not at all for the flower, but for the economic benefits of vanilla. If the flower could be coaxed to form a seed pod here in an English greenhouse, just imagine the possibilities of growing it elsewhere. Already he had arranged for the camphor tree and mangoes to be sent to his Jamaican reserves. Charles nodded approval, but with much less enthusiasm than his friend.

The morning was progressing and Charles missed an appearance by the Banks women.

"Where is Miss Sophie this morning? Did she not see it was I, or is she waiting in the hall for an interlude?" Charles teased.

"No, no, she has gone off with the wife to church. They insisted you stay for lunch. They asked me to inform you that if you departed before they returned that their sins would be forgiven and their souls would be whole, but their hearts would be broken." Banks sat forward putting his hand out. Charles passed him the sheet of paper he had been holding, waiting for a break in their conversation. Banks never missed a thing, Charles admitted.

"I found this in my library when I was leaving for Warwick. I believe it was dropped by an intruder," Charles stated.

"What? An artistic prowler do you think? Did you see the man?" Banks looked from the drawing to Charles with confusion and concern. Of late, many manors had been robbed by the poor. Jobless men were desperate for anything they could turn into money, but sadly, sometimes the thieves only took food.

"It was a woman," Charles said. He pictured the slender hand on the door frame, the nape of her neck, and the few curls of hair backlit by the sun. It excited him as any apparition would, but a female apparition caused an excitement in different parts of his body.

"A woman? Are you sure?" Banks inquired.

"Quite," said Charles, releasing the memory. "I will get to the bottom of it when I return. For now, I do not fear the intruder as you might expect. She apologized on her way out."

"How strange, Charles. You could not catch and confront her?" Banks asked.

"I did not follow her. I was a bit spellbound."

"The drawing is very fine. The view is the corner of your hothouse, yes?" Banks asserted as he took a magnifier to the lines on the paper.

"Yes, I have never viewed the corner from that angle. I am usually on the stool as the drawing indicates. It is as if I have been secretly observed." Charles shook his head.

"How curious it is. A secret admirer, do you think? I am very interested in what you discover. You must let me know when the mystery is solved." He handed back the drawing and scooted the blankets off his lap. He rose slowly, trying not to make a face that would cause concern.

"Come, let us have a small glass of something before the women get back," piped Banks. He gave Charles a wink as he hobbled out from behind the desk to the small stand where several glasses and a decanter of amber liquid waited.

As predicted, the gentlemen were barely able to empty their glasses before they heard commotion in the hall. Two large women rushed into the room with giddy laughter and a full round of hugs. Their large frames created a wind as they entered. Charles happily reciprocated their hugs with a peck of a kiss on each woman's cheek. Several dogs arrived with panting, clicking nails, and shrill barking which added to the hubbub.

"Oh, Charles!" Lady Banks exclaimed breathlessly. "You have been away so long. Isn't that so, Sophie?"

"Yes, indeed. My heart is all astir." Sir Joseph's sister teased.

Charles beamed at the ladies as they each took their turn at him. They were much fun, no fear of misunderstood attachments. Their friendship for one another had progressed past that distress long ago.

"Well then, I suppose I will not give you your presents if you are going to mock me," Charles quipped. He reached into his pocket and brought out two small packages wrapped and tied with string. He gave them both to Dorthea. She opened them carefully but quickly, so much like an excited child.

"I thought of you when I saw them sitting on the hall table at the castle, available to any of us who wanted the last trinkets from the bedrooms. My relatives had already ransacked the place."

Each lady was a collector in her own right. Dorthea Banks collected porcelain art of all types. She had barns of it. Charles did not think she needed another figurine, but the egg-shaped, lidded bowl and inkwell set were possibly of some use on the lady's desk.

"Oh look, Joseph, it is a lily, a snowflake. How sweetly it is painted. I would think a Hampshire native might have been the artist," Lady Banks said.

"I have no knowledge of their origin, just the pleasure they might give my porcelain queen," Charles interjected.

"I love them, Charles. Thank you so much for thinking of me."

Sophie cleared her throat, "Ahem." She placed one hand on her hip and the other she pushed toward Charles with an open palm. The lord tormented her by acting as though he were finished with gift giving.

"Oh yes, Miss Banks, I should give you something, as well?" Charles fiddled with his pocket and produced a coin. He tossed it her way as one might contribute to a beggar. Sophie struggled to catch it. Upon closer inspection, the large woman let out a small screech.

"Eeee, oh my, Charles! Where in the world...?"

"It has been in my cufflink box for some time now. I have been meaning to give it to you. Is it Roman?"

Sophie carefully held the small silver coin between her thumb and index finger. She collected coins, stamps, tickets, calling cards, and all manner of paper scraps from daily life. She let the light from the library window fall across the coin's face so she could read the inscription. The edges of the coin were irregular, obviously hand stamped.

"No not Roman, much older. To think it was in your cufflink box and traveled here loosely in your pocket, really Charles." She was obviously delighted with the gift. She came closer to give him a kiss, bending down as she was a full six inches taller.

Just like the wind that was created when the two large women and their canines rushed into the library, an identical wind was sucked down the hall as they scurried off to the dining room.

Banks once again insisted Charles stay after lunch.

"Your household does not expect your return until evening. You will certainly cause unnecessary upheaval by arriving home early. You would not begrudge your servants their Sabbath repose? I will get you home by dark." Banks said.

"As you request. I have need of civil conversation. The change of hands at the estate still upsets me though I know it is for the best."

As soon as the ladies were seated for lunch, they recited grace in unison. With a solemn "Amen," their questions began. The first round was traditional, questions of health and family. The conversation moved on, flowing freely as the men and women discussed a variety of topics. Then Sir Joseph gave his ladies a new topic.

"Charles caught an unknown female intruder in his library," he announced, enticing the women to question their friend.

"You did not follow the woman?" Sophia demanded. It was the very same question Sir Joseph had asked. Charles possessed no good explanation, so he merely told the truth.

"Oddly she declared her remorse. I believed I should honor that, forgive, and let her go."

"Oh, Charles, that is so romantic." Sophie chimed in with her head bent to the side and her hand above her large left breast.

"Was it a robbery?" Lady Banks asked. She raised her eyebrows and gave Charles a wary sideways glance. She was far more practical. Charles realized he had only briefly glanced across the top of his desk. He had not seriously considered the aspect of robbery.

"I cannot say. I picked up the notes I had returned for and left the room"

"Well, I am sure your dear Mrs. Lambert will get to the bottom of it," Lady Banks added with satisfaction.

Charles quickly filled his mouth with a spoonful of chowder, hoping to hide the horror that might show on his face. These few people at the table were the only ones who knew of the intrusion. Charles admitted to himself that his failure to tell anyone in his household might not have been a prudent decision. He resolved there and then he would be home before dark and summon Mrs. Lambert. Coleman would have much to say about the incident, to be sure.

Charles thought about showing the drawing, but he wished to end the exchange there. Guilt was creeping up on him, and he covered the new anxious feeling with attention to buttering a roll. Was anything missing from the library? He had many treasures in his cabinets there; jewels worth a king's ransom and small enough to fit in a pocket. He remembered the woman held something under her arm. He also remembered the hand pressed against the doorsill, young, slender, and empty.

"I am organizing a balloon ascent, with a grand picnic," squealed Sophie, excited by the new subject. "I will remain on the ground, of course, but I am anxious to watch it fly. You must attend Charles, I will send word."

Charles promised to attend though he assured her he, too, would not go aloft, but watch by her side. He had attended several of these ascents. Charles had personally witnessed more than one balloon go up in flames. He had yet to be a rider in the basket. It would be a very heavy load to send Miss Banks aloft, so they would stay put on the ground together.

After the meal, the two women took themselves off, so as to leave the men to their business. Sir Joseph had left the table from luncheon to lie down for a bit.

"We leave you two to solve the worries of the world," Lady Banks said. "Such great minds must not be disturbed by the chatter of trivial female conversation." Sophia mocked. This comment was received with a good dose of laughter, as the lord was well aware that these females each possessed superior intelligence.

After another round of kisses, the women giggled their way out of the room. Banks eased himself into the wheeled chair, allowing Charles to push him back to his desk.

11

"*Y*ou saw the Wedgwoods, did you?" Banks inquired when they returned to the library.

"Yes, the pottery has been saved. Their father would have been proud indeed. John came for one last view of the water lily he is using for a dinnerware design. They will use the new method of transferring an engraving to a print under the glaze; less expensive, more affordable," Charles answered. "I have had extremely good fortune with the water lilies. Thank goodness for George Blake."

"Have you any word from Flinders?" Charles asked before Banks could begin another subject. He hated to bring up the subject, but his curiosity begged for the news. "I know you are delighted with Brown and Bauer's return."

Matthew Flinders began his expedition to New Holland with Bank's own selection of Robert Brown as botanist and Ferdinand Bauer as artist. When his ship proved in need of repair, Flinders had traveled back to England with the first round of specimens aboard another ship. The vessel went down in a series of storms.

The crew was saved and transported to a colony under French control. With France at war with England, Flinders and his men had been imprisoned. The entire sad incident had been avoided by Brown and Bauer, both of whom had made safe returns.

"I have had no further word with regards to Flinders. He puts us all in a difficult position and our success at Trafalgar did not help. The British government will continue to implore those they can for his release, but there are no favors being granted to us by the French. I have no secret powers there." Banks admitted to his weakness when dealing with naval officers. Flinders' demise, though terrible, could not compare to the saga of the first officer of the HMS Bounty, Captain Bligh.

The discovery of breadfruit trees in the South Seas had stirred an interest in Sir Joseph as a possible inexpensive food source for laborers. It was Banks who had insisted that the breadfruit cuttings be fully rooted before moving them, as previous attempts had failed. During the five months needed to accomplish propagation, many of the men formed relationships with native women. The sailors' efforts to desert were thwarted, and the Bounty set sail as planned.

Several hundred miles at sea, fighting broke out, and Bligh lost control of his ship. The captain and his eighteen followers were ordered into a small launch. Amazingly, they managed to survive an arduous six thousand kilometers journey, losing only one man. Upon Bligh's return, he was further humiliated when he stood trial for his treatment of the mutinous crew.

Now Banks had ushered Bligh into position to be the next governor of New South Wales. Banks hoped he had not placed Bligh in another hellhole. A storm of contention was brewing between the new politician and the existing merchants who had set up an economy partially based on trading rum.

Changing the subject again before Charles could speak, Sir Joseph asked, "Will you attend the Lunar Society meeting next month? There are several members who wish to discuss the new theories concerning the origin of meteorites. I was hoping you would speak before we open up discussion to the floor," Banks prodded.

"When is the moon full?" Charles asked himself. "Three weeks, yes, I will be there." He was proud to own several meteorites and understand as much about them as anyone. "Will you have returned from Holkam by then?" Charles felt these meeting were so much more satisfying when Banks conducted them.

"We will have just returned from our trip," Banks assured his friend.

The two men talked for another hour until Charles noticed his friend stifle a yawn.

"I will take my leave," he said. He indicated to the footman his intention to depart. "I hope to see you in town, soon. Take care of yourself. I think the warm weather will be better for you. Please give my farewells to the girls."

His visit to Banks had left him tired but cheered. Teasing the young boys at Warwick had been a glad ending to an uncomfortable situation. With the subject of the changes at Warwick, he recalled he had his own ghost to think about. The idea of a paramour was very appealing. From the moment Banks mentioned "secret admirer," Charles felt a tingle in his senses. It was exhilarating to believe one might be watched unaware.

When Charles reached his bedroom, he found his valet finishing the sorting and folding of his clothing from his trip.

"How did you find Sir Joseph?" Coleman asked as he hung up his master's jacket and pulled a chair forward to remove his boots.

"He manages." Charles replied. Coleman heard the exhaustion in his master's voice, and did not speak again, allowing his master quietude while he undressed. It was the nobleman who spoke up.

"Coleman, I fear I may have misjudged a circumstance that occurred before we left for Warwick. I did not mention the situation to you, and I worry now I might have been in error."

For the master to start his conversation with such humility was indeed unusual, and immediately drew the valet's attention.

"Yes sir, what is it?"

"Do you recall I dashed back into the library as we were preparing to leave as I forgot some papers for Sir Joseph on the desk? You offered to do so for me, but I insisted, not sure which stack they were in?"

"Yes, I remember," Coleman said, still on edge for what was to come.

"When I entered the library, a figure stood in the doorway." Charles pictured the woman, her hair, her hand, and once again he shivered.

"A figure, sir, it was a person unknown to you?"

"Yes, quite. It was a woman. She took her leave with a curtsy and a quiet "I'm sorry" and that was all." Charles moved from his chair to the mirror on his dresser. He looked at his reflection vaguely, but gazed past his face to see his servant's expression of horror.

"You are saying a woman was trespassing in your library, and she left without identifying herself?" Coleman asked, the anxiety beginning to build in his voice.

"I fear it is so. I did not get the impression she meant any harm. She expressed regret at being caught."

"I am sure she felt regret upon your "catching" her, sir. What if you had not returned? What then? I suppose as you did not tell me, you also have not informed Mrs. Lambert or the magistrate?" Coleman recalled the woman by the hedge on the day of the Master's return from Wales. Might not this be that same person?

"The carriage was waiting, and I felt unduly rushed."

"Shall I ring for Mrs. Lambert now?"

"No, Coleman, let us not disturb her." Charles said quickly before the valet could summon a maid. "I will attend to the incident in the morning."

Charles splashed water on his face and turned to receive the towel Coleman held out for him.

"We can take comfort in the fact I heard nothing of a robbery or further intrusion while we were absent, but rest assured I will not sleep soundly tonight. If I hear any sound, I will call for Robert to search the grounds immediately," Coleman stated.

Lord Greville thanked his servant for his usual exaggerated concern, hoping that it was as unnecessary as he believed. The weary lord crawled into bed, ready for a much needed rest that no ghost would be able to disturb.

12

*U*rged on by his own worried conscience and Coleman's glare, Lord Greville made his way downstairs earlier than usual. His eagerness to have a conference with Mrs. Lambert had increased as he tossed and turned through the night. Charles sent word by way of the downstairs maid, "Becky" he believed was her name. This particular housemaid had made Charles fairly uncomfortable more than once, flaunting her bosom in his face. He had the mad urge to take out a comb and straighten her hair. Something about her was not just unkempt, but unsettling.

Charles was greatly relieved when his search of the library revealed nothing out of order. He panicked as he thought of his mineral cabinet, but he caught the glimmer off the surface of the gems inside and the lock was undisturbed. No books were amiss, no paintings awry. Charles reaffirmed that the woman was not a thief, helping to quell the fears that Lady Banks' inquiry had raised.

While waiting for Mrs. Lambert to appear, Charles looked over the two letters he had received while he was away. He recognized the embellished handwriting of his sister, Frances, on a note confirming her visit at the end of the week. The other correspondence concerned a cabinet of minerals he sought to buy. Several unique mineral examples could be drawn by James Sowerby who engaged in creating colored renderings of the best specimens from the top collections in England. Charles' apatite crystal cluster was already one of the book's earliest drawings.

Lord Greville would contact his friend, Henri de Bournon, to get his opinion on this latest assemblage, though he had already turned in a verbal bid. De Bournon had spent a great deal of time organizing Charles' existing collection. The Frenchman had a good knowledge of the chemical make-up of minerals while Charles felt he was still a student of the science.

The nobleman sat at his desk once again pondering the woman standing in the doorframe. Where was she now? "Perhaps she was a secret admirer?" he said to himself again, but he doubted that conclusion with a clearer head. Charles let his gaze rise to the portrait above the hall doorframe. For a moment he thought of another young woman he inquired about so long ago.

He took a look at the drawing he had found upon the young woman's exit. The view was unusual; he tried to remember when he had sat at the bench in such a way. When it came to him, he was flushed with embarrassment first, and then with anger. Had this girl witnessed his breakdown? Had he cried, while she looked on, sketching away without a care? How dare she?

Mrs. Lambert arrived as quickly as her large frame and small legs would bring her. It was not often she was summoned by the master. They often met on Monday mornings when the housekeeper would review the household accounts. He rarely made demands at all, so she was curious about the urgency of his request especially as he had just returned from an absence of a few days. Mrs. Lambert knew of the lord's visit to his ancestral home and the family's financial problems, though she doubted that would be the reason for the summons.

"Yes sir, you have had a good journey? I hope it was not too distressing."

"No, Lambert, it is done. I will not worry about it anymore," he said with a conviction he did not embrace.

Mrs. Lambert never questioned him, Charles realized, and yet she seemed to know the details of his life. She was always appropriate with her comments or silence, matching his mood and level of concern. In this case, she did not press further.

Louisa Lambert was a widow without family. She never admitted to being a widow. She had been married to the naval officer, Commander James Lambert, for several years before he failed to return from a tour of duty on the North Sea. Mrs. Lambert had received official word that her husband had been washed overboard during a storm, but she held onto the hope that he would reappear someday. She anticipated his return with an optimism most would say was impractical. She spoke of him in present tense and had celebrated his birthday and their anniversary alone for more than twenty-five years.

Mrs. Lambert was the lord's longest standing employee. The thrifty housekeeper had managed to spare his lordship from embarrassment and saved him from starvation. Lord Greville had given her full control of the household decisions long ago, as there was no other female to take care of the many responsibilities of that sort. He paid her a reasonable sum and gave her a large room downstairs in which to live. Though an elderly woman, she had more security than some. She had no wants really. The affairs of the house were her main concern.

As the mistress of the house, Mrs. Lambert took great pride in the cleanliness of the rooms, the supply of linens, the management of the household help, and a well-stocked pantry. Lord Greville had agreed to pay the servants a bit more than was customary on her advice. This decision proved worthy as the house staff to esteem his lordship and the running of his manor became important to them.

The lord was able to retain servants longer than many other establishments of a similar size.

Charles was fond of the elderly housekeeper. He thought of her as a relative and spoke more frankly to her than many of his close friends and most of his true relations. For Mrs. Lambert's sake, Charles held onto the hope that Commander Lambert would show up at the door someday.

"Sir Joseph, how does his gout fare? He is such a good man, so sad for him to suffer so," she said. Mrs. Lambert empathized with Sir Joseph as she experienced pains of her own.

"He is indeed in pain, but he sees a surgeon this coming week and his apothecary has prescribed a series of treatments. He keeps his mood up and speaks of improvement, but I saw little since my last visit." Charles took a breath and then continued.

"Lambert, I have two items about which I wish to speak," Charles began. "First, as you pointed out to me, the upstairs curtains are faded from sun and worn with age. Your choice of a striped fabric sounds appropriate and meets with my approval. I am truly sorry to have left it to the last minute as I have."

Anne's information about draperies at Welbeck Abbey had settled the selection in the elderly housekeeper's mind. Though the lord had no idea from whom she had garnered the information for her choice, he was happy she had made a decision and would see to it. He admitted that Mrs. Lambert made life so easy for him by tending to these things of which he had so little knowledge and even less concern.

The lord looked up at the matronly figure. She stood at an odd angle with one of her hips much higher than the other. She looked quite elderly. Charles wondered just how much older she actually was. Her round face sat atop a body shaped like a tree trunk with no definition between the breasts, waist, and hips.

"I am so glad you have come to that realization, my lord. I assure you they will be a delightful improvement."

"If there are any other last minute changes, please make the arrangements. I want to impress those sisters of mine!" Charles said.

"Of course, we will have everything ready for them. The entire staff looks forward to having guests in the house again. I'm sure the ladies will applaud your improvements to the manor and grounds. I hope we have many other such occasions in the future." The housekeeper smiled with pride.

Charles was pleased with her enthusiasm, even if he balked at the thought of increasing his social obligations.

"That brings me to my second issue, that of an intruder." Charles jumped into the subject.

"An intruder, my lord?" Mrs. Lambert retorted with a look of concern.

"Yes, I found a young woman in the library as I made ready to depart for Warwickshire. She was standing inside the door there." He pointed. "Her attire was completely unfamiliar; I do not think she was any of the housemaids. She wore no apron or cap. She had a considerable amount of dark brown hair, I can tell you that much." He did not go further into a description. That last detail, he remembered clearly, as heat crawled up his body. "I think she might draw, do painting, something of the sort," he added.

With that, Mrs. Lambert was sure of whom he was speaking.

Charles did not want to surrender the greenhouse likeness yet. He needed to be sure that the artist and the intruder were one and the same. He did not mention it to the housekeeper.

Mrs. Lambert shifted her weight. She rested her hand upside down on her waist as if she were in pain.

"Do take a seat, Lambert," Charles invited, pulling up a chair to the side of his desk, but the housekeeper declined the offer.

"It won't happen again, I can promise you that," Mrs. Lambert said firmly.

"You know the young woman, Lambert?" he asked. He was shocked at her reassurance.

"Yes. I am sorry if she has disturbed you, she means no harm." Mrs. Lambert tried to stay calm.

"Who is it? Tell me!" Charles could not imagine who this female might be that held such protection from his housekeeper. He demanded to know, his anger re-emerging. He felt excluded. "For Heaven's sake, is she employed here?"

"No, not quite. She is George's daughter," Mrs. Lambert so hated to say.

The elderly housekeeper was loyal first and foremost to Lord Greville, but she cared for the old gardener. She felt affection for the girl now reunited with her father. She could not guess what Anne had been doing in the master's library, though she knew the girl wandered about aimlessly. She would get to the root of the incident soon enough.

Charles paused in his questioning. He was much taken aback, trying to remember if he had knowledge of his gardener's family.

"I did not know George had any relatives, a wife?" Charles inquired.

"No, sir, his wife died many years past. She administered to the family of His Grace during the illness that took so many eight years ago. Though the great family one and all recovered, George's wife and son took ill and did not survive. The girl escaped the epidemic. She has been living with the family of the Duke. She worked as a nursery maid. Anne is her name. She is young as you guessed."

"Well, the girl I saw was not too young to know better. What is her employment here?"

Oh no, sir," Mrs. Lambert explained, "The young lady does not work in the house. She does help her father on occasion in your glasshouse, I believe. She awaits an appointment as a nanny. I believe the Duke's daughter and sister are seeing to it."

THE *Gardener's Daughter*

"Does not work here in the house, yet was clearly standing in my house? Let's get to the bottom of this, shall we, Lambert? Send for the girl."

"Oh no, your lordship! I will speak to her. I assure you, I will take care of the matter." Mrs. Lambert appreciated the master's fairness in past differences with servants. Foul language, tardiness, and an occasional drinker had been the misbehavior that called for her disciplinary action. Mrs. Lambert was the one who handled this level of household affairs. To be sure, Anne would need to receive a reprimand, but Mrs. Lambert hated to think of the shame George would feel upon learning his daughter had been called up before the master for trespassing. Surely, she could intercede for the master in this matter.

"No, Lambert, I find myself with time to take care of this matter myself. I wish to meet the young woman and see that she understands the boundaries of her wandering." He tapped the drawing on his desk. He wished to meet the source of such an intimate view and know of her intentions.

Mrs. Lambert wanted to protest, but knew the limit of her duties. She had done her best to spare the old man and his daughter embarrassment to no avail. She would send for Anne as directed.

Becky was the messenger Mrs. Lambert found in the hall when she exited. The housekeeper wondered if the maid might have been eavesdropping as she was in such close proximity. Becky was more than happy to take the master's demand to the gardener's daughter.

Anne was sweeping the stoop of the cottage. Her fear of retribution had waned some since the event of her trespassing. She had stayed clear of the house and garden all morning after learning of the master's return. When Becky came down the path, Anne knew her time had come. Becky gave Anne a smug expression shaking her finger and forming an "O" with her mouth.

"Oh, we are in a bit of trouble, we are," Becky said. "Lambert asked me to fetch you for the master wishes to speak with you."

Becky put her hands on her waist in an authoritative stance. She tapped her toe, mocking impatience.

Anne was speechless. She was angry it was Becky who came to "fetch" her. Becky delighted in Anne's situation. Anne removed her apron, and straightened her skirt. She tucked a few loose hairs behind her ears and smoothed down the rest with her hands.

Walking to the house before Becky could lead her, looking straight ahead, Anne prepared for the inquisition. At first, her view was clear, but then she saw her father leaning on his shovel off to the side of the path. He became curious as he saw Becky following his daughter in a march to the master's house. Anne passed by him like a soldier on review, never looking his way. She kept her gaze directly in front of her. Only the tears rolling down her cheeks belied her emotion.

There would be no entering Lord Greville's library through the open garden doors this time. She proceeded into the manor through the back hall and turned toward the larger hall leading to the library. At this point, Mrs. Lambert met her. She had been waiting. Anne slowed to allow the housekeeper to proceed alone. Anne was rigid with fear, but prepared to meet her fate. She wiped the tears from her cheeks and sniffed her nose quietly as she waited to be announced to the lord.

Mrs. Lambert gave Anne a smile and then a deep sigh as she exited the library, indicating with her outstretched arm that Anne should enter. Anne stepped into the library under the famous painting she never should have seen. She took three steps across the room and came to a halt with both feet together and her hands at her sides. She had lowered her head as soon as she came through the portal, afraid to look Lord Greville in the eyes. She slowly raised her face as she readied for the lord to address her.

Lord Greville turned from his position behind his desk, staring out at the threshold where he had last seen her. He looked her way, during what seemed to be a long silence, collecting his thoughts. He had not expected his reaction. He recognized her, though they had never met. Just the sight of her face had given him a warm feeling as if he was predisposed to have a good impression of this young woman he intended to punish. He was angry with his wavering resolve to be hard on the girl. Why did he feel so tender toward a young woman he did not know?

She was older than he had expected, but certainly not past twenty. Her dark dress was similar to many of his maids, but of a finer weave. She wore no apron or cap as he had noticed during her escape from the library. There was something to her countenance that denounced any underestimation one might have of her. Of course he should have known she would not arrive with dirty fingernails, cropped hair, and a worn dress, but he had not imagined so neat and attractive an appearance. She had not spoken a word, but he knew she was intelligent. She was strong enough to stand before him, though her cheeks held the damp tracks of tears and her lips quivered. The top half of her hair was pulled back with the remainder of the brown mass, familiar to him, curling down around her shoulders. He felt far less superior than he thought he would. He realized she waited for him to speak. He kept his face tight and his lips pursed, remembering his purpose.

"You are Anne Blake?"

"Yes, sir," Anne answered clearly, but softly.

"George, my head gardener, is your father?" Charles asked sternly.

"Yes, sir," she said again.

"You are not employed here in the house?"

"No, sir," Anne whispered as her mouth went dry.

"And yet you do own that you were in this room without permission last week?" He raised his voice as his anger returned.

"Yes, sir." Anne wanted to beg forgiveness and announce that it was his outburst that brought her into the room. She wanted to say she was out of her mind for those few minutes, and declare her feeling of compassion, having been a witness to his breakdown. Instead, she lowered her head a bit more.

"Do you have anything to say for yourself?" the master asked tersely.

Anne could hold back no longer and the words hiccoughed from her.

"I cannot justify my actions. I am most assuredly sorry. Please do not judge my father. I am the one at fault." Another tear ran down her cheek, she let it drop to her collar without making a move to stop it.

Charles was unable to continue in the vein in which he began. The woman had somehow beguiled him. His curiosity about the drawing took over.

"Do you draw Miss Blake?"

Anne was confused by this unexpected turn in the questioning. She had no reason to lie, but she worried what the question might have as a consequence in this current affair. Anne looked up, noting the look on the lord's face, trying to distinguish the direction this latest question was to proceed. It was the first time she looked into his eyes since the night of the hailstorm. His expression showed no sign of guile. He did not tease.

"Some, sir," she said slowly, waiting for an explanation.

Something about her made him want to know her better. He had an uncontrollable urge to employ her. He might make some use of her while she remained with her father. It was a bit of a gamble, but he had little to lose. He might have some record of the blooms in his glasshouse even if of inferior quality.

"There are flowers to be drawn, some orchids, the specimens in the hothouse, in particular. I have need of good quality renderings from which to make an engraving. Do you know what that is?" He kept his statements short trying to keep his voice severe. It did not matter if the girl was familiar with the process or not, and he imagined she was not.

Anne nodded her head, afraid to speak. She wondered how angry the lord really was, and yet this invitation to draw, so out of place.

Now he looked back at her. His gaze was not demeaning, and his voice was imploring, not demanding. Anne saw that his request was genuine, though she could hardly believe what was occurring.

"Do you think you could perform such a task?"

"I could try." Anne thought about his drawing of the vanilla orchid, but kept other thoughts at bay.

"Yes, well, I suppose so. That will be your restitution. You can draw the flowers in exchange for my excusing you from trespassing," Charles stated brusquely. He still held his judgment about her trespass in check, though she did not seem to be up to mischief.

It was all a little unsettling for Anne. Here she had worried that she might be sent off and her father let go from his position, leaving their future in peril. Instead, she was being invited to perform the very task of which she might have dreamt.

"I have an example of the drawings I need. This is a depiction ready for an engraver. This sort of detail is necessary and the colors must be accurate." The lord held out a sheet of paper containing a painted flower.

Anne took only one step closer to look at the picture. She examined the artwork from where she stood, not daring to touch it. She knew her hand would shake uncontrollably if she tried to take hold of the paper. She was aware of this sort of rendering; and though not a style she had taken for herself, she felt confident she could make something like it.

"You will have access to the glasshouse." The nobleman heard the haughtiness in his voice. She already had access to the greenhouse. Had not Mrs. Lambert alluded to her helping her father at times? She had drawn him at his bench there? Now, she would have his official permission. Did she respect him? He heard his tone and knew it was falsely superior.

"Monday, ten o'clock. The sun is out for light, but it is not too hot to sit in the enclosure for an hour or two."

"Yes, sir, however I can be of assistance," Anne stammered.

"Assuredly." He made some show of replacing the drawing she had inspected. He was fortifying himself against this girl who had won over some part of him already.

Anne resettled her arms at her sides, feeling some relief from the soldier-like stiffness she had assumed from the edge of her cottage stoop to her present position.

Charles caught the view of her hands as she did so, reminding him of the day in the library and something else.

"It is settled then, I will see you at ten o'clock Monday next. I will show you the flowers I am most interested in having you draw. That will do for now. You may go." Charles dismissed her, trying to retain some sense of master.

Anne turned to exit. She wanted to skip out of the room and laugh to let loose the nervous anxiety pent up in her stomach. She could scarcely believe what had come to pass.

"Oh, and Miss Blake," Lord Greville called out after her.

She turned back to face him, pulling the forward progression of her body back awkwardly. She reminded herself that she should keep the warm feeling in her glad heart from changing the cold emotion of her true humility.

"Yes, sir?" She asked in a soft and humble voice.

"When next you come into the library, do so by invitation." Charles was doing his best to remain aloof and in control. One had to put one's foot down firmly with this sort of thing. He could not let a servant get the best of him, well, not a servant's daughter either. He wondered if he had failed altogether on that score.

He kept his head down as he spoke to her. Charles hoped his first impression had not been incorrect. He hoped he had made the right decision. He was going to allow this daughter of his gardener a better look into his world rather than punishing her for taking a peek. He had made a decision to trust her, and yet he did not know why.

"Yes, sir, and thank you, sir!"

Anne curtsied and hurried out of the room with the beginning of a smile that turned to giggling before she could exit the house. She could only hope Becky was waiting by the kitchen door to see. Lord Greville kept his head down, but his eyes watched the girl as she exited the room. He was certain he saw a hop in her step as she went out the door.

The lord leaned back in his chair. He was amused by the girl's demeanor and his own as well. What was it about her face that seemed so familiar and even comforting? As he mused, the scent came to him, the smell of roses. He had to wonder if Miss Blake was the source.

The lord let his mind rest as his eyes drifted up to the portrait above the doorway. He remembered another young woman by whom he had been charmed. He recalled his first conversation with that girl, and how it changed events in his life.

Hard to believe that it had been over twenty-five years prior. Charles first spent time with Emma while visiting Sir Harry Fetherstonhaugh for a few days of hunting, cards, and camaraderie. As she was Sir Harry's mistress, Charles had given no real thought to Miss Lyon. She seemed to be quite entertaining at times, and although Charles thought her language and manners rather coarse, she was quite lovely to look at.

They were much thrown together one morning. Most of the party had gone off in the dawn's light to hunt. Charles was experiencing a sour stomach and preferred to stay in, spending his time in the library with a book of maps. He had not expected to find the room occupied, but on the sill of one of the large windows sat the lovely Miss Lyon. Charles thought he might exit and leave her alone with her thoughts; but as she turned, he saw that she had been crying. She gave him a most desperate look, a look he could not ignore.

"Miss Lyon, are you quite alright? What is your distress?" he asked as he approached her across the room.

Charles had pulled out his handkerchief and offered it to her. He tried to think of words to comfort her. He remembered he had winced when he bent toward her, his stomach still sore.

"I am sure whatever is bothering you must have a solution. There, there."

"Oh dear sir, you too have stayed from the hunting, and it is I who should be attending you as your hostess. I fail at my duties."

Charles had been repulsed by the sound of her voice and her accent, yet been enticed by her lips. Miss Blake had spoken with more controlled elocution than Emma embraced when he first met her.

Charles shook off the tension that was sure to make him ill if he continued with this train of thought. He removed himself to his dining room, away from the portrait and the memories brought forth, certain it was soon to be lunch.

Later in the afternoon, after a small meal, a glass of ale, and a look at a newspaper, Charles returned to his quarters to find Coleman waiting for him as usual.

"Well, Coleman, I believe we have solved the mystery of the female in the library," Lord Greville called out to his valet.

"Oh?" was all the servant commented for he felt sure he would hear the story.

"Yes, she is the gardener's daughter." A broad grin stretched across his lips. He thought of the young girl's hop as she left the questioning. He had to admit she had faced up to her crime quite bravely. He supposed she must wonder about his asking her about her drawing skills, but no matter, she could continue to wonder until such time he might return the drawing. His loss of control still worried him. What impression might she have of him? She had showed only a humbled servant's demeanor during her interview.

"Under which shrubbery has he been hiding her, sir?" Coleman asked snidely.

"Coleman, that is unkind!" Charles reprimanded.

"Sorry, sir, but I do not recall any children scampering here about. What is to become of the impudent girl? Shall you send her off?"

"No, I am indebted to George Blake. I might have paid three times as much to one so capable. Charles thought of the cabin at the back of the property where the old gardener lived. What sort of accommodations was provided to them?

"I have assigned her a task until such time she is otherwise employed," Charles answered.

"Employed here?" Coleman asked with disbelief.

"No, I believe she seeks a position as a nanny. She cared for the grandchildren of His Grace, and now she has been excused and sent off. There must have been some sort of incident, though Mrs. Lambert has no knowledge of it. The young woman seems innocent. She carries herself well, and I am aware she has some talent for drawing." Charles did not wish to speak further on the subject of the gardener's daughter or his decision to make use of her skill, as he knew Coleman would have a negative opinion. He had enough doubts of his own.

"Ah." Coleman commented. He would say more, but he noticed his master's eagerness. He would not judge the situation, though he sensed a discomfort within himself that was a sure sign of trouble. This girl was no doubt the one by the hedge on the drive their first day back. She would be a problem, he was certain.

Lord Greville mindlessly cleaned his face and hands in the basin Coleman provided.

"Will you dress now, or do you wish to wash further?" the valet asked.

"No. I think not. I will dress." There the lord stopped. He felt disconcerted about the young woman and lashed out to release the dam of tension building up.

"Remind me Coleman, why must I dress for dinner? I will see no one of consequence; you, a server, and perhaps Mrs. Lambert are the only persons I am apt to encounter the rest of the day. Why must I care how I appear?"

Coleman replied quickly, wishing to soothe his master's agitation. "Ceremony and tradition are the backbones of all great civilizations. If one chooses to ignore the need for decorum and the etiquette that accompanies it, then one begins the slippery slope down to the behavior of a heathen. By agreeing with the duties and following the manner in which things are done, one can be hurdled to excellence in all things of which one has control."

"You exaggerate as usual, my good man, but your words are very pretty," the lord teased. "There is a place for simplicity in all this, but I have yet to enjoy it." With submission, Lord Greville allowed his valet to remove his shirt.

In the cottage at the back of the property another conversation about the day's events was taking place. In this case, Anne was defending her actions by referring to the end result, but her father was too angry to accept such a conclusion.

"To be called up before the master is no small thing no matter how you might view it. It will be a mark against you. It may well be a mark against me, also."

"I begged his pardon on that score, and he seemed to hold no prejudice against you. That is when he questioned me about my drawing flowers." Anne remembered the conversation. "It was all quite strange, really. Perhaps someone had mentioned that I draw, for he seemed to know it already."

"I will expect you to attempt what the master has asked of you with the utmost humility. It would be a great honor if indeed you were to complete such a task, but I have concerns about the master's request." With that, her father went to his mat in the corner.

Anne felt a pain inflicted by her father's words. Was he concerned about her abilities or the nature of the master's request? Either way, it all left her unsettled where only hours before elation had filled her. She would certainly do her utmost to impress the nobleman, and of course she would remain humble for the chance. It had not been the ideal circumstance under which to meet Lord Greville, but she did not believe that the interview had left a mark against her as her father insisted. Instead, she felt the meeting had confirmed her connection to the man though she did not dare to tell her father.

13

*L*ord Greville's sisters were to arrive any minute. The manor had been polished from top to bottom. Though the lord was proud to show the women his home, he remained anxious about how the day might progress.

Charles met his sisters on the driveway with as much cheerfulness as he could muster. He tried to breath deep, hoping that would calm his nerves. He remained very much on guard against his elder sister, Frances. He clenched his teeth and smiled, bracing himself against the petulant manner with which she might choose to greet him.

Lady Frances Jane Harpur stepped from the shelter of the carriage into the dull sun with a straight-backed arrogance Charles tried to ignore. He tried to love his sister, though he found her quite shallow. He delighted in mocking her dramatic airs. For now, he was all smiles and "welcomes" as she began her saunter toward the house.

His sister's marriage had not changed her a bit. He doubted anything would improve her manner of relating to the rest of the world. Charles supposed she had controlled her husband, Harry, in much the same way she got on with her siblings. He was dead now, poor man.

"What is that on your arm, Fanny?" Charles inquired, taking the pointed object's end into his hand.

"It's my parasol. You've seen one before, Charles. It is for the sun. It may be too strong for my delicate nature."

"Delicate!" Charles scoffed with a smile, careful not to raise the lady's ire. Frances whirled away from him to remove the tip of her umbrella from his grasp. She gently pressed open the whalebone contraption to create a circle of shade.

Charles stepped forward and dipped under the umbrella to join her in the circle. Frances kissed him on the cheek. Although she decidedly tried to force her will on most of the family, Charles knew Frances loved him despite her failure to change him, and he came very close to loving her back.

In the past, Frances scoffed at her brother's lifestyle. In those days, he lived as he always had, well beyond his means. In certain circles, the discussion of his debts made for awkward conversation. Friends quietly inquired as to the state of his affairs and his financial resources. Frances had been obliged to stand up for her brother more than once, but she never gave him so much as a penny.

The fact that Frances never remarried came as no surprise to Charles. She would have certainly whipped the next unfortunate man into shape as she had the first. Frances gave birth to one son, heir to the baronetcy. That was the extent of her motherhood. As a widow, Frances traveled through many circles easily, impressing many and aspiring to nothing more.

What was important for Frances at this point was that her brother had come into their uncle's fortune. With no new scandals, she had nothing to complain about where Charles was concerned. Charles knew his failure to marry was a disappointment to his sister, but at the same time he knew Frances was of the opinion that a spouse could be a nuisance.

Louisa, the wife of Charles' younger brother, Robert, stepped from the carriage without the pomp his sister displayed. Charles took her hand before the coachman could offer his aid and giving her the true smile he denied Frances. Charles had not seen Louisa since his return from Wales. He missed her busy household more than many things in his life.

Louisa was still a beauty with green eyes, a well-defined nose and chin, and red hair that glowed gold in the sun despite the few grey hairs coming into it now. Charles had been much in love with her for an entire month the first season she came out into society. Louisa was his first cousin. Charles' mother and Louisa's mother were sisters. Charles and his brother, Robert, had admired their cousin, so suddenly grown into a beauty. She wisely set her eyes on higher sights and married a more fortunate prospect, the Earl of Mansfield. After the earl's untimely death, she had married Charles' brother, Robert.

Charles felt Louisa and Robert made a perfect match, their qualities meshed so well. She managed their households, Robert's relationship with the King, and her children with grace. Louisa's five children from her previous marriage were mostly grown when she married for the second time, but Robert had helped to raise the two youngest boys along with his own children.

"It is so good of you to accompany Frances on this visit, Louisa." Charles meant far more than his words delivered on a singular level. A visit from his sister alone might have loomed as a frightening event. With the addition of his sister-in-law, it became a more cheerful reunion. Charles and Louisa gave each other light kisses on each cheek.

"It is my pleasure. An afternoon away from home sounded most appealing. I have been in so much."

"How are the children? My little man grows quickly, I hear."

"Yes, he wears a jacket only once before we are looking for one a bit larger. He is quite the little soldier, always pulling the furniture together to "build a battlement" as he says. Then he makes war on the dogs or a maid, whichever comes by his castle walls first!"

"The baby is well? She is a pretty thing, and I don't feel all babies are so. I am sure she has grown since I saw her last." Charles was a doting uncle when it came to Robert's family. He appreciated their allowing him to be a part. Though none of his siblings turned their backs on him in the past, all but Robert chastised him either to his face or otherwise. Today, Charles met the two women with no shame or embarrassment, only trepidation caused by the typical familial hierarchy.

As Charles was growing up, his older brother, George, came into the world with confidence, knowing someday he would be the Earl of Warwick. George was promised a title, a castle, large parcels of land, and a great fortune. He had done nothing in particular to deserve these things. He had simply been born first. King George had not only attended his brother's christening, but also stood up as his godfather. Charles' mother produced an heir for his father, and then another, and in time, a third. Charles matured into no one in particular as his brother assumed a position of superiority. He watched his sisters take up the remainder of their mother's limited time. When his parents later divorced, it only weakened an already fragile bond.

Since childhood, Charles was impressed by his younger brother. Robert was the sort one could not dislike. He was fair, kind, considered all possible ways to look at a situation, made light of difficulties, and appreciated all good things. He excelled at everything he tried, yet remained humble and unassuming in a way Charles found most endearing.

Robert Greville earned the post as the King's equerry taking care of the horses and sheep for the King. Now he held the title of Groom to the King's Bedchamber. Robert was privy to much of what went on at court, but tended to discuss little of substance to anyone. It was the way in which he was able to keep his appointment. The position called for a high level of discretion and utmost secrecy.

Charles' father, the earl, became tired of calling his middle son forward to perform and compete with his brothers. Time and time again, Charles failed to put forth effort with the intensity the earl saw in each of his other two sons. George, though he tried hard, had little natural ability. Robert was endowed with a personality that could settle for nothing else than being the best. The earl died when Charles was twenty-four never seeing his second son amount to much.

As a family, Charles had watched relationships ebb and flow. Siblings teamed together one moment, and then fought each other the next, a natural occurrence in families. Only Robert had remained apart from these fickle partnerships, steadfast in his affable view of the world. Frances insisted upon acting as their mother. She wielded her sisterly power on them all. He had learned long ago to accept her advice, even if he rarely acted upon it. She seemed to be satisfied with the sense of authority.

"Come, Fanny, this way," he called, as he took each woman's arm. He was proud the walk was well paved and the ladies' shoes stayed dry. He squeezed each one's arm against his side, truly excited to have them there. He was much recovered from the dread he'd been feeling before their arrival. He looked at Frances on his left arm. The expression on her face indicated she was pleased to see him, and she seemed to be smiling. He peeked at Louisa on his right arm. She was beaming.

When Sir William had announced his intentions to create Charles as his heir many years before his death, the entire family had breathed a sigh, knowing Charles might come into it at any moment. The announcement was a letter of reference that Charles had used to pursue women of the higher order when he had no fortune of his own. Specifically, he had hoped to form an attachment with a Miss Henrietta Middleton, the youngest child of the Board of Trade's Lord Middleton. He had rid himself of Miss Lyon, Emma, in hopes of forming the union. The letter of credit from Uncle William had failed to carry the weight Charles hoped it would.

It had been unfortunate that Charles waited many more years before he received the due funds from his uncle. While Sir William remained alive, Charles suffered mixed feelings about longing for the relief the sum of money would assuredly bring and thinking of the man who must leave this life to do so. Uncle William was a jolly soul who treated Charles very much like a son without the expectations their own father had held for his child.

With Charles' need to separate from his mistress to find a wife with a fortune, Charles had sent Emma to his uncle in Naples. Emma had certainly done well by it, eventually marrying his uncle and taking up his title, as well. Subsequently, she had become Admiral Nelson's mistress; an odd kink in her relationship with his uncle. When Uncle William died, Charles came into a fortune of eight thousand pounds per year and the property in Wales. It was this fortune that allowed Charles to repair his home and landscape the yard.

"Shall we look at the garden first?" Charles asked as he helped his sisters up the path, holding each one's hand until ankles were steady on the loose gravel. Frances broke rank and moved quickly to the house without them. He hoped to stall her so that he could have her admire the upgraded entrance.

"Charles, we have traveled in a coach for an hour and a half. Can we not freshen ourselves and have a bit of something to eat?" Frances pleaded, looking at her sister-in-law for confirmation.

"I thought you came to see the grounds, not the kitchen," he goaded her, but led them through the front door without a word about the portico. Later he might mention it. Louisa was all smiles when Charles gave her a private look that excluded Frances.

"The parlor on the right will suit your needs, I believe. Can we eat outside on the terrace when you are ready?" Charles asked.

"So much out of doors, Charles," Frances complained, "we can wander the halls after lunch and then with the remainder of time, we will make a tour of your grounds. You know I do love your collections. No rocks, though," Frances said firmly.

"Certainly. We have new draperies upstairs which I know you will want to see." Charles knew approbation of his new residence and furnishings would not be forthcoming from his sister, but he would take pride in her lack of derision.

"The water closet is behind this door." He indicated the small room to his brother's wife.

Louisa Greville took a peek inside, her small frame almost disappearing. He cared dearly for her because she was simple and kind. Louisa had lost her daughters one by one, and Charles always thought of all the pain she bore with no demand for attention. Charles could only imagine the depth of her sorrow, as he too had grieved for those babies. Louisa loved his brother, assuredly, and for Charles, that was extremely gratifying. Charles felt he could name one hundred unhappy marriages.

"Oh that is wonderful, Charles, I am so happy for you." Louisa smiled.

He left the women to tend to their toilet while he looked through the letters the ladies had brought with them. Robert had sent a newsy letter, even though he had seen Charles two weeks prior. Robert had spared his brother the usual news of court, but he did give him a detailed account of his youngest boy's new pony.

14

*C*harles' sisters finished freshening themselves just as Coleman came down the hall to announce lunch. The ladies immediately directed their attention to him. They each felt an affinity for the old servant, and they took comfort in the knowledge of his diligent care of their brother.

"Coleman, it is good to see you," Louisa said sincerely upon the valet's appearance.

Lady Frances was about to speak, allowing a lull to pass. It was an expression of her superiority. She liked to have others wait upon her words. Coleman, however, spoke up first, in a hurry to proceed to the lunch table to help serve.

"I am very pleased to see you as well, my Lady, and my regards to you Lady Frances, as well." He bowed backing away, but before he could leave, Frances spoke.

"Still coping with my brother, dear Coleman? After so much time with my father and brother, one would think Charles' lackadaisical manners would have driven you mad by now!" Frances said, half teasing, half not.

Coleman understood Lady Frances completely, but he did not dare answer her directly concerning his master's etiquette. He merely muttered, "I do the best I can." He looked to Lady Louisa to see if she also had a comment, but was met only with her sweet smile. Coleman straightened his feet and bowed again, this time making his escape as Charles entered the hallway.

Charles led the ladies to the table set out on his new terrace. They spoke of weather and family news through lunch. As Frances swallowed her last bite and dabbed her lips with a napkin, she started in on her brother.

"Have you heard much of Emma, Charles? No one seems to have much news of her since Lord Nelson's funeral."

Charles doubted Frances was aware that he had recently heard from Emma. Lady Hamilton had continued to amass debt as she spent money on lavish entertainment in order to keep interesting and adoring people around her. Charles would never be one of them.

"No, I have not heard much other than that she has taken in a writer and his family. He is to write the story of Nelson's life. If the author has trouble putting the words down, she may never be rid of them. They say she has taken to carrying Nelson's relics with her everywhere." Charles finished with a sneering laugh.

"What will become of the child?" Frances brought up the subject all society tried not to; the "godchild" of Emma's who was indeed her own fathered by Horatio Nelson. Many in society were able to incorporate such "inconveniences" back into their lives. There were stories of noblemen in need of an heir, requesting a son they fathered to be raised in the care of the same nursemaids as his other children.

Charles ignored his sister's question about Emma's love child. He would not think any more of it. He could become miffed if

Frances chose to continue any further down this avenue of questioning.

Louisa spoke up in the widening gap of silence that extended between brother and sister.

"The terrace is lovely, Charles," she said.

"Yes Charles, a nice addition," Frances added in, as she looked about. The patio was landscaped with a lovely mural of bushes that provided privacy. It seemed she would not harangue her brother further as it made Louisa uncomfortable.

"I like the perfume you are wearing, Frances." Charles said, filling the awkward silence. He sniffed at the air, trying to be civil, hoping to change the course of the conversation. There was something familiar about the scent.

"It is Rose by Floris. Does "she" also wear Rose?" Frances teased. She offered Charles her wrist where she had placed a spot of perfume earlier, wondering about an unlikely paramour.

"It may be," Charles said without explanation. He took her arm and bent to smell the dot of scent as he thought of a silhouette in the doorframe of his library and Anne face as she had made her appearance in his library. He led the women back inside through the dining room doors as they glanced at each other with raised eyebrows.

After a tour of the house, the changes, and a close look at the new draperies and linens upstairs, they met Mrs. Lambert in the hall as they came back down. The housekeeper was bubbling over with effusions. The ladies slowly walked the hall looking at Charles' collection of watercolors while the elderly housekeeper chatted away.

"Ladies, I cannot tell you how excited we are to have you come pay a visit today. I hope the master plans to entertain more often now that his house reparations are completed and the rooms are so nicely furnished. The gentlemen who come for scientific discussions do not stay for supper or allow us to show off the master's home.

"Thank you, Mrs. Lambert; we will try to visit more now that Charles has engaged us so charmingly with this first visit," Louisa replied to the housekeeper. Frances only smiled and continued looking at the artwork.

The tour of the house finished in the library. They admired the new windows and double doors. Frances pursed her lips and shook her head.

"You will be taxed excessively for all this glass, Charles, but it is well within your ability to pay and the natural light is a great improvement to the room," she commented. Frances plopped herself down behind Charles' desk. Louisa found a chair by a window, as she understood her sister-in-law intended to rest.

"All in all, Charles, the house looks very nice. You have made a good investment with these last improvements. I told Louisa under no circumstance would I stay with you, Charles, but I would consider staying here one of the next times I come to town now that I have seen what you have done."

Frances meant to compliment Charles. It was as close as she would come, and Charles knew this. He felt cheered by the remark. If she did come to stay, he could tolerate Frances for that long, surely.

"I can think of nothing that would make me happier. Mrs. Lambert has urged me on my social way!" Charles announced to his sister.

"Dear Mrs. Lambert." Frances poised her face as if she would say more, but said nothing.

"That reminds me, were you in Warwick last week? How do the gentlemen get on? I spoke briefly on the subject with Fitzpatrick when I saw him at the charity ball several weeks ago, but as he was aware, I have stayed away from the whole situation."

It was true. Frances had not visited the castle since her brother's announcement that they would be moving to their house in Worthing for the rest of the year. Frances had left her quarters just as they were. Charles imagined that, when affairs were settled and any new tenants were comfortably installed, they would have the pleasure of their Aunt Frances' attendance from time to time. She would stay at Warwick without any qualms about the earls and their families residing there. In fact, Charles imagined she would act much as if she were mistress of the castle, commanding the servants to do her bidding by some divine right.

Frances leaned forward over the desk as if she were going to attend to the business of the few papers piled to the side. She dared not look up at the wall above the door in front of her, as she knew the portrait of Emma would be coyly looking back. She had picked up her brother's pile of papers and was straightening them together on edge when Anne's drawing slid out.

"Oh look here, a drawing of you in the greenhouse. It will be quite nice when it is finished. Who is the artist?" Frances carefully picked up the painting to look at it more closely.

"The Rose perfume," Charles said slowly after his re-examination. He raised his eyebrows brazenly at his sister.

Frances did not react to his comment; certain that he meant to draw her out.

"Louisa, our sister, was very accomplished at drawings such as these," Frances began. "She would sit on the long lawn and render the scene of the oak trees on the Avon with imaginary animals and people included. She was always painting a portrait of one of the dogs. Do you remember, Charles?" She looked over at her brother who was looking down at the drawing and nodding his head at the same time, but actually he remembered very little of his early childhood.

"Charles! I can see your roses from here!" Louisa called from where she sat looking out the window to the garden.

"Let us go out and see their blossoms, how lovely they are." Louisa had excluded herself from the conversation about the drawing by seemingly concentrating on the view outdoors. She wanted to look at the drawing and inquire after Charles' female acquaintance in a cheering sisterly fashion, but she did not wish to delve into Charles' life in the way Frances felt entitled. She might speak to Robert later on the subject. He might know if she thought to ask.

Charles opened the library doors, and the ladies followed him outside into the garden. They strolled up the path and turned into the semicircle of bushes.

"Oh, so lovely," Louisa announced again, "what did you do for these roses to have them so well in bloom for us, Charles?"

Charles had to admit that the roses were exceptional. He had not given any instructions specifically about this garden. In fact, he rarely passed this way and had neglected the area. Then he remembered the silent gardener who must have had a hand in the care of the bushes and thus their blooms.

"Ah, yes, I seem to have a mute gardener who has performed a bit of a miracle. They are lovely, are they not?"

"A mute gardener?" his sister-in-law asked inquisitively. She waited for her brother to elaborate, but he only looked pensive, unwilling to share the story or be chided for the man's insubordination.

At that moment, the "mute gardener" was cleaning rugs by her cottage. She heard the higher pitched voices of women in the garden. Despite her father's insistence that she stay clear of the garden that week as the master expected visitors, she left the rug on a branch to air and tiptoed along the hedge listening for the location and source of the voices.

Anne could just make out the women's skirts swaying down the path. She saw the ladies in patches as they proceeded to the rose garden. Anne watched the master follow them into the semi-circle of flowers and take a seat on the bench.

Although Anne could not hear the exact conversation, she felt sure they remarked on the flowers now in their proximity. The one lady with the parasol dipped with laughter as the other turned to smell a nearby rose. Charles went to sit between them shoulder to shoulder. Anne knew they were his sisters. The master looked very happy. She wanted to save this joyful moment.

She ducked down and made her way back to the cottage to retrieve her pencil and paper. She had misplaced her drawing of Lord Greville in the greenhouse. She was excited to have a new subject for a sketch. She snatched up her supplies and rushed back out to the garden to make a quick drawing of the ladies sitting on the bench.

After a few minutes more, Charles' sisters emerged from the garden bending to smell one last rose. Anne stepped back into the thicker cover, afraid of being discovered. Her apron caught on the thorns of the hedge and caused the branches to twitch as she tugged at the snagged fabric.

The flicker of the light cotton caught Charles' eye and he looked to see who might appear from the back of the garden, but no one did. As he turned back to his sisters, he looked into the rose bushes picturing the silent gardener. It was then Charles had an epiphany.

He saw a hand come up to point the way to where his head gardener had been. He knew that hand. Surely, the one pointing was the same hand he had seen on the doorframe of his library. Was it Anne Blake in the rose garden that day? He laughed out loud, shocked at the possibility, forgetting his sisters just in front of him on the path back to the garden and greenhouse.

"What are you snickering about back there, Charles?" Frances asked.

"If I tell you, you must not tell a soul." Charles replied.

"Never mind then," his sister said with a short laugh. "If it is so scandalous, I hate to be in your confidence. If it is not so important, I won't care to report it, so I have no need to know either way." Frances had not reasoned this out, really she just would not submit to her brother even if he were just having a joke. It did sound clever, though, and she was quite satisfied with her rebuke.

"I will let you know when I know." Charles said mysteriously. The rose perfume, indeed! This Miss Blake might be troublesome. It would all be resolved soon.

"Let us see the orchids quickly," said Frances, interrupting his thoughts, "I do not wish to walk on your lawn, the path will do, but if it is too hot in the glasshouse, I will not stay long. You do as you please, dear Louisa," she said, looking over at her sister-in-law and feeling quite righteous to have thought of someone other than herself.

"That's fine, I would rather see the greenhouse than the garden in the sun, but I can wander through on the way back to the house so Charles can show me his latest acquisitions and successes." Louisa smiled over to her brother-in-law, knowing his wish to show off his garden.

Anne began her picture with the outline of the vase in the foreground and the background of rose bushes as they were aligned against the wall of the house. She faintly drew in some lines for the path and then she started on the figures. She knew she would not draw two women. If it were to be the scene of a happy reunion, it must only be two figures, a man and a woman. She sketched Lord Greville first and was able to put a good impression of a seated gentleman down on paper.

Then she drew the dress of one of Charles' sisters, a silk over dress with small, embroidered flowers. She did not see the fabric closely, and yet she felt she knew its texture. She knew exactly how she would paint the scene and which colors she would chose to indicate the shadow and light.

As Anne drew in the features of the female in her picture, she could not help but make her eyes dark and then without any serious thought, she shyly drew long dark waves of hair on the woman's head. Surprising how much the sketch looked like her, she grinned. She felt mischievous as if confessing a beau to a friend, and yet it was only a painting and not a representation of anything real. It was all just romance and fantasy, Anne acknowledged.

"I will go on to the hothouse while you circumnavigate through the area there," the older woman informed the other two. Frances pretended to stumble, indicating another reason for her choice as she walked away.

Louisa was glad to have a day away from her busy household. It did not matter to her how they occupied themselves. Louisa let her mind meander as she followed Charles through the walled garden and heard him speaking of this and that. She smiled and said the appropriate responses, but she was thinking how different her life might have been had she chosen this brother over the other. Her love for Robert had made her choice easy. She was a lucky woman to have chosen for love twice. Louisa came back to the present as Charles was asking her a question.

"Have you given any thought to Robert's retirement? You could enjoy a flower garden of your own while Robert lurks in barns arranging trysts between rams and ewes."

"I hardly hope. It would delight me to see him leave court even if it is for a sheep." They both laughed together and locked arms the rest of the way to the greenhouse.

The orchids that were in bloom produced exclamations from the ladies. They remarked how all the tropical plants had filled in nicely since they had seen the display last year. The women lingered at the pond, sitting at the small table for a few minutes.

Charles took pride in the small pool of water in the center of the tiled area where they sat, the same area Wedgwood visited for his china design. A metal fish stood on its tail with water coming from its mouth in the center of the pond. It made a soothing noise and sent a light spray of moisture into the air. The flat circles of lily leaves floating on the surface supported blooms of pink and yellow.

"Charles, this is lovely. The temperature changes as you enter this part of the hothouse. It is amazing how comfortable it is here in the afternoon," Frances said.

Louisa stayed quiet, but her delight was in her expression.

Frances rose and proceeded to the door at the far end, and Louisa took off after her. Charles knew their visit would be ending shortly, and he dawdled to walk behind the two women, happy that the event had come off so well.

"It is all very nice. I am surprised, Louisa, I almost hate to go." Frances said in a low voice.

"You should tell him so." Louisa said. "He needs to know he has your good opinion. It would mean a great deal to him." Louisa knew how to play up to her sister. She did not deceive her, just swayed her.

"I suppose." Frances said. "Charles-" she began, glancing back.

Charles moved up to walk with the ladies.

"I want you to know I have had a lovely day. I will not let as much time pass before our next visit."

Charles beamed at his sister, knowing how difficult it was for her to compliment him.

"You are welcome anytime, Fanny," he returned, surprised by the warm feeling he felt toward his sister at that moment. He bent and gave her a light kiss on her cheek. Frances shrugged him off, but giggled as she did.

While the ladies visited the hothouse, Anne had continued to draw the drooping branches of the rose bush at the end of the bench. She worked on the details of the vase, and indicated the bricks in the wall behind the garden. She could hear voices coming closer again. Placing her drawing in her folder, thrilled to have a new project to work on this evening, she retreated from her hiding spot back to the cottage.

15

*M*onday morning arrived, and the hour of Anne's appointment with Lord Greville approached. She had not slept well, and she could not eat. She so wanted to meet with Lord Greville's approval. She worried whether she would be able draw the plants as he wished; the doubt to which her father had referred. What would happen if she could not?

Her father arrived to summon her just before the hour of ten, as there was no clock in the cottage. She noted the sun's position as she walked slowly, her knees wobbling beneath her. She opened the door to the glass enclosure to find Lord Greville standing just on the other side. His arms were locked together as if he had been waiting though she knew she was not tardy.

"Good, you are on time," he said sternly. He looked toward her but not at her. She carried a portfolio of paper and a box of supplies. Waiting as if for her to reply, she spoke up quickly.

"I ask only that if I am not able to perform the task you have set for me that you not censure my father for my impudence, sir."

There were almost tears, he noticed, but he allowed no empathy for the young woman. After the previous meeting, he was on guard to his position of authority. She had unnerved him.

"Miss Blake, I do not hold your father responsible for the actions of his ill-mannered daughter. We will hear no more about it. Instead, tell me what you know about the plants here." He released his arms to indicate the first bench of plants on his right.

The nobleman walked further into the greenhouse just ahead of her. Anne saw that the shirt he wore was stained lightly on the sleeve. He wore no vest, but a loosely tied cravat. There was no curl or powder to his hair. She could not guess at his age, certainly younger than her father or the Duke, perhaps older than Cook or her husband. Before she could answer, he asked another question.

"Do you ever help your father with the care of the plants?" Lord Greville was following up on a comment Lambert had made. He waited for the girl to answer.

Anne gasped, trying not to make a noise as she sucked in air. She had asked her father the very question the night before, "What if the master asks about my working in the garden? What should I say?"

She recalled her father looked into the flame of the candle on the table for almost a minute before he replied, "You must not tell him of your work. He will not approve. You are on thin ice with him already." Her father offered no further explanation and went to his bed at the end of the sentence. It was not what Anne expected her always-honest father to say.

Now, the lord asked the very question she dreaded he might. It was one of his very first questions. When she began to speak, she knew by the relief she felt that she would not lie.

"I clean the leaves; the plants cannot breathe when they are dirty. I help my father with some watering. I remove dead blossoms, and sometimes I sweep." Anne looked away as if looking at the perimeter, but she saw nothing. Her eyes were a blur. She did not want to cry. Her tears came with surrender and release.

"Tell me what you know about the care of the plants," the lord said, pointing to the area where most of the orchids were raised. Anne knew her father wanted the nighttime temperature to be lower than the daytime temperature there. He also wanted the temperatures in general to be lower than that of some of the other areas of the greenhouse. Was this the information the lord wanted from her? Surely, Lord Greville would know these things; she did not need to inform him of the care of his plants. Though she stepped over to the area where he pointed, she chose to be silent, patting a wet spot on her cheek.

This was their first formal meeting. Charles had put little thought into how he would conduct this interview. If the girl had the skills as indicated by her drawing, she might be able to render drawings of the plants now flowering in the hothouse. It was as simple as that. If she were not as talented as the painting suggested, keeping her busy away from the house and his library might suit as well. "We cannot have her gadding about the place without permission or purpose," he told Mrs. Lambert.

After some consideration, Anne began, "I know these few against the wall are fuchsias. Many came from Sir Joseph Banks. My father says the gentleman is the greatest of men and that you are well acquainted with him. I call them the dancing girls, as the flowers appear as ballerinas to me. The plants on this wall receive a good watering once each day." She stepped toward the plants with the dangling pink and purple flowers. "You have so many of them, all in different colors, sir."

Charles wanted to smile at her appreciation of the hybrids, but asked himself, did she understand the process? It was doubtful. George had surely spoken to his daughter of Sir Joseph, and she was correct that the original slips for these plants had come from him.

"I know these," Anne went on, pointing to the gloxinia. "They are watered only in the morning. The flowers are very delicate and their furry leaves are the most difficult to keep clean. We keep them tucked under the fig tree to keep them from the brightest sun."

The lord watched as she ducked in and out of the branch of the fig with graceful familiarity, well acquainted with the area. He was reminded of her painting.

"My father says many of your orchids grew on trees in the jungle, not in the soil at all! He keeps them moist, but not too wet. I have watched him put broken potsherds in the bottom of each planter and moss on top to keep the plant evenly moist." Anne was cheering up and feeling more comfortable, though it was nervousness that kept her talking.

The girl went from plant to plant as Lord Greville followed. He held his chin in his hand and his arms folded in a thoughtful manner, considering the young woman's knowledge of the plants. She talked on and on, sometimes with perfect clarity about cultivation and propagation, and other times with sentimental allusions. This odd young woman held a strange clutter of facts in that head of hers, indicated by the intensity within her eyes. Despite his efforts otherwise, Charles found her absolutely charming.

"This one I call "Yellow Beauty." This one I refer to as my "Duchess' Slipper." My previous mistress had a pair of shoes in that same pale pink. It reminds me of her."

Charles watched the girl's expression closely to take in the meaning beyond her words. She was all innocence and enthusiasm. He had not felt the exuberance she exuded for many years. The look on her face was contagious and urged him to know her better. He knew little of this girl's life. He had all but forgotten the untimely death of her mother and brother. He had never thought how it might have affected one so young.

"Ah yes, the Duke's daughter, Henrietta, was she good to you?" he interjected when he saw he had the chance. "The grandmother, the Duchess, was a wonderful lady. She was an important collector in her time and a good client, buying statuary and Roman trinkets. She had the most extensive shell collection." Charles let his voice trail off as he thought of his visits to the Duchess and the fine mind of the woman even in her later years.

"Do you miss the members of your previous household?" Charles asked the question with mild concern in hopes of discovering more about her dismissal.

"At times, I suppose," Anne said. "The ladies were very kind to me. They allowed me to draw when I had free time. In fact, they encouraged it as an acceptable diversion. I made some drawings of shells once when I was very young. The family kept them in the library, pressed in a book about the seashore. I was honored that they requested to retain them."

"Did they allow you to attend art lessons with the other children?" Charles asked, thinking that might explain her talent.

"No. The children engaged in a variety of activities that I did not attend."

"You were a nursery maid there, I believe?"

"I was to be a nanny soon, however it was decided I should do so in another household." Anne stopped there on the precipice of her demise.

"Do you miss anyone in particular?" Charles asked, beginning to have interest in the young girl's story. Usually when a governess was sent away, especially a young, pretty one, there had been an indiscretion.

"I do not miss the older children so very much; but the younger ones, I miss their laughter." She looked down shyly, realizing the topic was not altogether proper, but when she looked up again, the tilt of Lord Greville's head and a look of concern seemed to encourage her confidence.

"The boys were not so kind. They were devious in fact. I do not miss the teasing and hurtful ways of one boy in particular. I am very happy to be given this chance to be with my father even if I know I must begin to make my own way soon." Anne replied pensively. She glanced back at the gentleman, longing to be understood without saying more.

The lord thought she may have been removed by no fault of her own. There was no love lost coming from her side. He would not delve further on that subject. He could make inquiries if needed. Did she have a letter of reference from the family? What were her qualifications? Was George involved with her decisions after so long a separation?

"And how will you as you say, make your way, Miss Blake?" he asked.

"I will find some employment in a household nearby. Perhaps I will marry someday." She paused and then it slipped out. She had thought so much about Lord Greville and his past life with Emma Hamilton as she piped up, "Or become a mistress to a gentleman," she stated without thinking.

Charles burst out laughing. He could not control his reaction to the naïve summation of her choices. Her reference to a mistress and a gentleman most likely came from stories in his very own kitchen, but the innocuous delivery had been nothing to which he could take offense. She said the statement in such a matter of fact manner so innocent to the meaning. He could only receive it with humor.

"And that is it?" He was still chuckling. He folded his arms adopting an older and wiser position above her.

"I suppose I mostly hope I could be a nursemaid for a good family," she said in reparation of her previous comment, which she was beginning to regret.

"And the mistress choice, that is something you can fall back on?" The lord questioned her with amusement. He realized too late

THE Gardener's Daughter

what a horrible pun he made. Still, he would admonish the girl on the topic. "I hope you will never face such a choice. It is a rare thing for a girl to come of any good once she chooses such a path. What about love?" He had not planned to ask such questions, what did he care? Somewhere during this time together he had come to address this young woman quite differently, curious about her opinions. How odd he thought as he waited for her answer.

"I hope to marry for such an ideal, but I do not fool myself to think I would pass on a proposal from a good man because I did not love him. The security of a good skill or a piece of land could be equally important. I will not wait for love, if opportunity comes first."

Anne spoke as if she had thought this through, but she had not. How could she have intentions for her future when everything in her life was so undetermined? When asked by Lord Greville, she doubted her dreams would ever come true. She wondered if the lord considered her situation seriously. She had mustered up the mature reply, hoping he would not think her childish as his laugh had indicated.

Her reply was wise beyond her years or experience. He had pressed the young girl too far. He would not concern himself with her future. For the present, he needed a record of his plants.

"Well, in the interim, we will have you draw some flowers. Do you know the botanical terms, the Latin names, for each plant?" Lord Greville asked, getting back to their tour of the greenhouse.

"Oh, no sir, but I could learn them if it were necessary. I know some Latin."

"You know some Latin? How is that, Miss Blake?" Charles examined the girl again. This was yet another unexpected answer. Her skin was clear, her eyes, inquisitive. Her genuine smile might win over the most astringent critic.

"Yes, sir. My mother's family worked for a bishop when she was young. I once knew prayers and some Roman history in the language. Our mother schooled us in Latin and a little French. I learned more French as the Duke's grandchildren recited their lessons and conjugated verbs."

"Well, it is not entirely necessary for you to know the terms. It is right that all botanists can come to an agreement about a species because of specific traits, we will not discuss them now. Charles eased away from the subject of Linnaean terms, as he would not want to explain the sexual terminology to this innocent woman. "It will not matter. I can label later, and my good friend, Lord Banks, can make corrections as needed. He is indeed an acquaintance, and in fact, a good friend. The important thing is to get these plants recorded. Do you understand that, Miss Blake?"

Anne nodded, she could understand how it was important from the scientific standpoint, but she wondered how these wild plants ever truly adapted to their new home in this small enclosure in England, so far from their native land. It was her father's diligence that aided the effort toward success, and now she would have the chance to be a part. She smiled at the master, and he in turn smiled back an expression that replaced the fixed look with which he first began the interview.

"Let us get you started as I have work of my own to which I must attend." He turned and walked to the bench where she first observed him. He cleared the end and pulled up a second stool, a welcome new addition to the picture still etched in her memory.

"Let us see how well you can give me a drawing of this one here, the "Yellow Butterfly", I believe you called it. It is an orchid brought from China. It was one of the first orchids to be collected and propagated for Queen Charlotte in her garden at Kew, thanks in part again to my good friend Sir Joseph." Charles removed the plant from its shelf and brought it to the end of the bench.

"I hope my drawings do not disappoint you." Anne made the statement with utmost honesty and concern.

Charles looked at her and saw that she remained steady. She had backbone. She met him as a person of worth, not as a servant's daughter. She waited for him to move off, but instead he tapped his fingers on the bench beside her.

"Here," he indicated the bench top, "I like the light here. If a specimen is small enough, you may move it here if you wish." He fingered the paper Anne brought to the hothouse with her.

"This paper is of sufficient quality and will work well for your drawing and coloring. I see your paints are quite adequate and will do, as well."

"The paper, paints, and pencils were presented to me by the mistresses of my previous household."

"A nice gift, they will suit your purpose here." Charles dismissed any sentimentality Anne might have been leaning toward. The relationship was severed, and the sooner the girl accepted the fact, the better for her future.

"I will let you get to work then." He walked away to the other end of the greenhouse where the tiled area was cooler. He was hot around his collar though it was not exceedingly warm in the greenhouse. He tried not to think about Miss Blake at the other end.

He did not want to watch her, but he was equally uncomfortable to leave. He would dally for a while and return to look at her progress. As he turned the corner around the other side of the pond, he noticed a vase in the corner, one he had bought from a farmer's wife who found it in a field. He was sure it was Roman. He had not yet examined it fully or spoken to any experts about it. He just liked it and had the vase placed here. He had forgotten about it altogether until now.

He slid his finger along the top lip of the urn-shaped pot and felt the uneven layer of clay wondering who made it so long ago. When the woman sold it to Charles, she was shocked at the amount of money that he had offered to her, a partial payment of its true worth Charles guessed, but a pocketful of coins to her.

Remembering the gardener's daughter sketching at the other end of the greenhouse, the lord ambled her way seeming as casual as possible, when in fact he was excited to see what she had drawn. On first examination, Charles was delighted with the representation. The lines were timid and the shading not yet finished, but she had an eye for detail, he could see.

"I would like you to tint your drawing when you can. It is equally important that you record the colors as true as possible. I will see you again tomorrow at ten." With that, Lord Greville exited the greenhouse.

Charles was most pleased with how events were coming to pass. George's daughter was quite enchanting, really. Her conciliatory demeanor was pleasant. The servant's daughter would be unexpectedly useful.

Anne had been constantly aware of Lord Greville at the other end of the glasshouse. Now that he was gone, Anne felt at ease to continue to shade in the edges of the leaves of the orchid. She was not sure when she should add color, and decided she would wait until tomorrow and his acceptance of the drawing. Though she usually spent her time alone in the hothouse, she felt Lord Greville's absence acutely. She could barely continue.

Anne squirmed on her stool, trying to focus where her pencil met the paper, but her mind was wandering. She could draw only a few minutes more before the desire to look out and see if the master wandered his garden overtook her good sense. Anne looked back at her new special place at the workbench. For the first time she did not picture Lord Greville. Outside, she looked around the garden paths hoping the lord might have lingered, but he was nowhere to be seen.

"Silly me," she chided herself, "following after him like a puppy". She knew with a forlorn veracity that he must have much more important things to occupy his time. Still, she felt a connection and wondered if he felt it, too. She knew a gap in her existence had been filled even if only for a short time. She was fairly certain it was not so important to him.

Upstairs in the manor, Coleman waited for his master to return from the garden. He had caught a view of George Blake's daughter proceeding to the hothouse. The lightness of her step indicated one quite young. The morning sun reflected off the top of her head of dark curls, bright and shiny. He could not make out the details of her face, but he concluded she held some bloom to her cheeks. The view worried the old valet. It was not entirely proper that his master and the young woman be alone in the greenhouse for long periods of time. He did not know the girl. The father was a favorite of his lord's, and what of the sudden appearance of his daughter? What was the father's role in all this?

Coleman had no idea that the head gardener was equally concerned, but for different reasons. George Blake had found weeding and pruning to attend to just behind the hothouse while the interview proceeded. Though he did not enter the structure while the two had their meeting, in the same way as the valet, the gardener was not completely comfortable with the arrangement. His daughter was young and though level headed, she was apt to speak without thinking. He trusted the master would not judge her too harshly. He did think Anne showed some talent for drawing, and knew of the master's desire to record his plants.

It was not his place as a gardener to question the lord's decision to engage his daughter, but as a father, he held concerns. He knew it was Anne's delight to draw, and thus a happy task for her. It was strange that the lord had made such a request. He hoped Anne would not put too much store in Lord Greville's bit of attention.

When Lord Greville went to his room later in the afternoon, Coleman was waiting for him. As valet, it was not easy to approach the subject of the girl and the lord's interview, but there were ways to lead the conversation in that direction. The master did have a smirk of a smile on his face as he entered the room.

"You seem quite pleased with yourself, your lordship."

Charles knew his man was aware of his morning appointment with George's daughter. It was obvious that his valet had an opinion about the arrangement that he wished to share. This cat and mouse game of conversing had been going on between them for a long time.

"Don't start in on me, Coleman. The morning went well. Don't sour my evening."

Enough said, Coleman thought to himself. His lordship knew that he knew. For now, he would accept that as sufficient.

16

$\mathcal{A}$nne arrived to the greenhouse at ten each morning for the remainder of the week. Lord Greville would be there to instruct her as to the next flower choice, explaining a little about each selection as he did. He would tour his greenhouse for a short time and then exit, leaving Anne to work alone. On the third day, the nobleman stayed to work on correspondence he brought with him. He examined rocks, measuring angles with a pointed instrument and making notations.

From the moment of her arrival, Anne was self-conscience and aware of the lord's every move. Anne did not think her heightened awareness had any effect on her drawings. On the contrary, the atmosphere was one of serious endeavor. The proximity of the lord improved her work. They were seldom disturbed; even Anne's father rarely entered the hothouse. When he did, he was relieved to see the master and his daughter worked separately in silence.

At the end of the week, though Anne knew she should keep quiet, she could not control her curiosity. Anne was want for answers to so many questions. Lord Greville was pliant with his knowledge. Anne did not hear annoyance in his voice. With timidity, Anne approached the subject of Georgiana, the Duchess of Devonshire. The recent death of Her Grace had once again made her a topic of discussion. Anne knew Lord Greville might have personal knowledge of the legendary beauty. After introducing the subject, she gave him her rapt attention while drawing the leaves of a variegated begonia.

"I did not travel in her circle. I once knew her and we acknowledged one another in the halls at court. We shared very little of society these last years." he said. He would not go into Emma's connection with the lady and his attempt to steer clear of any eyebrow raising incidents.

"But, you did see her more than once? Was she as extraordinarily beautiful as they say?"

"Beautiful, yes, she was. I think it was the manner in which she projected that beauty that affected people. It was a humble vulnerability that made her beautiful. She did not use her beauty for power," Charles said. He was thinking deeply of what he had said. It came to him that Emma had been much the opposite, using her beauty whenever possible. The difference in their birth, upbringing and rank accounted for it, he supposed.

Anne leaned forward to examine the hairs on the stems of the begonia. She sketched a few, but realized the red hairs would be a challenge to recreate. She would wait to do so when painting, a dry brush would work. Lord Greville looked over to see the girl still sketching despite her animated speech.

"Did you ever attend a ball where she was present?" Anne tried to continue the conversation.

"Yes, we were at several balls together when we were younger, though she was several years older than I and quite established by the time I came into society. She married the Duke at a young age, so most men didn't have a chance to woo her." Charles suspected Anne knew most of the stories circling around the servant's back

144

rooms. If Miss Blake were going to continue with such questions, she would have to accept his sometimes-frank answers.

"I think she may have been quite lonely at times." Anne reflected on what Sybil had said about the Duchess of Devonshire. She said something about living a life so public that everyone knew your every word, but none knew what was truly in your heart. Anne paused there as she realized the master was quiet. She did not want to seem inclined to gossip.

The lord saw no harm in gratifying the young girl with stories of life at court. He enjoyed having such stories to share. He found it refreshing that the girl's disposition was such that she did not dwell on the negative; she seemed to want to think the best of people.

"Is Warwick Castle very much like the Duke's estate?" Anne asked, exploring a new subject.

"Warwick is much larger, stretching into many halls from the initial fortress." Charles answered. "You would love the grounds at the castle and the landscapes of Warwickshire. Have you ever been in that part of the country?" Charles had forgotten to whom he was speaking.

"No sir, I don't believe so."

"No, more than likely not," he realized. Charles turned from the bench where Anne sat drawing. He rose to walk off the anxious feeling the events at the castle caused him. He wished he could overcome the anger he felt about his brother's accounts and how they should have been handled differently.

Anne kept quiet, thinking she had overstepped her place, asking so many questions. She worked to draw overlapping leaves with lighter and darker lines so that she would know to paint them correctly later. Lord Greville looked over at her drawing. He noticed she was marking the layers of leaves probably to paint their different colors. Of course, many artists used this approach, but he was surprised to see Anne had created her own technique so quickly.

"The Bauer brothers are the greatest botanical artists of our time." He spoke up to her. "They have a method by which they color code the drawings for painting later. I see you have adopted the same sort of technique."

Anne knew the lord looked over her shoulder. She had hoped he might comment on her drawing. Instead he had spoken of the Bauers, and once again Anne felt very much put in her place. She could not expect to compete with "the greatest botanical artists." She could only do her best and work hard to impress the lord. She had been penciling two plants per day and coloring them in the evening. She hoped the drawings would please Lord Greville, as he still had never examined them.

"This next week, I will not be here as I have appointments elsewhere. I give you leave to choose another plant to draw from those I have shown you. The begonia was a good choice though it will bloom again. I wish to get back to the lilies, as each begins to bloom. There is the one from China that you call "Sunshine" in the other room. You may want to illustrate the poppies or the aster that I pointed out. I leave it to you to decide."

With that, the nobleman gathered his notes and left the glasshouse. Anne watched his distorted form through the glass as he walked away. He paid no further attention to her, dismissing her as he would any servant. She felt rejected, worrying that her perpetual questioning had driven him off. Perhaps it would be wise to limit her appetite for such information to smaller bites in the future.

After Lord Greville exited the greenhouse, Anne lost all interest in her drawing. She had the basic lines of the begonia down on paper, the patterns of the green and red variegation on the leaves. The rest of the coloring was suggested in her drawing and secured in her mind's eye. She could work on the drawing this afternoon or evening. She realized how hungry she was and hurried off to the kitchen.

146

Anne trotted to the hallway door and into the kitchen without any thought to what might be happening beyond. She burst through the doorway, running right into Peter, the boy who delivered the milk. They each stood startled, looking at each other for the first moments after her sudden entrance.

The boy was quite tall, as Anne was already aware. Standing beneath him, she saw just how much he towered over her. His blond hair was cut bluntly; a style Anne did not find attractive. His light blue eyes were lovely. She admitted as much to Sybil when they saw him walking around the Green.

Anne lifted her head to see an admiring face looking down at her. His skin was clear and he smelled of soap. There was a shadow of a blond mustache on his lip, and she knew he must be close to her own age. He was clean and well dressed for a delivery boy. His face was red from the sun, and his features were not angular or strong, but round and soft. Anne was aware that most girls would think him very handsome, but he did not hold the degree of attraction that a certain black haired delivery boy did.

The two boys were so unlike each other; it would be hard to find two so different delivery boys to compare. Tom's face was dark, rugged, and he dressed in the clothes of a worker, almost rags. Tom reminded her of a gypsy, with the manners to match. They were far from each other in their stations though their employment was much the same. Tom worked for the grocer, whereas this boy's family owned the cows.

"So sorry," Anne said, worried she might have hit him with the door.

"Good day, Miss." Peter doffed his hat and almost bowed. He was surprised to see the girl he had spotted on Paddington Green. Though she disappeared down this lane, he was not sure how she was connected to Lord Greville. He had kept his enthusiasm in check; she had appeared very shy when they passed each other on the Green. He had waited for an opportunity to talk with her, but as of yet, there had not been the chance.

Peter would have liked a conversation to ensue at that point and seemed to wait for one, but Anne moved away to the other side of the kitchen, headed for the breadbasket where she knew some ends of bread would be available for a mid-day meal.

Peter followed her with his eyes until his view included Cook who watched with amusement and waited for Peter to be finished with his delivery.

"This is Peter," Cook said, turning to Anne. "He brings fresh milk for the master."

Turning back to face Anne, she held her arm around the back of the girl as if to push her forward. "This is Anne. She is staying with us for a while. Her father is the head gardener." Cook tried to give Anne some position of importance. The older woman moved away giving the two a moment to become acquainted.

Anne curtsied to Peter and he once again bowed to her. Anne was aware of the look in Peter's eyes. She knew he was hoping for a conversation to begin. She tried not to look directly at him, fearing he might see she did not meet his gaze with the same enthusiasm. It was satisfying to know he looked at her that way, but Anne could not return his look with the same interest.

"It has been very pleasant these last Sundays," Anne finally stated.

"Yes. I was happy to see you enjoying the day," Peter returned with obvious delight at her remembrance.

"I often walk with another maid after church service. We see several of our friends. It is nice to pass time that way."

"Will you be walking Sunday?" Peter asked quickly.

Anne felt sorry that she did not fully delight at his inquiry. Rather, she felt constrained; as if saying yes would mean she accepted an arranged meeting. She paused to decide her approach.

"If the weather permits, we may take a walk next Sunday. Sometimes Sybil goes home to see her family and then I do not walk." It was a weak excuse, but Anne felt she must have a choice in the matter. She was sorry that she did not feel for Peter what she did for Tom, and she somehow knew she made a wrong choice. Peter was so predictable. Tom was wild and mysterious. Anne doubted Tom thought of her at all, considering his connection to the solicitous Becky. Anne felt somewhat ashamed that she thought so much of him.

She curtsied to Peter, and made her way to the door as Peter called "I will look for you, then." Anne gave him a smile and almost tripping as she retreated out the hall door. She felt relief as if she had escaped a trap.

17

*O*n Sunday, Sybil did leave to visit her family as Anne had mentioned to Peter. So it was that Anne walked to the parish church with Cook and Lucas. It was pleasant to accompany them. Anne liked to imagine they were a family. She loved to watch the pair hold hands or gently put their arms about each other, Lucas often guiding Cook's steps where the path was uneven.

The couple had lost a daughter to an accident. Anne imagined that such heartache had brought them closer together. They raised two sons to manhood, and now the couple looked toward the rest of their lives together here at Lord Greville's manor at Paddington.

Cook and Lucas had the perfect marriage to Anne's way of thinking. She saw them brush each other when they passed in the kitchen. She saw them exchange a knowing glance across the room in a way that showed they knew each other's thoughts. As a married couple who had spent more of their lives together than apart, the bond was unmistakable as something deep and lasting.

Cook's true name was Margaret. Lucas called her by the nickname, Maggie. It was the name she had used when she was young. It was the way Lucas said it that made it special for Anne.

"Maggie, I have the coal coming today, so do not fret for using what remains in the bucket." Anne heard him reassure his wife. "Maggie let me help you with that bag". He was always there to lift heavy items for her.

Lucas and Cook never exchanged cross words. Their relationship represented something of an ideal to Anne. She had not an idea if a chance for marriage would ever come for her as she had spoken to Lord Greville, but if so, she would wish for nothing more than the love these two had for one another.

Cook and Lucas' boys, now men, lived elsewhere. Matthew, the elder boy, worked as an apprentice to a mason in Oxford. He had loved to "stack bricks even as a small boy" Cook would say. The younger boy, Tim, had taken employment working on the Grand Canal loading and unloading barges. The flat boats could haul so much more tonnage than wagons. The condition of the roads limited the loads that could be hauled overland especially during the rainy season. More and more goods were being transferred by canal.

After church, as local residents filed onto the Green, Anne followed Cook and Lucas as they planned to walk the longer leg around the square on their way back to Lord Greville's lane. She spotted Peter dawdling by the church lawn. Peter cut a fine picture in his vest and waistcoat. She thought he was taller by inches every time she saw him. Though Peter did not attend the same church as Anne, his arrival seemed perfectly timed with the benediction and dismissal from her church.

"Miss Anne, will you walk around the Green today?" Peter asked. Cook and Lucas elbowed each other as they saw Peter come forward. Anne looked to them for permission.

"Hello Peter," Cook said. Lucas nodded his way. It was all fairly formal, as if they were her guardians.

"It is a nice day, Anne. You should take advantage of the weather and get a bit of exercise," Cook encouraged Peter's offer.

Cook had mentioned to Anne "his family has increased their property from one small farm to a large portion of the county. His father and uncle own one of the largest dairies and employ over thirty milkmaids." Cook thought the milkman might be a very fine match for Anne. It was obvious to her that the young farmer was enthralled with the gardener's daughter. She would do what she could toward such an end.

Anne did not want to think about milkmaids or the life of a farmer's wife. She was not ready to settle into such a fixed state of matrimony no matter how secure it might be. Her words to Lord Greville came back to her.

Anne enjoyed the attention Peter paid her, but feared any response might solicit his conclusion they were beginning a relationship. She still held onto the thought that the Duke's daughter would contact her with a position before winter set in, and she would be in very different circumstances. At any rate, she was not ready for any understanding despite Cook's obvious intentions. It would be so easy if she could care for Peter, but so far, those emotions were not forthcoming.

"The weather has been so much warmer this week," Anne said to Peter, keeping the conversation light and impersonal as they walked away together.

18

*E*ach day, Anne arrived to an empty greenhouse. Her initial excitement had worn down, and though she enjoyed drawing the flowers, it was an effort she pursued not for herself, but for Lord Greville. She settled into the task of drawing the next flower with a bit of disappointment that she would spend another morning alone. She knew she had little right to such feelings. She began a sketch of the vine she had spotted in the far corner of the hothouse. She drew the form of the stem and the pattern of the leaves along it.

Anne concentrated on transferring what her eye saw to paper. The passion flower was ornate with its crown of black hairs and purple tinges to the petals that circled out from the center. She did not hear footsteps, so she did not startle or realize Lord Greville had entered. He paused to watch her.

She was already pretty, but in a matter of years, she would possess the kind of beauty that all she met would reflect upon. He looked through the canopy of leaves and realized he stood just where the drawing he had found had been created. This was the location from which Anne must have spied on him. With horror, he thought of his breakdown. She had surely been a witness, a silent witness. He was thankful she had never referred to the event.

He wished he could have spent his morning in the hothouse with the young woman. He had enjoyed the previous week's visits, though Coleman made a stink. He did not mind her curious questioning; in fact, he felt important for it. Anne's obvious approval and admiration made him feel quite well about himself.

Anne turned slightly, adjusting her position and noticed him standing at the door.

"Ah, Miss Blake, hard at work, I see," he stuttered, regaining his composure.

Anne looked up and debated returning to her work without so much as a smile, but thought better of it and lifted the edges of her lips in a little smirk. She was angry and embarrassed for the anger. In a moment more, she corrected herself and replied with as much friendliness as she could.

"Yes my lord, I began sketching that interesting vine, the one in the corner with the elaborate flowers."

"Oh it has opened completely!" he said as he turned to take a look. It had been days since he last stopped by the hothouse. He was thankful Anne was aware of a possible subject for her sketching; the same he might have suggested had he been present.

"I have left you very much to your own good sense on which plant to choose. I see you have been quite attentive. Well done. I do have a request for one of the next flowers, as I am sure it, also, has begun to bloom. It is over in the corner on the opposite wall," he pointed. Anne looked over not sure which plant he indicated.

"The pot cannot be moved easily, so you will need to resituate yourself. Would you like one of the chairs by the pond to sit in? Perhaps you would be more comfortable using the stool?"

Anne put down her things and came across to understand where she might sit to sketch the tall plant.

156

"I think it would be simplest if I used my stool. I can move about easily and not disrupt furniture for the effort. What is this plant?" Anne asked.

"It is ginger, a spice used most frequently in the kitchens of India. You may have heard of its use in biscuits."

"I am familiar with ginger, but I never thought about from where it came, or that you would have it growing in your hothouse! The flowers smell so sweet." Anne could smell them from where she stood. "Are they the source of the flavor?"

"Oh no," the lord replied, "It is the root that is used."

"I thought perhaps it was bamboo. The vase is quite lovely also."

"It is an antique Chinese pot, but the lip is chipped and it suffers from a large crack that has been mended. I had your father make use of it for the ginger." Charles explained.

"I would happily make a drawing, though its tall features will require a different view of the plant and then a closer view of the flower itself."

"Yes, I think that would be the best way to represent it as it is indeed almost five feet tall in that planter, but you can decide," Charles said.

Anne did not mind these freedoms, but she was still acutely aware Lord Greville had yet to look at her drawings.

"I have brought you a sample of ginger root," he went on, "a treat I have enjoyed since I was very young. It is a good cure for a sour stomach." He passed Anne a small tin cracked open to reveal small sugar coated lumps of pale yellow candy.

Anne took the tin and selected a bit placing it in her mouth. The tangy flavor did not immediately leach through the sugar from the lump as it sat on her tongue, so she took a small bite. A spurt of spiciness shot through her mouth to the back of her throat. Then before it was too much, it subsided into a sweet heat. She chewed another bit off and enjoyed the sensation, happily awaiting the tang to come to her tongue and throat. She lifted her eyebrows in anticipation.

Anne looked up to see Lord Greville watching her with amusement at the faces she must have been making.

"I like it very much. I would want another and another," she remarked.

"Well, you will have to control the temptation or all too soon the treat will be gone. I leave it to you, though, for the tin is yours to keep."

Anne looked at the candy lumps which were suddenly more precious than gold as a present from the lord.

"Do you often suffer from a sour stomach?" Anne asked, thinking of the herbs that aid such a condition.

"Not often, but at times it can be a bother." Charles tried to answer off-handedly, not wishing to admit what had become a more chronic concern. He moved toward the door, ready to leave the enclosure.

Anne thought again of the scene in the greenhouse wondering if a stomach ache could have been the master's affliction that day. No, she thought, although he may have felt ill at the time, the sounds she heard had originated from the heart, not the stomach.

Anne wished she did not feel jealous of Lord Greville's other duties. She noticed he wore a fine waistcoat and his hair was pulled back and curled on the sides. He was certainly not dressed to remain in the hothouse.

As if he read her thoughts he continued, "I am once again off to town. I have three days of appointments and meetings this week alone. I had hoped for more serenity in my life."

Anne smiled through her disappointment. Lord Greville took the quickest look at her fresh paper with only a few tentative strokes of pencil upon it, but then hurried away to the door.

"Continue with your work. I do not wish to interrupt you."

With that, he was gone. Anne heard the sound of the lord's chaise pulling out of the lane. She shrugged her shoulders and tried not to feel abandoned. She wished she could have insisted that he did not bother her. His presence made her drawings better. Anne knew her life had changed due to the lord's attention, but it was difficult for her not to wish for more. She finished the vine before mid-day and started the sketch of the long stems on the ginger plant, all the while slowly sucking on sugary lumps.

Toward the end of the week, Lord Greville, her father, and two other men were already in the greenhouse when she arrived. The men gathered halfway down the side of the glasshouse, just beyond the area where the fuchsias were stacked. Their meeting took place around the corner from the workbench where Anne now tried to settle. She was just out of sight, but within earshot. They were discussing a project, measuring and postulating an imaginary, yet-to-be-built shelf for displaying more plants.

Plant slips were arriving from the New Holland hoard as Sir Banks had announced. Only a few evenings before, her father had complained about the crowding of the existing plants and the arrival of new specimens.

"I am sure Lord Greville will notice the disarray in the hothouse soon, but he has been very much away, and I have not asked for an audience," her father said.

"He has not given his attention to the greenhouse for the last while, so busy elsewhere, I suppose," Anne said with an irritated sigh.

A meeting must have taken place because now a new shelf was to be built. None of the men, his lordship included, so much as looked up when Anne entered and walked to her place at the workbench. After an hour, Anne realized the enclosure was quiet. She peeked around the edge of the bench to see that the men had exited through the other end of the greenhouse without so much as a word of acknowledgment to her. They failed to return anytime in the next hour.

Although she knew she had no right, she was miffed to have been ignored. For the first time, she was reminded that she was the outsider in the greenhouse; a servant, no one of consequence, and it both angered and frightened her.

The following day, the two men returned to finish their construction. They were not accompanied by Lord Greville. The men carried on their conversations, forgetting anyone might be in proximity to them.

"I'll bet a tankard, we don't get this done today," said the first carpenter.

"I'll bet you two we do," the other man replied, "if you keep quiet and bring that other board in. Be sure the edge is planed down, mind you. We don't want his lordship getting splinters up his nose when he's smelling his posies." They both laughed heartily.

Anne thought she might jump down from her stool to find her father and report the men's rude behavior. Anne's face was flushed and she could not steady her hand to draw, she was so infuriated. As she wiped the tears before they could fall onto her paper, her foot slipped from the step on her stool and slapped noisily on the floor. She listened for more, but the men, having realized they were not alone in the greenhouse, said nothing. She gathered her things, and left the enclosure with a bad-mannered slam that shook the panes all the way down the side of the glasshouse.

She hurried home to await her father's return from the garden for supper. She told him of the rude behavior of the workers, but he regarded the episode as none of her business. She would not have heard them if she had been intent on her work.

Befuddled by his reaction as unjustified, Anne sighed deeply as she looked out the window to see it was already dark. The days were growing shorter, and darkness would linger longer. She finished cleaning the few dishes accumulated after their late meal. Her father went to his bed almost as soon as he finished chewing his last bite. Anne was not the least bit tired. She was anxious. She decided she would take an evening walk to relieve her restlessness.

Anne pulled the shawl from the end of her bed and went out the door, closing it quietly. There was no moon. The sky was amazingly clear. The air was as clean and fresh as the sky. The smoke and soot that drifted in from the city had been scoured out by a mid-day shower. The stars were all out tonight, Anne noticed. It was warm and there was no wind, so she decided she would walk past the tall hedge marking Lord Greville's garden. Once there, she realized her view was obstructed to her right and if she went a bit farther onto the lawn, she would have an even better view of the night sky.

There was no light coming from Lord Greville's library. She guessed he was not home. The lights from the upstairs rooms were faint. With careful steps in the near dark, she made her way in between the beds and found a spot on the grass where she took a seat to watch the stars travel by, a phenomenon she had loved since childhood.

She stared out at the bright specks as she let her mind wander. How did she really feel about Peter? Their walk had been pleasant, and she enjoyed their conversation even if she knew how nervous the milkman's son had been. She feared that if she were to bend her attention toward him anymore, he would profess his feelings for her. Then the question presented itself; if Tom were to show such interest, would she be so shy? She thought not and blushed at her own thoughts. She lay back on the ground and rested her mind only for a minute before she caught the sound of footsteps coming from the house toward the area where she star gazed.

Lord Greville was agitated when he returned from town. Societal meetings often left him this way. His circle of friends were men of the globe, watching from their lofty states of mind as so many new theories, inventions, and discoveries came before them. They strived to understand the science of all of it. They knew of things that would change lives forever. There was power with this knowledge. He spent many hours pacing back and forth, sorting his thoughts on many subjects. His garden gave him relief from these mental examinations. He extinguished his lamp and made his way out into the dark of his small park, wishing to tame his mind toward sleep.

Charles wished he could invade a fellow's home in need of a good conversation. Sometimes ideas would come to him in the middle of the night, and he often wished he could have some confirmation so he might get back to sleep. If only Banks lived next door, or Robert, or any of his enlightened male acquaintances.

Charles shook his head and shrugged off the tension building in his neck and shoulders. He would have a headache soon if he did not turn his thoughts away from all this aggravation. He took a deep breath and looked about the garden though he saw few details in the darkness. He could picture the walled landscape he had created and let out a long sigh.

Charles Greville hated to admit there might be something to the fellow, Richard Payne Knight's, theories. Knight pursued the argument that true art must create sensations. The visual pleasure Charles' garden gave him would come as close as he could to Knight's theory, but he would not go so far as to agree with Knight that the feeling might enter the realm of sexual. There was a feeling akin to love when he saw his garden in good order. He had been truly moved by the sight of a flower. As usual though, Knight took things too far.

Personally, the lord thought Richard Knight an ass. He gave his opinions even if not asked. He had announced his plan to visit the marble sculpted fresco which Thomas Bruce, the 7th Earl of Elgin, had removed from the Parthenon. The interest in antiquities had shifted from Roman to Greek of late, partially because statues and such could be removed from Greece without paperwork. Charles had dealt with ancient artifacts for so long he was numb to any conscience guilt that might be associated with the removal of such wares as cultural items best left in the country of their origin. This was the argument that tainted the recovery of the Rosetta stone, now housed in the British Museum despite protest.

"I am off to see what is left of Elgin's marbles." Knight had proclaimed to the group tonight with his usual superiority. "I believe Thomas has overstepped his authority in this case. Several cornices were destroyed and the entire affair was underhanded. Still their beauty is striking, and the initial artwork was an incredible undertaking. He steals a fresco from Athena while his own Athena dwells in another's heart. Very sad trade off, I say." Knight referred to Bruce's wife who moved her affections elsewhere as Bruce was moving the frescos. It was this type of attitude that infuriated Charles and many others of their group.

"Are any of you ready to be aroused? Care to join me, gentlemen?" Knight had asked, lifting his eyebrows, proud of his pun.

Charles decided the theories Knight put forth came from too much time on his hands. Charles knew his disdain of the man began on the occasion when Knight had expressed such an effusion of delight over Emma's performance of attitudes, classical poses she would assume. She had often been asked to display these positions at gatherings. As usual, Emma had embarrassed him, Charles remembered with a grimace.

Charles continued his walk in the dark, now able to make out the marled pathway's light cover against the green of the grass. His mind still reeled from the discussions he had engaged in at the meeting. He thought of the other members present.

As much as Charles did not care for Richard Knight, he held Richard's brother, Andrew, in high esteem. Andrew was a diligent gentleman farmer. He looked on agriculture as a means to national greatness. He felt that they should all pursue such knowledge simply because food, feed for animals, clothing, and fuel all came from the tilling of the earth. Andrew Knight would receive this year's Copley Award for his diligence. It was very exciting to have known his work from the beginning. Charles agreed with him though he had no interest in saving the world, or even changing the world all that much. As long as he was free to enjoy it, he was satisfied. He wandered on deep in thought.

Anne saw the figure coming along the path toward her. It was his lordship, and he had not seen her in the dark. She could not decide whether to crawl away now or hold her position until he moved past. Once again, she would be the intruder on his grounds. She stayed where she was in part because her legs were asleep, tucked under her, tingling and numb.

The night sky stretched out around the lord, and he was surprised at its clarity. He let his thoughts subside. Nothing blocked a good view of the stars this night. The smoke from the chimneys traveled straight up. He spun in a circle to get his bearings, seeing Ursa Major and the North Star, the good friends of northern sailors. He thought of sailors triangulating their way across huge spans of water with nothing but these stars to give them their direction.

Charles spun back to his right faster than his feet could follow and he stumbled a bit. Trying to regain his balance, he made four large steps backwards and was just about to step on Anne, when she jumped to her feet, startling the lord.

"Gracious, what have we here? Miss Blake, is that you? What in the world are you doing here?" He was catching his breath from the jump she gave his heart.

"I am sorry, sir. I was watching the stars go by," she answered honestly.

Though the features of Anne's face could not be made out in the dark, Charles could see the silhouette her profile formed against the horizon. Though they stood in the night alone together, he did not wish to hurry away. How odd to think the need for conversation might be satisfied here.

"Yes, it is very clear tonight. It is easy to see them all," he remarked, looking up.

"They travel by so quickly. The three there in a row were over the elms only moments ago. They all move as one, never getting ahead of each other." Anne said.

"They do not move as you might think. They are more fixed, most of them. It is we who are moving," he explained.

"Is that so? Why do we see the same stars over each night and not another part of the Heavens as we move along?"

"Ah, remember we are standing on a sphere, a ball. It is held in the middle and spins in a circle around that point. Just around once is a day." He wanted to show with his hands, but it was too dark. He knew his explanation might be vague, but he was at a loss to make his description clearer.

"And what is a year?" Anne asked, trying to understand the correlation of these time increments.

Charles admired her following the subject so closely. Her question was very astute and appropriate. He doubted she had previously studied the subject.

"A year is how long it takes that spinning ball to move around the sun in a large circle one time."

Anne was silent as she thought about this. There was so much to know, she thought disheartened. She felt so ignorant of the world especially in Lord Greville's presence. She wondered if the master would shun her interest in knowing such things. Did he think a woman could or even should understand?

"Very soon, I intend to get a better look at those stars."

Anne heard a far off tone to his voice. She tried to think to what he referred.

"How will you do that, sir?"

"I am building an observatory with instruments to see into the night sky, mapping the stars and locating all that moves above our heads each night. There will be a large glass circle, a lens, to make objects many times larger than what you and I see. I will build a university for studying the stars." He imagined he'd gone on too long already, but he was encouraged by her attention.

Charles began to point out the brighter stars to Anne. "That is Vega, there is Arcturus. And there," Charles aligned his arm and finger up in front of the girl as if it were an arrow, " that is Jupiter, one of the planets. It is a very important planet." Charles was once more tutor.

"Why is it more important than the others?" Anne dared to ask.

"Jupiter has moons, just as we have the one moon. Fortunately, our moon has not joined us this evening for the darkness allows a better viewing. If I look through my eyepiece, I can see the moons of Jupiter travel across the face of the planet, which they do in a most timely fashion. If I know which moon I am seeing and how long it takes to travel across Jupiter, I know just where I am on this planet.

Anne let her head fall back as if surrendering to so much information. She looked fully at the sky. Until this moment, she was happy just to look at the stars without any knowledge of them. That was changed. She would never look at stars again without thinking of Lord Greville and this conversation.

Charles saw Anne relax her head back to look up and he mimicked the motion with his own. He scanned the sky toward her and caught another glimpse of her profile, dark against the spotted sky. The curve of her neck was a flawless road up to the hill of her chin. Her hair hung back escaping the ribbon tied around it. She had no idea of the allure she cast with the pose.

Anne looked back down and caught the master's eyes upon her. Her eyes had adjusted to the dark and she could see a curious look was evident on his face. Perhaps he judged her, thought her silly to try to learn.

"I think it is better if I do not try to understand such things, my lord, as a woman." Anne knew there would be no women at Lord Greville's school even if he suggested otherwise. While she could know of these facts, would she ever have need of this knowledge?

"It may be proper for you to say so," Charles said with a serious voice, "but I do not think you are such a woman. I think you do want to understand." Now his voice and his face held a smile she could hear as well as see on his face.

"Good night, Miss Blake."

"Good night, sir." Anne curtsied to the darkness and headed back down the path to the black shape of the cottage. She repeated the master's last comment to herself again. To be "such a woman" did not seem to be said in disapproval. No, the statement was indeed a compliment.

Charles watched her for a minute until she was close to the cottage door. He headed for his own shelter. When he thought of the brief encounter and conversation, he could not name another female with whom he might have had the same exchange. Most of the women he knew were not truly interested in gaining knowledge as Anne had mentioned about her sex. Most young girls were all giddy and decoration, no substance. Yet this gardener's daughter had enough views of nature to stir her curiosity and enough knowledge of what was around her to observe, comment, and learn from what she saw. Unique, really, Charles thought.

Lord Greville was surprised how well he felt, all the tension of a tight neck gone. Before he entered the library, he looked up at the stars one last time, letting his head drop back as Anne had. He slid his hand slowly down the underside of his chin imagining softer skin beneath his touch. It was becoming difficult not to think of the gardener's daughter as a woman, and a rather interesting one, at that.

19

*L*ord Greville made plans to journey to the London Docks. He knew he should not do so alone as there were often seedy characters lurking about such public places. He had thought to take Coleman, but realized the manservant would be little help if a circumstance were to arise. Coleman was apt to mutter and make rude comments, which might cause an altercation rather than avoid one.

A trip to the docks would be just the sort of outing Sir Joseph would enjoy if his health had allowed. They would have included his man and been quite safe together as a threesome. In the end, the lord decided to have Cook's husband, Lucas, accompany him. The man could not only drive them into town, but also his burly constitution would certainly provide additional security. So it was agreed, Lord Greville with Lucas in tow would make the expedition.

Early in the morning, the men departed with the expectation they would be away much of the day. It was to be a cool and misty morning expected to clear off by afternoon. Cook packed a luncheon his lordship could eat if necessary. If need be, Lucas could stay with the chaise while Lord Greville took his supper at a club on the way back. Lucas looked forward to the outing as he longed to see more of the commerce in which his younger boy was engaged.

By reaching the waterfront mid-morning, the twosome would miss some of the crowds of early arrivals and departures. Though the streets and alleyways of the area would still be busy with vendors and custom officers engaged in their daily duties, the hope was that the squeeze of passengers and delivery wagons would have dissipated. Lord Greville instructed Lucas to call for a hired chaise to take them within a few blocks of the dock while they left his lordship's carriage parked safely several blocks away.

As they traveled the short distance to the docks, Charles was cheered by the outing.

"I am most anxious to re-examine the warehouses along the quay," he explained to Lucas, though he did not expect the man to comment. "I have difficulty with the project in Milford as there is little level ground adjacent to the waterway. At this point, we cart most goods uphill to small storage buildings. We are limited in our abilities to offload in a way that is efficient."

"Your efforts at Milford are commendable, sir" said Lucas in a general reply. He knew little of the master's project. He would not assume to have any valuable knowledge or opinion that would be worthy of his master's audience.

The goods Charles wished to store included wool and whale oil, but he saw an increase in imports of tobacco, wine, tea, spices, and ivory. In no way was the harbor ready for larger loads of such products. He hoped to gain some ideas, perhaps the use of locks or any particular rope riggings useful in his situation for the movement of goods at Milford.

In addition, he hoped to look in on several merchants whose shops filled the side streets of the dock area with everything necessary to go to sea. He hoped to entice them his way or perhaps they might consider opening an additional business at Milford. He viewed the surroundings as a dreamland of the business his port might someday support.

Shops along the alleyways included the work of men who sewed sails, sacks, twined rope, and built barrels and casks. Without barrels for dry goods and fresh water, a man could not go to sea. If he wanted to increase his profits, he would also need to increase storage. It was as simple as that. As Lord Greville faded into the crowd that meandered between the river and the warehouses, the smell of wine, spice, tobacco, saltwater and the strange smell of dry rot filled his nose.

At all times, Lucas felt edgy with a heightened awareness. In this strange assortment of vendors, sailors of all different nationalities and costumes, and the general public wandering the streets, Lucas kept his eyes on the master as they weaved through the crowd. He protected his master from being bumped or perhaps pushed over by those who came at him from the opposite direction. For the most part, the crowd parted for his master, seeing the distinguished gentleman coming toward them.

As the two men came closer to the main area of activity, the masts of ships rose into view as a limbless forest against the sky. Some ships laden with goods sat well below the water line. Others, having already offloaded their steerage, rose up out of the water. For these ships, the planks of wood connecting the walkway tilted up the side of the ship. With the changing tides, these planks moved up and down.

The nobleman worked his way to the end of the block where another lane intersected the street. At this corner, two warehouses extended for one hundred feet in each direction. The lord peaked in the open doors to the dimly lit interior. He could barely make out the silhouettes of men moving about inside. The vast space was only partly filled. Hollow shouts from the dock workers bounced off the walls. The floor was sticky and stained purple where wine leaked or spilled. The next warehouse contained a mixture of goods, as some of the area held boxes and other parts casks and barrels. The building exuded a smell: warm, exotic, and altogether foreign.

Midway up the street, the warehouses gave way to a row of shops. Lord Greville plodded on, just barely aware of Lucas behind him. He entered one shop after another. Each time his lordship exited, Lucas noted the disappointment on his master's face. They circled back to the carriage.

"We'll head for home, Lucas. I have had enough narrow-mindedness for one day." The lord was perturbed that no merchants would so much as consider taking part in his Milford harbor project. The two men continued on in silence.

It was Lord Greville who spoke as they arrived back to his chaise, "Well Lucas, what did you think?"

"Ah sir, I find I am not the seafaring type as I never was. I have no love for the sailor's life. I prefer the land to the sea."

Lord confirmed what his servant remarked with a laugh and a nod. "Where are those cold cuts your dear wife sent along?" he asked, completely leaving the sea, sailors, the dock, and the merchants behind.

The men continued the trip home in silence, each lost in their thoughts. Lord Greville thinking of the swing arm he had seen off-loading cargo. Lucas hoping Tim never went to sea.

Anne spent another morning sketching alone. More and more she longed for Lord Greville to join her in the greenhouse. She longed to spend time with the nobleman, time he did not have to share. When she left the greenhouse, it was Cook's comfort she sought. The older woman always gave her advice in a soothing, motherly fashion that relieved Anne regardless of the situation.

The fresh air outside the enclosure renewed Anne's spirit, and she vowed to leave her peeved mood behind as she was almost certain Cook would advise her to do. What she did not expect in the midst of all her emotional control, was meeting Tom face to face on the other side of the kitchen door. Flustered and wounded as she was, she was not prepared for this meeting.

Seeing Anne enter behind Cook, Tom made a great show of the small load of bags in his arms.

"Could I prevail upon one of you to help with the doors?" he asked, looking Anne's way.

"Go on, then. Get the doors for Tom," Cook said to Anne.

Once again, Anne opened the kitchen door and stood aside while Tom exited, then caught up with him to open the storeroom door. This time, she was no longer so nervous. Her initial mood had quickly changed. She was intrigued at the repetition of the scene she replayed so many times in her mind. Though her imaginings had included a kiss she would never allow. And yet, here she was, waiting in the dark of the storeroom, alone with the gypsy boy again. She took short breaths as her heart raced. When Tom turned to leave the room, having emptied his arms of the packages onto the table and neatly arranged them as before, Anne realized she blocked the way. Before she could move, he came up close to her. Anne saw a crescent of light in his eyes and a sweet smile on his lips, a look both ethereal and sensual. Anne felt his look as if he touched her. He bent toward her, and she readied her lips for a kiss. Instead, he straightened and shook his head muttering, "I best not."

Anne moved out of the way, a bit stunned. Tom hurried ahead of her and back to the wagon, tipping his hat and saying good-bye without turning around. Anne might have felt rejected, but the close call told her all she needed to know. He thought of her sometimes, and may have imagined a kiss as well.

20

ord Greville was now the proud owner of the cabinet of minerals he had so coveted. His wish to own the finest mineral collection in England was well on its way to being a reality. The cabinet contained two specimens Charles felt his friend and engraver, James Sowerby, might wish to include in his book of British Mineralogy, a record that strived to reflect the geologic events that formed Britain through engraved pictures of rock samples from various locations.

And so it was that Charles found himself away from his Paddington manor once more. Charles left the boxed mineral clusters with James Sowerby's two older boys who had been involved in the process of engraving and illustrating since they were very young, first painting backgrounds and eventually carving and printing. They assured Lord Greville that their father would be very excited to see the specimens and add them to his record.

"Oh, I almost forgot, do you sell copies of your father's book of botanical drawing instruction? I believe it has "easy introduction" as part of the title?" Charles asked.

The oldest boy went to a shelf and removed a thin booklet, handing it to Lord Greville. Charles flipped through the pages and found it to be just what it claimed to be.

"Yes, thank you. That is precisely what I seek." He reached into his pocket for coins to pay the boys, but the older one, James, put out a hand as a signal to stop.

"I know our father would not accept payment from you, Lord Greville. He so appreciates your sponsorship. You can settle with him later if you feel differently," James said.

Charles knew it to be the case. Their relationship was reciprocal. Charles brought specimens to the man's museum and spoke highly of the Sowerby's efforts when in circles of society where money for such ventures could be found. In turn, the engraver called Charles when he had something of interest for the lord to examine. Charles felt Sowerby's work of assembling well-labeled collections of minerals, fossils, fungi, and ferns were of the utmost importance, creating a permanent record through his printed books. Charles felt honored to be in the man's circle of friends.

Though Charles was disappointed to have missed the senior Sowerby, it would give him more time to visit with his brother, Robert, at his next stop. Robert had actually spoken of leaving government service as his wife, Louisa, mentioned during her visit. It was an idea Charles adamantly supported. He hoped his brother would speak of it, so he could give a positive comment.

Upon arriving at court, Charles was welcomed by the guard who knew of him not only through his brother, but also on his own merit as a member of the King's Privy Council and a former Member of Parliament. His title of Right Honorable Charles Greville indicated he was a part of the inner circle surrounding King George. He had been less and less to court of late, but there was a time when he lived within its walls. Charles made his way down the long hallways to his brother's wing. He smiled and bowed to several current members of Parliament as he proceeded.

It had been a balancing act to dodge the political punches in these halls. Charles managed to stay on the edge of the faction pressing to install the Prince of Wales to the throne. The King was distracted with bouts of mental illness that came on so suddenly. Charles had no alliance with the Prince of Wales. The boy was self-indulgent and in no way prepared to rule.

Charles had heard that Emma allowed the Prince Regent to attend parties at her home with his mistress in tow. Lady Hamilton used anyone she could to get her closer to the annuity she sought. Charles did speak with Middleton, the Lord of the Admiralty, about her pension, as she had asked, but he would not worry anymore about her money problems. She had not asked for any news when she wrote for money. No doubt, she copied the letter to several of her "old friends," Charles thought bitterly. He heard talk that Emma continued to entertain whomever she could in hopes she might once again obtain the lifestyle and attention she enjoyed with Sir William in Naples. Charles' emotions were surprisingly raw on all that had to do with Lady Hamilton. He was angry with himself for even listening or caring.

He had new interests. His mineral collections took time and the chemistry of crystal formation caused him to study as if he were attending college. He thought of Milford. He thought of his garden, and then Anne's face came into view. She was a small part of his life now, but one of the more pleasant parts. He enjoyed the world from her point of view. The simplicity of their after dark visit had relieved him from the evening's anxiety. Still, he would not mention Anne to his brother. He might not understand his relationship with the young woman. He tucked the package from Sowerby's into his case.

Arriving at his brother's door, it came open before he could knock. His brother took his right hand in a strong grip pulling his brother to him. In their younger years, they might have wrestled at this point. Robert put his arm around Charles' back and gave two pats and a squeeze to his shoulder as he led him in. Charles barely could get out "good to see you" before Robert started in on him about a pair of handsome horses he had in mind for his brother.

"You need to cease this appeal!" Charles said, pulling away. "I have heard what you are saying, but for now, I am happy with the old cobs I own." Charles said. "I know you are quite adamant about my purchasing new equipage, but I am able to use my curricle for trips to town or local jaunts. My horses have no aversion or prejudice against being hitched to the wagon if I have need of them in that way. Lucas feels they are able to make the substitution well enough and has not mentioned any derision they have in that department. My current horses do not snub employment and consume a great deal of hay, even when I have no need of them during my long visits to Milford."

"You have no decent mount of your own to ride, few guns, and no fishing poles whatsoever. You do not engage in cards, dice, or gambling. You do not drink too much ale or port. You do no service to the reputation of our sex." He jested with Charles, as he knew his brother better than anyone. Neither of them gambled or drank in excess. Although Robert knew his brother had been in debt, none of it came from these vices.

"We have left Warwick in good hands." Charles began the visit to his brother with the subject closest to their hearts. "With economy and a careful watch over living expenses, George might dig out from the pile of debts he owes. We can only hope there is no scandal put upon George's name." Charles knew Robert did not wish to hear anymore of Charles' remarks about their older brother so he finished the conversation at that point.

"For me, I am glad to have it settled." Robert answered. He had not involved himself with his oldest brother's affairs as Charles had, but knew both John Stewart and John Fitzgerald well and trusted their efforts completely.

"I have decided to enjoy my life from this time on. I am thinking of departing court altogether." Robert declared. Charles' face broke into a broad smile, pleased to hear his brother's resolution even before he could bring the subject up.

"I will retire; raise horses, sheep, and dogs. Heaven forbid I spend time with my wife and family. I have never put myself first, and I am ready for a chance to try my own hand at farming as I have advised so many for so long. The thought of doing things my way without anyone's permission entices me greatly."

"I am very happy to hear you say such things aloud." Charles met Robert's plans with a degree of doubt, knowing such a change would be most difficult for his brother, tied to the needs of their sovereign as he was. His brother's fondness for animal husbandry might be just the ticket to get him out of government duty. During their childhood, Robert forever had a horse or a dog with which he had a close relationship. As they were growing up, Charles had preferred one mount over another, but never one horse above all others in the world.

"You have served your country well, Robert," Charles said. He moved from where he stood by a bureau of his brother's medals to stand close to Robert, putting his arm around his younger sibling. This retirement was something he had spoken of many times, but Charles never quite believed him. This time a new mood came across with his sibling's words. He was not just talking to convince himself; he addressed the topic with a certain conviction that Charles had never heard before.

"And yet, I hate to leave as Napoleon's campaign seems to be coming on. Emperor, ha! The man is insufferable. How many coalitions before we can be done with him? I had hoped this would all be over by now. He is intolerably obsessed with power. Pray, how can I leave at this hour?"

Robert changed the subject to one he knew would please his brother.

"What do you hear from Milford? I did get a report that the church foundation is set. They were bringing several loads of rock each day. They should be working on the walls by now."

"Yes, and they have come up several courses on the masonry. Laborers have started the chancels and we have purchased beautiful glass windows for each side. At least there is an abundance of help, so the project moves on," Charles replied, pleased that his brother kept up with the progress.

"I toured the London docks earlier this week." Charles' thoughts went to his demise at finding no suppliers open to the idea of setting up in Milford. "I accomplished little except to admire the rows of warehouses built along the waterway. I left cards at several merchant's shops, but I see they will not entertain a new outpost when they already have so much success here. I will look elsewhere for merchants with interests in new ventures," Charles continued.

"If you can get the Naval Board on your side, you will have all the support you need," Robert pointed out.

"Precisely," Charles answered. He was very much relieved by his brother's confidence.

"The brickwork on the observatory is finished and waits for the telescope to be placed," Charles continued, speaking of his favorite project on the hill above the harbor.

"I have made arrangements for the transit to be hauled to the observatory, but the weather has been wetter than usual, making the dirt road to the site impassable. I must be sure it is set correctly in the building, so I may have the men wait to move it until such time as I am present, perhaps at the end of summer." Charles mulled over the plans with his brother who had given more useful input and ideas than anyone else.

"You have monies left for an astronomer of some sort or a guard?" Robert inquired.

"I am working on enlisting the help of Thomas Firminger, as his work at Greenwich with Maskelyne is almost finished. I am hoping that, with enough money, I can install him as superintendent of the observatory. The life of an astronomer tends to be one separated from society by the hours that must be kept. Firminger is just the man, but I have little to entice him with as of yet."

Nevil Maskelyne, the Astronomer Royal, was well known for his work on the means by which to determine longitude and calculating Earth's density for which he received the Copley Award. Thomas Firminger had been his assistant in the later years. Now that Maskelyne was retiring, Thomas had expressed an interest in helping Charles with his plans for an institution for studying astronomy and navigation and in conjunction, setting up the observatory.

"What will you purchase next?" Robert asked. "The new chronographers have improved so much."

"Yes, that is another problem with the observatory. If I delay the furnishings until next year, there may be better instruments available." Charles said.

The conversation lulled and only seconds passed before Charles heard his brother ask, "And what is this I hear from Louisa? She mentioned an intruder, a female artist, and a scent of roses. She spun a strange tale of intrigue. I was not sure if there was a shred of truth to any of it." Robert looked to Charles to give some answer to the topic his curious wife had urged him to pursue.

"Yes, it was strange, but it is resolved now. The young woman is George Blake's daughter." Charles said.

"George, your gardener?"

"Yes the same."

"I think of George as ancient. How old is this daughter and is she pleasant to look at?" Robert inquired, raising his eyebrows and teasing his brother.

"She is quite young, not yet twenty, I believe, and very pleasant to look at. I am not so interested in her pretty face. I am more interested in her talent in making accurate drawings and have employed her to do penance for her trespass by sketching the plants in the hothouse."

"How did she come to be at Paddington? I had no idea George had family."

"She was removed from governess duties, perhaps a paramour, perhaps a misunderstanding. She seems unspoiled, so I doubt that any of it was her doing. She awaits another position, but nothing has been arranged as of yet. She is an intelligent creature, and has a thirst for knowledge I find commendable." Charles grinned, thinking of Anne and her incessant questions.

"Oh, and you are just the one to school her?" Robert asked in a suggestive voice, as he noted his brother's grin. "You seem quite pleased with the young woman. Take care, Charles."

"I enjoy her unobstructed view of the world," Charles answered with a sharp retort.

Robert heard his brother's tenor and backed out of the conversation. He would not pursue the topic further. It was not his custom to admonish his older brother. Robert invited Charles to join him for the midday meal. He led his brother out of the room with an arm across his back.

"Louisa will be glad to hear that the mystery is solved, but I think our sister, Frances, would still have something to say. I will not direct any information her way. I will leave that up to you."

Charles thought about the book in his valise, wondering just what it was that made his relationship with Anne so special he would protect it. He still had not looked at her drawings for fear they might be inferior, and her time in the greenhouse unjustified.

182

The two brothers visited for an hour after the meal, meeting with several close friends that the lord had not spoken with since his return from Wales. Charles found he was anxious to return home, hoping to find Miss Blake in the greenhouse in order to present her with the drawing book secreted in his valise.

"You must come for supper soon. The children miss your visits," Robert called out as Charles left.

"I would like nothing more," Charles replied with a wave.

21

The songbirds were the first to announce a new day in late summer. Their singing began even before Anne's duty-bound father moved about the cottage. Anne listened from her bed as the variety of tunes echoed across the tops of trees to the edge of the garden. She had seen birds hiding in the thick hedges, protected from the cats that wandered through Lord Greville's garden. Each individual song was melodious, but together they formed a cacophony of chirping and whistling. The noisy welcome to the day was testimony that Lord Greville's garden was home to a flourishing population of birds.

Rising to the greeting, Anne was dressed, had eaten a bit of jam on bread, and was out the door early. She set to work as soon as she arrived to the glasshouse. She did not expect to see Lord Greville. She had become accustomed to her lonely days.

The planter bench was finished and the plants had been rearranged according to her father's wishes. The fuchsias and a new display of some sort of ferns enjoyed the men's construction. The newcomers from Lord Banks were placed near Anne and the potting bench, where her father could keep a closer eye, watching for any suffering as they adjusted to their new home.

It was raining, so the greenhouse was not too hot. She had finished the rendering of the ginger. She decided she would draw the "pharaoh's lily" next. She had seen that several blossoms, the color of twilight, were opening at the end of a thick stem. Anne wanted to draw them quickly, anxious to paint the lovely shade of blue.

The plant was on the floor some ten feet away. The clay pot was not so large she could not carry it, and the blossom stalk had been secured to a twig, so she carefully lifted it to the bench rather than seek out any help. She had become accustomed to working in just the place Lord Greville assigned to her. She liked the way the light filtered through the glass on one side and the taller plants on the other.

As Anne let the plant down gently, one of the large, bladelike leaves caught the edge of a mineral cluster, dragging it from its place on the windowsill to the ground. The rock hit the flagstone, breaking into several large pieces. The dark grey rock broke in half and the white crystals that protruded from it broke into four smaller pieces all lined up where the rock hit the ground.

Anne was horrified. She looked at what was certainly a prize possession of his lordship scattered on the floor. At just that moment, the door came open.

Lord Greville was pleased to see the young woman at work when he arrived. Upon a closer look though, she looked distressed.

"What is it?" The lord asked as he came across to where she stood. She looked down at the shattered stone on the floor unable to speak or look into his face. She was paralyzed.

"I have broken your diamond!" Anne managed to exclaim. She shuddered at the sight of the catastrophe. "I am so sorry. I knocked it off as I was moving the lily," she whispered. Her throat began to close and the tears overflowed down her cheeks.

Lord Greville took one look at the scene and began to laugh. As soon as he could control himself, he came to her side.

"It is not a diamond, Miss Blake. You could not break a diamond just so, as it is a very hard material, one of the hardest in nature. What you have knocked down is merely calcite, not precious at all except for the lesson it can give you about minerals, if you are interested."

Anne thought perhaps he meant to give her a lesson as in a reprimand, but as she was thinking over his words, she saw him stoop down beside the chunks of broken rock. He looked up, beckoning for her to do the same.

Anne squatted, not more than a foot away as there was only room enough for the two of them between the bench and the wall. He watched her take her place alongside him, eager to begin the lesson. Anne let her knees relax, careful to keep her dress skirt evenly about her.

"See here, Miss Blake? This is the main crystal that jutted out from the rock that fell from the shelf." He looked at her to see that she examined the chunk as he handed it to her.

"Now see there, the small ones to the side? They have the exact same shape as the larger one. Can you see that?" Again, he looked to see if she was following his instruction. She closely examined the rock and then he saw her nod as she recognized the repetition of the cubic shape.

"Calcite always makes its pure crystals in this cube form. These smaller crystals would have grown larger if they remained in the earth longer, but that is another lesson for another day.

"A man by the name of Huey found that crystals formed uniquely for each mineral in just this way. When he accidentally broke a calcite crystal, it gave him the revelation. Now you have done the same!"

Anne could see that the larger white rock was the same shape as the small ones next to it. To think of rocks growing was something she could not quite conceive. She had never seen a rock move, let alone grow. She heard the excitement in the lord's voice. She believed him even if she had her doubts.

"How long does it take a rock to grow?" Anne asked innocently, thinking she would keep an eye on rocks from now on.

"Millenniums of millenniums," was the lord's quick answer.

"I fear that is a long time." Anne said.

"Much longer than you and I can understand," Lord Greville answered, shifting his weight to rise. He stood and waited as she did also. He decided not to offer her assistance, as he knew she was no doubt more limber than he. He also felt the touch might be inappropriate, beyond their schoolroom decorum; yet in his next breath, he made a decision that might have trumped the offer of his hand.

"Come, I want to show you something. Put up your drawing things."

Anne did as she was instructed, and followed his direction to proceed out of the greenhouse. He stood aside, letting her proceed first, and then pulled the door closed behind them.

George Blake saw the two proceeding across the lawn to the library doors. The old gardener noticed it was the lord who led the way. Anne tagged along behind him dutifully in the manner of a footman. When they arrived at the manor, Anne's father was shocked as he watched the master open the door for Anne and allowed her to go into the library first.

The head gardener had been in Lord Greville's library only on a few occasions; at Christmas to receive his annual present of tobacco, and once when the lord showed him plans for another man's hothouse. His daughter, in the short time she had lived at the manor, had been there three times. George vowed he would keep a better eye on Anne. He would speak to her about her station when in his lord's presence. He wondered at the master expending so much effort on the girl.

The only other person to see the lord returning with Anne was Coleman. He was examining a lapel in the light of a window, determined to remove a stain. He saw the girl follow the master to the door and proceed in first.

What was this young woman about? What would others think if they saw this gardener's daughter being treated with such regard? The valet shook his head and scrubbed with more vehement strokes as he considered his master's actions with disapproval.

Inside the library, Lord Greville took a key from his desk drawer to open his glass front cabinet. Inside, the shelves were filled with rocks and minerals. He drew out two mineral clusters and one small stone.

"I have not looked at these for several months, they are quite dingy." He set the clusters and the stone in the sun on his desktop and pulled a folded cloth from the middle drawer on the right side. Anne watched as he carefully held the cluster, tenderly wiping the sides of each of the crystals using small circular motions. The color began to shine much more vividly than before. Anne watched as he once again took up the other cluster and placed the cloth here and there on the top crystal formations, cleaning them until they reflected light. He used a soft brush from the same drawer to remove the dust from the rock's rough surface where the crystals appeared to sprout.

"Oh how they shine as you clean them!" Anne exclaimed.

The lord was pleased the girl paid such close attention. "Now, notice on this group, the crystals all point up with six sides each. These are common quartz crystals. They have little value. They grow quickly compared to others." The lord passed Anne the crystals pointing out the six sides at the tip.

"Now, look closely at the stone I hold here. It is a ruby." Anne knew something of rubies as the ladies of the previous house wore beautiful jewelry. She looked wide-eyed at the gem.

"Ruby is a form of corundum, a word coming from Hindi and Sanskrit," he continued. "In another language, they call the ruby Padmaraga, or red lotus, as it is believed it glows from within. Actually, the glow is caused by the mineral phosphorus. This sample came from Burma and it is worth a considerable sum. If you look closely, you see it also has six sides and a group of triangles at the top. The ruby is much harder and has other characteristics that are not the same as the quartz."

He passed Anne the stone and a small magnifying glass with which to examine it. She took them gingerly, worried about the value of the red gem. She put the magnifier by the rock and saw little difference. Charles bent toward her, taking the eyepiece and moving it up and down from her eye.

"Find where it is right for you. Then you can move the glass around to see parts of the ruby closely." He passed the magnifier back and she lifted it until the circle showed an enlarged view of the beautiful red crystal. As he had explained, the shape was much the same as the quartz, though a beautiful color of plum red with golden light deep inside. She looked up smiling and let him have the rock and looking glass back. Charles took one last look through the eyepiece and then replaced the specimen carefully in the cabinet.

"Diamond is the only rock harder than corundum." The lord resumed his lecture as Anne listened to him intently. "Now, look at this one. On this crystal, the ends form with three sides or a multiple of three: six or nine. They tend to be in columns such as this one, but can occur in many different colors. I like this one because the black crystal shows its form so well against the pale background of the rock from which it was formed. I cannot tell you how many thousands of years it took to make such a crystal. Leave it said, we cannot conceive of the length of time." Once again, Charles passed the rock and the glass to Anne.

The lord reached into the cabinet and brought out one other sample, which again he polished before setting it on the desk.

"This is the same rock chemically, as the black crystal you just examined, but created from different rock, so this specimen is a different color. As the story goes, a man had several of these specimens under the foundation of a barn he was building. Someone bought the rocks from under his barn, and with the money, he built a new barn. This sample is from Cornwall."

"Not nearly as far as Burma," Anne said, encouraged knowing worthy rocks existed in their own country.

Charles had not thought to wonder if she understood when he spoke of Burma as the home of the ruby, but her reply indicated she did. The duke's children were schooled in geography, of course, but once again, she surprised him with her strange array of knowledge.

"Sir?" Anne asked, interrupting his thoughts, "How do you come to know these things about the rocks?" She was feeling such a lack in her own knowledge.

"I have been curious about rocks ever since I was a boy. I spent much of my time playing by the river where I always found rocks I would carry home. My room was lined with my collection. Until later in my life, I had not thought to make a study of them," Charles explained.

"At school, I became interested in antiquities and from there I went into collecting, buying, and selling pieces of Roman artwork. After some time, I had free time and some money, so I took myself off to Scotland and attended lectures at the University. I studied the science of chemistry and natural history including the formation of our planet.

Anne merely sighed, "Umm." She was thinking of Lord Greville when he was younger. She leaned over the assortment of rocks, embarrassed to let her mind drift to such thoughts. He had always been such a figure of superiority, but as she spent more time

191

with him, that had changed. Yes, his vast knowledge was superior, but his teasing manner and his kindness when they were together made her consider him in a different light. He would never consider her beyond her young curiosity, she knew. But what if.... Though she had many more questions, her father's reprimands echoed in her head.

Charles looked her way. It was obvious that she was deep in thought.

"I think sometime soon women will be able to attend not just schools for women, but also the great universities. It has come to my attention there can be a great mind inside a female head." He thought specifically of the Banks women, and then looked at Anne and gave her a wink. She could take on such a challenge, he believed.

"Oh, I have a pamphlet I thought might interest you." He passed Anne the introduction manual from a pile on his desk. It was the one he brought home from Sowerby's shop.

"It is a good introduction, and perhaps your skill already surpasses its lessons, but I thought you would have an interest in it."

"Thank you," she said, astonished to receive another gift.

Charles heard the chime of the clock and saw that it was one o'clock already. Time had slipped away from him. He had planned to attend a meeting this afternoon.

"Well, back to work, then. You can draw the lily as you started. Your father either has cleaned the broken rock up already or if you wish, you may instruct someone to sweep it up because you know it is only a-." he said looking to her to finish the sentence.

"A calcite, and thankfully not a diamond," she finished, pleased to be teased. He took his seat at the desk. He sent her off as he thought he should. He would not escort her back to the greenhouse as was his first inclination.

She bowed a quick curtsy as she slipped back out the library doors. Anne returned to the greenhouse to finish the sketch of the lily, feeling renewed. She swept up the mess without alerting anyone.

Anne continued to think about Lord Greville the rest of the afternoon. Truly, she held great respect for his mind, but also she warmed to how generous he had been with his time, explaining things to her. He might just as well have waved her off. He might have sternly ordered her to take up a broom and clean up the mess she had made.

That evening when her father came in, he asked Anne about her day almost immediately. It took Anne aback as it was so unusual. She began, excited to have so much to tell.

"I was about to start a drawing when I knocked one of his lordship's rocks from its shelf and it broke into a several pieces." Anne paused ready to continue, but her father spoke right over her words as if he did not hear any of what she said. Her light mood was suddenly darkened as her father demanded, "Why did you enter Lord Greville's library today?"

The tone of his question was reproachful. Her father's inquiry made her uneasy.

"He asked me to do so," she said frankly.

"He invited you into his library?" her father asked in disbelief.

"Yes, he requested I follow him, which I did." Anne heard the concern in her father's voice.

"He wanted to explain how rocks are formed. It was a wonderful lesson. The rock I broke in the greenhouse was a calcite and though it looks like a diamond it is not worth nearly as much as the corundum, the ruby, that he let me examine with his magnifying glass," she said breathlessly.

Anne's father did not listen to her explanation. Entering the nobleman's library went far beyond his fear that her constant jabbering might annoy the lord. Lord Greville could invite his daughter if he wished, but he would advise her against taking part in such privileges in the future.

"You take too much of his lordship's time, Anne. He has much with which to attend. He has shown great patience with you. I do not approve of your taking such liberties."

Anne was confused by her father's remarks. Did he not approve of her sharing time with Lord Greville, or did he refer to her going into the lord's library with him alone? It had all been done so innocently. She had not burdened Lord Greville. She knew she had not. The flowers, the stars, the rocks would never be the same for her. The world had become a wondrous place, thanks to Lord Greville. He had given her knowledge that she would retain forever.

"Yes, Father." she answered. Anne did not wish to disobey her father or cause him to worry, but he was wrong. She was very sure that any interest she showed to Lord Greville had been equaled by the lord's own excitement about the knowledge he imparted. The nobleman's instruction was given by his own volition. Anne had only to envision the wink to reassure her. She could think of no one in her life who had taken such time with her, except perhaps her mother.

22

*L*ord Greville arrived home late the next afternoon from a meeting of the Royal Institution. He had endured a morning of embarrassment mixed with anger. His solicitation to establish a National Collection and Office of Assay had lacked sufficient votes to pass. It infuriated him that although he acted as Vice President of the Royal Society, the Royal Institution would not give merit to his entreaty. He had mistakenly felt it was an obvious necessity for progress, but it had not been obvious enough to get the backing he needed.

As he stood by his desk, a movement at the far right side of the garden drew his attention away from his mental deliberations. He leaned his body to the left in order to identify the source of the movement. It was the ever-surprising Miss Blake. She held on her left arm a gathering basket, wide and capable of carrying a large, flat load. She appeared to stop now and again to snip branches along the side of the garden and then move on. She was not at the kitchen garden gate, but had wandered out to the edge of the herb garden and now was making her way into his flower garden. She made a pretty picture.

Charles questioned the young girl's collecting until she paused at a foxglove spire, still blooming in the shade of a plum tree at the corner. She intently examined the flower, pulling the stalk to her. He was intrigued to think she might know the properties of the plant. He hurried to open the library door. He proceeded across the yard in large strides, very eager to learn if she could add herbalist to the rest of her odd bits of knowledge. He called out.

"Miss Blake, a word."

Anne was distracted and had not seen the lord's approach until he spoke. She was at once startled and ashamed to be caught gathering herbs in the master's garden without permission. She could not believe her lack of scruples. She had been so focused on what herbs might help her father that she had completely lost track of where she was. When she saw the leaves of the foxglove and a very small late bloom, she remembered its use for slowing the heart rate and curing congestion. The sprig might be a good addition to the already full basket.

"I am so sorry, sir," Anne said immediately after bowing, realizing she had moved beyond the appropriate boundaries of her gathering and into the lord's garden.

"I am afraid I have quite forgotten where I am and where I should be. Excuse me." She tried to curtsy and ease away, hoping he might forgive her and not seek further explanation. She bit her lip, so angry at herself and her ill luck at being caught once again.

"Miss Blake!" Lord Greville yelled to her before she could get more than three paces away, "I wonder what it is you are picking and for what purpose."

Anne saw that he looked down at the basket on her arm, trying to see what stems it held. It was awkward to be in the position of revealing what she had just stolen from his garden. She also was reluctant to speak of her father's illness. She did not wish to either alarm his employer or cause her father any trouble by inferring he was of a weak constitution. The honest and imploring look on his lordship's face led her to believe he was genuinely curious. She answered him as honestly as she dared.

"On occasion, my father has trouble with a cough and an accumulation of fluid in his lungs, just as he suffered last winter."

"I see you have quite a bit of hyssop." Lord Greville commented. "I have always enjoyed its smell though some are repelled by it. Your father tells me it is quite helpful to ward off the cabbage moth, and I have seen it used for lice on sheep. As you must know in gathering it, it is excellent for any complaints of the lungs."

Anne was surprised that the lord, just as with so many other matters of the natural world, was knowledgeable on the use of herbs. Most of the upper class hired apothecaries for such knowledge. It was the lower ranks that had need of folk medicines and herbal cures to doctor on their own.

"You have a lovely clump of the herb. I hope I have not disturbed the shrub by taking some sprigs." In her nervousness, she stuttered, "I-I will leave you to your garden, - so sorry I disturbed you." Anne stepped back another pace still anxious to retreat, but once more the master implored her.

"You misunderstand me, Miss Blake. I have not come out to remonstrate, but rather to learn what you know of these herbs."

Anne was somewhat soothed by the nobleman's appeal and moved the hyssop to one side of the basket to show him the other herbs she had picked.

"I took a bit of the feverfew especially along the path where it has spread and outgrown the bed from which it was first planted." She was still timid about her harvesting and believed she should justify her collecting. The lord paid no mind to her excuses, but shuffled the herbs lightly with his fingers to see what else she had. A light lemony scent rose from the pile of stems.

"Comfrey of course, we use comfrey for one reason or another, it has so much to offer." He looked at her for affirmation.

"Yes," was all she could say, still shocked at his knowledge of herbal remedies and the familiar manner in which he spoke to her. "Coltsfoot leaves here, I think?" he asked, examining the broad, arrow-shaped leaves.

She nodded and replied while pointing, "I pick the lemon balm because it makes the bitter herbs so much more pleasant to drink."

Lord Greville knew he had caught the young woman off guard and with the history of her library intrusion, she began their conversation fairly embarrassed and eager to leave. She was smiling now. He was pleased to make her easy as he enjoyed these discussions, as well. She did not balk at showing some knowledge of these things and he had to wonder how this part of her education had come about.

"You pause here at the foxglove. Do you intend to pick it also?" The lord was most curious about her knowledge of this plant above all.

Anne would have moved off at that very moment had she been given the chance. Yes, she was about to clip the foxglove flower top and some leaves also. Now, she realized how far she had overstepped. Still he assured her he meant no protest. He had sworn, so she softly replied to his inquiry.

"Yes, if it would be allowed. I saw the late bloom from across the path and it reminded me of its use for pluerisy. My mother would say you must be very careful with its use as it can slow the heart to a stop. Too much of the leaves can be harmful if not used in the correct dosage. I have used it before, but only a very little at a time."

"So, it is from your mother that you know of these things?" Lord Greville asked.

"My mother was respected as an apothecary of sorts when no physician was available. Her success was in preparing infusions, poultices, and salves. She was sought to administer to His Grace's family on occasion. She was also the midwife."

"I see." The lord noticed how proud the girl was when speaking of her mother. "And she died several years ago, is that correct?" he asked in a more somber voice.

"Yes, just before my father came here to work." Anne looked down. She was not so much saddened by the topic as humbled in the lord's questioning of her personally.

Charles returned to the subject of the herbs at hand, not wishing to make Anne uncomfortable by speaking of her long passed mother.

"I have read much about foxglove, Digitalis purpurea," he repeated the Linnaeus term. "An old acquaintance of mine, William Withering, studied the herb and its use with heart ailments. He has passed on some years ago now, but he did scientifically prove that the foxglove could be used with much success for heart ailments, and here you are ready to do the same." Charles cheered her. Anne felt bolstered.

"Where did you find the coltsfoot?" the lord asked.

"When I first came to your manor, it was blooming on the drive closer to the ditch than the oaks that grow along the side," she said, pointing toward the left side of the back lane. Though I collected a few flowers, I am more accustomed to using the leaves, as my father is very much in favor of smoking a tobacco of the herb in his pipe," Anne answered.

"Have you taken it upon yourself to draw any of these herbs?" Charles thought of the poor renderings in ancient herbals. There was need of better identification.

"I am afraid I have only drawn the coltsfoot and chamomile as colored bits under the oak trees. I sketched the view along the drive the first week I arrived." Anne added. "I have seen the drawing of the coltsfoot in Mr. Sowerby's book you so kindly bestowed upon me. Of course, one would never see the flowers and leaves at the same time," Anne chided.

"Quite so!" Charles agreed, smiling at her criticism. It was true. The coltsfoot flower bloomed first and the leaves developed later. Never did they appear together on the plant.

Anne noticed Lord Greville's eyes. She had drawn them in the past with the eyelid edges drawn down with the sadness she had seen. As she looked at the lord now, his eyes held a happy look of amusement with the corners drawn up into a smile of a wrinkle.

"I will leave you now to pick what you like, Miss Blake. I wish the best of health to your father."

Charles gave a slight bow and wandered off, allowing her to continue her harvest. He felt much improved for the visit. He wondered if his schedule would allow him to spend time in his hothouse tomorrow.

Anne could not stop the grin of satisfaction that spread over her face. The exchange had once again been so pleasant. Was Lord Greville as kind to others as he was to her? Leaning forward under the plum tree, she snipped the foxglove stalk.

23

The long days of summer brought the promise of blooms and fruit to a reality in a mass of foliage and color throughout Lord Greville's garden. Everyday Anne saw changes in flowers and finishing fruit as the peak of the season approached. The greenhouse was full. She could barely remember how sparse it had been when she first arrived.

When Anne entered the glasshouse in the morning, the scent in the moist air was a combination of soil life and dew. By the time she exited, the smell mimicked a perfume. The exotic odors of so many different flowers saturated the space with an intoxicating mixture, heady and sweet. She loved the smell, imagining she visited faraway places.

Anne sketched for an hour before she took a break to stand and stretch. As she was alone in the greenhouse, she seized the opportunity to examine the rocks on the window sill, hoping to review the information she had received from Lord Greville. She could not make out any similarities to the rocks in the library with these examples here. Anne looked to her bench and scolded her wandering. "You should be working!"

Assuming her place on the stool once more, Anne continued her sketch of an orchid's yellow spray of flowers. The brown spots in its throat were particularly interesting to draw. She looked into the throat of the flower, a deep well in miniature. She could see the rostellum hanging down, protecting the place where the flower's special pollen lingered. She did not know more of the plant's secrets, but she knew orchids could only be pollinated by insects specifically suited to enter through the small gap she studied.

Anne cocked her body sideways so that she could view the flower without leaving the bench. She didn't want to bother asking for help to move the pot closer as she did not wish to approach her father. His reaction to her visit to the lord's library left her disturbed and guarded. She certainly didn't want to try to move it herself.

Despite Lord Greville's absence, she continued diligently, eager to please. She felt she owed him for the mineral lesson and the kindness he showed when she harvested herbs for her father. Minutes later, the nobleman arrived.

Anne was pleased to see he wore no vest and his shirt was stained down the front. He was not off to town that morning. He brought an entire box of rocks, which he balanced carefully on his arm as he closed the door. After quick acknowledgements between them, the lord walked about his hothouse admiring the changes that had taken place since his last visit. He stayed at the end of the bench, but did not sit.

"Did you see that the vanilla is beginning to swell?" he asked. "Although it is early, I do believe the top bud may open tomorrow, at which point I hope to pollinate the flower." The lord went on to tell her a bit about the process he learned from Sir Joseph.

It was evident to Anne that the lord was excited. She turned slightly to look toward the vine and saw even from where she sat that indeed the end bud look noticeably larger. The lines where petals would form were more delineated and there was the slightest yellow ting to the otherwise green tips.

"It will be necessary to dislocate the pollen with a small stick. The procedure will be most delicate as there is so little room for error. I hope that I can practice on this orchid, the one you are currently sketching, in order to perfect my method for the vanilla. Your father and I will give it a try later today."

Lord Greville continued by making a drawing of the operation which Anne felt he did as a rehearsal for his own reassurance as much as to explain the intended mission to her.

"That is most exciting," Anne said with true elation. Her mind slipped back to the master's orchid drawing of months before. As Lord Greville said nothing, seeming to be deep in thought, Anne allowed the silence to fill back in between them, wondering where his thoughts might be.

She tried to return to her drawing, but after a few minutes, she could no longer refrain. She wanted to know about the woman whose name was written on the stem that day.

"I know that Lady Hamilton was painted by several famous artists. She was very young when you took her in. It was very kind of you, and you must have cared for her very much." Anne spoke as casually as she could, trying to entice the nobleman into a discussion of the woman. She did not raise her head, but continued to sketch.

Anne had not forgotten the portrait she spotted in the library. Lady Hamilton might be gone, but Anne sensed she was not forgotten. Anne wanted to understand why Lord Greville had never married. She wanted to know if he was still in love.

Anne heard Lord Greville adjust his position. He was trying to get comfortable in an uncomfortable situation. Anne was taken aback by her own lack of modesty. Certainly she should not ask such questions. Would he answer? Would he admit that he had traded her for money from the uncle, as everyone said? He might censure her for her impudence, though she did not believe he would.

Charles did not want Anne to think he was angry with her. Her curiosity was natural, and he had no qualms about giving her truthful answers to her questions, but he was tired of the subject of Lady Hamilton. He hoped Anne, too, would tire of the subject.

"Well," he said, collecting his thoughts, but then he paused again.

The seconds it took him to reply gave Anne cause to wish she had not spoken so boldly. What prodded her to delve into his past? Her stomach churned with a combination of concern and something like jealousy. She could not forget the master's sad display. She wished for answers as relief. She secretly wished to hear he no longer loved Emma.

Anne recognized that her feelings for the lord had developed beyond what might have been considered appropriate, but she felt no shame admitting to her high regard. She could not explain her emotion even to herself, she knew she tread close to a dangerous edge, thinking of Lord Greville as a man rather than her father's employer. Before she could chide herself for her forwardness any further, she saw the twinkle in his eye. He was not angry. She caught the edge of a smile at the corners of his lips as he answered her question still hanging in the air.

"Not as many thought of it," he finally replied. "The affair was not quite as everyone assumed. We were not lovers for long."

Charles could not believe what he had just uttered. Had he so forgotten with whom he kept company? He had grown so at ease with this young woman, that he had thought nothing of answering as close to the truth as he could. He did not consider the implications of what he had said, he had never admitted so much to anyone before.

Almost everyone in Charles' circle of friends admired his mistress. Men and women alike were jealous of their liaison.

Emma's behavior made men desire her and women fear her. Women wanted men to notice them in the same way, though they were not apt to pursue attention as shamelessly as Emma did. Did Miss Blake know any of this?

As if to answer him, she spoke. "I think you loved her, but you were forced to make a difficult decision to let her go because of debt. Money or the lack of it makes for few choices as I see it."

"Precisely, you have a good understanding of my situation. I am glad we have cleared that up." He hoped the sarcasm in his voice would not wound the girl, but he did wish to move on from the subject of Lady Hamilton.

When Emma was first turned out, pregnant and poor, Charles had taken pity. Though Emma had tried her best, she could not achieve the perfection he pushed her toward. When she could not please him, she tried to lure him with the tricks of her previous trade. Emma challenged him in the physical realm, and he could not respond. He did not wish to recall his life with Emma especially in present company.

"I would be happy with just a bit of money," Anne continued nervously, trying to sound as mature as possible. "I will not need much," she said.

"When you have money, be it a small amount or a large amount, it never seems enough. I have had little before, and plenty enough now, and I am ashamed to want for more," the lord said. "I have become quite stingy!" He added with a smile.

He looked up from his work to take a brief look at the person to whom he was speaking in such an unguarded way. It was an odd acquaintance he had with this lonely young woman. Before now, he would never have admitted that he, too, was a lonely man.

Anne could feel the gentleman's eyes upon her, but she did not turn around. She was glad her back was to him and that he could not see the smile of satisfaction on her face. She was pleased to hear the relationship with the beautiful Emma had not been as many people gossiped it to be. She turned slightly, still worried her face might betray her pleasure. Anne noticed his attention turned quickly back to his notes.

"I think she gained much from your kind consideration," Anne said, thinking of herself. "They say you remain her friend, even now, after the death of Lord Nelson."

"Why did you send her away? Was it to settle your debts as they say?" Anne was sure the answer was to square his accounts, but she longed to know more.

"She was a beautiful thing that I found like a gem in an Indian river. I saw a bit of beauty poking out and I polished her into a jewel that most admired and some coveted. I found a situation that better fit her lifestyle." Charles looked out the wavy glass as if looking into the past. He rose from the wooden counter.

Anne felt the finality of his statement and the way in which he closed the folder of his notes shut the door on the subject, leaving her outside and the lord once more alone with his private life. She rushed to put her drawing away before he could depart. She wanted to walk out with him if possible.

Charles noticed that Anne planned to leave the greenhouse as well and waited at the door.

"Let me see your sketch," he said. He had opened his heart a bit to this young woman. The quality of her artwork no longer mattered. She was part of his life now, and it did not trouble him that she had become so. He felt no threat.

Anne took the penciled drawing of the orchid spray from between the boards of her drawing kit and handed it to him as they walked.

The lord took the drawing from her, but did not move away to look at it. He left no space between them, their arms almost resting on each other. He bent a bit to include her in his view of the drawing.

"The deep lines down the middle of the leaf, the shading and bright spot where light hits the edge, you have drawn it perfectly. The flower is exact. It is very fine, Miss Blake."

A warm flush came across Anne's face as he handed back the drawing. Their hands brushed against each other as he let go of the paper and she took control of it. It was brief, but they had touched. Anne felt a tingle up her arm that accelerated her heartbeat. She beamed from within, feeling a strong attraction to Lord Greville.

Charles felt the touch also, and wondered at the effect of this girl's inquisitive nature. She calmed him. She had no aspirations beyond the obvious. She did not connive. He enjoyed her direct manner, and he had answered with an uncommon honesty of his own. He appreciated that she showed her admiration with respect rather than silly flattery.

The touch did not worry him. He trusted her. She would keep her emotions controlled. He had little worries when they endeavored in the bright glass enclosure together. They overlapped without commitments or expectations of each other beyond that time together.

There was a part of him that wanted to do something for her. He wished he could make her future brighter and offer some reward for her good-natured approach to all that was asked of her. He was not sure what he might do, but he would think of something.

Charles failed to notice the sun's retreat around the side of the house. It would be close to teatime when he went indoors. They had spent half a day together. He had not thought he had lingered so long. Neither Lord Greville nor Anne saw her father leaning on his rake beyond the greenhouse. Neither did they see the scowl that creased his brow as they walked together.

Anne was elated. Charles Greville was not only the smartest man she had ever known, but also the most considerate. He did not ignore her questions or tire of her curiosity. He took time with her that exceeded any necessity. Anne clung to these floating objects in the otherwise unknown and unsettled flow of her life. She could stay where she was, drawing plants for him forever if it could be so, but of course, her good sense told her it could not. Lord Greville was due to leave for Wales in less than a month. She would find herself in a new situation as winter came on. All that she knew now would be, once again, changed completely; a thought that frightened her.

Later in the afternoon, Charles proceeded from the garden to the greenhouse where he had scheduled a meeting with Anne's father. He did not mention to George his recent conversation with his daughter, and though there should have been no problem in doing so, he felt an uncomfortable tightness when it came to a discussion of the young woman with the father.

"I do believe the vanilla will open tomorrow," Charles announced.

"Yes sir," George answered in his usual fashion. Charles had asked the gardener to whittle some small sticks to be used for the purpose. George had some experience with hybridization; manually placing the pollen from one plant on the stigmas of another, but the process was difficult on orchids.

"I thought we might try our luck with the yellow orchid."

"Yes sir," George answered once again. The gardener gathered the jar of sticks he had prepared and moved around to his master's side by the bench.

"You will open the throat of the flower, and I will poke the stick in to unleash the pollen sacs."

George took the flower in his hand and proceeded to pinch the nose of the bloom down to open the hole in which the lord would place the stick. The old man's hand began to shake, tearing the edge of a petal. George immediately released the flower.

Charles looked up at the older man and waited to see if he could steady himself.

George made one more attempt, but once again, his shaking would not allow him to move the nose of the flower aside to allow Charles to carry out the pollination.

"My hands are not steady as they once were, my lord." George bowed his head somewhat ashamed.

The lord was disappointed, but another thought came to mind almost immediately.

"Do you suppose your daughter might be able to aid in this process?" Charles asked.

George, who would always do anything to help his master, answered before he thought more about it, "Yes, I am sure she could do so."

"Have her come to the greenhouse an hour earlier than usual tomorrow. We will hope the flower opens fully."

Charles was delighted he had come to such an easy resolve to the problem so quickly. In fact, sharing the pollination with Miss Blake would improve the experience. He was vastly satisfied with the solution.

"Yes sir," George said, reverting to his customary reply. Inside, though, the gardener had doubts. He recalled how closely they had been walking together just that morning. He hoped the master was careful in his dealings with his daughter, but he would not express his concerns. Anne would help the master pollinate the orchid. She would at least be useful to Lord Greville in this important task.

When Charles exited, he left behind a tension he felt building between his decision and his gardener's usual consent. It was an awkward situation to be requesting this young woman's presence. He had never before felt any reservations with his old gardener, but he had experienced it just now. There had been no discussion about Anne between the two men, and Charles preferred not to look too closely at how suitable his connection to the man's daughter was, lest it be as Coleman saw it, flawed.

24

*T*he afternoon had progressed slowly for Anne. She retreated to the rose garden to work on her sketch of the reunion, tired of flowers for the moment. She would finish her figure sitting on the bench. Her thoughts returned to her morning conversation with Lord Greville, remembering his comments about Lady Hamilton and the confidence about the relationship that the lord had shared with her.

She was disturbed by the sound of wagon wheels on the driveway. Excited to have a word with Tom, she hurried to look. At the confluence of the garden path with the back lane, she met Peter. The timing was perfect, as if planned.

Peter looked down at Anne as she arrived at the opening a little breathless, pleased that the girl might rush to see him, but he could not miss the look of disappointment in her expression.

Making a great show of moving her drawing things from one arm to the other as if she had important affairs to which she must attend, Anne turned on her heel and started back down the trail away from Peter, retreating to the cottage as quickly as she could.

She called out an apology, but continued on her way, leaving the milkman's son perplexed.

Anne's father came in for his evening meal an hour before dark. He was quiet and tired as usual. Anne let him remove his shoes in peace. Most evenings, the gardener would take up his pipe for a smoke. He would sit back with his eyes closed, puffing thin white clouds into the room while she prepared a late meal. Anne would wait to speak until he spoke to her. This was the ritual they had worked out.

Anne did not tell her father about the meeting with Lord Greville under the stars. She could not conceive of a way to explain their being together in the dark alone, though there was nothing for which to be ashamed. She told her father about the mineral lesson only briefly before he interrupted, insisting her time with the lord should be kept to a minimum, and that she should not delay his lordship in any way. She had yet to mention the meeting with the master while she was collecting herbs. If she did, she would not elaborate on the conversation involving her mother, as it was a subject she never approached with her father.

Anne's father did not know how far her relationship with Lord Greville had gone. No one did. She had no one with whom to consult; no mother, no sisters, no aunt or female companion she could trust outside of the household, and those within, she knew, would not understand.

Sybil would be shocked. Why would it be so? Anne knew the answer. The boundaries of society go both ways. As much as she should not attempt a step up, those of the upper crust should not bend too far to the lower ranks.

Cook would not comprehend the situation, either. She would no doubt give warnings similar to those of her father. There would be no compliments forthcoming on the fellowship she enjoyed with the master.

Do not bother Lord Greville, girl." Cook had warned her when the master first returned. "He is kind, but we, at our level, cannot take up his time with our business. You'd do well to keep to yourself, and if in his presence, keep quiet." Cook had instructed her, and Anne would have continued to do exactly as she had said if the scene in the greenhouse had not occurred. When she was drawn into the library's open doors, she had been lured by questions concerning Lord Greville's emotional display. She never would have imagined such an outcome.

Anne could not believe she was a bother to the lord. Why did he answer her questions beyond giving her simple answers? No, he was as much involved as she. Not one of them understood their association. It was a secret she would keep to herself. Did Lord Greville feel the same? She wondered how he thought of her if he did at all. For her, the gift of candied ginger and the illustrating instruction booklet proved he did. Her thoughts were interrupted as her father stirred.

George Blake had rested for a bit, and now sat up, blew his nose, cleared his throat, and began to speak.

"Lord Greville instructed me to tell you to arrive an hour earlier tomorrow."

Anne lifted her brows inquiring without saying a word.

"The vanilla will bloom. He hopes you will sketch the flower as it does." George did not mention the pollination process to his daughter. He knew she would be a good assistant to the lord, and made himself trust that it was important enough that his daughter should do so.

Anne held back her response, the excitement bubbling under the surface while she answered with a level headed, "Of course."

In the morning, as daylight changed from a dull grey to light blue, the hour of nine o'clock approached. Charles felt a youthful anticipation. If the orchid produced fruit, his fellow horticulturalists would certainly applaud him. He drummed his fingers on the bench top, becoming more impatient as each minute passed. Did she know the time? Did she have a clock? He realized he had given no thought to the young woman's life when she was not with him. Before he could be concerned, he heard Anne's footsteps and went to open the door.

"Will it be today?" she asked as she ducked in through the plants, placing her sketch paper on the bench. She was breathless. Apprehension was taking its toll on her lungs and her ability to breathe.

She walked with the gentleman to the pole that supported the vine. "Oh yes, I can see that the bud has swelled. It is no longer green and I can see the petals. Today you will make history!" she exclaimed, with an air of celebration.

Delighted at her excitement, Charles leaned over, trapping her small figure between the end of the bench and the pole. He smelled her rose petal scent and was alarmed at the effect. That smell stood for all that was new and unspoiled in his world.

Charles could not control the urge to touch her hair. He took a small lock that wandered away from the rest into his fingertips gently, so she would not know. He felt the soft bit of hair and saw it for all it symbolized. If she faced him, he felt he might actually kiss her! He fought a strong urge to take her shoulders and turn her into his arms. The excitement of the event was affecting his judgment.

Anne felt the lord behind her; warm breath on her neck. She did not move for fear their bodies would touch. She sipped at air, remaining steady.

The lord knew she had no idea of his attraction. She did not realize the temptation she placed before him. Her mental capacity alone fascinated him more than any woman he knew. He wondered if he let go of the reins holding back his feelings, what she might do. She would certainly expel such an advance and leave you much the old fool, he told himself. Sadly, he let the curl go.

Charles stepped back. Had he really stood so close? A moment passed before he could move, still under the spell of the rose scent and the young woman's proximity. He came across from her then and bent into the flower holding his body away from the inner circle, pulling a small magnifying glass from his waist pocket.

"I do see the other flower has opened slightly," Charles remarked when he caught his breath. He pointed the magnifying glass to the flower and then stood upright again appearing to be preoccupied, needing a moment more to recover.

"I will need your help," he said as he passed the glass to Anne too nervous to look her in the eye.

She took the lens carefully and held it in front of her face, and then moved it toward the flower until the distorted image became clear. Charles smiled at her, remembering their gem lesson in the library and her first use of a magnifier. Anne returned his smile, knowing his thoughts. The two of them formed a close circle around the vine. Once again, Charles thought how easily he might put his arms around her to close the circle, but he pulled away, regaining his senses. He would not spoil what was real and altogether pleasant in its innocence. She deserved better.

"We have some time. I leave you for a moment. I shall return shortly." The lord hurried out of the greenhouse, in need of a chance to settle his mind.

"I will take a quick sketch," Anne answered him with a smile of mutual excitement.

Charles left behind the heat of the moment and the humidity of the hothouse, sweat dripping down his neck inside his shirt. He dared not review the image of the way the young girl's hair poured off her shoulders forming into the curve of her body. The fresh air saved him as he rushed to the house.

"Cook?" the lord poked his head into the kitchen through the door usually used for the household staff. "Might I get a plate of cold cuts, cheese, and some bread, and perhaps a cold beverage as soon as possible, something simple for you to prepare?"

"Certainly," replied the robust woman, wiping her hands dry. He withdrew his head and proceeded to his library. Cook was aware that there was a flower of some importance about to bloom in the hothouse. No doubt, his lordship attended to the matter. The master seemed jittery, so she hurried to prepare a hearty basket luncheon.

Charles drew the door closed behind him. He went immediately to the shelf in his sideboard where a bottle of brandy waited with several glasses. He had not had a drink from this decanter for no telling how long. Alcohol made his stomach sore, so he was able to resist the urge to drink alone. This morning was an exception. He longed for a swallow of anything that might calm his nerves.

He poured two fingers of brandy into a glass, and then added another finger for good measure. Swirling it once, he drank it all, enjoying the burn it caused going down. He took two lemon drops out of his desk drawer and popped them in his mouth to cover the alcohol's smell on his breath. He headed back to the kitchen to find a basket ready.

"Cold beverage, sir? Cider? Ale?" Cook asked, trying to keep the language simple and speed the process of getting this lunch to him.

"No, not ale," Charles replied, as the burn from the brandy was just subsiding in his esophagus, his tongue slightly numb with a lemon coating. He felt perhaps he should not have indulged his urge, but carried on. Ale would not be an appropriate beverage to share with Miss Blake.

"There is fresh milk," Cook answered as an option, her face bright and smiley.

"Yes, that will do." Charles smiled back.

Cook poured a pitcher partly full and added a cup to the basket.

"Another cup if you please," he remarked, seeing her add only one cup.

Cook did as she was told, but wondered for whom the other cup might be. Who was in the hothouse that she had not heard arrive? Perhaps it was the fellow, Banks, or the artist, Bauer. She had no idea.

"Will you have guests at dinner?" Her only concern with extra lunch would be another place setting at dinner.

"No, I am not expecting anyone." As Charles took the basket by the handle, Cook interjected.

"Shall I have Becky bring that out for you? She is just up the hallway."

"No, I have hold of it. Thank you for your expedience." Out the door he went. Cook debated watching him, but she would hear soon enough what was transpiring in the glasshouse.

It was just at this time that Coleman happened to glance out the upstairs window, where he saw his master carrying a basket from the kitchen to the greenhouse. He shook his head, knowing he would surely make a comment when he saw his lordship. Someone must.

Anne set her hand on the paper to draw, but she found she could not steady it. Had she imagined Lord Greville's closeness? Did he feel any of what she felt? She quickly made some lines, defining the leaves and blossom bud of the orchid before his lordship returned.

The lord went straight to the orchid. Although the petals were continuing to open, he was pleased to see there was plenty of time to have a bite to eat.

"I come with sustenance," he announced to Anne, pulling back the napkins revealing the contents.

217

Anne took over as hostess, spreading the top napkin out on the bench. She grasped the pitcher with both hands careful not to spill any as she lifted it from the basket past the handle. A jolt went through her as she realized this was Peter's milk delivered the day before. Here she was, under very different circumstances, serving it to his lordship. Anne arranged the cold cuts on the one small plate she found in the basket. She admired the small picnic with complete joy. They ate in silence; Charles thinking of what Banks might say if they were successful, trying his hardest to forget his emotions of a half hour before. Anne thinking she might never be so happy again.

At the end of the meal, Anne cleaned up and moved the basket to the door. She placed her head in her hands and propped her elbows on the bench gazing at the orchid vine, trying not to be impatient. Lord Greville approached the flower again. When his focus rose a little, he was looking straight into the face of Miss Blake.

She was not looking at him directly, so he took a moment to take in her features. It was the eyes that drew him in, but the line of her mouth between her lips and the way she always appeared to be smiling that he found hard to ignore. Those lips longed to be kissed. He had a feeling that he had been this close to her before. Surely not, why would that be?

Her gaze met his, and he smiled, but moved away, embarrassed by his thoughts. The orchid was now open enough to see inside the entire column. He chose one of the whittled sticks from the jar and returned to the circle. Anne sat up again, feeling the excitement building again. She held the eyeglass out to the lord, but he put his hand up to stop her.

"You will hold the lens for me, I will need both hands." Charles positioned himself with his legs apart on each side of the pole that supported the vine. He took Anne's hand and placed the fingers holding the magnifier just above the flower. He touched her with such a purpose, neither flinched at the union.

218

"Can you tolerate keeping still just there?" he asked. Anne nodded and braced for endurance, steadying her breathing. She was so excited to be a key part of the procedure. She wondered where her father was. Then she remembered what the lord had said. She knew her father's hands were not steady. She watched him light his pipe as his hand wavered over the bowl. The lord had chosen her to help, and at that moment, she would have done anything to please Lord Greville.

Charles took the blossom firmly enough to control it without squeezing the petals, careful not to shake the pollen loose. He poked his little finger into the blossom and moved the lip down and out of the way. The movement was reminiscent of other recesses of long ago. His mind drifted to a love scene from years past.

He was with Emma. She was very much available to him. At that moment she would have done anything for him, anything to please him, anything to satisfy him. This he had known, yet he had held back just as he would this time, also.

Charles felt hot from the memory and looked up to see Anne's intent stare at his finger's hold on the flower only inches away. He knew she had no idea of his thoughts. He was assured of her innocence when she bit her lower lip and asked without moving, "Am I in the right place for you?" Charles swallowed, trying to get saliva back into his dry mouth.

He replied in a whisper, "You are perfect, just as you are." He carefully guided the stick under the rostellum lifting it out of the way. Charles pressed the head of the bloom down with his thumb and pollen dropped clinging to the stigma that was waiting moist and sticky below. He would press just a little more so that the top and bottom came together and the sides would remain stuck together, male to female.

Once more, Charles saw himself with Emma. He watched the scene unfold as he got up from the bed leaving Emma waiting, her

219

mouth open, her breath quickened, and her eyes closed. When she opened her eyes, she saw he stood at the end of their bed. Her face was tilted as she saw he would not finish what he started. He felt sick as he remembered Emma's face as she looked up and then down him with pity.

Charles hated that memory. He hated the pain it caused him. From that time on, their lovemaking would never be the same. Fear overtook any other urge. It was a torment he would never be rid of. He would never be the man Emma needed. It was cruel for the image to emerge now.

Anne saw the master's hand shaking as he paused with the stick in the throat of the flower. She remembered looking into the throat of another orchid and the delicate operation the lord performed. She did not know why he waited, but she had nothing but patience.

Charles felt Anne move slightly, he took hold of himself and the stick still poked inside the recess of the flower. He prepared to pull it out to finish the process. He would not look at Anne for fear she might read his thoughts. He touched the sticky surface of the stigma. Moving the rostellum up a bit more, he lifted the stick out from where where the balls of pollen had landed to complete the union.

Just as he began to move the stick, the door of the hothouse was thrown open, a gush of air came in and they both startled as George Blake approached on a march and called out to his daughter who was hidden by Lord Greville's form, "Anne, what goes on here?"

Anne looked up. She loosened the tight grip she had on the magnifying glass. Charles took a quick step backward from the pole, dropping the stick as he did. The jolt that traveled through him as the old gardener yelled had shaken the instrument in the throat of the flower. He had torn through the rostellum and the petals beyond. The flower hung damaged, no longer closed and stuck together, but open, bruised, and sterile as the clusters of pollen slid out, missing the stigma, their necessary target.

"Father, you have given such a fright. We have almost finished pollinating the bloom on the vanilla. It is so exciting."

It was then that George Blake saw the magnifying glass on the other side of the pole, where his daughter had been holding it for the master. George looked from the glass to the flower to the gentleman who stood as far back against the bench as he could. Although the lord had an odd expression, it changed as he looked at the flower he thought he had just successfully pollinated. George also looked at the flower as he recognized the disappointment on his master's face.

Anne witnessed the change in her father's expression from anger to apologetic. She was confused. She examined the flower in front of her before beginning to explain to her father how the operation had progressed. She stared with horror at the freshly open blossom now torn and withering.

"Oh my, what has happened?" she asked the lord with a great pain in her throat. "It was all going so well. Father, what did you - ?" She did not finish the sentence as the answer was slowly becoming clear. The way she stood so close to Lord Greville and the angle of the view, her father might have thought they were in each other's arms.

"Oh, Father," Anne said as she looked up at Lord Greville. He still had a look of shock and something else on his face. He was speechless.

"We were concentrating on the flower, I was holding the glass." Anne raised the magnifier for the old man to see, but then she let her arm fall back to her side. It was too late. For this flower, there would not be a second chance. There would be no fruit, no pod, and no future. The flower was already changing from its smooth, pale, yellow-green to a light brown. The petals were shriveling. Only moments before, that very same flower held so much hope for new life.

Anne could not control the tears. She looked at the flower one last time and stepped away from the pole to the bench where she set the magnifying glass down and picked up her tablet. She held back the sobs that began to erupt in her lungs.

Anne reached blindly for the handle of the hothouse door, turning back halfway and snatching up the basket. "Excuse me." She curtsied to the two men still in a frozen stance by the vanilla orchid's vine.

Her father's doubt, her love for the poor flower, her exhilaration and the proximity to the master; all came pouring out as she jogged to the rose garden to regain her composure. It was half an hour before she proceeded to the kitchen with the basket. She had done nothing wrong, she reminded herself. Her father had no grounds for his anger, but the expression on Lord Greville's face said something else. In his eyes, she saw a glint of guilt, and she wondered why.

Anne stepped into the kitchen. As she turned from catching the kitchen door before it shut in an attempt to be quiet, Cook was waiting on the other side.

"Well, what have you been doing all day? I have not seen you about."

Anne wanted to reply, but realized an obstacle in her throat gagged her from doing so. She bowed her head to keep her red eyes and quivering chin from Cook's view. It was the basket that gave it all away.

In a quick onslaught of knowledge, Cook realized that the other cup had been for Anne. Cook tried to calculate what it all meant. Her expression of question met Anne when she finally lifted her gaze.

"The vanilla orchid bloomed, and I was to draw it, and then Lord Greville wanted to try to pollinate it, but Father interrupted, and now the flower is dead. Only one chance, poor thing." Anne hiccoughed.

The sobs came as Anne ran out of breath. Cook went to the girl who appeared so very young and fragile at that moment. She took her into her arms to console her.

"Sh, sh now." Although Cook did not fully understand, she could see her young friend was distressed. Were Anne's tears caused by a flower or was there more to the story? Perhaps a serious conversation might be due if she was indeed spending time alone with the master to an extent her father was an interruption. She would not imagine Lord Greville doing anything inappropriate.

Anne's crying slowed to a stop. She could not say why she cried, so many emotions confused her. Her relationship with Lord Greville had been called into question by her father's accusation. Even now she could not tell Cook what she felt, though it was not guilt or even shame. No one would understand.

"There, there, girl. It is nothing for you to fret about. The master and your father can raise another, I am quite sure."

"Yes, there is another bud, but why-" Anne's lip quivered. She said no more. Hugging and thanking Cook, Anne left the kitchen with a strange dread of seeing her father.

After George Blake left the greenhouse, muttering an apology, Charles heaved a sigh and looked at the flower on the floor. What had just happened? He had done nothing wrong, and yet Miss Blake goes running off crying and her father wanders away leaving him without recourse about any of it. Thank God, there is another bud.

Charles thought back on the scene and how close they had come to performing the pollination. His lungs were filled with the scent of the young woman, rosy and sweet. He would not take advantage; he knew that. She and her father held his utmost respect. Her allure was her uncorrupted manner, a trait he would protect, not injure. It would be difficult to recover from his thoughts on Miss Blake, but he must!

When he returned to his quarters, he could tell by the set of Coleman's mouth that he had something to say. Charles could have guessed what it would be. He was already feeling pummeled by the gardener and his daughter. Now, another of his household had a comment to add. He prepared himself for the valet's admonishment by first asking him for a small brandy. He sat back in his favorite chair, closed his eyes, and listened to the sound of the stopper leaving the glass bottle.

"I have had a busy morning." Taking the brandy from the old servant, he let the door of conversation open.

"I see now you are taking meals with the young miss in the greenhouse. Next we will be moving a bed in there, I suppose?" The old servant spat the words having had hours to think of what he would say. The pressure of his displeasure had built up in that time. This was Coleman's way, Charles thought. He was always exaggerating, always brash, and forever concerned about propriety. Charles had put up with his grumblings for so long, it had little effect on him anymore.

"I am shocked, my man. I have done nothing to bring about such a rude conclusion. I was hungry. So was Miss Blake. She was busy drawing, so I fetched a bit of lunch. That is all." Charles sipped at the brandy slowly recalling his earlier gulps. He allowed the brandy to warm in his hands. The next sip went down smoothly, soothing his nerves immediately.

"Why did you not have the girl fetch the lunch or call for someone to serve you in the greenhouse if that was your wish?" Coleman asked, hissing like a snake.

"I had no reason or motive other than that we awaited the vanilla orchid's bloom, and I was free and she was not."

"It had all the appearances of a secret liaison. You toy with a young girl's emotions. She will fall in love while you are innocent to her design. Only too late, you will realize your folly, " Coleman reprimanded.

How wrong the old servant was. It was not the young lady who was in danger of falling in love. He had little to offer, and yet, to have such an inspiration in his life. It would make an old heart young. His valet's reprimand hit its mark, but for different reasons. He had pulled back from making a terrible mistake before "only too late, he would realize his folly."

"You have forgotten the fact that her father was also to attend and did in fact arrive in the middle of the attempt to pollinate the flower." Charles would not go into the details of the interruption, as Coleman would have concluded it was fortunate that the father came in when he did. Charles might agree. Though not guilt free, he could not be accused of any wrongdoing that Anne's father or Coleman could pinpoint. He would end the discussion here.

"I will hear no more of it. Nothing inappropriate went on, I tell you, is going on, or will go on, between Miss Blake and myself that any of you must be concerned with. Miss Blake has no design on me. She is quite sensible." He put down his glass like a judge's gavel and picked up the book sitting on the table beside him, pretending to read, and shutting off any further conversation with his valet, a boundary Coleman could do nothing but respect.

What Coleman first became aware of was that the master was indeed uncomfortable about the morning's events as evidenced by his anger. Secondly, he wondered who his lordship meant by "any of you." Perhaps, he was not the only one pointing out the lord's position. Who else? Coleman wondered.

25

*A*nne spent the afternoon alone in her room. She wished to avoid any confrontation with her father. She could not endure explanations of the day's events. Later, when they did eat together, he was solemn and Anne sensed an equal unwillingness on his part to speak of the morning's incident. A note had come from the master informing him of another opportunity to pollinate the vanilla the following day and requesting Anne's assistance once more. Anne's father spoke to her only to discharge the master's request.

As George Blake lay back in his bed, allowing the hunch in his back to straighten and ease the ache there, he found it was his heart that pained him more. He was once again in a state of worry about the future of his daughter. She was at a dangerous age without the experience to make her any the wiser.

He worried if she could make the right choices for herself. Anne had come through some sort of problem at the Duke's estate, and though he believed Anne was innocent, she had been removed.

That was just how it was for the lower ranks. He did not want to see such a circumstance here.

The gardener had come to realize that a letter of character was not coming. Anne's future as a nursery maid for a good family was in doubt. He would trust there was no harm in the bond that the lord had formed with his daughter, but if he sensed anything improper, he would find Anne employment immediately.

In the back room, alone with her thoughts, Anne tried to sort all that had come to pass with Lord Greville these last weeks, all the times they had been together. She ended with her father's storming into the greenhouse and thinking what he saw was an embrace. Surely she had done nothing to answer for. She only hoped the day's events had not changed her relationship with Lord Greville, but she felt different somehow.

In the morning, Anne took her time with dressing, not feeling in a hurry. She would arrive at the greenhouse at nine and not a moment early. She watched for the sun to come up over the roof of the house. Time passed slowly, and she was thankful for it. She calmed herself with a few deep breaths before leaving the cottage.

Anne lacked the eagerness to meet Lord Greville as she had the day before. She was unnerved as she walked down the path to the garden. Her father's false assumption had left her apprehensive. Nothing had happened or had it?

She had felt the lord's breathe on the back of her head, with the notion that he might address her in some intimate way. She was confused if what she conjured up had any truth to it, or if her imagination had run away with her. It was Lord Greville, after all, not Peter or Tom that stood so closely. She had made the decision to conduct herself with decorum today, determined to do everything with intention and correctness. The meeting was not about being together with Lord Greville, she reminded herself. It was about pollinating a flower. She would hold all imaginings in check.

Anne made certain that her father knew the time she planned to be at the greenhouse. She did not want any awkwardness to remain from the previous day. The old gardener mentioned that he would attend the event at some point in his morning rounds.

The hour was still early, not quite nine, and Lord Greville sat staring at the vanilla vine as he had been for the last hour. He was watching the bud slowly separating in preparation for opening. Though he had not commanded his gardener's daughter to be there this morning, he had sent word through her father that he would attempt to perform the pollination as they had the day before. Perhaps her father objected to her continuing with the project. Charles was irked. He should have demanded she be present at a specific time and that was that. He lost the upper hand in this situation. His need for help seemed no longer anything more than requests to the young woman and permission from the father.

He had done nothing out of order. He had nothing to answer for to his gardener or his valet. His momentary lapse into a memory of Emma had been a short span of time actually. The lord was quite sure that Anne had no idea of the picture that presented itself in the middle of their attempt to pollinate the flower. He would not think of how those brown curls and the light smell of roses almost influenced his judgment. How close he came to making a spontaneous declaration. He was thankful his thoughts on all scores had been private.

Anne came into the hothouse solemnly. How different was her entrance from the day before. She took out her drawings of the orchid, isolating her thoughts and actions away from his lordship. He sat on the other side of the bench. She took her place, glancing briefly at his smiling face.

"Good morning, Miss Blake. I hope you are as excited as I am at our chance to see the flower once again. I will try to pollinate it if I can call upon your help once more." The words came out easily. He was immediately relieved as she smiled back.

"I am glad you will have another chance so soon. I am so sorry about yesterday's failure." Anne could say no more for fear the overflow of emotions would swamp her. She was glad the gentleman did not seem disturbed by her father's actions. It was agreeable that he could return to the project at hand with such cheerfulness. Anne was relieved from some of her trepidation. The easiness of their connection replaced her discomfort.

"From where did this orchid come?" she asked, as she began a new sketch.

"Let me see, the vanilla comes from the evergreen jungles of Mexico." Lord Greville began, happy to have a chance to break the tension of her unusual silence. It was this part of their relationship he enjoyed the most. He enjoyed being so wise.

"The native residents of those jungles have a legend about the flower. They tell of a princess, Morning Star. She was given to the god of fertility and not intended for mortal man. Running Deer, a young man from the princess' tribe, fell in love with her and took her off to the surrounding mountains away from her intended. Evidently, their escape was interrupted by a fire-breathing dragon. The two young lovers were apprehended by priests who beheaded them and tossed their bodies into a deep ravine. In the spot where their heads were disposed of, a plant sprouted and subsequently, a vine covered with flowers, our vanilla here. Each time we smell the scent of vanilla it is a reminder of the princess." The lord concluded the tale, pleased to be able to enlighten the listener.

Anne enjoyed the story, but it had no bearing on the question she asked. Her question came from a much more humble interest. She was slightly embarrassed to admit that all she wanted to know was where Lord Greville procured the vine, so she tried again.

"How did you come to have this specimen?"

Charles smiled at her. "That is what you were asking, and I have given you a long answer and not what you sought."

"Oh no, I am happy to have heard the tale, as I love those sorts of stories, usually with a happier ending for the princess, of course." Anne dared to look the master in the eye for the first time.

He met her gaze. He was struck by how well he felt whenever he looked at her; a fondness he was not accustomed to.

"Yes well, such stories of forbidden love usually come to a bitter end." Charles sighed, not hearing the poignancy of his remark. He continued as he saw Anne waiting for him to reply.

"I received a slip of the vine from my friend, George Spencer, the Marchess of Blandford. He has a wonderful collection of plants. He has specimens he raises exclusively by the authority of the King as a safeguard for those at Queen Charlotte's gardens.

Anne coyly asked, "What is the meaning of these titles? Isn't he the son of the Duke of Marlborough? Won't he be the Duke of Marlborough when his father passes on?

Charles was amazed. Why would she know such a thing? Then he remembered her previous residence. The connection between the two families might have led her to knowing of the duke's family. It was another odd selection in her library of knowledge. He thought of his answer to her question.

"His elevated birth. Sometimes a title is given if both parents are of noble birth to indicate the child's position until such time that he assumes his ultimate title. It is an indication of entitlement to be a marquis, a baronet, or even a knight of some sort."

"Do you have a title?" Anne looked up from her drawing, waiting to picture the flower at the next stage of opening.

"I have been a Gentleman of the Bedchamber." Charles replied not thinking how the title might sound.

Anne blushed and formed an "oh" with her mouth but restrained a chuckle.

"The King's Bedchamber, that is. I was for some time a Chamberlain. It is a title given to a trusted ally to the king, available to do his bidding at whatever cost. Luckily, I was not called upon to perform much of anything important. I reported on naval operations and given the title of Right Honorable."

Anne was humbled. She knew of his connections to the court, but she had not pictured Lord Greville in a private audience with the king. It was truly amazing to be sitting with him under any circumstance. She retraced the lines already there on her drawing.

"I was a member of the House of Lords. As the son of an earl, I have the title "Lord" attached to me, and lastly, I have been a Lord of the Admiralty on the Board of Trade as part of my work on establishing a naval port in Wales. So, I am a lord many times over."

She did not like for him to speak about his plans for a harbor. Everyone in the household was fully aware he would return to Wales in a matter of weeks. He would not be back to Paddington until close to the end of the year.

Anne could barely tolerate the panic she felt when she thought of Lord Greville's departure. Without the master in residence, she feared her life and her soul might dissolve in the forthcoming winter's rains. She had little purpose beyond this time she spent with him.

Lord Greville stood by the flower and signaled to Anne. She took the magnifier from him and positioned her body much as she had the day before. This time, however, she could not avoid feeling tense and stiff. She let her breath out from her lips trying to hold steady, though her hands were shaking, and she felt her pulse thudding in her ears.

Taking up another small stick, the lord formed the other half of the circle their bodies created around the plant. He took the edge of the looking glass without touching Anne's fingers, and lifted the circle until he could see into the throat of the flower. He looked up quickly with a smile. He proceeded to move the rostellum up with the tip of his finger. In a natural state where the stingless bees pollinated the flower, this tab was the important means by which the pollen the insect gathered was reclaimed by the flower. It was the last chance for the flower to grab the pollen from the insect's body and become fertilized. For Charles, when he pulled the stick out carefully, it would bring the pollen sacs along with the stick. They would fall onto the sticky surface of the stigma completing the task.

He had no recollections of Emma today. His thoughts were lucid and present. He did not wobble in their circle, but remained a diameter away from her. He slowly pulled the stick out and watched the tiny pollen balls fall to the sticky wet surface waiting for them. He pressed the flower gently together to ensure the pollination was successful. The operation of joining male and female together had occurred with very little pomp and circumstance, certainly without passion or shame.

Charles was certain that the flower was fertilized. He took the glass from Anne's hand, as she remained perfectly still, staring at the flower, locked in the moment. He did not move his body out of the close ring they made around the vine. He wanted to stay just where they were for a moment longer; experiencing this together.

Anne lifted her head to look him in the eye. They gave each other a look built on their hours together culminating in this moment. They were alone in the knowledge of what they shared. Anne was the first to step back relaxing the tense pose she had assumed, humbled to have been a part of the lord's success.

"You did it! You can show Sir Banks and your sisters," Anne exclaimed with a bright and encouraging smile.

Charles marveled at how well she understood the importance of demonstrating his success to others. Yes, he had done it. They had done it! He could show Banks and the family, but for now, he wanted to slow time down, and enjoy the positive effect Anne's exuberance had on him. In the following days, if pollination were successful the ovary at the base of the column would swell as the petals fell off, an indication of a seed forming.

"You should be proud and your father, of course! Where is he?"

"I believe he was embarrassed for his actions yesterday. I did not have a chance to explain my father to you. I am so sorry, he worries so," she answered honestly.

"And rightly," Charles said to Anne. "He cares very much about you. He wants what is best. You are fortunate in that way." Charles was thinking of his own father and what a disappointment Charles had been to him. If he were younger, perhaps her father would have interceded long ago, or their time together might have been limited at best. He was recovered now, thank goodness, and he saw his position and her age clearly. It saddened him.

Anne looked at Lord Greville, trying to understand his meaning, but before she exerted herself too much he said, "There will be another bud soon. It is important to observe the changes in the flower in the next day or so, to see if in fact it will produce a seed pod. For now, would you make a drawing of the flower before it fades? I will also have Franz Bauer come soon if he can and make a sketch for Banks and our horticulture friends. I hope you understand."

Anne knew the limits of her involvement. It had been a privilege to have been allowed to participate. Tomorrow, she would be on the outside of the event again; but for now, she had a vivid memory of their time together. The gratification in his eyes as they shared the moment of the completed project was enough recognition for her.

"I must return to the library. Good day, Anne."

As he withdrew, Anne let out a lungful of air she was not aware she had been holding. A fresh smile spread up her cheeks. It was the first time Lord Greville used her first name.

Charles rushed off to post a note to Banks and Bauer, inviting them to attend the blooming and perhaps pollination of another flower. He doubted Banks was still in town, but he wanted to boast on any account. He needed time alone away from the greenhouse and the young artist he left there.

With the master's exit, Anne tried to calm her heart. She was still so excited about the morning's success. She finished indicating the coloring of the orchid. The yellow was so pale. By allowing the white of the paper to shine through at the right place, she made the throat of the orchid look very realistic as if the bright light washed out the color on the front edge of the flower. She would apply gray to the yellow to indicate the inside of the orchid's deep recesses. It was all but finished in an hour. She had only to shade the leaves to complete the orchid's representation.

Anne returned to the cottage, but found she could not sit still. She would avoid a visit to the kitchen, as she was sure Cook would have questions about the day before. She did not see her father, but hoped he had seen the orchid's flower by now. She stayed at the cottage only a few minutes before her restlessness drew her back outdoors.

Anne felt light and so happy. She took up her drawing of the rose garden and went out to sit across from the area. She sketched in the shadow of tree branches above the roses and the wall of the house where it showed through. Leaving her drawing on the short bench by the walk, she entered the garden thinking of her morning with Lord Greville, so different from how she had felt the day before.

Lost in her thoughts, she was startled when she heard two voices coming from the drive. She ran from the rose garden and across to the cottage path as quickly as she could. She wanted to see who interrupted. She waited for the couple to emerge toward the house. Perhaps Lord Greville had visitors coming to see the orchid.

No one came forward. Instead, Anne heard muffled noises coming from the shed where her father kept tools, ladders, and stakes. The voices joined together in a rhythm that seemed primal and unfamiliar to Anne. The sounds continued in unison, and then she thought she heard someone cry out followed by a moan. Too frightened to travel back across the lawn, she jogged back to the cottage distracted.

Her restlessness continued into the evening, but she did not venture out again as a fierce wind started up announcing an impending storm. Anne went to bed shortly after her father. They had spoken only briefly of the master's success and at no point did her father mention her involvement.

Still awake hours later, her mind was reeling from thoughts of the last few days and how curious her imagination had been. As she turned to a new position, hoping this time she could drift off, she remembered the voices on the path that afternoon. If she were called to give a guess, she would have said it was Becky's voice that belonged to one of the two people. She did not have to think very long or hard to imagine to whom the other voice belonged.

A feeling of panic made her sit up. She had forgotten to retrieve her drawing. What if someone found it? Oh! What if Lord Greville saw it? She did not even care how it might be spoiled by the storm, she only worried someone would find the drawing before she could. First light could not come quickly enough.

Anne awakened and dressed early. Though she searched the area, she could not find the drawing. She returned to the cottage as the morning was still cold and the trees were dripping, causing her to shiver.

Lord Greville was awake at first light, also. He had slept little as a rainstorm pelted the roof, and his thoughts reviewed the last two days' events. He planned to visit several friends to gloat. Anne's enthusiasm had been an important part for him, despite his more personal challenges, but he would not be mentioning her attendance. Charles turned that fact over in his mind.

236

He would be leaving for Milford soon. He had not given a thought to Anne's future. What would become of his illustrator? She had received no news of a new position. He might speak with Lambert on the matter, but he did not relish the discussion. Why? How odd the esteem he held for Miss Blake, and how difficult to admit to it. Some part of him wished her to stay.

Charles longed to do something for her. He mulled it over in his mind, a gift of perfume or a piece of jewelry? No, nothing of that sort. A book, perhaps, or a new set of pencils or easel? No, she had little need of more art supplies. He wanted to do something that would really please her.

The thought came to him as he sat at his desk staring up at Emma. Yes, that would do well. Excited about his idea and satisfied with resolving the issue, he hurried out to join George in the greenhouse to examine the vanilla's flower.

He meant to turn on the path to the hothouse, but something white near the rose garden caught his notice. He kneeled down to fish the piece of paper from under the bench that protected it from the previous night's rain. As Charles turned it over, he saw that it was a drawing. Parts had been drawn with details, and color had been added in spots; the woman's dress and dark hair, the roses on a bush, the man's face and clothes. He knew who the artist was. He even identified the two figures. What he did not know was how the artist came to draw these figures and make it look so authentic.

He knew he had never sat with her in the roses. The last time he sat in the rose garden was with his sisters. The white flash at the hedge came to mind. Just as it had triggered an epiphany as to who the rose gardener was, he realized Anne must have seen him with his sisters in the garden that day. How had the picture come to hide under the bench? The placement was most likely due to the storm. Odd that it had been allowed to blow about.

Luckily, it was in the right hands now. He felt only a small bit of guilt for not returning it to the owner. He wondered if the artist would be embarrassed by his seeing the drawing. Perhaps the question he should have been asking was "would he have been embarrassed if someone else found the drawing?"

The painting brought to mind Coleman's comments. The old servant's concern for appearances was annoying, though entirely proper. He had come close to a slip of propriety. To think the girl might fancy him. She appeared so well adjusted. He hoped he had not erred in his dismissal of the subject. To be sure, he planned no further advances toward Miss Blake.

26

"Is that you, Lambert?" Charles asked, as he heard his housekeeper's rap on the library door.

"Yes sir, I am off to town. I will return by evening." Mrs. Lambert stood at the entryway to the library pulling on her gloves.

Charles looked up from his work and observed that the elderly woman was dressed in her cloak and bonnet, ready to go out.

"I've quite forgotten, Lambert, to where are you off?" he asked.

"I will attend the wedding sir, the relative of Colonel Bligh. It is a naval affair that I feel I must attend." Mrs. Lambert straightened her posture for the statement.

These events were usually closed to the public, but Mrs. Lambert had attended several weddings and many more funerals. However she did it, Charles did not know. Perhaps she mentioned her long lost husband, and someone took pity on the would-be widow.

"Oh yes, of course, well, give them all my best wishes." Charles stepped back and gave a half bow indicating his full approval and releasing her from his employ for the day, but then remembered his plan.

"Lambert, do you have a minute or are you rushed?" Charles asked.

"No sir, I leave with plenty of time in case there are heavy crowds."

"I would think you are fine with no rain expected. We are nearing the end of harvest, and so many have left town with the end of the season. The weather will drive everyone indoors soon. I was wondering if you have heard if there is to be a ball at Westbourne?" Charles asked.

"No sir, I have not." Mrs. Lambert's world was a narrow slice. Other than the operation of Lord Greville's household, she had only these occasional duties as a naval wife and a church service on Sunday with which to be concerned. She made no effort to engage the world beyond that.

"I know they have given dances in the past, so I suppose it is that time of the year once more. I met my husband dancing," she said off-handedly. "I doubt I could manage a single dance of a single set before my knees would give out."

Charles looked where Mrs. Lambert's knees would certainly be and he felt pity for them. Such a narrow pass between the upper and lower leg would struggle under the woman's weight.

"Lambert, I want you to go," Charles hurried to say, "I mean for George's daughter, Miss Blake, to go. I think she would enjoy herself. I think it is appropriate, but she must have someone to stand up with her. I will make the arrangements if you will accompany her."

Mrs. Lambert usually saw eye to eye with her employer, but her immediate reaction about this was not in agreement at all. Did Anne possess the manners to appear at such an affair? What did she know of ballroom etiquette? Was she ready for such exposure? She knew the girl's history, but beyond that, she was not sure.

Thinking of the times lately when she had seen Anne, she was carrying her portfolio to and from the greenhouse. Many mornings the lord spent time in his greenhouse. Anne was drawing some of the plants in the hothouse for a record for the master. It had all come about because of her library intrusion. The housekeeper supposed that by now Lord Greville must have spent a considerable amount of time with the gardener's daughter.

Mrs. Lambert was surprised by the realization. As head housekeeper, she prided herself in keeping a tight household. A mouse did not move without her knowledge, but she had missed something of much greater consequence. She was horrified; horrified for her absent mindedness for one thing, and also for any inference that might be drawn from this situation.

Louisa Lambert respected Lord Greville, and trusted him to behave with honor as he always had. She did not know about Anne's behavior, though she had seemed like a sweet girl. No more the "girl" the elderly woman realized. She would not assume any scandalous conclusions of an involvement between his lordship and George's daughter without learning the facts of the matter first. What were her master's intentions, truly?

Mrs. Lambert fired questions like cannonballs at Lord Greville. Charles was surprised at the vehemence of her attack. He could tell by the shake of her head that she did not favor his decision.

"Is the girl ready for such exposure? Does she have any interest in such an experience? Does she know a reel or a rondo? Has she the manners to attend? What will she wear?"

The questions came at him in rapid succession. He saw the matron's pursed lips, held tight with reproof. Charles was caught off guard.

"Steady there, Lambert." Charles took a step back from her assault. "I am shocked to find you so uncertain. I am sure she has enough "manners" to get her by. It is a public ball, after all. As to the dances, she says she knows quite a few. She practiced dancing with His Grace's grandchildren, so I do believe she could perform the steps herself. I think she has spent a great deal of time observing and practicing during her time with the Duke's family. She will get a taste of local society and they, in turn, will meet one of the prettiest girls in the area! I think it is a grand scheme and a treat for her as well. You can discuss the possibility with the girl first, if you wish. I do not care one way or the other if she does not wish to go."

Charles knew this last sentence was not true. He did care and was disappointed by Lambert's reluctance. Anne had mentioned her doubts for her future. An introduction could make quite a difference in her opportunities. Upon re-examination however, he began to feel some hesitation.

Standing alone, the idea had been delightful; but in the larger picture, sending the young woman to the dance could threaten his position in the local society. Did he care? His mind had only just arrived at the subject of Anne making some horrible error, before the ghastly memory of Emma at the Gardens came back to him. Emma thinking she had arrived to Society and was somehow protected. She had acted so free with herself. She was so vulgar. He had been embarrassed to the point of losing control and had shoved her into the coach when they departed. Later he told friends they were tickling.

When Charles thought of Anne, who was all enthusiasm and delight at new things, he remembered the sentiment that drove him to the thought of sending her to the dance in the first place. He knew the girl better than Lambert. He knew Anne would love to attend a dance, and he was confident she would conduct herself well. He was not aware that Lambert's trepidation was due in part to his familiarity with the young woman.

The housekeeper was ready to take her leave. She would argue the matter no further. She worried for Anne as much as she was concerned with his lordship's behavior. He had little to lose in the idea, but Anne would be placed in a situation where her innocence and inexperience might lead to impropriety. The housekeeper felt the master was overly confident in the young lady's capabilities.

Mrs. Lambert did not meet with Anne until the following morning. Their conversation was brief, but it left the head housekeeper feeling somewhat reassured about the master's idea. Anne did know the steps for the various dances. She had attended several balls with the children. Mrs. Lambert felt that if she did stand with the girl, providing the proper introduction expected at such a function, Anne would have an opportunity to make a new acquaintance, have a turn to dance, and at least have a nice evening away from the small cottage at the back of the property.

After the conversation with Mrs. Lambert, Anne was anxious to find her father to tell him of the invitation. Anne searched in the flower garden and the hothouse to no avail. She could wait until the afternoon, but she sought his permission to attend the assembly as soon as possible. It would be so much more pleasant to imagine if she knew for certain she would be allowed to go. She could daydream with confidence.

So far she had imagined she would be asked to dance by a handsome stranger. Perhaps Tom mysteriously discovered he was the long lost son of a Baronet. Would Lord Greville attend? Would he dance with her? Anne groaned and shrugged her shoulders. She need spend no more time dreaming until she could find her father.

Maybe her father was at the back of the drive. She could not see beyond the hedges. She heard a rustling and felt for sure she had found him. She hurried around the corner.

By the time she caught a giggle coming from just beyond her view, it was too late to stop. Becky was sitting on the edge of the leaf bin. She was propped up awkwardly and held in place by Tom standing between her legs. They were entangled in an embrace, kissing. Anne focused on Tom's face, discerning what she had interrupted, frozen in place. As he turned to look her way, his expression changed from devilment to embarrassment.

Tom jumped back, and Becky came off the bin haphazardly. Her dress was mussed and her apron hung up around her collar. She was quick to straighten the fabric down. She looked over at Anne with disgust and a warning glare.

"Who do we have here?" Tom said, leering. "What brings you here?" He moved around Anne in a provocative circle, taking her in as a man might when examining a horse he thinks he will buy.

"She is the gardener's daughter, she likes dirt and manure." Becky answered for her.

"George, the gardener? He seems so old to have such a pretty young thing for his offspring."

Becky was frowning hard. The look she cast at Anne was poisonous.

"Was her mother a fairy?" Tom asked. "I thought she worked in the house." Tom reached out as if to pull one of Anne's curls, but instead of touching her at all, he made a circle in the air beside her cheek, never quite touching her skin.

Becky came up behind Tom and nudged him to the side as she passed.

"Never was a servant in this house. Wouldn't have her, I suppose. Or was she too good for it?" Becky said begrudgingly. "She slips away with the master every morning. Quite cozy they are, the two of them hiding in the plants." Becky came to stand directly in front of Anne, too close to be comfortable. Anne thought Becky might strike her, but she held her ground.

"You'll say not a word about what you may think you saw here." Becky hissed at her, nose to nose. "You'll forget you even spoke to us, if you know what is good for you." Becky added, a threat not lost on Anne.

Becky took Tom's hand and began to drag him away. Tom pulled out of her grasp and turned back toward Anne. He banged the heels of his boots together, and pulling his cap from his head, performed a deep bow.

"Forgive me, My Lady, but I must leave you now." He tripped down the path to catch up with Becky. "See you in the garden!" Tom called back with a gesture of throwing a kiss.

Anne winced at the laughter the two lovers shared as they cleared the end of the dense bushes and then split off in different directions. Though she agreed that it would be best to forget this encounter, she spent a few seconds trying to recall what she had seen. She knew what transpired between the two. Anne shook her head, trying to shed the implications. Becky's naughty giggle and their taunting laughs echoed in her head. Yes, she would like to forget what she had seen. She would look no further for her father. Mrs. Lambert's invitation no longer lifted her spirits or directed her actions.

The circle Tom drew above her cheek burned as if branded there. She would never admit to anyone that she enjoyed the attentions of the delivery boy, despite how inappropriate his actions were. She was so angry with herself for ever thinking he would have any interest in her when he had Becky dripping off of him like honey. Anne ran to the cottage where she would await a meeting with her father in the evening.

Charles Greville returned home from his business in town. He had contacted Sir Joseph, Franz Bauer, and his neighbor, Robert Symmons, an avid plant collector as well, inviting each to witness the vanilla flower and possibly perform a pollination. As Lucas led the horse around the back side of the manor, Charles proceeded to the house just in time to see Tom leaving in his wagon and Becky heading into the hall door. At the edge of his view, he saw Anne running toward her cottage at a hurried pace. The three parts, though perhaps coincidental, occurred in a proximity that intrigued him for the minutes it took him to enter his home through the front door.

Hours passed slowly for Anne as she waited for her father and his permission to attend the dance. Finally, with the end of their evening meal, Anne began the conversation. It would be only a short time before her father would turn his face from the fire and the day to retreat to his bench along the wall. Anne let him have his supper in peace, but now she could wait no longer.

"Mrs. Lambert requested a meeting with me this morning." Anne paused to make sure she had her father's attention. He stared off, but had not left the table.

"Father, there is to be an assembly next Friday evening. Mrs. Lambert plans to attend and has requested I accompany her. I have so wanted to go to such an event. Surely, you don't object to my attending with Mrs. Lambert?"

George Blake was tired. His bones were sore, his hands and feet ached, and the hard-working body he always prided himself with was giving up. He worried about the workload ahead and whether he could keep up. With all these personal concerns, none were as important to him as his worry about his daughter.

Anne was growing up before his eyes. These last months with her had been a delight on one hand and a bit of torture on the other. He worried for her idleness and now this situation with his lordship. He worried his daughter put too much stock in her drawing for the master. His only hope was that she would be moving on eventually. Now this idea to attend an assembly, he could not fight against her, he had no energy.

"Yes, you may go, but it will not be a usual pastime for you. Do not set yourself up for disappointment. These affairs can bring as much trouble as pleasure."

Her father's admonishment fell on deaf ears. All she heard was his first word. His reservations about the importance of such public assemblies and an overall concern with her emotional safety should have penetrated her thoughts, but his words failed to. She did not hear him warn her, or think to ask to what he referred.

Anne waited until he stopped talking and moved across the room to give him a hug from behind and a kiss on his scratchy cheek. He smelled of earth and life. She wished he could respond, but she knew he would not. He shook his head, "Now, now, let a poor man rest." He leaned away from her, never comfortable with her bursts of affection.

It was still early, and the excitement of her father's decision kept her from wishing to sleep. Anne stayed awake for another hour before she retired to her bed. She arranged her hair several different ways. She examined the three different dresses that might be suitable to wear. She settled on the pale yellow one. Though secondhand, the dress was like new. The simple cut and the quality of the fabric made it an elegant choice. It fit her well, and would be appropriate. Some girls might wear a darker color or a warmer fabric as the season was changing, but there was still time for thin muslin and lighter colors.

Anne closed her eyes and forced her breathing to subside. All her planning could not insure acceptance. She wanted to fit in and not be an obvious novice when maneuvering the patterns at the dance. She wished to be a credit to the invitation and reflect well on Lord Greville. She fell asleep in the midst of imagining an interesting partner.

27

*I*n the morning, Mrs. Lambert approached his lordship in the dining room to request a private audience after breakfast. Charles was curious about her need for a conversation behind closed doors. He hoped to hear something positive on his idea to send Anne to the dance.

"Good day, Lambert. The wedding went well, I trust?"

"Oh yes, sir. It was well attended and the couple seemed quite in love."

"Now, what is it that you wish to discuss?" Lord Greville asked, expecting a certain answer.

"I wish to bring some mischief to your attention." Mrs. Lambert continued before he could interrupt with any exclamation. "Cook has come up short on several kitchen supplies this month. She has no explanation as to why stores such as a bag of sugar and a tin of coffee have disappeared. She feels sure they were delivered by Tom from Suttons Grocery. We have the bills, but the supplies do not seem to be anywhere."

It was not a coincidence he could ignore any longer when Mrs. Lambert came forth to say, "in addition, a box of candles is missing from the cabinet in the dining room, twenty four in all. I am also missing a silver brooch from the top of my dresser. It has been lost since two weeks past. I thought perhaps I mislaid the piece, and I hoped to find it. I have searched and have concluded that it is not misplaced, but absent from my room altogether." She did not want to alarm the master, but she decided she had waited long enough before informing him.

If the thief were part of the household staff, she would know soon enough, she told the master. Mrs. Lambert would arrange interviews with each of the maids individually. She had her suspicions, but she told the master she would be fair and reserve judgment until there was proof of guilt.

The nobleman began pacing, thinking came easier that way. Mrs. Lambert awaited his thoughts on the situation.

"We must be vigilant, Lambert. Yes, as you say, no jumping to conclusions until we have more evidence.

"Did you discuss the dance with Miss Blake?" Charles asked at last.

"I have, sir. She has informed me that she has her father's permission to attend."

Just the mention of George changed Charles' expression. He had forgotten the young woman would need her father's blessing. Perhaps the father should have been informed initially. Of course, her father would have many of the same worries as Lambert, but still the old gardener had given his consent. The girl could be convincing, he mused. His thoughts returned to theft.

"I will question Miss Blake about the missing stores, myself," he told the matron.

Mrs. Lambert thought it curious that the master insisted on speaking to Anne. She revisited her fears from the day before. Surely, the master knew what he was doing. She would not express an opinion or mention his involvement with the young woman until she felt it was absolutely necessary. She rarely commented in such a way.

Early in the afternoon, Charles spotted Anne leaving the greenhouse. He stepped from the library to intercept her.

"May I have a word with you, Miss Blake?" He looked around and although there was no one, he thought it best to remove their discussion from the view of others.

"Would you come into the library for a moment?"

Anne wondered what his concern might be. The lord's manner seemed very formal, as if he approached her on a higher level than their usual conversations. Here she was entering his library again! She hoped her father was in some other part of the garden. Once inside, the master faltered before he began his inquisition. Anne held her hands behind her back, and gripped them tighter as she noted the lord's struggle for words.

"You do not have many friends, Anne. I think, on the whole, your life is a lonely one." Charles addressed her directly.

"No, sir, I do not have many friends. I am lonely at times, but I have enjoyed my duties, limited as they are." Anne was confused by the subject of his questions. She did not dare announce how she felt about their meetings. Their relationship was the most important thing in her life, but she could not tell him so. She hoped it was not in jeopardy.

"Your life may not have been arranged in a way that would promote deep friendships, I am afraid."

"No, sir, it has not. I have enjoyed meeting many people of different ranks and ages, but as for friends, I have few. I have a friendship with Cook and Lucas. I hold them very dear. Mrs. Lambert has always been kind to me, but we do not share our thoughts as friends do." Anne did not hide how she felt about the question he asked. She gave him as straight an answer as she thought appropriate. In her inner thoughts though, she felt that he, Lord Greville, was closer to being a friend than anyone else. She wondered where all these answers would lead.

As he had predicted and expected, Charles knew she would be forthright.

"Do you count Becky as a friend?" Charles asked, looking straight at her.

Anne took a breath at the name. She kept the image in the yard at the back of her mind. She heard the shift in the topic with a change in the master's tone of voice.

"No. She is not a friend as one would understand the term to mean. She does not think of me in that way, either." Anne answered curtly.

"And you? Do you like her? Would you wish her to be your friend?"

"I don't know why she does not think well of me, perhaps because I do not work in the house. Sybil is much more of a friend." Anne found she was afraid to say anything derogatory about Becky, as if it might get back to her.

"Are we friends, Anne?" Charles was almost teasing an answer from her. He wished to hear what the girl would say. He took a step toward her, but stopped himself from coming closer.

Anne was startled. She stopped staring off and turned her head to look at the nobleman. She sought to understand if this were the reason he questioned her. Surely not. She was perplexed to admit to her private thoughts. To say "no," they were not friends due to his station would not be altogether true. To say "yes" and reveal the connection she felt for the lord would be inappropriate, especially if he did not share in that association. She was perplexed as to what answer she should give. She looked him in the eye and saw nothing but kindness.

"We might be, I suppose, but our time together is short and so much apart from all else in our lives."

"Well said, Anne!" She had put it into words what he could not. He wished he could embrace her, she addressed him so truthfully. He moved back toward his desk resisting his urge.

"I do believe we are friends when we are together, but we do not face life together for so much of the rest of the time. You are so right. We could be good friends in different circumstances," Charles said with surprising truthfulness. There was so much of what was not being said. "I, too, have few friends. The few I do consider as such have stayed with me through hard times as well as the present. I think I am lucky to have perhaps four such people in my life."

Anne felt relieved that she had answered the question as she had, pleasing him. This was the comfortable place where their conversations lingered.

"Did you see Tom and Becky behind the garden yesterday?"

Anne was shocked by the suddenness of the question. The previous questions had lulled her senses. Having reassured herself about being honest, she wanted to tell the master what she had seen, but she would only answer the question asked, and hope no more were to follow

"Yes."

"Did you see anything inappropriate?"

After a moment she answered, "Please sir, I do not feel comfortable passing judgment on what I may or may not have seen." Anne could not stop her hand from shaking and pretended to scratch her arm. She feared her eyes told more than she had said.

"I do not wish to make you uncomfortable, but I believe you were all in the garden at the same time yesterday, and I am of the opinion that Becky and Tom were together when you saw them," he continued with authority to his statements, justifying his need to know.

"Becky has been lax in her duties according to Mrs. Lambert. Cook thinks that there may be more to this than laziness. Did you see them close together yesterday?"

"Yes, sir." Anne thought of their position of entanglement together. It would be impossible to tell the master.

"Did you see them kissing? Do not worry, Anne, I do not plan to confront Becky with your information as an accusation." He waited for her answer, but as none immediately came, he persisted.

"As you do not deny it, I will deduce on my own that they were. Is there anything else I should know?"

"No sir, nothing else," she forced herself to say. It was enough. He did not need more to understand the connection between Becky and Tom.

"Thank you. You do a service to the household." Charles rubbed his lip as he thought about the situation. He could be angrier, but not now in front of Anne who showed more discomfort than interrupting a kiss should have caused. There was more here, but what?

Charles saw the girl's face growing darker. He had not meant to trouble her. He knew she would give him honest answers and he needed them. Perhaps he should include her in the goings on of the household, but was it wise? He trusted her explicably, and knew above all considerations that she had nothing to do with the disappearances. He changed the subject altogether.

"Well, enough of that, how are your paintings coming?" Charles inquired. He took a seat behind his desk keeping his distance.

Anne felt the change in the mood. She was put at ease.

"I have quite a few that I have completed. I have several others to which I have not put all the color, and I have three drawings to finish."

"I would appreciate if you could leave any completed drawings on my desk within the next few days. I attend a meeting next week at which I would enjoy showing them to my fellow horticulturalists. It will be your debut, so to speak, even if anonymous." Charles gave Anne a bright smile.

"I will have Sybil leave them on your desk as you wish," Anne said.

Anne wanted to ask about the dance. Lord Greville did not mention it, so she would keep the prospect to herself in case attending the dance was insignificant to him.

"Yes, that would be fine," he said, turning over the letters on his desk. He would have liked to put an arm around her and escort her out, but Coleman's words came back to him, again. They forced his eyes to stay down.

Feeling dismissed, Anne curtsied and left the room. She was still ruffled by his questioning. She hurried home fearing a confrontation with Becky more than anything.

28

*A*nne finished her drawings, stacking the papers neatly together in order of their completion. The renderings would be a record of the flowering time of each plant. She anticipated Lord Greville's view of her work with some timidity. She took the portfolio to Sybil to place on the master's desk.

"May I look?" Sybil asked as Anne gave her the stack of drawings.

"Oh yes, I would like you to see." Anne opened the folder to the first drawing allowing Sybil to thumb through them. Even Anne could see great improvement between her first drawings and those she had just completed.

"Oh they are lovely. The master will be well pleased," Sybil encouraged.

As they stood in the hallway, Becky stopped to take a look, realizing they were Anne's drawings. Becky pulled one of the pages out of order and held it for a moment before throwing it back on the top of the pile.

"If you ask me, it was a waste of time, you and the master in the greenhouse. Makes me wonder, what else were you two up to, all those mornings?" She laughed her ugly, piercing cackle and headed off down the hall. The edge of the paper was stained. Anne brushed it lightly, but the smudge remained.

Anne had spoken to Sybil about attending the assembly with Mrs. Lambert. The upstairs maid had been very excited for her and did not display a hint of jealousy. She knew Anne would be excellent company to the old housekeeper. She hoped Anne would have an opportunity to dance.

Two days before the assembly, Mrs. Lambert asked to see the dress that Anne had chosen to wear. When the matron saw the pale yellow muslin with eyelet embroidery, she immediately liked the color and simplicity of the dress. As Anne held the gown up against her body, the elderly woman was surprised at how exquisite the gardener's daughter appeared. Anne, with her fair complexion, dark eyes, and auburn hair against the buttery color of the dress, ensured the young woman would not only look appropriate, but stunning.

"Lord Greville has called for a carriage to pick us up at eight, Anne. You will need to walk out to the back drive, so mind the hem of your dress on the paths. Please do not keep me waiting," Mrs. Lambert warned.

Anne had put no thought to how they would be conveyed to the dance. Walking after dark near the canals could be dangerous. How nice of Lord Greville to order a carriage for them.

At the end of the week, Lord Greville had not heard back from Mrs. Lambert, wondering how she fared with her investigation. He had informed Coleman of the mischief and as usual the elderly valet had reacted fervently.

"If I see so much as a doily in your parlor moved, I will contact the magistrate! To think there is a possibility of a robber in our house. One thing awry, I tell you! I will not sit by and wait for worse!"

"Calm yourself, Coleman. You will keel over." Charles did feel violated, but also felt they had a good chance of catching the thief in the next little while as he was almost certain of the identity of the culprits. Charles changed the subject to that of the dance. He would need suitable attire aired out and ready for the evening of the ball.

Once again, the manservant went off. He had nothing good to say about the idea, but when the lord held up his hand against his caustic remarks, the valet merely muttered something and finished with, "mark my words!"

Charles' only concern was for the girl's enjoyment. The dance was only as interesting as the young woman's attendance. He devised to make one additional purchase for Anne. It had been many years since he engaged in such entertainment, but he knew that women had not changed so much in that time. He knew exactly what he wanted, and hoped he could choose correctly.

The afternoon of the assembly arrived. Anne brushed her hair one hundred times having aired her dress and spot cleaned her shoes. She thought of her mother, but she would not allow any sadness to enter her mood.

Anne twisted her hair up in a knot the way Jane had shown her. By winding the mass in a circle and flipping it over, it formed a twisted bun that when pinned down the side, kept most of her hair under control. Anne felt quite sophisticated with her hair up, and carried her head differently because of it. As usual, a few curly strands escaped the knot and hung softly along her hairline. She could do nothing to include them with the rest, so she circled them in her fingers to form matching curls on each side of her neck.

While Anne was preparing for the dance, Lord Greville was in his library relaxing before the evening's event. The folder of drawings sat on the corner of his desk. He was still reluctant to look, but it was time. Why had he questioned her ability, he did not know. For when he started to peel off the paintings one by one, he was delighted. The lines of her first drawings were timid, but as time went by, the quality became quite fine with good dark lines. Charles was equally amazed at the quantity of drawings the girl had completed, forgetting she had continued to work even in his absence.

He was pleased with himself for solving the problem of the trespass with such enjoyable consequences. He was glad to be rewarding Anne with her attendance tonight, and the gift he had purchased for her. She had certainly done her penance for any inconvenience she ever caused. When it came to thoughts of Anne Blake, they were altogether pleasing.

At last, the hour approached. Anne stepped into her gown as she had no maid to help the dress over her hair without catching on some part of her coiffure and pulling strands loose. She was thin enough to get her hips through the opening and nimble enough to fasten the two hook and eyes at the top. She wore her mother's gold cross and small pearl earrings as her only jewelry. Though plain, Anne felt a small confidence about her efforts. Her father was waiting to see her as she departed. When she came into sight, he was awestruck. He pondered his decision to allow her to attend. She would turn heads. George Blake had to hope the heads she turned would respect her age and innocence. He thought of the master and his intentions, but it was too late for all that now.

"My daughter is a princess tonight. If only…," but he did not finish his thought about her mother.

"Thank you, Father. I know." She too did not wish to dwell on thoughts that might jeopardize the happiness she felt. Anne slipped her silk shawl around her shoulders and went for the door, but her father reached it first, opening it for her and bowing as she walked by.

Anne kissed him on his forehead, "I will not be too late."

The proud father watched his daughter walk away down the path, her dress hem carefully folded on her arm. She wore her boots to the house where Sybil had agreed to help her finish dressing. Sybil was as excited as Anne when she met her at the door.

"Oh Anne! Here, let me put your shoes on for you." Sybil, once a lady's maid, reminded Anne about her stockings and straightening her chemise so that her dress showed no wrinkles. She even coaxed Anne into taking a fan, which Mrs. Lambert procured, but Anne doubted she would ever remove it from her purse, as she would not have a steady enough hand.

Anne was to borrow a pair of gloves from Mrs. Lambert, but the fingers were stretched out and the tips of her own fingers did not match those of the gloves, giving a clown-like look to them. Mrs. Lambert thought it better if she just not use gloves. She had absentmindedly complained about the lack of suitable gloves to Lord Greville when he inquired about Anne's dress.

"Her dress is appropriate, Lambert?" he had inquired.

"Quite, sir."

"Is she excited at the prospect?" Charles asked more specifically, wishing to hear something of the girl's appreciation for his plan.

"She does seem so, sir. She reins in her emotions well, as she should," the housekeeper replied, not fully to the master's liking.

Now the time had arrived and the reined in emotions were brimming over in a nervous smile.

Mrs. Lambert stepped into the hall. "I have one last touch for your outfit tonight, my dear, a gift from the master."

Anne opened the thin box with shaking hands to find a pair of white gloves within.

"Oh, how lovely!" Anne lifted the smooth white fabric from the box. As she pulled them on, she saw there was a small yellow rose embroidered at the top edge of each glove where it lay against her arm. They were a perfect fit, tight to put on this first time. The seams at the fingertips were well sewn, accenting Anne's dainty hands. The gloves had been perfumed and now gave off a light smell of roses; the same scent Anne had used herself.

"The master did well on the size. The coach is here and will pull up to pick us up shortly. We leave by the side door," the matron instructed.

"You look very nice," Sybil remarked to Mrs. Lambert. Anne glanced over at her escort. The housekeeper wore a black dress with a squared neck embellished with a small lace ruffle. She wore white gloves and a small pearl hair decoration.

"We are both from fairy tales tonight," Anne said to her chaperone. She gave Sybil a light hug and tiptoed out the door.

"No dear, you might be, but I am dressed much as I did years ago at the many naval balls I attended."

Anne chose not to think too much of Mrs. Lambert's remark, as she feared it might frighten her from proceeding to the coach. The idea of being one in a crowd and finding a possible dancing partner wore on her courage.

As Anne stepped from the house, she saw that her father had spent his afternoon sweeping the path so that it was clean and stone free. Tears waited at the corners of her eyes, but she would not cry now, she lifted her head and walked on to the waiting coach.

At the corner of the manor, Anne caught a glimpse of Becky, standing alone with her arms crossed. Anne did not expect any acknowledgement from the girl, certainly not any approval. Becky wore a strange expression as she watched Anne depart. It was not a smile of approbation, but a smirk containing evil satisfaction that made Anne's skin crawl. Anne supposed the look came from her jealous nature. The excitement made it easy to shirk off the sensation it had given her.

The ride in the satin lined carriage was a magical one. She spied into the dimly lit interiors of the small cottages along the road. The outline of the church spire gave her bearings so that, as they pulled up to a long drive, she knew they were soon to arrive. Mrs. Lambert allowed Anne to look out as they drove, but now the matron leaned forward, touching the young woman's hand.

"Lean back now, my dear. We will be there soon enough, and you must hold back your enthusiasm and depart from the coach slowly, watching your step." Anne's emotions sharpened every point about the evening. She sat back thinking how fortunate she was.

29

*W*hen the coach pulled around the drive at the front of the Hammonds' manor, Anne wished they could have continued traveling for another hour. She was so soothed by the splendor surrounding her, the shine off the fabric inside the carriage, the ornament in Mrs. Lambert's hair, and her new, beautiful, white gloves. It was difficult to believe that this moment was real.

Mrs. Lambert descended the small steps of the chaise slowly, cumbersome as her figure was. She completely depended upon the coachman's arm as she did. The leather straps and springs that held up the body of the carriage rose up with a jerk as the woman stepped off the last stair. Anne waited patiently, catching a glimpse of the well-lit entry room at the top of the stairs. When it was her turn, she felt as if her feet did not touch the ground. Anne believed this must be how heaven would be.

Mrs. Lambert produced Lord Greville's card at the door. Anne stayed close to her as they spilled into a large room. Her chaperone directed her to leave her shawl on one of the many benches as she was removing her own wrap. The mood of this large room progressed from confusion at the entry door to chaos at the other end as the gatherers funneled into a short hallway leading to the great hall. Anne took the lead ahead of Mrs. Lambert who put her hand on Anne's back as they plunged into the flow of the crowd. Anne was pushed through the hallway's narrow inlet to the sea of people waiting beyond in the large ballroom.

At the back of the first room, Lord Greville stood watching as Mrs. Lambert and Anne made their way through. He had a wide view of the lobby. The movement of the mass of finely dressed persons was slower as it went through the narrow section. Slower, and yet the lord could not make Anne out in the multitude, nor did he see her emerge on the other side. He would hurry to go in, relieved now that he had witnessed the pair's safe arrival. The anxious weight in his stomach was something new.

Lord Greville met several other guests with whom he was acquainted as he made his way through the hall. He had a social obligation to acknowledge a few in the crowd around him. He might not have known who several of the guests were, but they all knew who he was. As he came into the ballroom, he could not see Anne from his vantage point, but he felt she must be just ahead in the thick group of men and women, feathers bobbing and voices murmuring. They made their way to the middle of the room to dance.

Charles Frances Greville was always a subject of interest when polite society gathered. His connection to an ancient family made him a celebrity. He heard whispering as he walked by. His reputation as a single man made women curious. His new found fortune only made him more interesting.

Anne took a breath when she finally landed safely in the room where the music was beginning to play. There were so many candles that the room was shimmering with their heat and glow. Everywhere were decorations of bouquets and garlands of fresh flowers accented with gold and copper painted leaves. The magic feeling she experienced in the carriage was little compared to the sights and sounds around her now. It was even more wonderful than she had imagined.

Mrs. Lambert was still standing with a few women from their neighborhood when Anne looked back. She wanted to catch her chaperone's eye before proceeding any further into the room, but the housekeeper seemed lost in her own enjoyment of the evening, surrounded by grey-haired women all talking at the same time. Anne let the current of people push her forward closer to the dancing area.

An older woman in a pale blue dress overtook Anne by placing her arm under Anne's in an assertive manner. Anne faced the woman to curtsy. She came up smiling as the woman returned the smile and a nod. Anne noticed how elegantly plain the distinguish woman looked. She wore no jewelry except large pearl drop earrings. In front of the nest of hair drawn to form a bun, the woman wore a large pearl pendant also in a teardrop shape. The grand lady was simply elegant. Anne was reminded of the ladies of the Duke's household.

This dowager must be one of the committee of women who directed the assembly. Mrs. Lambert had explained that usually the mistress of the hall or a group of older women took charge of these gatherings. This governing body was responsible for keeping order, making the decisions about refreshments, the music, and who would be allowed to assemble. In some areas, a small entrance fee would be charged and the group accounted for this money, which was used to fund the next event.

Mrs. Lambert had also made it clear that this dance would be a public affair, rather than a private or subscription ball. The guest list for those types of events was very select. Public balls were much more open and accepting, Mrs. Lambert clarified, patting Anne's hand in a conciliatory manner.

The elegant woman's arm guided Anne to the left side of the room. There, Anne noticed other young women were lining up to wait for a perspective dance partner to seek them out. Anne took her place in the line and looked over at the other attendees. Some of the women were her same age, but most were a bit older. Anne was pleased to see that her dress was appropriate. She noticed her new gloves. They gave her a feeling of sophistication. Spying the embroidered rose, she smiled to think of his lordship's possible intention. Did he know it was she working in the roses that day?

Introductions were being made around Anne. She feared that not having Mrs. Lambert to point out worthy prospects or help her establish a connection, making a partner out of a stranger, might disadvantage her. She might wait quite awhile to be able to dance. Just as others were moving off to the dance floor, and Anne's heart began to sink, she felt someone at her elbow and turned to see Peter's smiling face.

At that moment, she could not have been more pleased. Her smile was genuine, though it came more from her feeling of salvation than her delight with the person who saved her. She curtsied to Peter and he bowed to her. Standing this close to him, he rose nearly a foot above her.

"You look so changed from when I see you at your home or on the Green. I mean you look very nice." He stumbled through the short speech.

"Yes, in Lord Greville's kitchen, we all have different roles. Even on Sundays, we never wear clothes as fine as these." She pointed to the young boy's outfit. He looked every part a gentleman. There was difficulty in his use of the word "home" for Anne. The kitchen where she met Peter was not her home and in fact, her role there in general was vague. By referring to Lord Greville, she wished to set the record straight, though Peter appeared not to be listening.

Peter was pleased to be standing next to the prettiest girl in the room. The lovely girl took all reasonable thought away from him. He was overwhelmed by the natural air of her self-esteem. It would be said she carried herself well.

Lord Greville could not spy Anne as he entered the grand hall. He knew in time he would spot her and witness others seeing her for the first time. Her pale yellow gown fit her personality perfectly, Charles thought. He did not linger on the thought of how well it fit her figure. The gloves he had purchased offered an appealing outline to her arms and hands. Charles had a weakness for women in gloves. He wondered if she had found the small roses embroidered on the cuffs and guessed at his discovery.

Charles could see couples forming a line on the dance floor and now he was able to pick his artist out of the crowd. Anne was still standing to the side. He searched for Mrs. Lambert and finally spotted her clear across the room, having only made a little progress from the entryway. If Anne held a position along the outside edge, there was a possibility that she might not be asked to dance at all, but when he looked again, she was on the dance floor, dancing with Peter, the dairyman's son.

Peter's father had done very well for his family. They were from Germany originally, hardworking and determined. They had come to be landowners with considerable holdings. Anne and Peter must have met at some point, perhaps at his manor. Not a bad match for Anne, thought the nobleman, as he watched them together. Most would in fact consider such a connection to be a step up for Anne.

Lord Greville watched the girl as she danced. She had an uncommon grace as if she'd danced a thousand balls. Her turns and twirls were timed perfectly to the music. When the dance set ended, Peter escorted Anne from the dance floor, not ready to let her go, the lord supposed with a smile. But then, he left Anne sitting by one of the large windows along the opposite wall as he went off for refreshment.

Anne had forgotten to look for Lord Greville in all her nervousness. Mrs. Lambert had informed her that he would attend. Now, waiting by the window, she had the wits about her to do so. After scanning much of the interior of the room, she finally spotted the lord leaning against the wall on the far side of the hall. He leaned in a way that made Anne think of him in his younger days, perhaps a little cocky, with a sideways glance at all that took place in the ballroom. She looked away quickly before he saw her stare.

How many balls Lord Greville must have attended including far more gala events with a much higher echelon of attendants? How many women must have caught his eye and vice versa? How many women sought him out, the handsome son of an Earl and Member of Parliament?

Did he take any of them out to speak about the stars? Did he talk to them of rubies he might give them one day? They might sketch, but none of them would have talked with him about herbal remedies. Had any of them sat with him in his garden?

Anne looked up and saw Lord Greville meet her gaze. He must have been dashing, Anne mused, as he was still a handsome face in the crowd. For that moment, in the company of close to two hundred people, they singled each other out. With a look of sheer delight, Anne lifted her gloved arms for him to see. The look that connected them tingled. She felt as if he were standing right before her and not across a crowded room. The feeling was every bit as strong as if he had touched her. She heard her quavering exhale as she received a glowing smile from the lord.

He would dance with her! Damn the gossips! His pulse sped at once, excited by the idea, but first he would have a glass of wine. The lord made his way to the refreshments himself and found Peter. He wanted to acknowledge some part of the boy's success. "A lovely evening and a lovely partner," Charles said, looking up to the tall young man.

Peter realized the lord spoke to him. He was surprised and caught off guard. This was his partner's guardian, he was uncertain what he should say. What was the connection between Lord Greville and Anne?

"Yes, I am quite lucky," Peter replied truthfully.

The statement drew a broad smile from the lord who responded as he turned to go, "Yes, I envy you." He moved off to close the gap to Anne and wait his turn at a dance with her.

"Miss Blake?" A voice startled Anne from outside the window. She looked out to see the dark silhouette of a man just at the edge of the square of light coming from the window.

Tom stepped into the light, making pleading gestures. "Miss Blake, I need to speak with you at once. Come quickly. It is very important. Your father-," and then his voice trailed off as he ducked away into the shadows.

How could this be, Anne thought, she was in the middle of the most exhilarating night of her life, and now the delivery boy, the artist of the hot circle, wished to speak to her. When she looked at Tom, he looked particularly disconcerted. "Come quickly," he had implored.

She looked back toward where Lord Greville had been standing. He was no longer there. She wished for his confirmation, a mutual wave to explain she was summoned. Concerned for her father, she was drawn forth. Not for an instant did she consider that it might be a ruse.

Anne was no longer sitting at the window when he began to move across the room. The spot where she had been sitting was empty. He looked to the right and saw a brief glimpse of her standing by the open doors. Perhaps she felt faint from all the exertion and the excitement, but when she stepped outside, his heart raced. Where was she going? The lord panicked, staring at the door where Anne exited, hoping she would reappear.

The lord broke through the crowd with many apologies, using his elbows as necessary. He created a small commotion as he left an open trail behind him. For his life, he did not know how he could get from one place to another with such agility. He was extremely agitated and empowered by a strong internal force.

271

Anne passed several couples standing on the terrace outside. They stayed close enough to the opening that all could see them, but enjoyed the fresh air the short escape provided. Anne descended three steps to the garden and turned in the direction from which Tom had called. Her skin formed goose bumps under the thin material of her gown. Some of the bumps were caused by the cool night air and some by the prospects of a conversation with Tom.

Lord Greville came to the door where Anne had departed and looked down the length of the building. There, in the light of the ballroom were Tom and Anne together. She seemed animated in her speech to the boy, the same boy about whom the housekeeper had made inferences.

"There are no prettier girls here," the dark haired boy said. "You look to be one of these fine ladies."

Anne was disturbed. His compliments meant nothing to her at that moment.

"What news of my father?"

"I came in the hopes of seeing you," he said with his eyes on hers without a glimmer of distraction. "Ever since the first day I met you, I have wished for a chance to explain that things are not as they appear," he said awkwardly.

"I did not see anything." Anne lied, confused and no longer willing to give Tom her attention. She looked back through the window. She knew she should return. Tom took a step toward her.

"Becky means trouble for you as she has been trouble for me."

Anne saw an odd look in Tom's eyes just before he leaned closer. He took Anne's hands and yanked her into the shadow of the hedge. He turned his body in toward Anne's taking up the space that separated them. He forced her arms behind her with his grasp, bending into her to plant a kiss on her partly opened lips that tried to object. The attack surprised her, and though she tried to move her head away from him in rejection, she could not break out of his strong hold. She thought the kiss would end quickly, but he pressed tighter on her lips, forcing his tongue between her teeth.

Anne struggled against his body, turning her face away from his kiss. The boy moaned, kissing her neck as his hips pressed against her, rubbing his leg up and down along her side. The sound was unmistakable. She had heard it before, the afternoon of the pollination, by the tool shed. Disgusted, Anne pulled her arms free and pushed Tom backwards in an effort to escape.

When Lord Greville saw Tom and Anne kissing, he was enraged. He launched himself from the steps, tripping in his descent. He caught up with his feet and bound down the path, colliding into the middle of the two with the jolt of his body.

"Step away!" he shouted at Tom, frightening him with the ferocity of the assault.

"Lord Greville!" Tom saw madness in the nobleman's eyes.

"Miss Blake, make haste to get back inside immediately!"

Anne did not wait to ask any questions. She went back to the heat, lights, and noise of the hall. Before she could catch her breath, Peter approached.

"I am sorry. I did not think to look for you out of doors."

"I saw someone I knew_," There was no explaining what had just happened."

"I would have accompanied you if you had waited," Peter added, reminding Anne again that she overstepped propriety.

"Drink up and we will dance again if you would like."

"Yes, that would be nice," she answered, trying to recover from all that had just occurred. It was not Tom's kiss she thought of, but Lord Greville's anger.

There was a sudden rush of people to the window. The dancing was disrupted though the musicians continued. As people came back to the dance floor, she heard the master's name and something about blood and a fight.

Anne did her best to stay in the dance line with Peter and pay little attention to the crowd returning from the windows, though she worried what might be happening. Inside her stomach, a sick feeling was building. The reel ended and once again, Peter took Anne's arm gently and led her from the dance floor. At that same moment, Mrs. Lambert arrived breathless and flushed.

"We must go now, dear," she announced between gasps.

Anne did not dare ask why so soon or so suddenly, because she was sure she knew the reason. Peter did not voice any objections either, and Anne wondered if he had heard something of what had happened moments ago. She could not think clearly for herself, so many confusing and conflicting emotions were running through her mind.

Anne curtsied to Peter and thanked him for the dances. She spoke briefly about seeing him again soon. Anne followed Mrs. Lambert as she made her way back through the narrow hall to gather her shawl. They hurried down the stairs to the waiting coach.

The coachman opened the door and Anne carefully took the step to enter. The interior of the carriage was dark. She moved to the far side to allow room for Mrs. Lambert. She was shocked when she bumped into another person.

"Do not be frightened, Miss Blake. We will ride together, if you do not mind. It will be your second close encounter with a man tonight." Lord Greville mocked her.

Anne sat dutifully to the side of the dark figure and waited for the doorman to help the older woman in. As the carriage turned around in the drive, the lights from the hall swept across the inside of the chaise showing Lord Greville sitting with his handkerchief held up to his nose. She could see a large red patch of blood on the linen pad.

Anne was horrified by the quick view of the lord and the extent of his injury. Though she wished she could inquire and see to his wound, she was certain he would not take kindly to her concern, as she was the cause. His tone of voice had confirmed that he was extremely angry with her.

They traveled in silence, each deep in thought. Charles fumed in his corner, still livid. He was irate for a variety of reasons, and he needed time to sort them out. Anne might have exposed herself to real ridicule. How foolish to have brought her out. He had learned this lesson before, he insisted to himself. However, what had he done but allow for mockery by his own actions? His missed delivery of a fist to the face of the boy had concluded in his falling forward into a stone wall injuring his nose and lip in the process. The scoundrel had never touched him, nor suffered any blows.

Mrs. Lambert feared she had not performed her chaperone duties as she should have. She had never raised a child and did not really understand the responsibility. She worried that the master would rebuke her, so she stayed quiet in her corner of the coach.

Anne desired the chance to talk about all that she had seen and experienced at the assembly, but all the glimmering images seemed tarnished by Tom's actions and Lord Greville's injury. She could only guess what the master had surmised seeing Tom kissing her. She had not solicited that kiss. She had no time to shame Tom for taking it. She could only guess that a fight had ensued between the lord and Tom. Had she embarrassed Lord Greville irrevocably? She was angry at Tom, but much more so at herself.

Anne wanted to thank the lord and Mrs. Lambert for their kindness, but she could not speak into the silence, thick with unsaid thoughts. She kept to herself, tense and alert, trying not to move on the seat next to the master who seemed to be dozing in the corner. As they pulled up beside a lamp on the main road, she saw he was not asleep. His face was tight with an expression so harsh it frightened her. He appeared furious to the point of menacing.

The bleeding had stopped, but Charles' entire face was pounding with pain. Though he was looking at Anne as they made their way back to his manor, it was another young woman he was seeing. He imagined they were riding home from Vauxhall, where that female had embarrassed and enraged him with her vulgar behavior, attracting the attention of several men of dubious intentions.

"Once again, you have made a spectacle of yourself," he murmured looking back at Anne with murderous eyes. She looked away quickly. To what did he refer when he said "once again"? Truly, she had never before been in such a situation.

They pulled up on the drive and before coming around to the front portico, Lord Greville knocked on the roof of the carriage, signaling the driver to stop. This would give Anne the shortest way home. The doorman opened the door, and Anne took his hand to steady her descent. She leaned back toward the carriage and the silent adults within.

"Thank you for a wonderful evening I will never forget. It was more wonderful than I even dreamed it would be. Lord Greville," she began, but was cut off by the closing of the door and the lurch forward of the carriage to the front of the house. She stepped back from the drive and onto the gravel walkway where she waited alone in the dark for a moment before heading to the cottage with the heaviest of hearts.

30

$\mathcal{A}$s Anne woke the next morning, she enjoyed a moment's peace before remembering the calamity. She knew Tom's actions, her behavior, and the subsequent harm that came to Lord Greville had serious implications still to come. She wanted to think only of the golden glow from the candle light, the pearl drop in the elderly matron's hair, and Lord Greville's bright smile. She did not want to think of Tom's forceful kiss or the blood on the lord's handkerchief. The view of the lord's swollen face, ugly and askew in anger came to her as did the lord's voice, so harsh and hateful. It was all a catastrophe.

She was not thinking of the dance and the delight she had shared with Peter. She had laughed and enjoyed herself even with Peter as her partner. It was those few minutes outside that made her heart plummet as she came awake.

It was Sunday. She would attend church with Cook and Lucas. She would pray for forgiveness for her actions, and pray for her father as usual. In addition, she would ask that Mrs. Lambert was not ashamed of her. Her last request would be for an expedient recovery for Lord Greville.

Would he forgive her? Was she such an embarrassment that he would remain angry? She feared she had severed the bond that grew stronger each time they met, a connection that approached much more in her heart.

Thoughts of Tom came to mind. How could she ever face the boy again? Would he still deliver to Lord Greville's kitchen? If need be, she would avoid the kitchen forever to never see him again. When Anne thought of Becky, anxiety and fear brought sweat to her forehead though it was a cool morning. How would Becky punish her if the maid had discovered any of what had occurred. Anne trembled at the thought.

After church, Anne would come right home and make bread for her father. She would not go out of the cottage in the afternoon, as she might want to do. She would stick to chores within the small cottage. She would stay away from the garden.

When Anne met Cook at the drive on their way to church, she asked if the master had made his way downstairs that morning. The head of the kitchen seemed to know nothing of what had occurred.

"Oh, no dear, he left early this morning. He took no breakfast and wished to get on his way, I suppose before church traffic clogged the roads. It was still dark when I heard the carriage pull away. He must have arranged for a chaise last night when he came home."

Anne was heartsick. She would not have a chance to speak to the lord. She would feel so much better if she could but apologize for any discontent she might have caused. There was no relief from her anguish this morning.

"And how was your first assembly, Anne? You looked so lovely, dear."

"It was so beautiful there." Anne could not go into details, as they would all lead to the same ending. She was not sure how to speak of the event knowing repercussions were still to come. In fact, she was not sure of much of the evening anymore. The lights, the flowers, the music, and the dancers were slowly fading memories lost to Tom's grip and the silent ride home with Lord Greville.

After church, Anne was weary from self-examination. She was exhausted, and fell asleep for a short nap. Her father came and went from his midday meal. He had not bothered to wake her. They had yet to speak of the evening.

When she awoke, Anne went to the manor in the hope of finding Mrs. Lambert. She was surprised by the hubbub she encountered. Excited language came from the kitchen as she recognized the housekeeper and others speaking in loud voices.

"She is not upstairs, either," answered Sybil to the obvious search for someone.

"I do not think she is here," chimed in another maid. "The bedding is gone, and all her belongings excepting her caps and aprons."

"Good afternoon, Anne," Mrs. Lambert said. Anne could not tell from the matron's voice if it held any resentment. "Becky has left in the night," Mrs. Lambert explained. "Sybil states that Becky expressed the intention to leave service for a factory job. She had some sort of liaison with Tom, the delivery boy, with whom she was planning to travel. Becky spoke to Sybil about biding her time until she had enough money to leave the master's manor and strike out on her own. It seems that time was now."

How long Sybil was aware of the connection between the two lovers was unclear. Anne so wished she had spoken to Sybil about Tom. Sybil might have warned her. Anne would have shunned the boy, and all would be well this morning.

Anne's heart sank as she pictured Becky pressing herself into Tom. He must have been planning to go all along. His words to her at the ball were all false. They were only an attempt to take a chance with her before he left. He had nothing to lose, but she lost so much.

Anne was so angry at her naiveté. She had been so stupid. Somewhere inside, she had always known that Tom was not the type of boy she should be hurrying after, and yet she had more than once made excuses for his behavior.

"Continue to search the house for anything out of the ordinary, girls," Mrs. Lambert called back to the maids. The elderly woman limped out of the kitchen. Anne followed the old housekeeper to her apartment's door. "Perhaps the run in last night hurried them on their way," she added to Anne.

"What did happen, Mrs. Lambert?"

Mrs. Lambert sighed as she began.

"I was not as attentive to you as I should have been, I suppose. When I last saw you, you were dancing with the dairyman's son. You looked well cared for, and I did not concern myself." The elderly woman seemed very fatigued, not from lack of sleep, but from the heaviness of the burden of her responsibilities. "The master observed you leaving the hall and feared for your safety." Mrs. Lambert opened the door to her room and gestured for Anne to follow, closing the door behind her.

"It was neither wise nor proper for you to leave the room without an escort or permission, my dear. Many common people lurk outside these affairs. Muggings and robberies have occurred. The master saw you go out the door, and when he saw the young man speaking to you he was evidently very concerned."

"I must tell you," Mrs. Lambert went on with a quieter voice as if any of the others might be listening at the door, "the master, Cook, and I came to the conclusion that Tom has been swindling us a little at a time in his deliveries. Where two sacks of sugar were charged to the master's bill, only one sack was delivered. This sort of thing had been going on for weeks. Becky, too, had taken tea and coffee from the pantry, which Sybil found under her bed. The master was loath to make any accusations until we were quite sure. Lord Greville has every intention of speaking with the owner of the market. It is more than likely the boy shorted more than just our household, selling the supplies for extra money in his pocket. I suppose it is too late now." Mrs. Lambert sat down on the edge of her bed, obviously tired.

Anne looked down trying to focus and fight back tears. She felt so ashamed.

"The master became very angry. They say he took a swing at the young man. Tom stepped back just as he did, sending my dear master into a stone wall as he lost his balance. He suffered a cut on his lip and a bloody nose, which in turn caused women to scream, as they thought the injury much worse than it was. The young man took off down the street. My acquaintance, Mrs. Grayson, saw the entire unpleasant incident, so embarrassing for Lord Greville. As sure as she was to tell me about it, she will no doubt tell others," Mrs. Lambert said ominously.

"The master left early this morning to take breakfast with his friend, Lord Banks. I received a note from him, and he sent along an additional note to you." The housekeeper took the note from the desk and passed it to Anne.

"Now, if you would not mind reading it elsewhere, I am sore from standing too long last evening. I think I will put my feet up for a bit. There is nothing to do about Becky's departure today. We will inform the authorities in case the girl is so foolish as to return to the area." Mrs. Lambert removed her shoes and lifted her legs with obvious stiffness. She leaned back on her pillow.

"Lord Greville will want a full account of what is missing and as of yet, it is only the supplies and nothing else that seems to be absent. I thought I misplaced my brooch, but I am now of the opinion that Becky took it from my dresser. I will include it in my report to the magistrate.

"I am sorry that the evening did not end as pleasantly as it began, but I believe you still had some fun, and it was nice to see you dance. Perhaps I should have kept closer to you and advised you better." With that, the elderly woman said no more.

"I too am sorry for the trouble I have caused, "Anne said. Mrs. Lambert put up her hand and shook her head.

Anne left the room, apprehensive about the note and feeling humbled by the older woman's evaluation of the evening. Indeed, Anne would have liked the matron to have stayed closer to her and given her guidance. She did not blame Mrs. Lambert for what transpired, though it seemed the housekeeper blamed herself.

Anne took refuge in the rose garden. She could find peace there away from the household and her father who knew nothing of the night's events. She carefully opened the note, the first she ever received from the master. It was special, even if she feared its contents.

31

*J*oseph Banks was dressed and in his study early. He expected the usual Sunday crowd including Wedgwood, Brown, Davy, and perhaps one or two others. They would converge as if it were an arranged meeting of one of the various societies to which they each belonged. This was no official meeting, however, but an informal, friendly congregation of thinking men. They longed for more of their communal discourses on those things in science they deemed most important than a society meeting could grant.

Sir Joseph had the maids clear some of the surfaces of the bookcases and the desk to provide an area for any maps, bureaus of collector's objects, or any other renderings of new discoveries being presented for consideration. Several times, experiments were carried out on his desktop.

Astonished but delighted, he waved his hand when he saw Charles was the first to make an appearance at his door.

"You have missed so many Sundays, I never expect you anymore. What a wonderful surprise."

"I hardly knew it was Sunday, forgive my intrusion." Charles was all seriousness. As he came across the room to where his friend sat chair bound, Sir Joseph saw the bruise and cut on his upper lip. His friend's nose was enlarged and red.

"I trust the other man looks much the worse?" Banks asked Charles, having decided that humor might be the best approach. He did not really suppose Charles engaged in a boxing match.

Lord Greville looked at his friend considering whether he already had news of the previous night's scuffle. He then realized his friend meant only to make a joke. Sir Joseph most likely assumed his injuries had a far different explanation.

"I fell down before I could deliver the blow I intended to give the fellow. I did not come for breakfast. I leave for Wales and stopped by to see you, as I will be away for some months. I have much with which to be engaged at Milford." Charles was tired. He stopped by Bank's Soho home to gather himself a bit before his trip. He felt he had to get away from Paddington. He had dawdled far too long.

"This seems sudden," Sir Joseph remarked.

"A problem with a servant." Charles answered, as it was too difficult to explain.

"Let Lambert handle those affairs, you should not be troubling yourself with such things."

"Yes, I suppose I should have done so, but I did not. Do you remember the phantom in the library?

"Ah yes," Banks replied, looking up his desktop. "Did you discover the identity?"

"Yes, it was the gardener's daughter." Charles said, feeling squeamish.

"George Blake has a daughter?" Banks looked at his friend. "I did not know he had a wife. I am astonished." As Banks thought about the girl and her family, he suddenly came upon a different picture in his mind.

"Oh, no Charles, you did not get yourself involved with the girl?"

"No, no. I merely showed an interest in her ability to draw," Charles answered.

"Oh, I do remember, now. The picture from inside the greenhouse, she is the artist? More surprises!"

"I have allowed her to make drawings of several of the plants in the hothouse. She has a fine eye for detail, and an enthusiasm for life I find I enjoy. I regret that I overstepped my position and the girl's by having Lambert take her to the assembly in Westbourne last night."

"How so, my friend?" Banks was not so interested. These types of relations with servants rarely added up to much. Charles had certainly dealt with worse than this in his past. Who couldn't think of the lovely Lady Hamilton?

"She had not the upbringing to handle such affairs. She left the hall to visit with a young man outside. She might have been exposed to even more ridicule if I had not separated them before he could further compromise her."

Banks began to smile. "Ah, and at what point did your fists come into play?"

"No, I tripped and fell into the stone wall. The boy took off and has not been seen since.

"And George's daughter, did she run, also?"

"I sent her back inside before others saw what had occurred."

"Well, no harm done. She could not be expected to be more than what she is. You had higher hopes for her perhaps? How old is the girl?" Banks thought again of the lovely Emma. Charles had groomed her into quite a gentlewoman. He had done well enough to please the uncle and then Nelson. The woman was legendary, even if Charles' involvement was not.

Just as the clock struck ten, Charles heard someone at the door. The arrival caught Sir Joseph's attention as well. The lord was not ready to explain his facial wounds to anyone else.

"I will take my leave at this point, my friend. I have no wish to hold up the discussion, and I am not in the mood for fellowship. I will let myself out the side door." He rose and shook the seated man's hand.

Sir Joseph patted his hand.

"Take care, Charles. Send word of your return. I have some new ideas for the Royal Society's speakers for next year. I want you to help with the schedule. You will want to attend at least two that I have planned."

"I shall. I hope to come back before the holidays, or the end of the year at the latest."

With that, Charles slipped out to return home and finish his packing for the journey that would take him to his refuge on the coast of Wales.

32

*A*nne heard the master return. She had been listening for him. She hoped for an interview, a meeting she could not solicit. She made her way to the kitchen.

When she inquired how long the master would be staying, the kitchen maid shook her head.

"Not so long. There are several cases packed and ready in the hall. He has given Mrs. Lambert instruction to close the upstairs rooms. He will be away for months."

Anne so wanted to speak with him. She had never had the chance to redeem herself, or repent the impropriety she had committed. She had not been given an opportunity to explain her feelings about Tom's kiss.

The note from the master had been short. The missive gave Anne no relief from her guilt.

Miss Blake,

As you took it upon yourself to leave the ballroom, I was forced to take on the responsibility for your actions. I am sorry if you feel you received undue rudeness. I was greatly disappointed by your choice of company. We are both to blame for the evening's events.

The note was signed without salutation, simply, "CFG."

Anne felt the coldness of the nobleman's words. Anne dreamed of being summoned to the greenhouse. They would talk of her actions at the dance, and she would have the opportunity to make her excuses. The talks in the greenhouse, under the stars, and in the herbs seemed far off memories. The present reality was that she was waiting to hear from a man no longer connected to her with more important affairs on his mind.

Sybil had learned of the master's plans to leave for Wales by afternoon, but thought to build a fire in the master's library as perhaps he would be using the room before his departure. The grates of the fireplace were full of ashes. As Sybil collected them into a bucket, she noticed the edge of one of the papers held a green leaf and a little yellow where part of a flower remained. As Sybil looked closer, she realized the whole stack of papers had been drawings. Her heart sank. These were Anne's drawings. Had the master burned the papers? No, it did not make sense. Then Sybil thought of Becky, and she knew she had the answer. She fished out a few charred paper fragments and rushed off to inform the head housekeeper.

Sybil found Anne in the kitchen. Anne was excited to be summoned. When she asked how the master's mood appeared, Sybil had answered "Grave, very grave, but it is Mrs. Lambert who wishes to see you, not the master."

Anne tried to keep the disappointment in her heart from appearing on her face. Sybil turned to Anne and said, "I am so sorry" as she led the way. Anne could only guess her friend referred to her indiscretion.

Mrs. Lambert called Anne to the back of the hallway and there on a table, she displayed the burnt fragments of two drawings.

"Sybil found these in the library fireplace. Are these your drawings, Anne?" Anne did not need to look any closer. She could only nod at the housekeeper. She was stunned.

"Is it Becky's doing? Do you suppose?" The matron asked the rhetorical question to which they all knew the answer. "The master has been made aware of the loss. I believe he felt you had completed the task you were given with some satisfaction." It was encouragement Anne could not feel.

It was difficult to conjure up what must have happened; Anne could not imagine the depth of Becky's resentment. She remembered Becky's expression as she left for the assembly, sure that the maid had burned her drawings at that point and not subsequent to the dance and Tom's kiss. Anne did not comprehend such bitterness.

"Yes, I can see they are. What a shame," she said, only beginning to comprehend the extent of the housemaid's action. "Did Sybil think they were all burned?"

"Yes, I am afraid so," Mrs. Lambert replied. "I am so sorry, dear. We all are." The elderly housekeeper paused, but then in a lower voice added, "The master expressed his regrets as well."

Anne's thoughts went from the hours of work to thoughts of Lord Greville. She did not think of the destruction of the drawings as a personal loss. As the lord's record of flowers in his greenhouse, the injury was much worse.

"The master wishes to see you after I have spoken with you. He waits in the library." Mrs. Lambert used an austere tone of voice that Anne had never heard before. Anne felt hollow and knew no fulfillment waited at her meeting with his lordship.

He was still angry, as she remained guilty for the shortcomings of the evening, a battered face, and an embarrassment for all still to come. Anne walked numbly through the hall to the library. The feeling of dread was similar to that which she had felt when she answered for her trespass in the library. She could not expect a happy ending would be the result this time.

Anne found Lord Greville staring out the window. He stood with his hands behind his back. He was dressed in his waistcoat for the journey. As Charles turned to face her, she bowed and dared not lift her head until he addressed her. She felt very much put in her place, a very low station indeed. She cowered, waiting for him to speak.

"Come in, Miss Blake," he stated without emotion. She was not "Anne" to him now.

Lord Greville waited several uncomfortable seconds before he spoke. With a sigh, he began.

"It has come to my attention that you have been living on my property without purpose or duty to my household. We are going to put an end to that," he said. He paused, but she kept her eyes down.

"Mrs. Lambert will make inquiries to find you a suitable position elsewhere as soon as possible." He flipped papers on his desk with rude disregard to her presence. He was thoroughly annoyed with her. That was obvious. Anne felt her chin quiver with the knowledge.

"I am aware that you wish to be in the proximity of your father, and that may or may not be a consideration. He is welcome to move closer to you if such a situation presents itself. In the meantime, I expect you to report to Mrs. Lambert, who may give you such duties of which you are capable and which will account an exchange for your food and living quarters here." He hung his cane from his arm and took up his valise. He spoke toward Anne, but never looked her way.

"I have spent too long away from my affairs, and now have much to engage me elsewhere. As the drawings are now unavailable, it is my opinion that a great deal of time was wasted in the cultivation of your artistic endeavors. You are hereby released from any past debt for your trespass in the library." His voice had assumed a haughty air, a baritone full of disdain. He looked at her momentarily.

He paused at the end of his desk before he proceeded. He had seen her face, full of pain. His hard demeanor was no match for the sadness he saw in her face. He wanted to tell her of her talent, a fact obvious to him now. He knew she had done nothing to provoke the burning of the drawings. He felt he might have been just as much to blame. Perhaps it was best this way, he convinced himself. She would have no unfounded expectations of the world. Charles thought of Emma as he looked at the young woman in front of him. He would not play Pygmalion again. He had learned his lesson twice.

Anne heard the man before her make his speech with no evidence they had shared anything special over the last few months. His looks, his manner of speaking, and the way he moved about ignoring her; he was not the same person she had come to know. He seemed to have no disdain for Becky or what the hateful maid had done. He had no thought of the sad situation in which she now found herself.

He was not her Lord Greville, but the one she heard common gossip about, the man who could be cruel and abhorrent in his treatment of others. Perhaps he had sent Emma off as they said. She could believe that now. Who was the man with whom she had spent those precious hours?

"Sir, I will strive to be of help to Mrs. Lambert in any way I can. I am so sorry-," she began, but he interrupted her.

"There is no need for that now, Miss Blake. We must both go on with our lives. I take my leave now, you may go." He waited for her to exit before he moved toward the door, fearing he might catch up with her in the hallway. His austere presence might give way to the aching core within.

Anne curtsied and left at a steady pace, but as she rounded the corner into the short hallway, she ran into Coleman, almost bowling over the elderly valet.

The startled face of the lord's manservant held an expression that changed from surprise to admonishment to disgust. The metamorphosis was unmistakable, and Anne felt soiled by his look, as was the man's intention.

Escaping to the outdoors, Anne ran back to the cottage before the distress of sobs erupted from inside, stealing her breath and pulling her legs out from under her as she stumbled across the threshold.

The master had not given her a chance to explain. He did not care. She had been a fool to think she had meant something to the nobleman. He had made use of her mediocre skill, and her efforts had turned out for naught.

Now, she knew the one evening at the ball had been a singular event. She had failed, failed to stay within the bounds of propriety. She would not have another chance. The limit of who she was born to be was obvious. She had fooled herself for long enough, thinking that by some lucky circumstance her life would turn out differently. It was not to be.

She would not hear from the Duke's family. A vision of Jane's kind face provided little solace as she realized that her departure from Lord Greville's household would also come with some degree of shame. It would not take long for the likes of Mrs. Grayson to spread a story that would carry serious repercussions for her future employment. She would regret even more that she had brought dishonor to Lord Greville and his household.

Anne hoped her father would be spared any insult. That Lord Greville referred to her father moving on from his manor with her was especially frightful. Her father would be appalled at a change in his relationship with Lord Greville. Anne knew her father was too elderly to move or take a new position.

The impending separation from Lord Greville and his household loomed as her greatest distress. Such melancholy came upon her when she thought of it. It would take all her strength to face her future. A door on the world Lord Greville had allowed her to look through was slamming shut, leaving her on the other side.

Lord Greville sat back in the seat of his chaise as it pulled away from Paddington Green. He was still trying to convince himself he had been right to dismiss Anne so mercilessly. The sadness of what he had done bore down on his soul, and he rubbed his forehead, weary with emotion and distraught by the empathy he felt for the girl. He could only tell himself it came about as it should have.

He should never have grown so close. Somewhere during his amusement, he should have seen her for who she was, not making her up to be something she was not. If he had only sent her off at the start, none of this would have occurred.

Yet, he thought of her entrance to the ball. She was a bright spot in that room. She did not look out of place. The matrons had paid special attention to her. Peter had immediately stepped forward to claim the first two dances. Tom lured her outside; it was as simple as that.

He remembered trying to explain to Coleman his motive in allowing the girl to attend the dance, and the old valet had argued back.

"The girl is found guilty of intruding your house, and you reward by codling her. Then you wish to show your appreciation by including her in your society? Perhaps next time you will take me to the dance. At least, I would not embarrass you. The girl is the gardener's daughter. She is not in any way your responsibility. I cannot understand your thinking on this situation, my lord."

Coleman was still in a foul mood that morning. The lord had avoided any further discussion with his manservant. He did not wish to admit that the old valet had been right. He would think no more about it. Let Lambert find the girl employment as soon as possible. Leave the old gardener where he was, unless of course he wanted to go.

The lord stopped his thoughts there with the shock that George might leave as he had mentioned. Charles could not calculate the loss that would be. The gardener's knack for knowing each plant's needs was irreplaceable. Here he was leaving for an extended period of time with an easy spirit knowing the old gardener would take care of everything outdoors as Lambert would take care of everything indoors. What had he said? He tried to recall his threats to Miss Blake.

It would be no easy task to install a substitute. A new gardener might know how to trim back irises, but would he know how to tend an arctic moss? It would be risky allowing the care of the hothouse to a novice. He was leaving his garden for a period of months. He thought about any of the undergardeners who currently worked at Paddington. His thoughts went back to Anne.

The afternoon when his sisters were visiting, Charles had realized that it was Anne in the roses. The hand on the doorframe of the library was the same hand that pointed the way to George's location; the same slender hands for which he had purchased rose-scented gloves. She really looked like a young man to him that day, and then that fragrance. He could not restrain a chuckle.

The young woman executed some fine drawings, lost now to the maid's jealousy. Charles imagined his attention to Anne might have added some degree of hostility. More than once, Becky had appeared in his library without reason, giggled a sentence or two, and curtsied out again. If he had desired an arrangement with the girl, it would have come easily.

Lord Greville knew two of Anne's drawings were saved. He had held onto the drawing of inside the greenhouse that he found when Anne hastily exited his library months ago. He had planned to one day return it. In addition, he had the drawing of the man and woman in the rose garden. The picture was a souvenir, a trinket of what never was. He patted the valise that held the drawings beside him.

"Have a good journey, sir," Lucas said at the door after his master's cases were loaded. "We eagerly await your return."

"Thank you, Lucas. Tell Cook I want as much pear preserves as she is willing to make. Please arrange for the additional gravel on the drive. Do not, under any circumstances, allow my brother to exchange my horses for any others! And one last thing, Lucas, please keep an eye on George. He is failing, I fear."

This last comment he made blithely, avoiding overstating his concern for the elderly gardener upon the separation from his daughter, which was inevitable. Lambert would find some use for the girl and set her right for a position elsewhere. Some part of him hoped he would see her again

33

*W*hen Lord Greville climbed into the waiting carriage, he chose to sit on the seat facing the direction from which he was leaving. Usually, he liked to sit on the other side of the carriage facing where he was going. When his traveling partner, a Mr. William Hartley, joined him, he sat opposite, and they set out immediately. So it was that the nobleman spent the first day of his journey looking toward Paddington rather than away.

The lord and Hartley shared the acquaintance of Samuel Pepys Cockerell, an architect and great, great nephew of the famous diarist. Hartley, a surveyor and also an architect, was making the trip to Carmarthen to aid in the building of a tower in honor of Admiral Nelson. Strange to think that even here he could not avoid thoughts of Emma.

Lord Greville spoke of the plans for Milford of which the man had heard only a little. He was pleased that Hartley was not overly verbose. The traveler relaxed and fell asleep shortly after their conversation. The nobleman kept his eyes focused out the window.

As the hours of the journey passed, they traversed from more populated towns to less inhabited villages. Traffic lessened and the countryside opened up as the coach made its way west toward the now setting sun.

Coleman would follow in an economical conveyance with the additional luggage. The valet felt it was not fitting to be seen accompanying his master in such a luxurious accommodation as a private coach. He would be delivered to care for his master at each stop within hours of the lord's arrival.

That evening, as darkness descended, Charles surrendered to the sometimes lulling, sometimes jarring motion of the carriage box, allowing it to rock him to sleep. He startled awake when they exchanged horses. Hartley also napped, so Charles felt no embarrassment for his own dozing. It would be only a few more hours before they stopped for a longer break and a meal. By then he would be weary of the journey.

Each time he traveled to Milford, the distance seemed shorter and the time passed more quickly. He counted off the miles with the knowledge of what came next, but the journey was still a long one. He could endure the trip, aware that a different life waited at the other end. In Milford, the Right Honorable Charles Greville was treated as a king. He had a secretary, two footmen, several maids, and a local woman who came in to cook. He even had a cat, a continuous annoyance to his valet who objected to the fur.

"The animal sheds, my lord. It is in my nose. It is on your jacket, now. The animal is unclean."

"Coleman, I believe I see "the animal" bathing here in the sun every morning," Charles said, pointing to the wool rug by his desk.

"Humph" would be the valet's only reply as he stormed off.

Charles did not revisit the fiasco at the ball. No need to worry about the delivery boy or the maid who ran off with him. It was doubtful they would be seen again. With a little more difficulty, he tried not to picture the face framed in dark curls, stricken with tearless pain.

Her innocence was her enemy. He felt a bit of shame that he did nothing to protect her. He would not be there when the rumors made their full rounds and the damage was complete. He was far removed from doing anything about it now, a thought he should have found comforting.

Once again, the carriage was moving. The lantern on the corner of the coach's frame created a circle of light on the glass window at his side. The wavering light was hypnotizing. Once more, he slipped into a shallow sleep, full of dreams.

He was inside his greenhouse, looking for something lost. He felt panic as he did not know what it was that was lost, and so it was impossible to look for it. He floated around the corner by the large fig tree and saw a girl with shiny black eyes and long tendrils of hair that touched the ground, spreading out like roots of an old tree. She held a giant crystal in her hand extended toward him as if offering a gift. Her hair completely obscured her face.

As the dream continued, he was not sure who he was dealing with, but he knew he wanted that crystal. When he reached to take it from her, she balked saying, "I will gladly let you have it, but remember it is my heart." Without any thought, he took the jewel from her. As he held it in his own hand, he realized it was merely ice, which melted into a handful of water. Shocked at the outcome, he was about to console the girl when his body jolted forward and he was awake. The carriage came to an abrupt stop, this time for a warm meal.

He could not entirely shake the image of the girl in his dream. With that came the expression on Anne's face and the residual shame for treating her so poorly. Had not Lambert tried to warn him?

"Is she ready for such exposure?" the housekeeper had asked. Charles had failed to examine this question earnestly. Though he did not blame Lambert, he might have chosen a more suitable chaperone. Even Coleman had aided him seeing things more clearly.

"You are a kind man, but you have obligations to fulfill in more important matters. It is ludicrous for you to spend the time on one of the thousands of less fortunate cases compared to the help your harbor or your scientific work will provide for us all."

It was Coleman's usual overstatement, but the man was a poet of sorts. His grand statements had the sound, if not always the substance, of something profound. The loss of the drawings added to the frustration. His time with Anne had not been as much of a waste as it might have appeared to others. He had feelings for the young woman that went deeper than anyone was aware. Charles shook off this inner debate as the footman opened the carriage door and he entered the inn.

Two days later, early in the afternoon, the coach began its descent to the town of Milford. Charles was fully revitalized. He had slept soundly at night. As the miles continued to pass, he put an end to his mental torment over everything he had left behind in Paddington.

When the carriage emerged from the wooded hills onto the peninsula of wasteland and moors, he was excited to be close to his destination. He had come to love this landscape of grays and purples, the soft roll of terrain, and the spaciousness of the treeless horizon. The journey had made him stiff and sore, but all would fade quickly with the activity and warm exchanges upon his arrival. He looked out the window, waiting to catch the first view of the estuary that waited like a giant lake below.

As they came along the edge of the coast and he caught that first glimpse of the ocean inlet, a strong fishy smell filled the coach. Charles found the salty stench invigorating. Life here was of the sea and the men who traversed it; ships, tides, and a wonderful world of riches.

Milford was a grid of only a few intersecting streets. The inn and the best houses stood on the street overlooking the ocean from a safe distance above. The harbor's protection from wind gave the deep port the appearance of a calm body of water rather than part of the giant tidal ocean. It was a safe and secure place where even ships heavy in the water were able to dock. There was room for thousands to be harbored if necessary.

The late Admiral Nelson had claimed the location the single, finest harbor capable of safely housing the entire British Navy! His comment may have been excessive, but Charles had appreciated his opinion, as did much of the nation. What a strange visit that had been, Emma and Lord Nelson viewing his harbor, and Charles so needing the show of support from the naval veteran. How awkward it might have been if not for Emma's conciliatory manner that had put them all at ease.

Charles resided in a small house at the end of a row of homes. It was quaint and close, giving the nobleman a coziness he loved. He liked to pretend he was a member of the group of seafarers with whom he lived so closely, decorating his home with sextants, charts and a telescope at the window.

When his own countrymen failed to show interest in his plans for a harbor, Lord Greville sought the help of the people from New England. He convinced the Quaker folks to return to the home of their forefathers. As smart business men, the triangle with America, England, and the newly explored world did not elude them.

The lord had high hopes of developing this corner of Wales, and specifically the local seacoast, into an asset. Though the whale oil production surpassed the needs of America, it was just catching up to British consumption. Other goods were coming through the port from which fortunes could be made.

Looking out along the cliff above sea level, Charles loved the way the rocks surrounding the structures of the village matched the gray of the weathered wood and slate. The spots of color from planter boxes on the porches of many of the homes adorned the otherwise colorless landscape. The sea's mist softened the edges of the entire scene.

The Folger and Starbuck families came first. Eventually, the Starbuck's cousins, the Roches, joined them. All three families held title to several whaling ships, which used Milford harbor as their homeport. They brought their families, their religion, and their customs.

It was the father, Timothy Folger, who with the aid of his cousin, Benjamin Franklin, made a map of the Gulf Stream current which proved indispensable to the success of ships sailing across the Atlantic and home again. The warm current rode on top of the colder water like a river in the ocean. Whales tended to live and travel along the edges of the flow.

The Folger family also engaged in candle making, using whale oil for a brighter, smokeless flame. As the oil was slow to congeal in the cold, it gained popularity as a lamp fuel, even though the price exceeded that of other lamp oils. Charles made use of the candles as well as purchasing several whale oil lamps with which to light his home here and at Paddington.

Whale oil was not only important to London for lighting, but also as a lubricant for machinery, leather making, batching flax and jute, and oiling wool. The whalebones were a by-product of no small account. The largest bones and cartilage were used for the body of carriages, the smaller bones for fishing rods, buggy whips, umbrellas, and women's skirt hoops. The very smallest cartilage was used as stays on articles of clothing such as corsets. The holds of ships returned with not only the valuable oil, but these products as well.

Charles kept trading at the forefront of his development ideas, but it was a naval shipyard that he ultimately planned for the harbor. Products and worldwide trade could suffer under the whims of fashion or change with new discoveries or ideas. A shipyard, especially in a time of war, would provide the constancy he needed for success.

Lord Greville's arrival to Milford was met with celebrations. The heads of household gathered outside the lord's door to greet him as he stepped from the carriage. Although he was weary from his journey, the reception renewed him as he knew it would.

"Thank you, all!" Charles shouted to the crowd. "I am indeed as glad to see you as you are to celebrate my return." He retreated into his house as the crowd dispersed. He wished to stretch his legs and take a short walk before making a formal appearance at a dinner given in his honor.

The mist was not unusually cold, and the wind was light as he made his way along the coast. The nobleman was not usually prone to bird watching, but from this vantage point, he could not but notice the various beach dwellers. He did not expect to see any puffins this time of year, but he did think he might spot the impressive oystercatcher with its black feathered coat, and large, red bill. It gave the nobleman great joy to reunite with these birds and this life.

As Charles made his way down to the water's edge, he was thrilled by the prospect of this first walk in the sand. His boots made the only footprints in the otherwise blank canvas washed smooth by the last high tide. He breathed the moist salt air deeply. It relieved his sore heart, and he did not allow any thoughts of Paddington to interrupt the healing.

The evening was filled with stories and laughter, toasts and prayers. Tomorrow would be busy with plans to inspect the church, the new storerooms, and the docks. He would keep in mind what he had seen in London.

Most mornings began with fresh biscuits and coffee. The Folgers opened a bakery to make the dry biscuits that sailors took to sea. The thin, dry, flat bread did not develop mold easily or weigh heavily, an important factor when loading the holds of ships heading out over the sea for months. The coffee came as an import from several locales. It was new to the trading scheme, but the drink was rapidly gaining in popularity. The beans were roasted into a dark, oily, and invigorating drink that Lord Greville found he preferred to tea.

Afternoons included a meal prepared and served to him with some ritual and great pride. His cook made chowder that he preferred to the finest fillets. He could have eaten it daily if she would have permitted. She also created a constant flow of sloe berry tarts and apple pies.

The nobleman watched ships return to port when the North Atlantic ice sheet extended into the blue water. The town bustled with the new arrivals. Except that his plans for the naval college moved forward so slowly, life in Milford was altogether pleasant. And so it might have continued if not for the shipwreck of the vessel, Jane.

Storms hit the coast with a vehemence Lord Greville had never experienced in either Warwickshire or London. The ocean bred squalls that churned up sea swells, crashing into the first land they met. Boats in the harbor were protected, but those just coming to shore were in jeopardy of being thrown on the rocks and broken into bits by the strong waves of a violent sea. As a storm subsided, fog would form, making the outline of the coast invisible, a recipe for disaster. So it was for the Jane. Eleven of her crew met their fate on the rocks just a mile from shore. The village suffered greatly. Each villager was either related to or friends with one or more of the crew from the ship. Funerals were held in twos and threes until all the men were either buried or taken back out into the salty graveyard if their families preferred.

Not one of the villagers looked to Lord Greville with blame, but he felt responsible for the disaster. Over and over, his thoughts reviewed how they might have saved the crew. He deliberated over what could be done to warn ships away from such a catastrophe, so close to land. He took on the people's sorrow with his own and deemed himself a failure.

Lord Greville wandered the hills above the sea, quieting his mind and escaping the sounds of quiet mourning that had taken over the shouts of progress. He found the beach much wider than usual with a low tide. He steered around large piles of seaweed ripped from the kelp beds by the strong waves of the storm. The long brown strands were twisted together and their color brought forth an image of a mass of curls. The view of the back of Miss Blake's head and one wandering curl played in his mind. He tried to escape, but the vision stayed with him as he left the beach and started up the cliff. He hurried on as if pursued; his eyes glued to the ground.

Directly above him a hawk let out a shrill cry. His attention to the trail was interrupted, and he lost his balance, sending him off the edge. A patch of thorny gorse broke his fall from the rock cliff saving him from a more serious injury.

Charles stayed where he was to catch his breath; his heart thudded as adrenaline ran through his veins. He leaned back and another image of Miss Blake came before him. She was bending over him, with her hand on his forehead. It was a comfort to have her so close. He remembered the night of the hailstorm. Indeed, she must have been there. The doctor had commented on the care of his wound. The words" my angel" came from far away, yet exited his lips.

He allowed the thoughts he had locked away to emerge. He had a sudden urge to see her. She could ease his aching heart and calm his questioning soul.

He wondered about the aftermath of the dance. Had she been fed upon by the gossips in Society papers? Had they mentioned his involvement? He certainly would have made tongues wag by dancing with her, but he never had the chance. Perhaps, she had moved on to another position. He would pen a letter to Lambert to inquire of the general state of Paddington, how George Blake was, and off-handedly ask about his daughter.

Along the bottom edge of the outcropping where the going was easier, he found a clump of sea lavender still in bloom. He picked several of the purple spikes. Coleman was sure to complain about the "weeds," but the bouquet again reminded him of Miss Blake. That day in his garden seemed so long ago.

When he came in from his walk, Coleman cried out in alarm as if the gentleman had returned with a missing limb.

"Sit down, immediately! You are bleeding! Your arm has a serious wound." Coleman took the cuff of his master's shirt and gingerly rolled it away and up the gentleman's arm.

The lord turned his head to see that he had scratched the back of his arm, probably when he fell into the gorse bush. The blood had seeped through his shirtsleeve and caused Coleman's reaction. It was not a serious scratch even if it had bled profusely. He smiled at his servant's concern.

"Ah yes, it looks as if the bush might have scored one in this battle, but I will live to fight another day," he joked. Sitting back in his chair, knowing that resisting the valet would do no good, he surrendered as Coleman knelt to take off the master's salty boots and ran off to get a basin of hot water and bandage for the small scratch, muttering something about infection.

After Coleman finished doctoring the cut, Charles asked him to bring paper, pen, and ink. He would write to Paddington immediately.

34

*A*t Paddington, life had slowed down to a monotonous pace as consistent as the dreary weather. The days were an endless grey fog that merged morning into midday and midday into afternoon. The only change came about when the fog disappeared into the dark. Rain and wet snows came and went, but it was the fog that persisted in between.

The flower garden was clipped back to ground level, removing the disorder of the dead and dying remnants of the once lush and colorful landscape. The last roses had disappeared. Only red hips dotted an otherwise bland view. Most of the vegetable beds were covered with loads of rotten leaves. Outdoors, all was dormant, covered with silver frost.

In the glasshouse, some plants lost their leaves and died back to stems. Many of the potted foliage plants would remain the same with no new growth for months. Here and there, tropical plants attempted to bloom, confused by the season's change.

No rumors were heard about the night of the dance, though in time the household knew something of the matter. Mrs. Lambert's fears about Mrs. Grayson were unfounded. The elderly gossip had taken pity on Lord Greville's ward. The matron found it important to accept any young lady presented by the son of an Earl. She spread the word that the scuffle between the young man and Lord Greville was the result of a lewd comment directed toward the girl who had stepped to the door for fresh air.

Anne did not care what account came of the evening. It was the last conversation with Lord Greville that tormented her. The night of the ball only signified the end of their relationship, a loss she could barely endure. A sad depression came over her that went unnoticed. She stayed quiet and to herself. She did not complain.

As the daylight hours grew shorter and shorter, Anne's father slept more and more. In the dark, she could hear his breathing; a gasp in, a wheeze out. Anne tried a variety of herbal teas, but he did not seem to improve. She sent him off each morning with increasing concern and the strip of wool she had knitted tucked into the collar of his jacket. He balked at her efforts insisting "I am fine, girl," and waved her off.

At first, Mrs. Lambert found small tasks for Anne as she had been instructed to do. She also made an attempt at finding a suitable position for the young woman elsewhere to no avail. With Becky gone, the head housekeeper decided to employ Anne with the maid's share of the chores.

Mrs. Lambert was also aware of George Blake's failing health. The elderly gardener moved about hunched and slow. Reassured that leaving Anne be was the right decision for the moment, Mrs. Lambert thought no more about finding other employment.

"I have decided Anne should help here in the house for the time being," she told Cook. Cook agreed that removing Anne from her father at this time might put the elderly gardener's well being in jeopardy.

The housekeeper had Anne scrape the old wax from the banisters of the stairs, redefining the curved designs carved into the wood. She instructed Anne to wash, press, and drape the curtains downstairs, room by room. She had Anne wash the windows, cleaning each of the small diamonds of glass in the leaded frames with the fold of a rag.

By the third week, when no further duties were obvious to Mrs. Lambert, Anne offered ideas of her own. The sting of Lord Greville's words was still fresh. She took on the hardest tasks in an effort to repay the master for the trouble she had caused. Mrs. Lambert and Cook watched the once happy and spirited girl turned into a shadow of her previous self. She was silent and undefined.

One afternoon when the sun had made a rare appearance, Anne spoke to Mrs. Lambert about cleaning the minerals in the cases in the library. The housekeeper had no knowledge of such a task.

"Do you suppose they need to be cleaned, Anne?"

"I have seen the master do so. I have heard him complain that they needed cleaning. I know where he keeps his polishing cloth and brush."

Mrs. Lambert was well aware of Anne's remorse, knowing the girl would indeed pay close attention to the master's prize possessions, his rocks. It was evident she had spent some time in the lord's company discussing such a chore.

Anne found the key to the cabinet where she had watched the lord retrieve it. She took each specimen from the bureau and arranged it in the same position on a rag in the sun on the floor. She took the tools from the desk drawer. One by one, she polished the crystal surfaces and dusted clean each specimen with the brush, then returned the sparkling mineral example to clean shelves exactly where they sat before. She pictured Lord Greville as he had performed the duty during her mineral lesson. It was a small consolation to think Lord Greville might admire his collection when he returned.

"Those do look so much brighter," Mrs. Lambert remarked when she came to check on Anne's progress. "I did not know the master's rocks could be polished to such a shine."

Weeks passed, and though Cook and Mrs. Lambert watched the changes in Anne, neither knew what could be done for the girl. Though she completed each task required of her, she took no joy from her life, and no longer visited the house otherwise.

At church, Anne prayed for forgiveness. She prayed for her father's health. She prayed for Lord Greville's safety. She would have prayed for a change if she had felt she deserved it. These Sundays, Anne came straight home from church and did not walk on the Green even when others were doing so.

George Blake watched his daughter's mood become somber as fall became winter. He believed life was made of much hard work and little pleasure. He never asked about the dance. He was satisfied that his daughter had come to accept her station, and he no longer questioned her working as a housemaid. Each evening they ate supper together in silence, and then each would retire to their beds.

Lord Greville had been away from the manor for close to two months. It was yet another grey day, exactly like the day before. Anne went to her room after their evening meal as usual. She was weary, a fatigue that left her with aching bones and a throbbing head, yet unable to fall asleep.

Late in the night, Anne was alerted to her father's coughing. Though he often coughed, this time it was unrelenting. When she heard him gasping for air between spasms, she pulled on her robe and went to him. She found her father sitting on the side of his bed, barely able to catch his breath. She bent to him, but he waved her off.

"The fire is so low, it smokes," Anne said, frightened by the choking cough.

Anne stirred the fire and set another log on which quickly flamed up and lit the room. In the firelight Anne saw the elderly man shaking uncontrollably. She went to him again, putting her arm around him. She found his shirt was soaked through and cold. As she helped him into the dry shirt, she felt his skin burning through the fabric. It startled her.

"Father, I will make some tea to calm your cough."

Her father made no answer, but slumped into the corner as if asleep.

She helped him drink a cup of the tea, a combination of herbs she had harvested the day she spoke with Lord Greville about her mother. Though she worried about her father's cough, it was the fever that troubled her most. The herbs would lower his body's temperature and give him comfort to sleep, as well as ease the congestion in his lungs, the shortness of breath, and rapid beat of his heart.

Anne rolled an extra blanket into a pillow to support his head, keeping him upright. After a time, her father seemed soothed, his coughing eased, his temperature declined, and his breathing, though shallow, was no longer as difficult. As he slipped back to sleep, his throaty wheeze was the only sound. Anne returned to her bed.

In the dim light of a new day, Anne awoke to hear her father coughing once more. She went to him again, worried he might leave the cottage as he saw the pale sky of morning. His whole torso seemed to lift in his effort to take a breath. Anne repeated her rounds. Once again his shirt was wet, and his body trembled, but this time when she gave him the tea he almost choked trying to sip between coughing. She sat with him in the corner and he finally dozed off. She was also tired and napped as he did.

Throughout the day, Anne repeated her nursing, adding herbs to the tea she prepared and coating his chest with an aromatic liniment. Each time, her father would sleep a bit before the cough resumed. His fever came and went, but his lethargy increased and in time, he seemed to slip from grogginess to a stupor in which he was no longer able to drink. The cough was replaced by shallow, raspy breathing. Late in the afternoon, the fever returned and his chest heaved harder with each breath, Anne realized this sickness needed more than her care could provide.

She was afraid to leave her father, but resolved to do so before dark. She would consult with Cook and allow Mrs. Lambert to call a physician. Anne knew her father did not wish such attentions, but she feared he was in grave danger and in need of medical knowledge she did not have.

When she woke from a short nap, she was alarmed that she had slept at all. She was stiff and sore, propped up against the wall. It was early evening and not quite dark. The fire showed only small coals and there was little light left outside coming through the small window. Anne adjusted her position slightly trying not to disturb her father now at peace and quiet. He did not wake. She looked down at him in the late dim light and saw with horror that his chest no longer moved up and down.

Sometime during the short time she slept, he had slipped away from this hard world. She offered a faint smile to the darkness. She could find some peace knowing he would be reunited at last with his wife and son.

Anne sat paralyzed. As long as she lingered here, she would not be forced to acknowledge her father's death. She could not swallow. If only she could suspend the beating of her heart and still the pulse that throbbed in her wrist, she too could join her family's happy reunion. The harsh truth was that she had been left behind, alone.

Anne could not think beyond holding her father close as his body formed into hers for this last time together. With nightfall came the reality of the inevitable, and what she must do. She cleaned and dressed her father before going to the house and the beginning of her life without him.

35

*M*en took her father's body away. She was kept in the kitchen until they were gone. Everyone in the household was subdued and quiet. They gave Anne their sincere condolences. Cook watched with sadness as Anne hurried back to the cottage as soon as she was allowed. There was nothing to do but leave her to grieve.

For two days, Anne stayed in the cottage. On the third day she was drawn outdoors. She stared ahead without any thought of where she might be going. She proceeded through the sleeping garden like a wandering spirit. Her mind matched the dormancy of winter.

As Anne drifted through the door of the hothouse, the warmer interior embraced her. Her gaze rested on the bench where she first saw Lord Greville. That view changed her life, a secret she would hold forever. Anne walked to the bench and took her seat as if she were to draw, though she had buried her art supplies deep in her trunk on the day Lord Greville left for Wales.

Sunlight washed across the area where she had sketched for so many hours. Anne noticed the clusters of minerals still sat in a row on the windowsill. They had not been touched for months. The long rays of the winter sun came sideways through the glass panes of the hothouse and at just the perfect angle to shine through one of the rocks.

Beside the clear quartz crystal stretched a tiny, bright rainbow. It was a small miracle and a clear message to Anne. She was sure it implied that Lord Greville would soon return. She did not need to expound. Lord Greville was her only hope, and she rested in the knowledge he would soon arrive.

In Milford, Lord Greville had been pensive, sharpening the point on his quill before dipping it in ink to write his note to Lambert. He searched for the words that might bring him to the subject of Miss Blake. Before he could do so, Coleman rushed into the room.

"This has come for you, my lord," he said anxiously.

Lord Greville recognized Lambert's handwriting. He noticed she had paid an extra penny to post as quickly as such a missive could travel. He ripped the letter open, his interest piqued. After the usual salutations, Mrs. Lambert informed the lord of George Blake's illness and subsequent passing. She noted that the undergardener, Danforth, had come to tend the greenhouse since George's death. Lambert was not sure what arrangements should be made for continuing the man's service.

The housekeeper referred to Anne briefly, saying that she still had not found a situation for George's daughter; and now with her father's death, she wondered what should be done. She mentioned that Anne seemed quite lost. Lambert let off saying she felt the household was well in hand for now, but awaited his instructions with regards to the care of the gardens and any other thoughts he might have about Miss Blake.

"Is there a reply, your lordship?" Coleman asked.

314

"No, no reply. It is necessary for me to return to Paddington at once."

Coleman was surprised and could only guess at the content of the letter. It was not his place to inquire. He sent the messenger off and left to pack the lord's bags.

That day in Milford the skies were clear, but a dark grey layer could be seen far out to the west, making its way slowly toward land. If Charles left without delay, he might travel inland ahead of the impending storm. He explained to Coleman that George Blake had died. He wanted his trunks packed and his papers organized for the return trip. Within two hours, the nobleman was on the road home, having sent word and payment ahead at the tollgates to expedite his trip.

He spent most of the journey thinking about Anne. He should have never left her without seeing to her situation and making some arrangement for her. How could he have been so thoughtless to the point of being cruel? He believed he loved her, but what good could come from such a declaration? He did know he wished to comfort her more than anything else. The slow passing miles prolonged his agony.

Two nights later, Lord Greville arrived home after dark. Upon his arrival back in London, he made one important visit before he returned to Paddington. He stopped briefly to see Sir Joseph. Though he thought to seek Anne out upon his return, he dreaded the state in which he might find her. He would wait until morning.

With the first light, Charles summoned Lambert who spoke about the events surrounding George's death. She spoke of the change in Anne.

"She is so forlorn. I would say almost empty. She is, after all, quite without relatives or connections. Yesterday, Lucas took coal and some wood for her stove. He says she sits at the table much of the day and has rarely gone out. She has never come to the house to my knowledge."

Charles stood with his elbow cupped in his hand and his finger patted his face as he thought of the girl's previous temperament, so cheerful and full of life. His gaze looked out toward the back corner of his property.

Anne had napped with her head on the table using her father's sweater as a pillow. She came quickly awake with a thought. She staggered to the shelf above her father's bed. Dust had settled on all her father's treasures. She looked across the items, the symbols of her father's life: his favorite trowel, a knife and sharpening stone, the tools of his trade. Her fingers held his burnt out pipe, the single indulgence he allowed himself, and then moved to the silhouette of his wife, his one true love.

Anne took up the oval frame that held the crumbling portrait of her mother. Her tears cleared small spots on the glass. The lack of features of the silhouette was similar to her memories of her mother; nothing specific remained. So much of her mother existed only as a shadow of what had once been so real. Now her father was gone, and she could not allow the same to happen. She found paper, pen, and ink in her trunk and set about drawing her father's profile at once, fearing each moment took away a little more of her memory.

Cook sent Lucas to take Anne bread and cheese. He stirred her fire and brought in wood enough to keep it going for another day and night. He also brought the message from Lord Greville requesting Anne's presence in the library at ten. She nodded. She would come to the house at ten.

Anne looked down at her clothes and realized she would need to bathe and change from the dress she had worn for two days. She looked at her figure. There was much less of her than months ago. She moved the teakettle to the stove and began to organize a bath.

She brushed her curls, working to remove tangles she had no energy to comb out during her mourning. She felt she did not deserve any beauty outside until she reckoned with the shameful state of her inner self. She no longer thought of Tom. She had been fooled, and she felt no animosity against the dark-haired boy. She did not loathe him, but herself.

Anne tied up her hair with the same bit of black ribbon she'd been wearing for days, without concern for how it might look. As she took the first step out of the cottage, old memories came to mind.

She entered the hall from the kitchen. Mrs. Lambert opened the library door and waved her through, patting her back as she did. The old housekeeper closed the door quietly, leaving the two to their solemn reunion. Lord Greville came around to the front of the desk as Anne entered the room. The lord was shocked at the girl's appearance. It broke his heart to see her so slight with flat dark hair, grey circles under her eyes, and a dull complexion.

Anne did not stop. She came with a steady cadence, making her way across the room to where he stood. Lord Greville witnessed her non-stop progression and opened his arms to receive her. She came into the waiting half circle, shuddered, and let the tears come. She could be brave no longer. She surrendered. Charles let her cry as he held her in his steadying embrace.

He supported her as the sobs came on and her legs seemed to give out. When she regained her footing, she tilted her head up to look into his face. He, too, surrendered to pressure his heart could no longer struggle against. He placed a small kiss on her forehead and continued to kiss her cheeks, salty with tears. As she offered no resistance, he moved his lips to hers, hesitating for only a moment before placing them gently where he had thought he might so many times months ago. Their embrace strengthened as the kiss continued and Anne responded to his advance.

She did not think. She did not question. She allowed her heart to tell the lord all she felt in her kiss.

He had imagined this moment on his journey home. He did not reason with himself about the meaning of his approach or her submission. He just let it be.

The lord led Anne to a chair and set her down. He pulled another chair close to hers. He passed her his handkerchief, waiting as she regained her composure and his own breath returned. He took her hands in his.

"I must speak with you," he said. "Your father has been buried." He looked at the girl's face to see if she could tolerate this conversation before he continued.

"I have sent word to the church for the procurement of the plot and a stone marker is to be made. The date of your father's birth was given to me by Mrs. Lambert. The church warden will take care of the setting of the stone." Those were difficult sentences. He paused to swallow and proceed as the girl seemed to retain her calm. "I did not offer more inscriptions, but of course you may. Some like to indicate a sentiment, but it follows that your father was a simple man of few words. If you wish to make an addition, I will make the arrangements."

Anne looked into the lord's eyes. She tried to read what she saw there. She did not wish to imagine more than what was real, and she could not be sure of anything that had just happened.

"No, you have served my father as he always enjoyed serving you." She could say no more as tears were waiting to flow.

"I don't want you to worry. I must travel into town this morning, but when I return, I would have another meeting with you. You may wait here if you wish."

She shook her head and he escorted her to the door. She did not understand how their relationship might progress. She did not attempt another kiss. Later she would make it clear. Her desire was to be with him always.

In the afternoon, he sent word through Sybil that he wished to meet her in his library once more. This time, she entered unannounced as she knew he expected her. He saw her come to him directly, but he only held her in his arms. He closed his eyes as he put his cheek in her hair perhaps for the last time. He drew in the scent of her, but did not turn her for a kiss.

He was surprised by his strength. He pulled himself away from her as he fetched another chair and sat her close, but not touching. He thought to take her hands again, but he would want all of her if he did. He leaned to her, but kept the gap that was necessary for what he was about to do.

Anne felt him pull away, just as he had in the greenhouse when the orchid had finally brought them together. He held her in his arms, but there was no kiss. He did not sit next to her. She would not tell him of her feelings though they wanted to be shouted out. If he did not love her, he did not need to know. She would keep her love with her other secrets.

Charles heard the words he spoke as if they came from someone else. They were indeed so opposed to what he thought he would say. He had imagined so many other conversations on his way home, but his selfish desires would be denied. He would not misuse this woman's youthful spirit for his needs. She deserved a young strong love, not the kind of relationship a future with him could offer. Though he felt she would have agreed to any decision he made for her, he would not let her commit. He would push her away quickly before he changed his mind.

Anne did not speak what shouted from her heart. She could stay and take care of him. She could make new drawings as spring came on. She could be a housemaid if necessary to be near him, but she could tell, he intended to send her away.

"You may remain until you feel you are able to travel, but of course, you cannot remain here. I have found a position for you, but we can discuss that when you are ready. I do not wish to compel you to do anything to which you are opposed, but there is little for you here now."

Anne reckoned with his plan. He was entirely right in all he said. Without his love, there was little here for her. The roots of connection she thought she had spread since her arrival did not hold against the wind of the events that followed. She had come up empty handed in it all, and that is what frightened her. Having never faced the world without someone else's direction, Anne had no experience in steering her own course. She wanted all to be well with the world even as her small corner crumbled. She would follow his advice and direction. He did not want her to stay, that was clear. His kiss had stood for little in his life, but she would always have it as a memory and nothing more.

Blotting her tears and wiping her nose, Anne sniffled away the last of the tears and took a deep breath so that she could speak.

"I am obliged to you for taking care of these things. I have no path in this world. I can pack the few belongings I own and be prepared for the new situation as soon as possible. I do not wish to be a burden to any here. You have all been so kind. As you have said, there is little for me here now."

Anne could not look at the lord's face, at the edges of his eyes or the brows she tried so often to draw. He had truly been kind; and when it mattered most, he had been the aid she knew he would be. She was embarrassed to have kissed him with the passion of the lover she wanted to be. Soon enough it would all be forgotten. She would be forgotten.

Her time here was finished. She had prevailed upon Lucas, Cook, and Mrs. Lambert's kindness for these last few days, and she knew they all had other responsibilities especially with the return of the master. To show the utmost diligence for this next employer was her new goal. Anne would live her life to please the nobleman. Lord Greville would hear nothing but platitudes if he ever inquired.

36

ithin two days, Lord Greville sent word that her new employer, an elderly lady of some distinction, expected her as soon as she could be delivered. Anne felt the master was extremely eager to discharge her to this new situation. No doubt he longed to see an end to any responsibility he felt. He did not see Anne again, but word came through Mrs. Lambert that she should organize her things, as she was to move at the end of the week.

"We will miss you, dear," said the elderly housekeeper. "I know you are sad to leave, but the master has found you a fine post in a small household."

Although Mrs. Lambert tried to encourage Anne, telling her how fortunate she would be as she would "fit in" so well at her new station. Anne felt she usually "fit around," molding her life into the lives of others. She had no expectations beyond doing the same for this lady.

Anne had heard nothing about the woman for whom she was to work. The butcher's wife would have told the story about an affair involving the famous miniature painter, Thomas Cosway, with whom Mistress Moser traveled quite openly while the man's wife waited for his return. Miss Moser's father was highly regarded as he had been the art instructor to the king. The connections protected the woman.

Anne was determined to accept Lord Greville's choice of her new employment with grace no matter what. Cook had made her own inquiries into the household when she learned of the master's plan. She did not want to send her dear friend off to a household with a reputation of mistreatment. Mistress Moser was a well-known artist. Her father held the position of Keeper of the Royal Academy. Queen Charlotte had enlisted the lady to paint floral banners in one of her rooms at Frogmoor House. All this was such a pleasant surprise to Cook. She happily shared it with Anne.

Anne listened to these details with little acknowledgement. She wondered what her duties would be as a housemaid to the lady. Most of her thoughts could not overcome the sadness she felt leaving Paddington. She would miss Sylvie, Cook, Lucas, and Mrs. Lambert, but it was the separation from Lord Greville she felt the deepest.

The remainder of Anne's personal possessions had been packed for two days. With only one candle for light and a small fire to keep away the cold dampness, Anne had gone to her room for the last time though she did not sleep. She met the morning with tenacity. She believed her family, all gone now, would wish it so. She would meet her new assignment with humble acceptance, eager to begin anew with purpose.

Anne planned to write or even visit Paddington someday. It was the only way she could tolerate the separation. She had imagined what Peter would think when he heard she was gone. Would he feel absolved from any connection? As a whole, thoughts of visiting made Anne squeamish, as she knew she would struggle seeing the master from afar. She should not expect to be received by the lord from this time on. The connection between them would weaken more over time. Ultimately, she was to be separated from her past.

The cottage was empty, resonating its hollowness as Anne walked to the door. In her bedroom, she left her mother's chair, a bit of herself. She looked upon her father's sleeping bench one last time before walking out. It was much for one so young to bear, but Anne held her head up and smiled to those present, accepting her fate.

Anne turned to board the chaise where Lucas waited for her. She had not expected to ride in fashion to her new destination, but Mrs. Lambert explained that the wagon was not as easy to drive through the crowded streets of the city. The lady's home was not so far that Anne would need to ride a coach, and Lord Greville had offered the chaise.

Anne saw the master exit from his library and walk toward the drive. She thought it a coincidence until he stood before her, and she understood he came to wish her off. He offered his hand, and as she took it in hers, he said, "I hope for a bright future for you Miss Blake. Come back to see us when you can."

It was an invitation she would hold dear. Anne took comfort in the knowledge she would indeed visit again one day. She smiled at him but did not try to speak. She did not look for the man who kissed her. He was gone forever.

Lord Greville helped her into the carriage. Lucas shut the side and stepped to the front to take the reins. Anne looked up for a last glimpse into the nobleman's face. She did not anticipate the obvious emotion that showed on his quivering lips and creased brow. He cringed at the edge of tears. The look held the proof of their connection. So many questions hung between them; questions he had not answered and neither dared to ask.

Anne smiled as she sat straight in the chaise, looking out, but not actually seeing as they made their progress from the quiet landscape of the Green to the thick rows of stone houses with ironwork porches and columned entryways. It was not until Lucas stopped the horse that Anne realized she was unaware of the direction from which they had traveled. It was a frightening thought. The links on the chain that connected her mother to her father to the present were broken. She could not follow them back to any of her family. She did not know which way to face to look toward Paddington Green and Lord Greville.

"We will miss you, Anne," she heard Lucas saying, as he helped her out of the carriage and passed her bags to a footman at the edge of the street.

"You know you have become something special to all of us. If you have need of anything you have but to send word."

Anne dared not speak. There was a throbbing in her heart that hurt so deeply. It would not do to arrive at her new destination with a fit of crying. She answered Lucas with a nod of her head as he moved back to his place as the driver. Anne watched her trunk being carried inside, and followed a smiling maid who was waiting for her. As the door was closing on all connection to her past, Anne fought the urge to dash back out before the clink of the latch.

The maid informed Anne that the mistress was waiting for her and led the newcomer up the stairs. Mary Moser sat at a table surrounded by jars of brushes, a tray of paints, a stack of paper, and a bouquet. Closest to her was a very large magnifying glass and another smaller eyepiece. Her back was turned to all of it as she faced the brilliant window. It was a hazy winter sun, an early reprieve from rain and fog. The maid showed Anne in upon the mistresses' request.

Anne saw the woman in the nest of her art supplies. On the corner of the desk stood a gold-framed picture of a man dressed as a military officer. Anne knew this to be the woman's late husband. Cook told Anne the story of the lady's later life, marked by a happy marriage and unfortunate sudden death of the naval captain. The thin-faced woman was elderly, but her age lessened as she turned to look at Anne with approval and a kind face. She smiled and beckoned Anne forward.

"Come in, dear." She looked over with a blank stare.

"Sit here where we can talk." The seat of the chair she indicated was covered with a fine needlework of flowers with a border of leaves against a dark blue background. Anne guessed it to be another artful representation by the lady. Anne sat as directed and looked around the room.

The bright light that illuminated the desk came from a large bay window that took up the entire wall facing the street. The workplace gathered light from all three angles. The two side walls of the room were covered in wallpaper of honeysuckle vines. The pattern reminded Anne of the lord's walled garden. A twinge of regret came to her, but she forced it back down inside. She would have time to herself later to allow such painful memories their due consideration and tears.

From where Anne sat, she was able to see what was previously behind her. The third wall was white, showing off small framed flower paintings, three frames in two neat rows. A similar honeysuckle design with butterflies and small birds perched on the vines was painted around the doorframe from which Anne had entered the room. The furniture and decorations in the rest of the room were feminine, floral, and lightened the heart with its overall cheerfulness. Anne melted into the chair, relaxing for a moment, realizing how tired she was. The spirit of the room gladdened even her sore heart. She reasoned that the lady who designed and lived in this room would surely be a pleasant mistress.

"So, you have a talent, I see." Mary Moser pulled out two sheets of paper from the side of her desk. When Anne leaned forward to see what the lady gave attention to, she was amazed to see first, the drawing of the rose garden she misplaced weeks ago, and then the drawing she made so long ago of the master at the bench in the greenhouse. She took a hiccoughed breath, controlling her surprise. How had this woman come to have these drawings? Why would they interest her now?

Anne had been so sure she lost the picture of the rose garden in the storm, and yet here it was. It had not blown away with a gust of wind. Then it became clear. Lord Greville must have found the drawing. She had never guessed such a circumstance. Now the portrait sat before her in the possession of her new employer. She must have dropped the portrait of the master in the greenhouse when she was caught in the library. He must have kept the drawings, but why? And now here they were on Mistress Moser's desk!

Anne exhaled in exasperation. It was all too confusing to consider at this moment. Her heart was in a whirlwind, not knowing what this interview would entail. Why should Mistress Moser care about her drawings? Did she need the service of a maid who had some knowledge of her paints or someone who could correctly clean and store her brushes?

Mary Moser interrupted Anne's wandering thoughts. "Don't misunderstand me, we have work to do. For me, the colors are fading. My eyes are like sunset, with only so much time before the day is done and all is dark. We must hurry."

Anne knew the woman referred to the onslaught of blindness Anne had been informed might be some part of the lady's need. Though Mary Moser spoke of it poetically, as a fellow artist, Anne could only imagine how devastating it would be to lose her sight; the tool with which she took in the images she so finely recreated. This kind lady met the inevitable with dignified resignation.

Miss Moser held the magnifier over the top of the drawing in places.

"I see you care for roses." She looked up at Anne with the inexact glance.

"Yes, Madame, I do," Anne replied.

"I have a few bushes myself, but nothing as lovely as this garden. Is it a real garden somewhere?"

"Yes, it is Lord Greville's rose garden."

"And the man, who is he?" Mary Moser asked a question Anne had thought she would never have to answer. She replied truthfully, "He is fashioned after the master, I suppose, but it is all romance and is not real." Anne knew there was never any truth to her drawing, not in the way she had depicted it. The world had divided her from Lord Greville, but she had been closer to him than anyone would ever know. She thought of his kiss.

"I am very impressed with your abilities. You have looked closely at nature and the awareness comes through your work. That is our gift, you know. We display nature's gifts to others. We are moved to reproduce the beauty. That is not a thing I would be able to teach, so it is very important to note you have an eye, and even the heart, for what you see. Perhaps, that is because you were a gardener's daughter?

"Let us begin at the beginning. Let me see just how you hold your brush," she said. She handed Anne one of the brushes from the jar on her desk.

In the moments it took Anne to lean over to receive the brush from the woman's wrinkled hand, a vision came to her from months ago. A dream Anne could barely recall. A rush of thoughts came all at once. Anne picked the words "we" and "teach" out of the lady's speech. The situation was becoming clearer to her now. The manner in which the lady addressed her was reminiscent of conversations with Lord Greville. Mary Moser spoke to Anne as a teacher would to a pupil. Anne's lips wiggled into a small smile as she realized what the kind lady with the cheerful room intended.

Anne knew now that Lord Greville cared a great deal for her. He cared enough to send her away to a situation he judged best for her. In that moment in Mary Moser's upstairs study, Anne knew Lord Greville loved her. She remembered him sobbing at the bench. She pictured the drawing he made with the word "Emma" up the stem. He had loved Emma as well. He had sacrificed his happiness to give the beauty a better opportunity than he could offer.

She recalled the talks about stars and minerals. She remembered Lord Greville's hand on hers as they prepared to draw the first pollen from the orchid. She thought of her father's angry entrance into the greenhouse and his quiet exit from this world. She thought of one kiss, rude and rough, and another so close to her heart. Finally Anne reviewed her newest memory, Lord Greville's face as the coach pulled away that morning. The grief was unmistakable, and Anne understood. The lord had found her a situation not as a maid to this elderly woman. Anne was here to learn.

It was Anne's turn to speak. She took the brush into her right hand with a nod of approval from the elderly artist. Anne had spent hours contemplating what she might say to the woman, her new mistress. She imagined the interview and worried what she should reveal about her life. As she saw the kindness in Mary Moser's eyes, all preconceived notions faded away. Anne knew the artist expected nothing but her true feelings. The lady would not judge her. Anne was close to tears, but the tears were joyful. She scooted her fingers down the brush as she would if she were about to paint.

"Yes, I was a gardener's daughter," she answered, with a long slow sigh of relief.